Sorr

Mended

Re-encounters and Reconsideration

Sorrows Mended

Re-encounters and Reconsideration

William Paley

BROWN
DOG
BOOKS

Published under licence by Brown Dog Books and
The Self-Publishing Partnership Ltd,
10b Greenway Farm, Bath Rd, Wick, nr. Bath BS30 5RL

www.selfpublishingpartnership.co.uk

ISBN printed book: 978-1-83952-675-6
ISBN e-book: 978-1-83952-676-3

Cover design by Andrew Prescott
Internal design by Jenny Watson Design

This book is printed on FSC® certified paper

Also by William Paley

Fiction
The Magic Canopy
Four Ways to Keep a Secret
Oceans of Regret
Raking the Sands

Poetry
Visions and Illusions

Anthologies in Kindle format
Original texts with English translations

101 French Poems
150 German Poems

Website
poemswithoutfrontiers.com

Dedication

To Laura Foster-Thompson

Contents

Chapter 1

Bentley Railton was a man of many talents that he had exercised successfully in establishing his business in finance and strategy development, and expanding it over the decades with the aid of his friend and partner, Hector Barratt. At forty-eight, he was affluent, well regarded in his circle, happy in his achievements but, in recent months, had necessarily reverted to the enjoyment of his own company now sadly diminished since his companion, Heather, was no longer with him. In those months with her, he had found the challenge of business satisfying enough, but she had known only the limitations of domesticity. With her absence, he had become aware of how unpalatable his existence must have seemed to her, but he knew no other and simply continued to pursue the uneventful tenor of his ways that had sustained him through the years and to which he had now been undisturbedly returned.

Business had become his life, perhaps his drug. It kept his mind alert whilst he was at his desk or with clients with whom he could readily establish friendly, if disengaged, contact. How deficient he must have appeared to them when he had to admit that he had no family whilst they enjoyed full lives with wife and children. Mostly wife, but very occasionally husband when he had had the good fortune to work with his more infrequent female clients. They were a breed apart; people who managed businesses but also had, somehow, managed to bring up families in addition to their daily grind.

Whatever failings he may have had, however, his clients had full confidence in him, feeling that he was a valuable contact full of experience and one who was able to offer advice as well as criticism and to create survival strategies if required. He could even, to the admiration of his clients, negotiate terms with other parties on their behalf should the occasion arise, but his entertainment hardly stepped beyond the occasional invitation by them to open days held at their office.

Both he and Hector usually dealt with several projects simultaneously, though they tended to be the more complex negotiations, but some projects required a degree of concentration that precluded too great an admixture of distraction. One such negotiation had fascinated Bentley over a period of three months or more, a complex merger of Overdale Engineering and Lowfield. They were the two leading groups of companies in a field under pressure from competition abroad. Overdale had commissioned Railton and Barratt Consultants to negotiate a viable entity of the two in a process that demanded a delicate handling of the chief executives, each of whom sought leadership of the combined business. Bentley's skill on behalf of Overdale's Norbert Grantley in exploiting the few weaknesses of the opposition and his resort to bankers with an ample supply of capital had won the day, although with a rather reluctant acquiescence of the targeted company.

Only when that highly lucrative project had been completed could Bentley relax into what he had always regarded as a satisfying routine. But, after all that hectic activity, he felt a strange feeling of loss at experiencing the return to normality. Business as usual without the strain and without the adrenaline that had characterised his recent workload seemed rather lacking in excitement. The smaller projects lacked the tension and the challenge that, despite the accompanying stress, he had found exhilarating.

One Saturday morning, he awoke with the thought that the day ahead, in contrast to the previous weeks, was totally without interest. The transformation from the pressure of the recent stimulation to the inactivity of the new dawn was a contrast that he found hard to bear since he had little to occupy himself over the weekend except the prospect of resuming life at his desk on the following Monday. That was consoling, but the business had encountered one of those disappointing periods in which new approaches had slackened and few current projects required his attention. For almost the only time in over twenty years, it occurred to him that the next Monday morning would be not quite as appealing as all those other Mondays to which he had looked forward with so much eagerness.

He was, nonetheless, relieved when, at last, the weekend was over and he could resume the week at his normal hour. He dealt with a little newly received routine correspondence, but by mid-morning sought Hector's company for an exchange of words on an equally brief account of his activities, at which he mentioned the lull in their normally busy schedule.

'Just a temporary decline, they've happened before. Business will probably pick up soon,' Hector reassured him.

'I hope so. I get a bit bored when there's nothing to do. Where's the excitement?'

'There's plenty if you care to look for it,' Hector replied with a helpful smile, but only too well aware of Bentley's sheltered life. 'Get out more. You have too few outside interests. Go somewhere lively where you can find something to do. Take a holiday whilst business is slack and come back when it picks up,' Hector told him with a liveliness quite contrary to that of Bentley, who had seldom raised a smile for several weeks.

'Holidays are not my sort of thing,' Bentley responded. 'I wouldn't know what to do or where to go,' he admitted, feeling somewhat inadequate in having to confess his weakness.

'We are booked for a fortnight in Bologna later in the year. You should try a trip abroad, too. A bit of sun, a cruise, perhaps?' Hector suggested.

'Sounds a bit too adventurous for me. I prefer an outing to the National Trust or a picturesque garden.'

'Well! Try that then. You've had several months of intense negotiations and, now, you are plunged back into normality. Once you've emerged from your enforced idleness, you'll feel a lot better and come back excited enough to tackle the influx of new work that will, hopefully, have arrived by then.'

After having fretted through the days, Bentley sat in his armchair the following weekend thinking how strange it was that, after several years at the grindstone, he no longer had any pressure of work or necessity to resolve the latest problem. He thought of Heather, whom he had regarded as a close friend and partner, but he knew that she had wanted more sparkle in her life than he had been able to provide. The recurring thought that he had enjoyed his workload, which had, in the meantime, become deadly dull to Heather, reverberated around his mind. They had parted amicably and undemonstratively but that was not to say that he had experienced no disappointment. He had felt that she was companionable whilst it had lasted, but he was confident that he could manage without her, or, at least, was stoically determined to do so.

Many years before, he had survived a similar occasion, even if that one had left him with a deep and lasting sorrow. He remembered that dark period of his life when he had preoccupied himself in work with a diligence and creativity born of that sad time. It had occupied him through all the following years, but he had gradually become aware of how barren that intervening period had been and, in an attempt to clamber out of his despair, he had sought a more satisfying existence with Heather. Their relationship had never had the binding attraction of his first and endearing love, however, and it had sunk into mere routine. After her departure, he had been compelled to resume the uneventful and unrewarding existence that he had thought he had enjoyed before he had met her; but the feverish activity that his latest project had provided had now ceased, leaving him to the realisation that, with his lack of social contact, he was now lonelier than ever.

Hector had told him to get out more, to do something. He would if he knew what to do, but cruises and pretence at liking some other place than home for a week or two was not his forte. He had always spoken from the heart and preferred to tell clients the unvarnished truth about their business plans as he perceived them, and he was equally forthright with his own lifestyle, telling himself that he had no interest in frivolity.

He recalled that almost the only time when he had enjoyed holidays away from home was decades ago when, as a boy, he had spent a week with his mother on holiday on the south coast. But he also remembered the disappointment at leaving so soon after their arrival. It was a superb place for a boy, he remembered; running about on the sands, taking a bicycle over the hills where one could see for miles over land as well as out to sea. But that was all in the past. He might just possibly ride a bicycle but definitely wouldn't run over the sands now. A slight smile spread over his face at the contrast into which he had now sunk; an upright citizen with a dignity to uphold and no longer the boy without cares. That was a life best viewed from a distance, he thought, lest he be sucked back through the years to those days of abandon. That would not do; his usual weekend occupation would have to suffice, and having come to that resolution, he heaved himself to his feet and trod the well-worn path of his afternoon walk.

His route took him past the manicured lawns of the salubrious district in which he lived, into the park and along the banks of the stream. He wandered past the football pitch and the copse to the church near the main road with a spire just like the spire that he remembered from those childhood holidays spent with his widowed mother at the seaside. The recollection of how he had looked forward to the change, the sea and the scenery that he could visit, recurred as a pleasant thought that entertained him throughout his walk. His mother was no playmate but had simply sent him off to enjoy his freedom whilst she was content to form new friendships with other similarly situated ladies whom she was sure to engage in conversation. She could thereby pass a happy week and also enjoy a Christmas card exchange with them if they proved amenable, whilst he could borrow a bicycle and explore the area even if he was not used to making friends except for a few equally undemonstrative boys he would meet occasionally. He had learned to like his own company and, later, to value the independence it had forged.

Bentley knew that his mother must have been lonely after his father's accident and he reflected that his views on the world had been shaped by his being an only child thrown onto his own devices. They had usually spent their summer holiday on the coast at Hurton Grange, a small hotel with a welcoming atmosphere and handy for both beach and country. He remembered how he had loved the thrill of arriving and running over the not-too distant sands or of taking a bicycle from the hotel collection of three and cycling over the hills. He had loved the wide-open countryside with views from the top towards the sea and over the land. There was a map in the lobby with which he had navigated to all the local villages often with a packed lunch and a bottle of pop, but the break had always concluded far too soon before he had to return to home and school.

Sometimes, he had met one of the local children with whom he had gone off on a joint excursion, but their acquaintance was inevitably short lived regardless of how ideal it might have been. He had once been caught out in a rain storm and returned drenched to the skin, but he could, now, look back at that with an amusement not felt at the time.

On the return route of his walk, Bentley remembered those days of yore. There must still be sand on the beach, he supposed, but he wondered what the interior of that church looked like that he had never entered; and were there still bicycles to borrow or to hire? Hector's advice and that memory of days spent at the seaside running about, climbing rocks and cycling over the hills brought the thought that he might enjoy a brief holiday in a place where he had been so keen to arrive in the summer holidays.

His mother had no car in those days and they had always taken the train, which was an adventure in itself. He wondered whether the old hotel in that small town was still there but, to his pleasure and surprise, he found it on the internet as 'a family-run hotel offering comfortable rooms with sea views'. The photographs showed a building much as he had remembered but the interior shots revealed rooms much improved from his memories of the days that they had spent in that idyllic spot. He could visit at any time but would he find the area as attractive as he remembered? And the hotel was rather small; would rooms be available, he wondered?

His curiosity was soon solved when the receptionist informed him on the telephone that they were terribly sorry but all rooms were taken and that they could not offer a room with a sea view until the following month. That proved more an enticement than a rejection merely prompting a brief period of delayed gratification that, within a few weeks, could be satisfied. He booked the week and sat back proud of his achievement. He had something to look forward to, at last, wondering whether he should take the train in deference to the old days, but he would have to wheel a suitcase and heave it onto and off the bus. He would take the car, even if that were a departure from the old routine; they would have a car park at the hotel, he assumed.

Decisions had never posed any difficulties for him in his business life, but he knew that he was somewhat dilatory in matters concerning his personal affairs. That was one of the reasons why Heather had walked out. He remembered how she had chided him on the matter and how he had told her that he was quite happy to follow any wish of hers and how that had merely led to her sighing at his lack of initiative. It was only now that he realised that she would have liked a change of scene, but she had left and it was too late for recriminations. He could have taken her for a holiday at the hotel if he had ever thought of it whilst he was working, but it was not just those idyllic weeks that he had spent as a boy that he wanted to remember. The ever-lingering thoughts of his much later visit to that town for just one short week formed a memory that he did not wish to disturb; recollections of the girl who was the only person whom he had really loved.

Bentley bought an OS map of the area when he passed through the shopping centre and was able to pop into the stationery shop. Once more at home, he spread the map over the table in order to study that long-since unvisited area. Hurton Grange was marked just where he remembered it, only about two hundred yards from the front. Those memories stirred again. The pier was still there. Was the beach still as sandy as he had remembered? Were there still endless fields just over the hills? He felt a bustle of excitement at the prospect of visiting that place of far-away youth. He would visit the town in just under three weeks but would he find the days as rewarding as those that he had experienced all those years ago?

'It will be a big break,' he told Hector to the latter's amusement, 'but I've thought about it very carefully. The job has its attraction but everything has its limits. Now that the desks are clear, I thought I would take your advice, seek the sun and leave all the routine to you,' he said with a smile. 'But I'm happy to leave everything in your care. We've both had a good relationship, grown the business together and made it a well-regarded name. It will be safe with you for a few weeks,' he joked.

Hector congratulated him on his announcement. 'Good for you!' he said with a beaming smile. He sensed that Bentley might be a little nervous at the unaccustomed break to routine and sought to allay any fears he might be harbouring. 'If anything big comes up, I can always contact you, but summer is coming and business activity generally declines then,' he said, quietly confident that he could handle any eventuality that may arise.

The weeks passed with little activity, but that increased the appeal of the holiday, although Bentley was happy to have booked only a short stay away from the office just in case some new prospect came up that he would find exciting. He would not be running over the sands as he did all those years ago and had begun to wonder how he could fill even the short time that would be at his disposal. But in the days immediately before the holiday, his desire to renew his acquaintance with Sandley grew sufficiently to dispel all trepidation at whether he was wise to depart from the practice of recent times.

They shook hands not for the final time as long-term friends and neither for the final time as business partners. But it was a time almost as notable, a most unusual occurrence when, almost against precedent, Bentley had announced that he would take a holiday. 'Business is bound to slacken off, now, Hector, and I thought I could do with a change,' he had said apologetically. Hector responded with the slightest of mockery that Bentley had, at last, returned to the world of normality and was no longer the drudge he had supposed him to be who preferred to spend his time wrestling with the business of the day. With a fond look around the office that had been his haunt for most of the last twenty years, Bentley walked happily away into an unusual period of relaxation.

Hector watched him from the window regretful that, for a week or more, their partnership would not witness Bentley busily working at his desk, but he could now feel the unusual prospect of being in sole charge of the business. He suspected that Bentley's desire for a holiday was not so much as simply to move on from his success but more owing to the fact that Heather had walked out eighteen months previously after their having lived quietly together for several months before that. Bentley had never been demonstrative but that was why he was so suited to the demands of a job that required some deep thinking and a determination to achieve results. Hector was convinced that beneath that calm exterior lay a feeling of unexpressed injustice. Bentley had given Heather a home and security but she had wanted a more lively existence than he had provided and had finally sought a life elsewhere. From hints that he had gleaned from long conversations with him, Hector suspected that Bentley had never overcome his first loss and that his quiet personality had consigned him to solitary deprivation, and, now, he would not even have the business to entertain him. Hector concluded that he would probably want to return after a brief absence only too keen to get back to work. 'Unless he develops a liking for holidays, of course, but that would be very uncharacteristic of him.'

Bentley walked out of the building and into the wide-open spaces of those without a care. He would miss the intensity of action to some degree but he had persuaded himself that he would welcome a period of freedom in which he could enjoy the blessings of idleness, at last. No more frantically working through weekends, no more placing his expertise in the service of others or chasing deadlines for early completion. He had done all that and enjoyed the several years of an excitement that had never lost its charm, but he could please himself now. Precisely what he could do in Sandley had not yet fully formed in his brain, but, the day before he left, he had joked with Hector that he would not forget his bucket and spade.

The next day, as he loaded his suitcase into the boot, brought confirmation that he had entered a new era, perhaps one of adventure. He could have driven that way at any time in his life, he thought. A few hours brought him to the town and a glance at the street map brought him to his destination, a much-improved building from the days he remembered. His arrival brought a reminder of how he and his mother had formerly carried their cases from the station but it was the modest car park behind the building that persuaded him that the holiday had now undoubtedly commenced. His smile matched that of the receptionist who hastened from the back office to greet him. He looked about. It was totally changed from the old days, and for the better. He told her that he had last come over thirty years previously, to which she replied light heartedly that they were always pleased to receive regular guests even if his last visit was well before the new owners had taken over ten years before.

On entering his room, he had a feeling that he had travelled back through time. His mood changed from that slight remnant of doubt whether he had made the right decision to one of delight at the prospect of rediscovering his youth. The room had a satisfying view over a few rooftops and onto the sea. The pier was visible to the east and the bay swept invitingly round to the rocky headland in the west. The hills he had cycled as a boy were not visible but he was conscious that they were there just waiting to be explored again.

He set out for a brief preliminary walk down to the prom from where he ascertained that the beach was as extensive and as sandy as he had recollected. He stood at the rail and gazed at the view. How near the sea, how near his memories and how far that dreary office at home! An unaccustomed smile crossed over his face as he felt his happy days returning.

Chapter 2

Hedrick Tarrant's first visit to the Pelham Gallery was when, as a boy, he had taken part in an afternoon school visit conducted by their rather prim teacher, Miss Kilder, who had reminded the class to observe the rules of quiet admiration and respect for the hallowed surroundings. He and his classmates had consequently assembled in front of the building and were ushered inside to file slowly through, sharing the paintings with a few respectful adults who were also enjoying a day out of their own. Hedrick had been more impressed by the adults' admiration of the pictures than by the paintings themselves, until his group passed into the Batista del Mano room where several stunning paintings were displayed.

One, in particular, had arrested his gaze: *Girl with a Harp*. It must have measured almost one metre wide, his mathematical brain noticed, but his gaze was drawn to the light on the girl's face illuminating her countenance in a miraculous glow of innocent youth, and the strings of the harp seemed almost to be vibrating with sound. The background was also crowded with figures seeming to have more interest in a fair than in the music which he thought must be more enticing than those costumed clowns whom he perceived on the stage behind them. The label beside the painting gave the artist and the year in which the picture had been painted, 1644, but having been cleaned a decade ago it now looked as if it had been painted only yesterday. He had vaguely heard of del Mano but had no idea where he had lived or what he had created. The adjacent painting was one entitled *Lady in a Garden*, a picture of a young lady seated among flowers with a small dog nearby on the lawn. On noting the date of creation as 1651, he wondered whether she were the same person as the girl with the harp. He seemed to have been captured in a magic cave filled with wonders, but most of his classmates had filed through to the next room and he had to hurry as he realised that everybody had progressed to further discoveries.

Before exiting the building, they passed through a shop selling souvenirs to visitors. Hedrick had very little money but there was a slim volume giving a brief account amongst others of the little that was known of del Mano's life and creations. It would absorb all his spare cash but a quick glance gave him a depiction of *Girl with a Harp* and a short commentary. He bought it and showed his good taste to Miss Kilder, who gave an unaccustomed smile and congratulated him on his purchase. 'An artist who deserves a better reputation,' she commented.

She had embarked on a teaching career imbued with the enthusiasm of one intent not only on the education of her pupils but also in raising them to a higher level of appreciation in the arts in which her holiday country of choice had such a rich history. At least one of the class had shown some appreciation of her efforts in proposing the outing and had been stimulated enough to enquire further. 'A little ray of sunshine may have pierced his mind,' she thought, unaware that it was the light bathing the girl in the picture that had stimulated his interest and one that he would treasure through all the years to come.

A few weeks later, Hedrick met his older friend, Bamber Stapleton, who had just finished his fresher year at university. Conversation turned inevitably to future ambitions, but whereas Hedrick spoke fulsomely of the gallery visit, Bamber was politely dismissive of Hedrick's praise.

'Collectors pay millions for a picture that is hundreds of years old,' he said. 'That can't be simply to have the pleasure of looking at it every day. They just want an investment that can be sold on in a few years. They talk about art but their real objective is to create a more vibrant market, which has the effect of raising prices. They should keep the pictures because they like them and not want to part with them, but their real motivation is to increase values by competing with one another in praising the merits of their possessions. It's all a big plot to ensure that the upper classes can retain their wealth and status,' he concluded as they walked on to meet Bamber's elder sister, Cora, at her new flat.

The years passed quietly by with Hedrick having obtained a mildly interesting employment at the local stationery factory and Bamber having been awarded an additional year at university. One day, for want of other activity, Hedrick sauntered into the gallery shop with no intention of buying anything, but merely to recall the day when he had visited with his class. After browsing the books, he glanced slowly through the full-size reproductions on offer, suddenly stopping at one of *Girl with a Harp*. It was just as fascinating as the original he had seen those few years before. But the price was too high for his limited budget and he reluctantly gave place to an older man quietly waiting for him to finish.

'A beautiful painting,' the man remarked.

'Yes. I saw it in the del Mano room when I came on a school visit,' Hedrick replied. 'I bought a little book about him but it gave only a short resume of the painting. I remember my teacher saying that he deserved to be better known.'

'I agree with your teacher. I've been employed in the workrooms for over thirty years and have access to all the paintings in the gallery. Working on these Old Masters is a joy and there is always much to do, but I sometimes feel a little selfish at having a painting all to myself when I am working on it; and they are jobs that cannot be hurried.'

'It had never occurred to me that there must be workrooms here,' Hedrick replied. 'But I suppose the paintings have to be examined and moved around; and looking closely at these Old Masters presumably for hours at a time must be very satisfying.'

'Not hours, but days and sometimes weeks. Yes. Very satisfying.'

'And *Girl with a Harp* is absolutely fascinating,' Hedrick replied.

'One of my favourites,' the man admitted, and noting an unusual spark of interest in a young person, offered to show him the workroom.

'Oh, yes. That would be marvellous, but I don't have an entrance ticket,' Hedrick replied regretfully.

'Don't worry about that. They all know me here, and we are allowed to bring in a guest from time to time.'

The man took him to the back stairs and through a door controlled by keypad. The workroom was on the third floor above the exhibition rooms accessed through yet another security door. The man gave him a mask and unveiled the picture in order for them to look closely at his current work. 'Not a del Mano but one of his contemporaries, Edwardo Farrero,' he said, looking lovingly at the art before him.

'It must be worth a fortune!' Hedrick exclaimed, looking at the interior of a florist shop full of flower displays portrayed in the current work on the bench.

'Probably, but, to me, the value of a painting is in the artistry, that's all we think about. We can pretend to own it whilst we are working on it but we must eventually return it to an admiring public,' he ended with a smile.

'What a marvellous job! Sole ownership of an Old Master even for a limited period!' Never had Hedrick been driven to such admiration.

'I've never regretted taking my job here,' the man said. 'I applied after I had graduated in fine arts, but you could check with the office if you're interested. They keep note of anybody who expresses interest. Tell them that Garrard Portman recommended you.'

'But I don't have a degree or know anything about art. Much as I'd like to.'

'That shows a certain amount of eagerness. Tell them you are keen to learn and that you know a bit about del Mano. I'll take you to the del Mano gallery to see *Girl with a Harp* if you like.'

'Oh, yes. It's years since I saw it on my school outing.'

Mr Portman conducted him down the back stairs via another secure route and led Hedrick to the exhibits. 'There you are. Almost four hundred years old and still a marvel of human creativity,' he said, standing back fondly. 'It is not due for inspection until probably ten years from now. It was cleaned more than fifteen years ago and, now, looks as if it were painted yesterday.'

'How often are the paintings inspected?' Hedrick asked.

'The conservator examines them biannually and withdraws them for renovation if a problem is detected. Otherwise, a thorough inspection is scheduled only after several decades have elapsed. A visual check might be sufficient but they may need cleaning or a slight repair or, in very rare cases, if the old frame is beyond saving, a new frame might be required. I do all of that,' he ended with a quiet note of pride in his voice. 'I'll show you the other Farrero paintings we have,' he said after a while. 'Only two still hanging but I should finish *Flowers* within a week and, then, I'll go on to the next one. But it is the art director who determines the activity we undertake.'

Hedrick left the gallery having enquired at the office whether he could fill any vacancy they may have, careful not to omit his recommendation from Mr Portman, but the attempt ended as he had expected. They expressed great regret at having no vacancy but assured him that they would contact him if a suitable position were to arise. He felt disappointed but simultaneously emboldened at having almost entered a new world that may have offered him an entrance to a more elevated social status.

'Mr Portman had the ideal job,' he thought, working among art that had been created several centuries ago and with a satisfaction that was obviously far greater than could be achieved at the factory where only a limited attraction was offered. That would probably not reach much beyond the level to which he had already acceded, whereas the gallery offered several interesting job activities. 'If only I could also work in the gallery. Do something that would last at least for decades if not for the centuries that those great artists had achieved.'

Back at the factory, he spoke to his colleague, Grant Temperley, about his day off. He was always somebody keen to impart a little advice to a younger man who had shown a willingness to learn and prosper within the confines of his employment. 'You should contact the Fine Arts Guild in order to enquire about training courses on that sort of work,' he advised, 'But whatever they offer would take time and dedication.'

'Yes. That was the problem,' Hedrick thought. They would also require fees and he would have to continue to earn a living.

Meetings with Bamber had meantime become occasions of decreasing frequency. In one reencounter after several years had elapsed since their last meeting, Hedrick was shocked to learn the news that a very distressed Bamber brought him. Several years before, his sister had met with a fatal accident when she had fallen from a cliff whilst on holiday with her fiancé in the Hebrides. It was clear that Bamber was deeply troubled by the loss as he stumbled through an account of the death. 'Cora was always very careful but she stepped too close to the edge, and fell. She and her fiancé were photographing the cliffs but he testified that she trod on a loose rock, slipped and fell. Accidental death, the inquest said, but she was always very cautious. If I'd been there, I would have told her to keep her distance. Her fiancé said he told her not to go too far, but that she insisted on taking another photograph; and that was her last.'

Bamber was understandably too upset to be in the least bit comforted by Hedrick's struggles to convey his condolences, and was not easily calmed by his poor attempt at sympathy and sorrow. 'He put her in danger. He should have caught her. He should have saved her,' was all he could respond, only too wretched at the recollection of the verdict. 'We've been close all my life and now she's gone. On the brink of marriage, she was on the brink of the grave. A tragedy that shouldn't have been allowed to happen! And, now, full of apologies, Frank has run away to Italy. Good riddance to him!'

Hedrick was almost as troubled as Bamber. He remembered his sister as a very generous and welcoming person whom it had been a pleasure to know, and felt totally unable to utter anything of comfort. The next time they met, several months later, it was for Bamber to announce that he had been awarded a position at a leading American university where he could continue his studies in electronics.

Much to Hedrick's surprise a few months after his encounter with Mr Portman, the gallery contacted him to ask whether he would be free to speak to the art director, Spenser Ferndale, about the possibility of a job as workroom assistant. He made an appointment and nervously entered the director's office to be greeted by a rather learned, slimly built and neatly dressed man in his mid-fifties who apologised that the job he had to offer may not be precisely what Hedrick was looking for but, because he had stimulated some interest with Mr Portman, he thought it worth sounding him on his intentions.

Hedrick managed to mention his interest in the world of art, his school outing to the gallery and his scant knowledge of del Mano and Farrero. He felt a certain amount of courage when the director smiled appreciatively at Hedrick's admiration for *Girl with a Harp* and *Lady in a Garden* and his theory that the depictions might have been of the same subject. That gave the director the opportunity to inform him that the girl was, indeed, the same subject and had been a favourite model of del Mano. Hedrick mentioned the girl depicted in the Farrero painting that was created at about the same time as the del Manos, which allowed the director to relax into an opportunity to display his area of expertise by expressing a few sentences about her and expressing the art world's indecision whether she had also been the model for del Mano.

At Hedrick's mention of his interest in framing and the Fine Arts Guild, the director smiled his satisfaction and also paid mild interest to Hedrick's knowledge of stationery and the differing qualities of each grade. That all seemed to add to Hedrick's qualifications for a workroom assistant where a high degree of care, discrimination and respect for the art was required.

He left the gallery with the offer of a new job and prospects for a future in the highest forms of art. Within a little over a month, he had been enrolled on the staff and been assigned to Mr Portman, who would mentor him, but he also had unfettered access not only to all the exhibits but also to the workshops and the restorations conducted by craftsmen with decades of experience.

He learned that the gallery had been established as a charitable trust managed by a small board of directors under the chairmanship of Marcus Carlton. From having held several posts at the county council, Marcus had been nominated to become chairman of the board and was occasionally asked to speak at local functions. He had brought his wife, Mabel, a status and standard of living envied, he presumed, by all her friends. For his part, he was conscious of being what others might think was merely a dependable administrator, but he had prided himself in having a deep devotion to duty that was an essential part of a senior manager's role, and, over the years, had developed a facility for speech from which he could not now depart. He had been aware of his inferiority to undoubted experts such as Spenser Ferndale, whose knowledge and capability were of a level he could never attain regardless of how much he tried, but he was content to consider that his position was one that outranked them all. He had found that a flamboyant way of expressing himself to all his staff, whether high or low, had always compensated for any deficiencies he may have had, but was aware that it would also act as a deterrent against disagreement from them and endow him with an authority that none could challenge.

Several years after Hedrick's entrance into the world of art, the Pelham directors learned of the death of their founder, Lewis Pelham, a man of very advanced age who had created his fortune in engineering and had retired two decades previously. He had long before entrusted his industrial empire to his grandson, Frank, who, with no interest in art, had raised his elder sister, Laura, to the board.

Laura had a greater interest in art than her brother, but that was because she had no necessity to be the slave to duty that he preferred to be, and she had been introduced to the subject by no less than her grandfather. She was also grateful to have an occupation that had helped distract her from the constant emptiness of her several years of widowhood since her husband's early death. She remembered how, years before, her grandfather had taken her into the exhibition room and had pointed out various features that were obviously of meaning to him although, at that early age, their importance to her was less striking. In adulthood, however, despite being not quite as devoted to art as he had been, she was conscious of her responsibility as a director to protect and preserve the works that he had bequeathed to the gallery.

When she attended the next monthly meeting, she graciously received the heartfelt condolences of her fellow directors on her grandfather's death. As a direct descendant of the founder, she responded with effusive thanks, remembering him as a man of great generosity who had not only founded the gallery but also the local museum some twenty years before that. She praised him as a man with artistic aspirations despite his overruling practical endeavours in engineering and one who had been always gentle with her, especially during the fifteen years of his life in bereavement.

Ever aware of her position, she turned quickly to the agenda, noting the omission of any reference to security measures, which she was keen to revue. Recent negligence at an American modern art gallery that had enabled a man of troubled mind to throw paint at a new acquisition gnawed at her conscience. She was not prepared to ignore the possibility of a similar occurrence in the gallery for which she felt not only responsibility but also the lingering memory of her grandfather in his lasting legacy to an admiring public.

Security had been a matter that had already been addressed by the board on previous occasions. The collections were not those that ranked with the greatest in the world of art, but several exhibits were of great antiquity and extremely valuable. The directors sought to preserve them free of any calamity that may be encountered by having long since created a watchful team to patrol the exhibition rooms. Laura's three colleagues and the chairman were sceptical at the prospect of an occurrence in their gallery such as that to which she had referred. Surely, nobody could possibly contemplate such an action even in this age when freedom was readily claimed to outrank self-restraint! Their recognition not only of a drop in valuation but also in their reputations in the art world if they were seen not to have taken preventative measures set uncomfortable considerations in their minds, however, quite at odds with their usual, unhurried routine. Nonetheless, disturbing though the news may be, they took comfort in their current practice and expressed confidence in their precautions that they maintained were sufficient to prevent such disastrous occurrences on their own premises.

Laura paid scant regard to those assurances, knowing that even one occurrence would not only be a desecration but also a blow against the reputation of the gallery. She insisted that each picture should receive the protection of anti-reflective, 99% UV-blocking glass, a suggestion that continued to be dismissed with regret. 'That would mean that all our art would have to be reframed,' they chorused 'and some frames are in themselves objects of great age and veneration.' One director was favourably inclined but changed his mind when the financial impact was broached. 'Reframing would cost a fortune,' was the almost unanimous response.

'But values would quite likely be diminished,' Laura protested. 'Precautions may be costly, but how much would a restoration cost?' she added with slight annoyance. 'We don't know how many paintings could be irretrievably damaged in a single incident, or even whether a madman may slash the canvas.'

The board temporised by agreeing to initiate a cost investigation. Laura sighed inwardly at the prospect of a long wait that she feared may well be extended in order to postpone the decision even further. She therefore proposed and insisted that the resolution be passed at the next meeting, at which the directors nodded to one another in silent, if reluctant, approval. She was fifteen years younger than most of her colleagues and confirmed in her opinion that they had no wish to change the beaten track of their blinkered management of several decades but would remain intransigent to all matters outside their experience until a calamity forced them into action.

The meeting closed with renewed expressions of condolences to Laura. She and the conservator left both grumbling at the reluctance of the board for any change and the danger to which they were exposing the collection. For her part, she had some concern for her grandfather's endeavours but they were merely paintings rather than persons. But if one were damaged, she thought, the fact that others were available would be no consolation.

Spenser had been fairly supportive of the proposal even if they were inviting a conflict of modernity against tradition, but he took comfort in the thought that safety measures would always be a wise precaution.

Chapter 3

The gallery directors finally authorised the new glazing policy, not at the next meeting but at the one after that, and then only at Laura's impatient insistence with that of the conservator, whereby they achieved the concession from the others that early action would be prudent. The directors had pleaded the cost involved, interruption to routine, lack of resources and loss of admission fees. Restoration work would have to be paused, pictures removed from show for lengthy periods and rehung, and some would need skilful and therefore protracted cleaning. The total cost barrier was presented by the opposing directors as exceeding the acquisition costs of most of the paintings.

Laura responded that the reframing proposal need be carried out only one room at a time and routine inspections could be postponed for one year without adverse consequences. In addition, she pointed out how fortuitous the gallery had been in her grandfather's bequest. He had bought the paintings over several decades at what was now regarded as very beneficial values and they had been transferred from his company balance sheet at cost price into a charitable subsidiary controlled by her brother, Frank. With the huge appreciation of art values, the gallery had a duty to protect the value of its assets, she argued, adopting her most persuasive tone made the stronger by her being the founder's granddaughter. The debate proceeded more as a substitution for the otherwise little business to be discussed, but the wisdom of acting before any calamity might strike was finally agreed and the reframing project received consent.

Spenser was fearful that an infringement of routine may lead to unfortunate consequences, but he had to admit that the arguments for the proposal were well founded. Laura was one whom he regarded highly for her concern. She had had the good fortune to be born into the Pelham dynasty and therefore had a voice that was likely to be more influential than others, and on this occasion, he was happy to support her.

Marcus Carlton, as general manager, whenever confronted with Spenser's reputation for expertise, could not forgo his customary deprecatory manner of one floundering in comparative ignorance. 'An excellent point, Spenser,' he would respond, 'but I would like to hear the views of the others.'

Spenser heaped these habitual dismissals upon an accumulation over the years of the petty rebuttals that he had heard from Marcus, who had been appointed solely because of his long service in local government but whose ability resided in fine words rather than fine arts. He may well be recognised as a good speaker, but he was nonetheless ignorant of the art that Spenser had studied for decades, and a mere pen pusher who took all the limelight whenever called upon to represent the gallery to the outside world.

The burden of his opinions being repeatedly deprecated by an ignorant bureaucrat had, long since, become a source of irritation to Spenser who, despite not having reached even the age of sixty, would have retired long ago if it were not for his love of the art with which he was surrounded. But the option of retirement was becoming more attractive than ever. Writing about art and a few radio or television appearances had already offered a more satisfying prospect than his recommendations being constantly overridden. Now, at a time when the gallery could boast a history unblemished by any incident of managerial failure, there was reason for him to depart with a clean record, but, since that would conflict with his duty to preserve the exhibits, he resolved, as usual, to persevere.

Some of the little consulted workshop staff also greeted the announcement of the new policy with concern, fearful that routine would be greatly disturbed, that the project would be rushed, that restoration would be impeded. Others welcomed the initiative because it underlined the gallery's dedication to safeguarding the work of centuries.

Hedrick was more delighted than most. The gallery had over one hundred Masters in its collection and all would be scheduled for reframing, which would offer him a new opportunity to expand his field of craftsmanship. He had now spent nearly a decade in the gallery, but this was an opportunity for him to become productive in an extended process in which he would play an important and creative part. It would demand a major change of practice and take over a year to complete. On consideration, he thought the new policy a worthy precaution; he loved the pictures with almost equal interest and would not like any to be vandalised. Furthermore, he would also be presented with an opportunity to participate in a major project and to see several works of his hung in this leading, provincial gallery. Back in his house, as he viewed his own modest gallery of three full- size reproductions, he felt the opening of a new chapter in his life.

Some months now passed during which consultations had taken place and the reframing schedule had been devised. Hedrick and Garrard had almost completed the two pilots that had been critically examined by the conservator and Spenser, both of whom, after a lengthy examination and discussion, had approved the first works for rehanging and applied a code to the back of the frame indicating authenticity and the current year for future examiners. The pictures were the least valuable in the collection, but any nervousness at any slight damage that may have been caused had been allayed.

Neither Hedrick nor Garrard had expected any adverse comments on their work; they had undertaken routine reframing to complete satisfaction on several occasions in the past, but they understood the importance of their role in the glazing project and had approached the work with even greater care than usual. They attended the reintroduction of the pictures into the gallery, which amounted almost to a little ceremony entailing isolation of the security and rehanging with great solemnity, succeeded by appreciative views from all angles until closing with reactivation of the security code. The participants congratulated one another at the conclusion of a process that would inevitably be followed on numerous other occasions. Hedrick and Garrard returned to the workshop happy to have completed the first of many more successes to come.

Spenser sat at his desk feeling that his care and worry at the project had been alleviated by the standard of workmanship he had witnessed, but he could not entirely dismiss his misgivings at what he still regarded may be a policy fraught with risk. The frames that he had just inspected had shown a high level of craft, but could that be sustained over the whole of the next year with equally high standards throughout? If the more valuable pictures were to suffer even the slightest damage that fool of a general manager would be the first to direct the blame onto him. The thought of retirement welled up again to persuade him that the time for a decision on that matter was nigh. His nerves were frayed enough, but he was appreciative of the work that had been carried out and felt that the staff concerned deserved an extra word of thanks.

A quick telephone call brought them to his office where, with an unaccustomed smile wreathing about his face, he explained his delight in their having relieved him of a great worry at the start of the project. He had known how skilled his workforce was but that had now been reinforced and he knew that he could rely upon them in the future. Garrard expressed his thanks at this unusual expression of confidence and both he and Hedrick assured Spenser of their devotion to the art they served.

Spenser added that he would retain a certain level of anxiety until the project was finished because he would not be able to relax completely until it had concluded satisfactorily, but he now had conclusive evidence that, together, they would achieve a commendable result. At the same time, he assured them of his determination to assist in advice and helpful comments throughout the project as it progressed.

As they left his office, Hedrick told Garrard that that was one of very few occasions when they had been congratulated so warmly. Garrard responded that the praise was very welcome, but all the more so owing to Spenser's rather withdrawn and lofty character when they had met on frequent occasions in the past. 'We are all devoted to those works of art, but he carries the greatest responsibility for their care. That must be quite worrying for him.'

Over the next few months, the project made its slow but steady progress. On one of his occasional visits, Hedrick told his mother about the gallery and how enthusiastic he was at the prospect of safeguarding all the Old Masters in their care. Despite her earlier doubts, she had now accepted that he had made a good choice in exchanging his stationery job for a vocation; he was happy and his future was assured. An atmosphere of increasing confidence also pervaded the gallery both in the workshop and throughout the management. No problems had been encountered, the framers settled into a satisfying routine and Spenser gave his approval of the work and to the dedication of all concerned.

As the day approached for the del Mano paintings to be examined and reframed, Spenser became more cautious. He had noticed that the existing frames originating from over a century before had been refitted after the last cleaning but were showing signs of wear. The frames were not exactly suitable but had gained a certain amount of acceptability merely by long association. Spenser declared his preference for a change of style in view of the fact that, given their current condition, the existing frames would need to be exchanged within twenty years and may as well be exchanged now. Hedrick reported that almost similar designs were, fortunately, to hand and could be utilised without exciting too great a comment on departing from the old. Spenser critically examined the sample expressing a little caution at its suitability and, promising to return his verdict in good time, took it to his office for closer examination before reaching a final verdict.

Once more, in his office, Spenser held the sample before him with a gathering current of exultation passing through his veins. The design would suit but he was keen to prolong this close association with their oldest work of art and asked Hedrick to demonstrate a trial frame on a reproduction from the shop. That was an unusual request but perhaps it was better to follow the instruction; Spenser was the expert and he had offered Hedrick the job all those years ago. But the convincing reason to adhere to the instruction was that he could apply himself to framing his favourite painting in the gallery, *Girl with a Harp*, that he had so admired ever since he had first glimpsed it in that school visit. That would offer him an enjoyable time despite its being a reproduction.

Several days later, he viewed the finished job, careful to scrutinise it with a keener eye than he had applied to any task he had handled hitherto. After another loving glance he carried it to Spenser's office who examined it minutely, finally declaring himself satisfied but reserving judgement for a while. Hedrick returned to the workshop happy to have attained the standard of craftsmanship that had met Spenser's approval, but he was now bereft of his favourite, even if it was a reproduction, for whatever length of time may now elapse until the final verdict.

Spenser summoned Hedrick to his office, next day, where he explained that the picture before them was splendidly framed but wondered whether Hedrick could frame another using the alternative design.

Hedrick looked a little startled at the idea but Spenser explained that with a painting of this age and importance, it would be prudent to explore the alternative when the frame was destined to last for more than a hundred years, perhaps two. Hedrick replied that he would be happy to comply and, together, they both drew another reproduction from the store. He promised the work to be ready within a week. He cleared the work bench for a repeat project which he delivered to Spenser several days later.

Spenser placed both reproductions side by side and feasted his eyes on the picture, conscious of making a decision that would echo through the gallery for a century or more. He compared the two frames, declaring both to be highly suitable, but with the attraction of the new, commented that the second design seemed to him the more suitable. 'What do you think?' he asked Hedrick, who stammered the reply that they were both superbly appropriate to the subject.

'The rounded corners seem better to display the glow on the face,' Spenser commented as if thinking aloud. 'Wouldn't you agree?'

Hedrick thought that it added very little to the subject but cautiously mentioned that 'They do give a certain resonance,' a comment that seemed to please Spenser, who stored it as another little gem he could use on a future occasion, elsewhere.

'That's it, then,' Spenser concluded with some decisiveness. 'We'll use the alternative frame for the original. I know you are very careful in your work but you will have a genuine Old Master this time. Remember that you will also have both the past and the future in your hands.'

Hedrick did not remark that he had often handled Old Masters before, but, when the time came, he did indeed treat the painting with even greater care than usual. The transfer from the old frame into the new was witnessed by Marcus and Spenser, who applauded Hedrick's work but then left him with Garrard after the delicate task of positioning the glass just clear of the original paintwork.

Marcus gave his congratulations to Spenser. 'The project is advancing very well,' he said. 'All attributable to our excellent work force. A job very well done.'

Spenser noted the omission of any praise specifically directed towards him, but he was secretly content. 'Quite right,' he replied. 'It is they who deserve congratulations. Despite management having a role to play, we are all dependent upon the craftsmen who have the skills that support us in our endeavours.' He wondered whether Marcus had deliberately sought to demean his role and whether he had detected that little riposte in defence.

Hedrick brought the finished product to his office a few days later and Spenser stood it next to the reproductions. 'There!' he exclaimed enthusiastically. 'You'll never again see three identical paintings of Old Masters together. You've done an excellent job.'

At that moment, Hedrick was as proud of himself as he had ever been. His favourite painting multiplied by three! There could be no better view than this. He left the office with Spenser's fulsome praise ringing in his ears.

Once more at home, Hedrick viewed his little gallery with Spenser's congratulations still resounding in his head. He had achieved the highest accolade that a young man with his background could hope for. The art director himself had singled him out for special praise, something that even Garrard had seldom received. His gallery of reproductions looked back at him, and he felt a surge of pride in having achieved a level of skill that he had envied in others in those earlier years.

Back in the workshop, he received the message that the del Mano would be rehung that morning and that both he and Garrard were invited to attend. At the appointed hour, they assembled with a beaming general manager, Laura and an unusually smiling Spenser. Marcus made a few remarks to his expectant listeners emphasising the importance of the painting and the art of del Mano. 'The oldest and most venerable of our entire collection,' he announced. 'We owe a debt of gratitude to our dedicated and skilful staff in the workroom, whose great endeavours have ensured that our reframing project for the entire gallery is well on target.'

Spenser noted with his habitual disdain that, yet again, he had been excluded from acknowledgement, but this was not a time for recriminations; he had reasons of his own for satisfaction, having indulged himself over the months in a closer contact with the exhibits reframed so far. The code was verified and the picture rehung. After the security had been reset, the group broke up and Hedrick took the opportunity to ask Spenser whether he could buy one of the test pictures. Spenser was in excellent mood and told him. 'Yes, of course. You deserve a reward. I'm in the same mood myself. A Master in the house would, to a casual glance, be just as beautiful as the original,' he announced with a broad smile at the experience that each would enjoy.

Laura told Hedrick that she had taken great satisfaction at the progress in the reframing project in which he was a major participant. 'My grandfather would have been very grateful. We all owe our positions to him for his foresight in creating the collection in order to save it unharmed for future generations.'

Spenser added, 'Yes. We have all contributed to the start of a new era and can relax in the knowledge that the collection is under the beneficial management of our board of directors, particularly of Marcus and his expert management of the project.'

Marcus smiled broadly at this unexpected tribute from the least expected quarter and preened himself at the remark, totally oblivious to Spenser's gentle sarcasm. 'Very generous of you, Spenser. Yes. Top management competence is essential in a project of this nature. As well as teamwork,' he added with resort to the slightest of faint praise.

Spenser received the response with his habitual distaste. 'No generosity whatever the occasion,' was his reaction, but, because he knew that it had been uttered by a master of speech, he also knew that the slight was deliberate and just one more sign of insecurity erecting a flimsy wall of defence. But it was also another disparagement that heaped yet more weight upon Spenser's delicate frame.

Chapter 4

Frank Pelham turned away from contemplation of his carefully tended garden, more than pleased by its setting over the lake and the Italian sun that shone upon it. It was some consolation for the loss of his great love many years before, after which he had exiled himself from the country of his birth. His constant sorrow was that Cora could not be with him to share the scene.

The news from his aide in the engineering sector of his industrial group was more than a little disappointing, but, at least, it offered some activity for a change. He no longer had any appetite for the day-to-day running of the business, having ably delegated most authority, but that had left him with very little excitement and he was almost glad at news of the failure to acquire his latest target. He had been keen to acquire the Lowfield group not simply because of its engineering capability but mostly because it contained the company managed by Bamber, which he hoped might enable him somehow to rectify the regretful relationship that had arisen between them. Even after all this time, he remained greatly troubled by a schism that weighed heavily upon him as a constant tarnish on his memory of Cora. He knew that she would never return but he had no wish to cloud his memory of her with a conflict that would remain forever unresolved; but his merger strategy had been dashed. He would have to think again.

Several years before, he had engaged Sylvano, a newly retired gardener and landscaper who had transformed a former nondescript layout to unsurpassed beauty in which Frank had found some consolation and a distraction from the everlasting sadness that had blighted his existence.

They had both enjoyed discussing the works required and modifying them gradually over the years. Sylvano had rejoiced in the opportunity presented to revive his love of gardening and also to boost his modest pension, particularly as Franco was a generous employer and had accepted almost all suggestions. He was not the least bit reluctant to support any scheme that was tentatively proposed and even contributed his ideas at extending them.

He knew that Franco was some sort of industrialist, and thought him rather reclusive, but he was unaware and uninterested in the precise nature of his background. He knew that Franco had moved there after several years in Milan where he had settled when he had first arrived in Italy, but it was sufficient that he was definitely a man who exuded an atmosphere of substantial wealth. Despite whatever background he had had, he was very approachable, acceding to, and contributing to, much of the advice that he had tendered.

In exercising full authority to commission contractors from the town if heavy works were to be involved, Sylvano had revelled in his work and the transformation that he had been able to bring to the gardens, but the opportunities to demonstrate his skills had diminished over the years as the garden took final shape.

He wondered why Franco lived alone in that big house. He must rattle around in there, he thought, and as a degree of friendship grew over the passing years, he ventured to ask why he had not married, to which Franco responded that he had been married to his business and had never had time for domesticity. That was a most unlikely reason but one that he sensed he should not press too hard because a completely different and rather personal explanation seemed more probable. It was enough for him that Franco received several visitors on social occasions including sometimes small gatherings in the garden when his sister had visited with her now teenage children, whom he had gladly introduced to Sylvano and Selena.

Selena was particularly proud that it was her husband who had been the main creator and she marvelled at the transformation from the poorly presented plot of years before to the splendid gardens of the present. She also experienced great enjoyment at their invitations to occasional evenings at the big house, particularly after the death of her great childhood friend, Tandrina, whose husband had lived in the cottage just a little over one hundred metres from Franco's house.

Many years had now passed, however, and time had taken its toll as first Tandrina had died followed by her widower some years later. Their son had moved away to Milan many years before that and, no longer with any contact with the quiet spot where he had grown up, had decided to sell the rather neglected cottage. Little interest was shown by prospective purchasers until, after several months, it was bought by a woman who, after modernising it and transforming it into a desirable residence, lived there alone. Her arrival proved beneficial to both parties because Selena could cultivate relations with her near neighbour and be welcomed by the new occupant for the opportunity it gave the latter for her gradually to extend her small circle of friends in the neighbourhood. It also gave Selena the chance to introduce her husband, who could help her with garden design and cultivation.

He had reported back that the new resident was a woman who had practised a career among the well to do, but seemed still to be in search of a role. She was called Cordelia and had retired into this secluded location following an apparently successful career as a photographer to the elite, but had become sated with the milieu of luxury, beautiful dresses, big houses, opulence and waste.

Selena replied that it would be nice to retire with a plenitude of wealth, but she agreed with him that they had had their small rewards that, in some ways, had been augmented by their having seen their family thrive and grow to maturity.

The new neighbour had subsequently shown some of her albums of photographs to her when, after several weeks, they had formed a closer relationship. Some were of high-end cars but most of them were haute couture dresses. 'This was at Milan, this was at Rome, this was at Florence,' she had been told proudly but also sorrowfully as Cordelia turned the pages. 'But it's just waste,' she had declared, dismissively. 'Rich people with too much money to spend on trifles and having nothing worthwhile to do. Children raised in an atmosphere where everything was granted and who would grow up thinking that the world owed them the same.'

It had never occurred to Selena that the spendthrift habits of those city types was mere waste in irresponsible families of affluence, and she was not particularly persuaded by her new neighbour's denunciations. She had never known riches, herself, but had enjoyed her career as a mother, a housewife, a carer and was happy to note that that was something in which the new resident not only found value but had also expressed a measure of envy. 'I was no different from most other people,' Selena assured her. 'Hard times when the family was young, but lovely memories. I wonder that you didn't do the same.'

'I thought about it but life has many turnings,' came the sad reply. 'I went in search of happiness but never found it.'

'You must have gathered some memories that you treasure, though,' she responded encouragingly, trying to forge a closer relationship that might compensate her for the loss of Tandrina.

Cordelia smiled as if recalling days long ago. She had kept one memory a secret divulged to very few; but Selena was a homely woman, and they had achieved a special status as good companions. The cottage would also be a long-term residence where Cordelia felt she should encourage a promising relationship with her neighbour. She reached for an album and opened it at the last page, where she showed her a picture of two young people clasping each other and smiling with unbridled happiness into the camera. 'That was when we were captured by a seaside photographer. A day when we spent a week at the coast. But that's almost the only record of him that I have.'

'What happened to him?'

'The usual story,' Cordelia replied with a sigh. 'Two young people with no money. We said we loved each other and meant it but, in the end, I grew disillusioned with waiting and we drifted apart. It seemed that he didn't want me and I didn't know how to stimulate his interest in a formal relationship. To be honest, we were both tongue tied and neither of us could approach the subject. I received an offer of a job in London which I thought would bring satisfaction. They paid well and gave me opportunities to travel but after two decades I had to accept that it had brought financial rewards but no real satisfaction. So I bought this cottage and left all that nonsense to the others. Now, I'm content to watch the view. Almost,' she added quietly.

Selena glowed with reminiscences of her younger days and the romantic films she had seen with Sylvano. Days of courtship floated back into her memory and she responded with an unrestrained rendering of how they had met, how restrained they had been and how joyful had their marriage been ever since. Nor was she silent in expressing her sympathies with Cordelia at her revelation, but chided her very gently in having placed a career before romance, at which Cordelia could only shrug at the opportunity lost, although in the depths of her being, had to concede that Selena was right. But it was too late now.

Franco's house was the biggest in the area and his garden the envy of all who visited. Not that he gave many invitations, but his wider family was important to him. Without a family of his own, he enjoyed meeting his sister and his nephew and niece. Sometimes Laura rang to announce that she had planned another visit and would fly in with her children for 'a duty call' as she described it. But that was also a welcome interruption to his routine or, rather, lack of routine. She provided a joyful interlude and was always full of news about the children, gossiping merrily away for a few hours, staying for several nights whilst attempting to bring order to the house. He was happy in her company, even though he knew that she was always very subtly demonstrating that he, too, should join the matrimonial world. Some of those hints seemed to support that theory, but he valued his sister's quiet understanding of his inability to break away from the anchor that held him to the past. When she had first broached the futility of his continuing loyalty and inability to forget the incident that had burdened him for years, he had protested, 'Just forget it and carry on as if nothing had happened!' Having noted his sensitivity, she had desisted from the least criticism, but she had adopted the practice of subtly illustrating with her family the benefits of matrimony and was encouraged by her brother's happiness with them when they visited.

Since then, Laura had always been diplomatic on the subject, knowing how delicate was the matter that had driven him into bustling activity for several years. But she had understood his real and abiding love for Cora, the girl who had died on that otherwise blissful mountain holiday so long ago. She also suspected that his sorrow had been deepened by his feeling of guilt at not having been able to save her. Years before, his mode of living had changed radically from unambitious to frenetic business leader in charge of his grandfather's company until he had realised the pointlessness of constant striving and then, at an early stage of life, had moved to Milan and then to Bologna, where he appeared to have sunk into a semi-retirement accompanied by a pain that had gradually subsided into the everlasting wound of a bleeding heart.

He had almost dismissed all contact with humanity after the accident, until one day, several years afterwards, when she judged that Frank had suffered enough, Laura had returned from one of her visits full of compassion and the resolve to raise him from the depths of melancholy. Whilst she was in Bologna, Laura had called on Rosa, who had been one of their tightly knit group of friends since their teenage years but had returned to her native town after her two years as an au pair. They both agreed that Franco needed a little female company. Rosa concurred, but noted that it was Franco who was the object of his sister's concern.

'You could have asked him to console me,' she said in a somewhat resentful reply. 'Cora and I were always together. The news of her death was almost as much a tragedy for me as it was for Franco, but he received all the commiserations whilst I was cast into a pit of despondency, not quite as deep as his but only in recent years have I been able to climb out of it.'

Laura felt immediately contrite. 'You're right,' she responded apologetically. 'I placed him before you because he is my brother. I knew you were close but I've conveniently overlooked your claims to condolences. I'm sorry. You must feel that I've been very inconsiderate.'

'I've missed her deeply over all these years, but we have to pass on. There's no sense in continually brooding about it even if there is nobody who could be such a good friend as she was.'

'There is someone,' Laura prompted.

'Who is that, then?' Rosa asked, rather puzzled whom she could mean.

'Frank, of course. You were the nearest and dearest to Cora,' she told her. 'You have the perfect qualifications for easing him out of his misery and he will do the same for you. Both of you have the same memories. Go to him and persuade him to break out of his tortured soul. Smother him with the love that he has missed and mourn for Cora together with him; she would have wanted you to save him. Do it for her and for him and for yourself. I know you are already close, and don't hesitate to use any weapon,' she told her hinting heavily at the strategy she should adopt. 'He must be aching for a loving relationship.'

Rosa was not averse to a closer contact with Franco, the friend with whom both Cora and she had spent their days of innocence travelling around in the holidays and messing about with boats, but she knew that he had built an invisible wall around himself. Those days of innocent pleasure had passed into history and he had entered further into a more formal adulthood, still friendly but more inhibited and self-constrained. 'I can't just go to him and make a business proposition to him: you comfort me and I'll comfort you,' she responded.

'Rosa, I know Frank better than anyone. I know you, too. You would make a perfect couple. You are both romantics. Throw caution to the winds and melt into a single being.'

Thus encouraged by no less than his sister, Rosa meditated on being selected as the saviour of a man in turmoil. But she was in turmoil, too. Why shouldn't it be Franco who rescued her? They were both victims of the same misfortune; that terrible time when the most beautiful day had been shattered by the moment that had changed history. Cora quite literally shattered, her body hidden from view by the emergency rescue team, and then enquiries by the police, followed by the inquest and a remorse that had lasted for years; and a beauty spot that remained forever a place of grief.

Laura had her family as compensation, Franco had his businesses, but Rosa had memories that occasionally returned as nightmares. How could there ever be a perfect or even partial resolution? But she and Franco had more than a casual friendship; they had a bond of unspoken love; for Cora, for each other. They were survivors who had clutched at each other but loyalty to Cora had intervened to hold them apart until the moment when Laura had told her that the moment of resolution was nigh.

Somewhat uncertain of her strategy, Rosa had rung Franco and spoken for some time about not very much, but hinting that she was missing the times they had enjoyed before, and, when she had identified that he would be free for several days, told him without tolerating any refusal that she would visit next day.

Franco was only too aware that he had locked himself away from those days when nobody had any cares except to find some new scene of enjoyment. Rosa brought back the flavour of his yesteryear and they spoke of the good old times and the things they had done, inevitably bringing the image of Cora into their minds. Rosa noticed how he became a little distracted, but he could see that she also missed her former friend.

'We have nothing but memories, now,' she admitted. 'Even if I knew her for only two years,' she mused. 'But, I think of her a lot, even now, years later. Fate is a cruel visitor,' she commented. 'That's why I came, really,' she continued in a genuine sadness. 'I've bottled up all my feelings and carried on as if nothing had happened, but the more I think about it, the more unbearable it becomes until I feel I am going to burst unless I can release all that pent up despair to the only person who can understand it. We are both deprived of a deep and lasting friendship all because of some freak accident. I'd give anything to bring her back.'

Franco had remained silent, feeling a magma of emotions raging inside him, but he finally managed to respond. 'It was all my fault. I told her not to go too near the edge, but not sharply enough. I'd give anything, too. All I have now is a big, empty house and, like you, no one I can talk to about it. Everybody tiptoes around the subject, but, sometimes, I want to shout my frustration to the skies, to tell them how cruel they are, to plead for her return. But, of course, they never hear me.'

'We'll remember her as she was. The most wonderful friend either of us could have had,' Rosa replied, embracing him for the first time. Franco felt that he was holding the nearest thing to Cora that he could ever have imagined.

Rosa's contact with Franco proved highly successful and her visits more regular. He had even confessed his private thoughts of himself, a shell in which he hid himself from the world, but she had responded that her object was to bathe him in the soft light of love. 'That is a commodity that has no limit,' she said. 'It radiates from the soul and penetrates the hardest exterior.' Franco felt the glow of love upon him once more.

All these years later, Franco reflected that Rosa had provided the sympathy and comfort that he needed and the support for him to turn his efforts into more productive directions. He wondered what Laura felt about his relationship with Rosa, unaware that it was his sister who had hinted to her that she should be the one to drown his sorrows and had joyfully approved of Rosa's success. Cora's loss had left her bereft of a dearly loved friend, but had robbed Franco almost of existence.

His relationship with Rosa had encouraged him into further activity and a fresh impetus with which to launch a remorseless career of industry takeovers in which he had been highly successful and intended to remain so, and as a result of his increased reputation, he had become one of the most important people not only in the district but also in the company of a number of leading industrialists.

Chapter 5

Franco had known the pressures of business, the hectic round of negotiations and the unremitting stress that had been his faithful companion, but he had overcome all that by delegating almost all authority and withdrawing not from daily affairs but from the intensity of the struggle for detail. Using his secure telephone system, he could still keep as near to business via frequent updates as he had formerly been able to do from the office. It was peaceful here, he had discovered, and very conducive to thought. He had also had the pleasure of organising the reconstruction of his garden which, mostly thanks to Sylvano, presented very satisfactory views wherever he looked.

He was keen to display the product of their joint creation to his new neighbour, somebody who displayed more appreciation than ever Tandrina could have done. Cordelia therefore became a frequent visitor to the house and garden where they could sit admiring the view, yet again. On one occasion, he coaxed her into a few words of praise before returning to the house to mix the cocktails, but he stood at the window from where he could see her seated in a director's chair gazing over the lake into the far distance beyond. She often sat there like that just looking at the view with the trace of a smile on her face. He had wondered what thoughts passed through her mind as she absorbed the sight of those gently rippling waters. It was a view worth looking at, that was why he had bought the house and moved from his former residence in Milan, but he felt that she was not just feasting her eyes.

At least several months before, he had divined that she was thinking deep thoughts of the past, but, whatever it was that passed through her brain, he did not press her for an explanation when she visited him, sensing that they must be those that he felt she did not, or would not, wish to reveal. He had his own history to guide him. Somewhere in the depths of her mind was the nostalgia of a time before she had moved to the cottage, perhaps something triggered by the view that seemed to fascinate her so much, or perhaps her former high life that had been innocently relayed to him by Selena. He was confident that it was not a troubled time that she had experienced but one that she had found to be incomplete. She was highly intelligent and had held a well-paid occupation among the glitterati but had given it up and, over a year before, had retired to the edge of this little town to think or to recover or just to dream of the past.

Despite being aware that several people of distinction lived in the neighbourhood, he was delighted that this graceful lady had taken the place so sadly vacated at the death of Tandrina and of her husband. Her being an incomer and therefore possessing a little mystery added to her attraction, in addition to which she knew little about the area and had readily accepted his hospitality. He had paid a courtesy visit soon after her arrival, waited a few weeks for her to settle in and, then, had invited her to lunch, whereupon he had become captivated by her charm and her skill at reserving a little privacy at her antecedents; they each had their secrets of the past and neither enquired too deeply about them. She also had an additional aura of fascination in that her name reminded him of his first love. He knew only too well that she could not be the reincarnation of the girl he had loved so deeply. His memory was too scarred for that; but she possessed a personality that he had known in Cora, whom he had lost, but had, now, it seemed, returned in spirit.

On his first invitation to her, she had remained silent on the affluent surroundings she found in his house: the furnishings, the drapes, the carpets, but he was also very perspicacious and easily detected a slight animosity in her at his mode of living, despite her having expressed polite approval of it. She was a very attractive woman with a slight reservation behind her smile and he admired her for her bearing, her speech and her gracious behaviour. A woman who had mixed with the best of society but one who had a certain reserve in expressing her approval of their lifestyle. Diplomacy was his forte, however, and he adopted the politeness of a man skilled in the customs of human relationships.

He had reason to be highly considerate towards this new neighbour who had suddenly appeared from nowhere as one who may rekindle a spark of life, reason that easily drew him into conversations that elicited a little of her background and tastes, and to the discovery and approval of her achievements as well as to her sense of discrimination that echoed his own. His only regret was that her visits were rather too infrequent, but they were enough for him to accept her as a lady of accomplishment and to adopt the deference of the well-bred gentleman of distinction. That was an accolade that he had earned not because of having been born into a family that could have given him the air of good breeding that he now possessed, but, as merely the grandson of a self-made man of industry, his awareness of the rough edges he had acquired had become an embarrassment, and he had striven over the decades to eliminate them. From his beginnings in an unexceptional town in England, he had gained useful business training working for his grandfather in his engineering company and had travelled on an upward journey through society to become recognised by his peers as a man of sound judgement and one with a talent for management.

He enjoyed Cordelia's company and invited her to his little parties that he arranged from time to time in which he sought to alleviate the boredom that occasionally enveloped him as well as to repay his business colleagues for their loyalty and his affluent neighbours for their occasional hospitality. She guarded a little of her former mystery, which merely ensured that his interest had never waned, but he, nonetheless, found her reticence to unveil her complete history somewhat tantalising. That was merely a temptation for him to explore further with the consequence that the relationship had blossomed over the next months into the sort of friendship enjoyed by like minds thrown together by the accident of neighbourliness. He knew enough about her to be quite confident of her spotless character, although still rather puzzled by her habitual resort to daydreams of the past, or of the future, or even, perhaps, of the present, but he diplomatically maintained a studious lack of open curiosity, sensing that penetrating questions would tend to alienate her rather than to draw her more closely to him.

Out there in the garden, Cordelia had sunk into her habitual resort of staring over the lake and thinking apparently of nothing except a dream. But it was not only of the time through which she had passed but also of the time that might have been. A strange weaving of times that had carried her through that procession of experiences without resolving her constant wish for a diversion onto another route. What a strange path she had taken! A childhood spent satisfactorily at boarding school and university, a brief period of junior service at a little-known magazine followed by just one glorious year in the company of her great love, during which she had matured into a thinking, independent woman finally breaking free to travel Europe for the magazine.

The route that she had not trodden was merely a fancy; a wish that had not been granted but had remained throughout the years as an unfulfilled aspiration, often vague, but sometimes strengthened into the possibility of achievement had she but sought to retrace her steps and cross back into those halcyon days.

In her new profession, she had at first been pleased at the revelation of how others enjoyed their luxurious lives but, as the decades passed, she had gradually become jaded by the continual sight of waste and superfluity. After several years of regret, she had to face the fact that she had taken the wrong turning and now yearned to return to the simplicity of a former existence, one spent among more deserving people whose modest interests centred upon their families and not the spendthrift style of the super-rich.

But it was to this place and to this view to which her path had brought her and not to the realisation of that dream of long ago. As she sat in the garden, she reflected upon her life and wondered what she had done with that precious commodity. It had launched her into a career as a leisured woman of means but, now, having been transplanted from living among the rich and powerful and a lifestyle that she abhorred, she had merely moved elsewhere and assumed the idleness that her affluence had enabled. What had all that striving to reach the giddy heights of fame, such as it was, brought to her? Simply, the loneliness of a woman who had not followed the route which she had craved all those years before.

It was pleasing to be regarded by those few visitors she received as one of the more important personages in the area, but that was mostly owing to the fact that her promotion in everyone's eyes had been attributable to her acceptance into the local high society and not for qualities of her own. Franco's family and almost all his acquaintances had welcomed her into their circle as a sign of an emergence from his strictly guarded privacy of so many years, regretting only that it had been undertaken well into his fifties.

Cordelia had wondered whether they would regard her as an interloper seeking advancement in the lofty realms of an affluent family, but Franco's sister, Laura, regarded her as a welcome guest which, she confessed, gave her an opportunity to speak of topics of which her brother, wrapped up in his pursuit of wealth, was entirely ignorant. The only woman in whom Cordelia had detected a little well-disguised jealousy was Rosa, the family friend from Franco's early days, a woman of similar age, always well dressed and one who had been educated in the arts and languages. She was also one who had bristled at the news of Franco's interest in his neighbour and the thought that, after all these years, her hopes of finally achieving her desire for a permanent relationship with him must now be endangered.

For her part, Cordelia had a feeling that a reproachful finger had been raised to trouble her conscience once more with a sense of not belonging, of not wanting to belong, of having taken another wrong turning in the maze of her existence that had merely led her to the realisation that she was in danger of falling into a trap from which she would never be able to escape. Perhaps she had already fallen into the trap. Franco had come dangerously close to hinting at the desirability of finding a less troubled existence, but she had extricated herself from that subject with her usual tact and diplomacy, although remaining plagued by her habitual indecision at what her destiny should be.

As they sat on the terrace one evening following another of Franco's invitations, he reached out to touch her hand and to look at her with a genuine feeling of understanding. 'You always seem so melancholy,' he said. 'Is there anything that I can do? I hope you are not having doubts about the cottage.'

'No. Of course not. There's nothing to be doubtful about. I just think I should be doing something. Helping the village children, perhaps, even taking a job somewhere. But not the sort of job I had before. That was just a never ending round of gaiety and parties. They are just a constant reminder of how inherited wealth bars all knowledge of the real problems of the world.'

'That makes me grateful that I made my fortune from a dedication to hard work,' Franco replied. 'But it did mean that I had to wait too long to produce a family. Now, I have the wealth but there will be nobody to inherit it.'

'I can't help reproaching myself for being able to live in a style denied to most, even if not that of those super-rich whom I finally came to despise,' she responded. 'At least, you don't squander your wealth on needless parties, but I see myself as a hypocrite and a traitor to my ideals. I've travelled Europe, been regarded as an excellent researcher and earned a decent living, but I have nowhere to go, now. Somebody without a goal except to be a dutiful citizen,' she added as if that were a poor aspiration.

'That's a worthy enough ambition,' Franco responded encouragingly. 'But I think you are needlessly repressing yourself, Cordelia. You need to settle into a life that rewards your capabilities and assists you finally to attain the role for which you were destined.'

'I wonder what my destiny is. To float through an existence with no further effort or to become a society hostess? For all my regrets, I have had active employment, but being among all your friends and family on infrequent occasions is not enough. I need something to do. I hadn't realised that I would ever say this, but those days witnessing one extravagance after another had their compensations.'

Franco had been pleased to find that his new neighbour was an educated lady of taste and decorum but he sensed a past that had enveloped her in mystery. She was a puzzle

– very forthcoming in speaking of her former activities but simultaneously guarding all reference to her place in that society. But everybody had their privacy, he thought. Even he had his secrets, and dark ones at that. He was intrigued by that enigmatic background that seemed to waft about her, and was tempted to ascertain what lay behind that persona and perhaps to be able to allay any reticence she may have about revealing her past. 'What sort of life did you like best?' he asked, somewhat cautiously.

Cordelia thought for a moment before mentioning, 'I met plenty of high-ranking people who were happy to talk about their plans and careers. Fashion photography, business journalism, executives, factories, offices. They welcomed all the publicity when my magazine syndicated my photographs and articles, and I gained an education in a wide range of economic activity. Not that I ever started my own businesses but it was interesting to write fulsome reports about them. Some of them even led to business expansion.'

'I'm surprised that you gave it up. It sounds a very interesting career. My business could have used someone like you. We are always looking for information on competitors, particularly in engineering.'

'I became sated with too great a focus upon the empty lives led by the super-rich. Rich men's palaces and their families who squandered thousands on cars and haute couture,' she continued as if she had not heard his comment. 'When I realised that, even as an observer, I had unknowingly been supporting their lifestyle, I just fled the scene of extravagant waste and bought the cottage in order to return to the simple life, the life that I used to lead, a life when I had no money and only the riches of the poor: simple things, walking the hills alone or with friends, the photography club or theatres; but I foolishly left that undemanding world for the tinsel of the social whirl lived by the demigods of industry. I thought I wanted to be independent and as wealthy as all the others but it took two decades for me to realise that I had made the wrong decision. Now, I have left that hectic world where one outrageous expense follows another. I have re-entered the calm I knew before but not regained the days of youth.'

Franco commented sympathetically, 'None of us has been able to reach back into those innocent days.'

'No,' she agreed. 'But they remain like a flower remembered for its beauty although long since faded. How I would like to visit those places I knew before! To relive the days of no regrets, the days before the winds of change!'

'Take a little holiday. Go back for a few weeks and relive the times you loved.'

Cordelia remained thoughtfully silent. She had contemplated going back several times over the years, but had hesitated, not wishing to confirm her fears that everything would have changed radically. 'The world would no longer be the same and I would merely be wandering through as a ghost of former times,' she replied with a regret tinged with wistful longing, but quickly recovering, she added with the trace of a smile, 'And what would you do with no one local to invite for drinks?'

'I've lived here alone for years,' Franco replied. 'You said you preferred to follow the quiet paths. If you can do that, I certainly can. I'm used to it. I can invite Sylvano and Selena. They are totally decent people who always have something sensible to say. And I shall be able to look forward to your return,' he added. 'When you come back, I hope it will be with the satisfaction of having relived your memories and, with a new resolution, to step into the future unencumbered by the past.'

He paused while she seemed to be reconsidering her answer, but added as a further contribution to her thoughts, 'May I also express the wish that it would be a future that would find us as even closer neighbours.'

Cordelia heard the words uttered in such considerate tones for her delicate sensibility and was poised on the edge of indecision. She wavered between the memory of those sunny days in an unfettered youth and their inevitable loss behind the clouds of a new maturity. With Franco's words, she felt the past receding ever further and being replaced by the future sweeping over her and ever near at hand. Life would begin again and she could cast all her hesitations aside. But reliving those past times that she had loved or adopting the life that seemed now to be offered added further confusion to her thoughts. Only a word was needed, one that would start her upon a new voyage and cut her past adrift. But a past that, before it was lost completely, could be retrieved, if not relived, by accepting the suggestion of a little holiday.

After a short pause, she replied to Franco's assumption of her imminent acceptance, 'I'll have to give it some consideration,' but it was to her dream of recapturing those days of old to which she was referring, and to his mystification, added, 'I've never been able to make a wise decision.' But however puzzled he was at her response, he noted that she had not refused and thought her already half persuaded. She would, no doubt, use the intervening time to think advantageously of his offer.

'Would you prefer cities? London, for instance, plenty to do there, or a country retreat, very restful? Or a coastal town. You like looking over the water,' he suggested.

'There was a place on the south coast that I liked. But I'll have to think about it.'

'Of course, but don't waste the summer.'

Cordelia thought about it just as she had thought about it for years, but this time, Franco's invitation was an additional element that intruded into her deliberations. The thought that his words could have been a proposal of marriage formed more persuasively in her mind, and he had, no doubt, wrongly linked her reply to his proposition. Another decision was required. Would it be yet another wrong turn? She had very nearly decided to return to the old days and the more she thought, the more she was tempted by that prospect of renewal while she was still free. To revisit the days that were in total contrast to what she could now afford became almost an obsession; days of penury, days of love and laughter that had left indelible memories in her mind, days of unforgettable happiness lost. But she had fled the scenes she held so dear and knew that they could not be reinstated.

'Take an absence of a month or even more,' he told her. 'Stay at a decent hotel and don't worry about the cost. I know you want the simple life but don't economise too much,' he advised her with an understanding smile.

Prompted by Franco and his advice, she announced with an unusual decisiveness her intention to transform her memories into action. She did not want to lose them but simply to tread again the scenes she had known all those years ago and to recall her long-lost past. Her memories would be refreshed to serve another twenty years.

A week later, Franco drove her to the airport, told her to think about his offer and she replied that she would. He waved goodbye upon parting, reassured by her apparent acceptance, happily believing that he could manage even if he were left to his own amusements, but on returning to his empty home, he was struck by the feeling that it was less appealing than before. The several hours that elapsed until the telephone rang for Cordelia to report that she had booked into a nice hotel in London proved lonelier than he had imagined. He wished her an interesting time and not to worry about him, assuring her that he had a few business matters that would occupy his mind, even if he privately realised that he would miss her visits.

Franco was puzzled that she seemed to harbour the same conflicts of action from which he, too, had suffered – past conflicts that had so impressed its stamp upon their minds that they could not be erased. Both of them, he reasoned, had placed a veil of unspoken sorrow over their former lives that, even if its cause remained a mystery to the other, had united them in an abiding grief.

Chapter 6

The Pelham Gallery buzzed with an unusual excitement and commotion. A palpable atmosphere of urgency pervaded the normally calm and measured pace of activity as senior staff consulted each other in hurried exchanges of puzzled expressions. Something was afoot. Something never before encountered, but something that demanded immediate action. All ears were cocked in order to understand the cause of this tension but the junior staff were denied knowledge of whatever it was that had so upset their managers, but were simply told that an announcement would be made later that morning.

Before the morning was out, the cause of the uproar had been established from a few sentences released by the security staff in tones of incredibility imparted to those few people who had access to them. The news spread quickly around the building transmitted in sensational flashes faster than a forest fire leading to clusters of whispered conversations on the likely cause.

The directors of the gallery attended a board meeting hastily called by an unusually nervous Marcus, who ensured that the door was firmly closed before he addressed the meeting. The assembled board directed puzzled glances at Marcus, aware from his set features and portentous manner that something big was about to be announced. They looked silently and expectantly at him as this man of normally flowing speech returned their gaze with an air of solemn silence before swallowing a deep sigh of desperation. Suddenly rousing himself to the task in hand, he said simply, 'We have been the object of a cunning theft of one of our most valuable paintings.' He stopped in an agony of despair, during which the directors expressed incredulous gasps of surprise.

'Theft! Robbed!' were among their most intense exclamations, followed by 'Which one? How?'

'The del Mano, *Girl with a Harp*,' Marcus announced. 'Gone! Stolen! Four hundred years of safekeeping that has ended with a huge measure of ignominy on our conduct. I need hardly say how damaging that will be for the gallery and for our administration.'

'But how?' they chorused. 'We have very secure premises and alarms at every door.'

'I'll give the floor to Spenser in order to convey the full story. Needless to say, it is he, as art director, who is most affected and best able to relate the circumstances.'

Spenser noticed the implication by Marcus that it was he who was somehow culpable, proving yet again how quick he was to offload any blame that would otherwise be sure to fall upon himself. But with a calmer manner than that adopted by Marcus, he briefly explained that they had been duped by a substitution of the painting for a copy, and that that had, no doubt, been sourced from their own shop. The original had been exhibited for over four months since the last verification at the rehanging of the picture, but at a routine change of security code he had noticed that the current painting on display showed no identification number. A cunning replacement had somehow taken place.

He was interrupted by a chorus of 'But we installed the most modern security system only a few years ago, and it is tested daily. Why wasn't that triggered when the theft took place? Has the theft been reported to the police? How could the theft have gone unnoticed until now?'

Marcus attempted to calm the meeting. 'We have not yet reported the matter to the police. That could have very adverse consequences on our internal investigations. The indicators are that the theft may well have been perpetrated by one of our own staff. Somebody who knew the testing regime and presumably could have removed the original and rehung the copy within little over a minute.'

Spenser reminded the meeting that the painting, together with several dozen others, had been reframed. Two copies had been produced as test pieces, but both had been accounted for. The reproduction had also been available to the public through the gallery shop, which had registered several sales of that picture over the course of the years, but no details of the purchasers had been recorded. He sought to alleviate any concerns at the prospect of damage by reminding the meeting that the original had received a glass covering which should provide protection against accidental damage during removal or in inappropriate storage conditions. That calmed the meeting a little but did nothing to quieten the protests that the painting was no longer in their care. If it was an inside job, it may still be hidden away on the premises and a thorough search must be undertaken. Spenser warned that the date of the theft was unknown and that the painting could have been moved elsewhere at any time in the last four months, but the meeting, nonetheless, insisted that they direct their efforts to examining every possible hiding place.

Marcus closed the meeting, having agreed to implement a thorough search. He turned to Spenser. 'This is going to ruin our reputation for good management. There is no way we can keep the theft secret for long, and the publicity will destroy all the credibility that we have gained over the years. We'll have to notify the insurers and they are sure to splash the news all over the media. We'll also have very tricky negotiations on values, not to speak of ransom demands by all manner of crooks and cranks.'

The staff were shocked by the news. Routine was interrupted, benches were cleared, cupboards searched, store rooms examined. Nothing was found.

The directors gathered next day to be told that security records had been checked and found correct with no interruptions, all obvious places as well as the least likely had been thoroughly searched but nothing had been discovered. Laura drew the obvious conclusion. 'The painting has been smuggled out, somehow. We now have to report the matter to the police and they will question everybody in the building, as well as anybody whom we can identify as a frequent visitor and who may have been checking our routines. The media will swarm all over us and probably demand an examination of all remaining exhibits in order to verify their authenticity, which will slow down or even halt the project. And we can expect our own conduct to be critically examined,' she added. 'Fortunately, we can claim that if the del Mano is ever found, it is unlikely to be damaged owing to the protection it has received from the glazing that we recommended.'

The directors were silent in their horror at referring the matter to the police, but they finally admitted that they had no other option. Marcus, with the bustle appropriate to a dutiful manager beset by a crisis, bravely undertook to notify the authorities, despite feeling great trepidation at whatever interrogation he would have to face, and, even worse, how he could defend the gallery to the press if, but more probably when, the news became public knowledge. He met Spenser's stony expression with a fleeting, downcast glance of submission, having thought that this job would be the pinnacle of his profession but, instead, now felt that it had brought him to the lowest point of his career.

Spenser returned to his office and slumped disconsolately at his desk, thinking that Marcus's crisis management had little to be praised; he was a man full of words but empty of courage.

The door opened and Laura entered. 'It's more likely to be an inside job, Spenser. No employees have left gallery employment for well over a year and only the security staff could have known the regime. They will be the first to be questioned.'

Spenser sighed. 'My thoughts entirely,' he responded. 'But I have complete faith in their integrity. Both security men have been long-term employees and neither has any motive to deviate from years of loyalty to the gallery.'

'Money?' Laura suggested. 'That's a powerful incentive.'

'Possibly, but the painting is not quite of the first rank, although its antiquity does add fame and desirability. It would be difficult but not impossible to sell it on the private market. It is more probable that the painting will be retained by the perpetrator in his own gallery never visited by the public and never to be seen again.'

'Perhaps the Art Squad can track it down. They may have leads to a likely purchaser.'

Spenser simply spread his hands to indicate a total lack of knowledge of where it could be. He was as mystified as she.

Laura telephoned Frank in order to inform him of the theft and to express her horror to somebody who would not only keep the matter confidential but also be a comfort in her despondency. Her duties consisted merely of attending board meetings but, as a direct descendant of the founder, she felt as if she had suffered a mortal blow.

'I was too insistent upon all the exhibits being reframed. If I hadn't persisted, this may never have happened.'

'Quite the contrary,' he replied. 'That would have had no bearing on the theft. Don't blame yourself. The more quickly they can be glazed, the safer they will be from violation,' he assured her. 'Does anybody have any ideas of who could have perpetrated the theft?'

'No. We'll just have to wait for the Art Squad to investigate, but they may never find the painting. The oldest and most valuable painting in the gallery! I've no idea what it could be worth, but, obviously, several millions. What on earth can we tell the press? It's a huge failure of management and that means me as well as Marcus and Spenser and the others. And it's also a huge blot on the gallery's reputation. We've never had anything like this since we were founded.'

Frank told her not to be so upset, but he was also wondering whether all this turmoil would reflect upon himself as main trustee. He was a thousand miles away but, now, rather worried that the repercussions would impact heavily upon the local staff.

Hedrick felt the loss more sharply than others. That was the painting that had drawn him to the gallery, and he felt that he had suffered a personal disaster. He stood in his own little gallery at home of just a few reproductions in which was his *Girl with a Harp*. It stirred deep memories of that school visit; an eternal reminder of a youth now fading into the fog of passing years. 'What had he done with his life, since then?' he wondered. 'Built a role in an important part of somebody else's gallery only to have his work stolen by thieves. Such was his reward for diligence!'

His disgust at being beset by the fortunes of age was somewhat alleviated by once more encountering his old friend, Bamber, who had returned from several years in the US and announced that he was now a married man with a wife called Lois and a family of two daughters. Hedrick was delighted to meet him again and looked forward to meeting his family, but was even more aware that his own existence was one becoming more isolated than ever. Bamber had entered the world whereas he had remained as if cloistered in a monastery garden.

Inspector Yardley and Sergeant Forbes had appeared within two hours of the report and were met by Marcus and Spenser.

Marcus explained the security routine and showed them the empty space where now there was only a label announcing 'Withdrawn for examination'.

'Any ideas on who the culprit was?' Yardley asked. Obviously a man of few words, they realised, but one who would get directly down to business.

'None at all. All our staff have been with us for years and all are completely trustworthy.'

'The security staff?'

'Two people, and security records are complete and without incident.'

'Could be a team job. One to switch off the security and another to switch the painting.'

'No interruption has been recorded, though. There are also gallery patrols. They would have observed any attempts at theft.'

'Unless the theft took place at night. Any official movements of the painting?'

'The building is secured at night and we don't risk sending any of our paintings to exhibitions,' Marcus replied, settling into the role of authoritative manager who was fully versed in the administration of the gallery. 'The picture has been with us from our formation and never been moved except for periodic inspections, which we carry out in our own workrooms. The last time it was examined was when we commenced a programme of reframing for all our exhibits. We rehung the painting about four months ago. Both the art director and I were there together with the framers. We checked the code and I gave a little speech to celebrate the return to exhibition of our most valuable picture,' he ended with a note of pride that betrayed just a slight amount of bombast.

Spenser explained that several copies of the painting existed. Their own shop had sold several reproductions over the years and he had, himself, drawn copies from the store for study purposes. Test framing had been carried out to professional standards. Two copies had been framed in their workroom as test pieces but they had been certified by him. 'I know that the framer has bought one for his own gallery and I bought another for my little gallery. I suppose you'll want to examine both of them,' he ended with just a hint of a sneer at the mere thought of a violation.

'Yes. But we shall take them to our own expert for that purpose,' Yardley told him. Spenser wondered who that might be and what he would know about the painting.

The police had commissioned Walter Tilson, from Westerton, a leading expert on paintings of the del Mano era and one known to Spenser from a previous television programme in which both had participated. He looked forward to meeting him again; they would have an enjoyable day together in reminiscing about del Mano despite the calamity of a disappearance that was shrouded in mystery, but, until the theft was resolved, they would have to observe the integrity of silence.

Yardley and Forbes, in discussing the theft after Tilson's examinations, gave the summary as, 'Valuable painting stolen within the last four months, no breeches of security recorded, several copies circulating among the public, copies in the possession of two employees but found to be legitimate purchases.'

Forbes added, 'Tilson has reported back that his examination of the test pieces has revealed that they would have been very nearly indistinguishable from the original. Comparisons of other exhibits indicated that originals and copies framed behind glass were virtually identical and would not, without detailed perusal, have raised any suspicion.'

'And there was no reason to suppose that the original had been replaced by a copy,' Yardley commented, thoughtfully.

Forbes continued, 'Both copies held by Tarrant and Ferndale have been verified as copies lawfully sourced from the gallery, both of which had been framed in the gallery workroom. I suppose we'll have to compensate them for breaking up their lawfully acquired possessions.'

Yardley dismissed that with a curt, 'Not our responsibility,' but added, 'No intelligence received of any interest from the private market.'

'A complete blackout,' Forbes commented. 'But how could it have been smuggled out given all that security?'

'It's obvious how it could have happened,' Yardley replied. 'It's an inside job. It was smuggled out in plain sight.'

'By whom?' Forbes asked, wondering how his chief could be so certain in the midst of all that mystery.

'The smuggler,' Yardley growled, unable to identify the culprit yet. 'No security alert, copies masquerading as originals, no rumours from the private market, and why must it have been smuggled out in the last four months. The painting had been verified when it had been rehung but perhaps it had already been switched by then. Precautions taken against possible mad men intent on damage would provide sufficient distraction. It's an inside job, all right; but a carefully orchestrated one.'

Hedrick returned to work not a little annoyed that his *Girl with a Harp* had been violated. His protests that he knew the picture to be a copy drawn from the store had been met with the blank face of officialdom, who argued that it was a police investigation and he might be considered culpable if he did not consent to it being examined by an expert. Hedrick was, nonetheless, aggrieved at the dismantling of his work. It was the equivalent of unveiling centuries of abstinence in an innocent girl by wreckers who would lack the love and dedication that he had devoted to the job; and his fury was reinforced by the totally inadequate apology he had received when the examination had confirmed his claim. They had trampled him underfoot but, even worse, had insulted the *Girl* with impunity.

Several weeks after the theft, Spenser was still fuming at the lack of any advance in locating the painting. But he had also been racking his brains for a possible method of how the switch could have been made. He had selected the painting from the three framed pictures he had examined with Hedrick. He had taken one for exhibition at his home and Hedrick had taken the other, thereby leaving the genuine picture to be hung next day. Walter Tilson had verified his and Hedrick's pictures as copies. Had the genuine painting been lifted later in some sort of Topkapi theft, or had it been switched the night before hanging? He had locked the painting in his office overnight and no intruders had been recorded by the CCTV. The only possibilities were that the picture had been switched either minutes before rehanging, a most improbable possibility, or before Hedrick had brought the painting to his office for comparison with the two copies. But he had viewed the painting in the workroom, and he knew that it was genuine. He despaired – two months missing and no ransom note. It seemed that whoever had committed the theft had no wish to publicise it. The painting must be in a private gallery somewhere, and be in the possession of someone who had no other thought than to keep it hidden from view by everyone except himself.

'At least, Laura had proposed glazing the exhibits,' he thought. 'That might have protected it, but thieves would probably have no consideration for safety,' he fretted. 'Now we are laughing stocks throughout the art world. How sorrowfully everyone had greeted the news, how condescending they had been, and how neglectful they must have thought us!'

Marcus sat at his desk tortured by the memory of the interviews he had been compelled to grant not only to the investigators but also to the press who had impertinently accused him of careless management of historically important and valuable paintings. He had had to resort to the full extent of extenuating circumstances: the wisdom of protecting the exhibits from damage, the full array of security measures employed and the dedication of all his staff who had never had to experience anything similar in the entire history of the gallery.

The greatest annoyance he had suffered had been the necessity for him to remain calm under the hail of accusations he had faced from people who knew nothing of art but revelled in demeaning a man with an impeccable record of management. How he wished he had been able to release the full force of his considerable vocabulary in castigating those teenage scribblers for the injustice of their allegations and then to have had the satisfaction of slamming the door in their faces! But they revelled in the freedom of self-importance whilst he was the innocent prey surrounded by slavering hounds; but it was some hidden figure shrouded in the fog of delinquency who should have been their target, and not he.

Chapter 7

Franco's memory of the day that had changed his life troubled him with increased intensity as he returned to business after taking leave of Cordelia. He had never forgotten Cora but now bore the additional burden of very nearly having deserted her for another. His attempt to justify his action with the thought that the living were present and the dead were not was dishonourable and left him with an uncomfortable feeling of guilt. He resumed perusal of his papers with the intention of spending a day or so refreshing himself with the business strategies he had adopted, but all the while with a sense of discomfort that he had deviated from his veneration of the past.

His considerations inevitably focussed on what policies he could now follow in order to recover from the failure of his merger deal that had collapsed at the last moment. It had been concluded more by persuasive argument rather than cash, and he had lost out because, he was convinced, he had not been the principal negotiator. He was sure that he could have won the deal if only he had not been so reluctant to risk the renewal of his acquaintance with Cora's brother, Bamber, who managed one of the companies in the targeted group. He had therefore appointed his director of development for that task. 'So much for delegation,' he thought wondering whether the failure was caused by his director's inadequacy or by his own decision to stay firmly in the background in order not to reveal his interest to Bamber at a too early stage. The fact of having had a redoubtable opponent in the opposing consultants could also have proved decisive, but whatever the reason for the defeat, an opportunity to renegotiate the deal was hardly likely to be presented in the near future.

He was irked at the halt to the plan that he had been considering for several years. His attempt at forging a closer link to the company managed by Cora's brother, whom he had good reason to wish well, could have provided a means by which they might resume their former good relations and lessen the burden of that unhappy day. Bamber must have suffered almost as much as he had but he thought it unwise, even so many years later, to act in an adversarial role which he feared would merely prolong an antagonism with somebody whose feelings may be as raw as his. He wanted peace of mind on that delicate subject and preferred to remain remote with the consequence that he had distanced himself from the negotiations. Perhaps he was fearful at stirring the embers, perhaps he did not wish to summon the Furies; but he was being worn down by the constant reminder of that unforgettable calamity. Perhaps he should renew contact and assert his goodwill before Bamber finally perfected the device that he, Frank, had learned may soon be unleashed against him.

The telephone interrupted his thoughts and he heard Rosa's voice inviting him to a little party at her house for a change. Franco had a sixth sense that informed him of her not wishing to meet Cordelia again if it were he who were the host. Cordelia's silent criticism warning him against constant parties sounded a cautious note, although there was no reason for him to feel any admonishment. Perhaps it was the impact of his long-sought isolation that had now engulfed him together with a growing awareness of how incautious he had been that led him to decline Rosa's kind invitation. 'I have a few business matters to think about,' he told her, but not without a twinge of conscience knowing that he had made a poor excuse for prolonging this interval of privacy. That immediately led Rosa to prickle with suspicion, however.

'I suppose you've got that new neighbour to talk to, occasionally,' she said in a slightly accusatory tone that Franco detected as an undercurrent of restrained jealousy. He hastened to explain that Cordelia had flown to London for a holiday, and that he would be on his own for a while, despite thinking that he was almost extending an invitation to her and for the opportunity for a visit not to be lost.

Rosa immediately sympathised with his predicament and told him that she would postpone her invitation until a later date, but upon further consideration, she proposed a brief visit in order to alleviate his solitariness. Franco hesitated. He had known her for years but Cordelia had only recently been the recipient of his admiration, which therefore troubled him with the mixed feelings of constancy and betrayal. Rosa was more than an old friend and he would not like further prevarication to impose any impediment to their relationship. He had not seen her for a while and would welcome an interruption to his melancholy and required only a moment of weakness to summon an end to his current seclusion.

Rosa arrived next day determined to smooth any fissures that may have opened in her absence. She had known Franco for years and felt that she understood him perfectly. They had enjoyed the closest relationship throughout all that time, the only imperfection being that he remained stubbornly committed to the girl whom he had known from childhood. Rosa knew that he had been, and remained, haunted by her death, but she had invested all her efforts in a so far unsuccessful attempt, whether as lover or as hostess, to restore him to rationality. Now, she was concerned that he would be diverted from what she regarded as her rightful place in favour of a mere newcomer with no background, almost a recluse and one who had little interest in identifying herself with the locality.

Although Rosa felt that she was on unsafe ground in talking about Cordelia to Franco, she could not refrain from registering her protest. 'I must say, Franco, I don't understand why you regard her so highly. We have had such a lovely relationship for so many years. You must have known that I had my eye on you even if you always shrunk from discussing – anything permanent. And you just go and bring her into our circle, a woman you've known for one year at the most. What has she got to offer you? She's intelligent, attractive and homely, but so am I. And I've proved it over all those years. Any call, and I come running, throwing everything aside.'

Franco lay quietly beside her, confirmed in thinking how foolish he had been. 'You're right,' he had to admit to the only person to whom he knew he could confess and confide. 'She was a mystery and I was intrigued by her. I was distracted by the business and just lost my senses thinking that she would fill the void.'

'I know you've had the stress of those businesses you run but you've always had that. I didn't mind being the girl who calmed you down and gave you all that satisfaction over the years. I've never had anybody else, nor wanted anybody else. Haven't I made you happy? Haven't I loved you all the time? She's just a money grabber looking for a fortune, and, now, she's run away somewhere. But I've stayed at Bologna in order always to be there for you whenever you needed me,' Rosa continued with a note of bitter disappointment in her voice.

'Well,' she continued reassuringly after a short pause, but with a note of resignation, 'I'll be there whenever you want me, I suppose, but always waiting, always wanting. Now I'm wondering what I've never wondered about before.'

She hesitated, thinking that she might already have spoken too much.

'What's that?' he asked, but she remained a little reluctant and felt she might say something that could end or, at least, damage their relationship.

She finally said, 'Whether you have anybody else. That woman for instance.'

'There's nobody else,' he responded to her great relief, and suddenly feeling that Rosa was, indeed, the choice he should have made years before. His recent thoughts of mysteries melting into a single solution for both him and Cordelia now seemed to have been totally misguided. He had constructed a fantasy which was most unlikely to have been replicated in Cordelia's mind, but the reality of the present had now superseded the darkness of the past. It was a comfort to think that Rosa would always be there. To her anxious anticipation after a lengthy silence, he confessed, 'The reason why I never married you was that I still felt obligated to Cora. Cordelia was here and only an occasional but, admittedly, welcome guest, but you were in Bologna.'

'We all knew how close you were to her, Franco,' Rosa responded with the sympathy she had always used on that subject. 'But Cora died over twenty years ago! I knew her for only a short time but she has been a constant presence ever since, and we have hardly mentioned her since she died. You've kept your feelings bottled up for so long, but you would have benefited by speaking to me about her. You think it is as if we would be disturbing her grave but you know that I would never reveal anything of a private nature. She's with the angels, now, but I can't help wishing she were here, still.'

They lay in silence as thoughts and memories of Cora flooded their minds. Rosa valued her association with Franco but was only too aware of how he adored the memory of his fiancée even until the present time. She had formed a close relationship with him and over the years had become the image of her in Franco's mind, perhaps the substitute for her, and had provided the comfort that he had valued. Franco thought of losing his first and greatest love and began to wonder why his loyalties to Cora had persisted for so long. He had not wanted to extinguish his happy memories, that was why, and he had bound himself with a promise of lifelong loyalty, but he had become stuck in a mind-set of venerating her and had ever since held to his resolve never to betray her even in death. Until now!

The realisation that he had committed himself to the wrong woman hammered at his conscience as another burden that he must bear but could not confess. Cordelia would soon return refreshed from her holiday and, once released from the bonds that had tied her, would have expectations of permanency, but he had been distracted and, in his fascination for her, had overlooked Cora as the woman he should have remembered. He had become suddenly aware that he had let slip his resolution never to forget his deepest love. For one brief moment, it had been dismissed by his fascination for a woman with as mysterious a past as his but he had kept that as a closely guarded secret. He was horrified and distressed at his error knowing not only that he had betrayed his vow of dedication to his fiancée, but also that he would have great difficulty in extricating himself from his predicament.

He had promised Cora that they would never be parted and he had been determined to abide by that sacred promise, but the thought now occurred to him that he may have been too rigid in his loyalty. He had always known that Cora was in the company of angels but, now, Rosa had confirmed it. She had uttered the words that cleared his mind of a guilt that had pursued him whenever he had thought of abandoning Cora for another, however worthy she may be. A veil fell from his mind and the future seemed suddenly brighter. More than twenty years was long enough to grieve, and, together, they would honour Cora with a double devotion. With a huge sense of relief at the realisation, he confessed that he had been too blind to realise that Rosa would be his constant partner. She responded that Cora had not been lost but had shone her light upon them.

With that encouragement, his immediate thoughts were to resort to his usual hectic strategy that had served him for years as the best means of diverting him from matters uncongenial. He would have the embarrassment of having to disappoint Cordelia when she returned but that was a task that he could place in a category to be dealt with later. Business called with the prospect that it would keep him occupied and free of worry for the foreseeable future. He might also be able to stimulate further contact with the new group that he had only narrowly lost to the competition.

But he hesitated at the realisation that he was on the brink of resuming the life of melancholy that had been his constant companion for over twenty years. A window had opened through which he perceived the image of Cora smiling approval of Rosa. She would look down from her balcony in the sky and be his guiding light rather than his golden chain. He flinched. Was the Catholicism with which he was surrounded converting him from dismissal to acceptance? Surely not. But need he resist if he were enabled to exchange his baleful existence for the lighter burden of redemption? A new strategy dawned upon him as he opened to a wider world.

He had lived in anguish for over two decades not only because of Cora's death but also because he had felt the antagonism of her family and of Bamber in particular at his having somehow contributed to her death. The injustice had so seared his soul that he had fled the scene in hope that he could flee the accusation; but he had merely carried it with him to a distant land and had buried himself in work with the forlorn hope that he could earn forgiveness. It was all too clear that the family were not convinced of his innocence even if their accusation centred solely upon a conjecture of his having carelessly endangered Cora on that holiday of a lifetime. He knew that he was without guilt of any illegal act but he had to concede that, if he had not taken her there, she would be with him still; but he had and he had borne the everlasting burden for which there was no consolation either for him or for all those so long bereaved.

Frank now sensed a future as a man about to enter a new world, but a world still tainted with the unjust accusation of what would remain a denunciation for ever even if unfounded. He wanted to rid himself of that black shadow but he would need to plead his case to those whom he feared he could not approach with any expectation that they would hear him. His foiled attempt to acquire the group to which Bamber's company belonged had been dashed with the consequence that a further approach so soon would be pointless.

All those years ago, he had attempted to defend himself but was conscious that his case had met with an unforgiving distain. Would it be any different now? Rosa would want an early date for a wedding and he would not wish to perpetuate a predicament that may become a cause of stress between them. There was no alternative now but to seek a meeting with Bamber direct, but, first, he would have to clear away every vestige of the past regardless of the cost. He would have to find a convincing pretext that would ensure his acceptance. An invitation, he feared, would quite likely be ignored; a letter would be too formal and destined for the bin; a proposal to visit him in person would be declined; and an unexpected encounter would lead to instant dismissal.

Was he being too dramatic? Possibly, but he wanted to expunge this ever-present trauma for which he had to leap a chasm of unknown width. He knew that it was affecting not only himself but also Laura, who had already suffered enough from her husband's long illness and subsequent death. They had both endured their suffering but his affliction remained whilst she had, he thought, recovered, in contrast to his selfishness of wallowing in an ocean of sorrow. He immediately chided himself at minimising what must have been a loss beyond measure for his sister who had two children to comfort despite her undoubted grief. But apart from that constant hive of buzzing bees in his head, he had no cause for anguish. He had worked himself into and through his torment – but not out of it. Despite his big house and fortune and the respect of all he met, he would have to stoop, once more, and plead with Bamber or meet his nemesis – an encounter from which he would emerge either with his mind restored or plunged into perpetual madness.

Rosa wandered happily about the house and garden. During all those years in which she had been Franco's loyal companion, consoling friend and passionate lover, she had ensured that he had retained his interest in life and not sunk too deeply into morbidity. It had not been too difficult a time. She had enjoyed her role helping with his infrequent parties and family gatherings or simply being with him in the calmness of the evening or setting the household into order. But the years had passed in an acceptance that he would never change, and be always subject to that abiding thought, one that lingered still and would not fade.

She had little interest in his business affairs. Engineering had no appeal but it seemed to generate a decent living for him and he was generous in his success. He was also well regarded by all the other residents around the lake, whom he invited for special celebrations, and she would shortly become the focus of a very important event in which she would play the long desired and much envied role. One that she had almost concluded would never come but in which she would, at last, occupy a place as the equal of all their neighbours.

She could now plan a grand reception for the villagers with musicians and that duo from Bologna whose concerts she had attended. She wondered whether that neighbour whom she did not dislike but had regarded with no more than the politeness of a gracious hostess would attend. No objection would be raised. Quite the contrary. The woman who had seemed to her to be the only one who might pose a challenge to her long-sought position had been vanquished. A rather questioning look would suffice to emphasise her victory; but she resolved to be magnanimous with the defeated, whom she would greet with her habitual smile but, perhaps, just a hint of triumph.

Chapter 8

The streets of London awoke once more to the procession of buses and cars as if the night had lifted its sanction on the city in order to permit the sun to shine upon another brief period of bustling activity. Crowds walked purposely along the pavements intent on reaching offices or punctually to attend their appointments. Tables were being set out on terraces to await the tourist trade, and discerning shoppers were viewing garments in shop displays.

Revelling in the recollection of times long ago, Cordelia experienced the welcome of her almost forgotten streets. After all those years away, she wanted to renew what connections she had had before, thinking sadly that most of her friends from those days would have melted into history. 'This is the time when we should be meeting again and exchanging stories of our lives,' she thought, 'but I'm too well practised at leaving life behind.' Reviewing the scenes she had known was, nonetheless, a quite acceptable occupation. Her first objective was to find the building where her student accommodation had been in her teenage days and after only a very slight confusion in the long unvisited surroundings, she found the door through which she had so frequently passed. It had been updated and furnished with an entrance phone but she did not want to do more than view from across the street that second floor window behind which, with Harriet and Rachel, she had spent her years of study. Pausing simply to wonder whether it was occupied by other students, she reflected that it might now be those who may not even have been born in the days when her flower had begun to bloom.

Only when she had left the security of home had she felt that the world had accepted her into the immensity of the future that contained not only space but also adventure. She had explored the space and had had her adventures, despite the space having proved to be without limit and all the adventures, except one, being of little consequence. But here she was, back where she had started upon a journey that had meandered through unexplored territory. The terrain had held spectacle and excitement enough to hold her admiration until it had transformed into a land of trifles and the revelation that she had trodden the path of false reward.

Now that she had found her student flat, retracing her steps to her old college was a joy only slightly diminished by the thought that the walk was not as long as she had remembered. A rather longer walk would have given her more time to indulge her reminiscences but, upon turning the last corner, she saw once again the imposing building that it had always been. The façade was completely unchanged, but she wondered whether the interior had been introduced to this later age and ventured into the reception area where she was pleased to find that it had been modernised from the Edwardian splendour of her day. Nothing too drastic, but it breathed an atmosphere more suited to present times, she thought. It also had a small coffee area served by a slot machine where she sat among the waiting students and drank from a plastic cup.

A girl placed a bag full of books on the table, fetched a coffee for herself and asked abruptly, 'Waiting for someone?'

'Just looking at my old college,' Cordelia replied. 'I haven't been back for over twenty years and thought I'd like to see whether anything has changed.'

'Has it?' the girl asked.

'Not a great deal. But it's nice to see it again.'

'What did you study?'

'Economics and law.'

'I'm doing pharmacy. My dad has his own shop. What did you do with economics?'

'Very little. I travelled the world photographing properties and fashion shows and living the life of an international journalist.'

'Sounds interesting.'

'I don't recommend it. I was always on the edge and never settled down.'

'Independent. Show people they can't kick you around. Your own boss.'

'It has its drawbacks. I should have married and had children but that's gone now,' Cordelia confessed.

'Very old fashioned. But it's some sort of life, I suppose.' The girl picked up her bag and left without farewell.

'Not the sort of student we had in my day,' Cordelia thought and walked on to explore her next memory.

She booked a show for the following evening at the Taggard Theatre that she and her flat mates had visited occasionally to find that the décor was almost exactly as she remembered from all those years ago; but perhaps a little shabbiness was an indication of endurance. The show was new but she was determined to enjoy it as much as she had enjoyed the old ones, and, as she exited later quite satisfied with her entertaining evening, she reflected that she need have had no apprehension about that. The dark cloak that had swathed her in its gloom was beginning to slip from her shoulders to reveal the rough cast clay that had been formed in the mould from which she sprang. She was back at the beginning and could set out on another journey but, this time, armed with an experience she had not known before.

Her days were filled with one tiring round after another, but they were all rewarding in their way and her only regret was that, in her hotel, she dined at a table for one. Dining alone at home was a frequent occurrence but the thought that she may be the object of several curious glances in this almost public arena made her slightly uncomfortable and she resolved to find a less conspicuous place after her revue of the sights had finished next day.

All that was left now was wandering through the bustle of Covent Garden with its shops and cafes that neither she nor Harriet nor Rachel could hardly afford to have enjoyed in their student days. But that prohibition held no terrors, now. She reflected that, whatever she had done with her life, there would be no barriers to face that could not be raised. Her very slow perambulation around the plaza brought to mind the change in the presentation of the wares for sale through which the old days had been driven away by new excitements; brighter shops, better displays, more prosperous times. The café tables were almost all occupied, but she was grateful to find a seat and to view the scene as if it were a film set created by a master choreographer.

'Excuse me,' she heard. 'May I join you? There are no unoccupied tables.'

A well-dressed, elderly man had spoken and she politely indicated her consent to his joining her. 'I'm waiting for my granddaughter. She said she would just pop into that shop over there. She shouldn't be too long.'

'I shall be moving along soon,' she replied. 'I'm on holiday and just enjoying the day.'

'We're on a trip to town. Bunty needed an escort,' he smiled. 'But it's years since I was here and I told her we would see the sights together.'

'My holiday is almost over. I'll have to think of booking a flight soon.'

'A flight! Where to, may I ask?'

'Italy. Near Bologna,' Cordelia replied.

'Posso parlare con la signora? The only Italian sentence I know,' he smiled. '*May I speak to the lady?*'

'No need to translate. But congratulations, anyway. I've travelled around for several years and picked up smatterings wherever I go.'

'I travelled a bit in my job in stress testing before I retired, but I'm happy to stay home now and meet my granddaughter occasionally. What did you do in your travels?'

'Fashion photography, mostly. But it was not the glamourous life one associates with the elite. I was always travelling from one show to another.'

'Not good for family life,' he commented.

'There wasn't a family. I've missed out on that.'

'All I can say is that you've missed a lot. I've never regretted having a family. I meet Bunty as often as possible for outings,' he continued. 'An investment in the future and a huge consolation since my wife died.'

'Sorry to hear that,' Cordelia responded automatically, but the man merely shrugged helplessly.

'Hello Granddad. I've bought a new top,' a young woman said, sitting down next to him and casting a quick glance at Cordelia.

'It's time I moved on,' Cordelia said. 'It was nice meeting you.'

The granddaughter gave a polite smile and the man ordered two coffees as Cordelia left to relive the next reminiscence and, inevitably, to reflect upon her contacts, so far. One had told her that her objectives were very old fashioned and another had told her of his granddaughter being a huge consolation to him. She decided that striding across the world was a positive action, although one the wisdom of which could not properly be assessed until several years had elapsed; but whatever the judgement may be, that lapse of time could never be retraced.

Her review of those days before her wanderings had begun was now very nearly complete, and, reminded by that latest conversation, thoughts of her cottage floated again into her mind. A calm and relaxing home, a home she had always wanted and now possessed and one to which she could retire to spend the rest of her days in peace untroubled by her thoughts of the past and of what might have been. But she was a little disturbed by the thought that she had no granddaughter for consolation. 'Or anybody else,' she added. And then, the reminder of Franco and that half-understood proposition of his loomed dimly over her mind. Had she made a decision that would bring her the peace that she craved?

A shadow seemed to pass across her thoughts to bring an uncomfortable reminder of her fate, but the old haunts she had revisited had refreshed her and lent a certain amount of encouragement. Those doubts that she had harboured over the years had now very nearly been exorcised and laid to rest, but the thought that she had not indulged herself in a return to that town on the south coast that she had so loved many years before recurred with greater insistence. Despite her new certainty, she wondered whether that would be wise. If it had changed, it might erase a part of that fond memory that she wished to retain unblemished, a memory that stood out so strongly from all the recollections with which she had been assailed, but now that she had returned to her old days, the temptation to visit it grew more strongly upon her. She would not know whether it had changed if she did not, and she was nearer to it, now, than she had been for over two decades.

With a fresh resolve, therefore, no longer burdened by her former hesitations, she checked out of the hotel next day and booked a ticket to Sandley. 'Change at Skettering,' the inspector told her in response to her enquiry as she boarded the train, and, as she sat by the window watching the countryside pass by, she felt her years falling away. Away from the glitter, away from the waste and back to the days of those innocent times.

The train rolled comfortingly on through the beauty of the blossoming countryside, stopping at every station until reaching the junction at Durnley, where it waited for passengers crossing the footbridge with unnecessary haste from the Halford connection. Her delight increased as she looked out at a scene that appeared as if it were a film set from old newsreels, but those few minutes of delight soon passed and her journey continued to Skettering, where she alighted in order to wait with a girlish excitement for the shuttle. Fifteen minutes later, she had boarded the train that would bring her memories to life, and as the route soon revealed a glimpse of the sea, she knew that she had made the right decision.

On stepping onto the platform at her destination, she inhaled a breath of sea air, pleased to note that the town was just as she remembered. She wheeled her case to the taxi stand where a taxi driver whom she asked for advice, assessed her as one who would prefer a leading hotel and suggested The Grand. 'That's the best hotel in town for sea views and just a short drive away along the prom,' he said. He stowed her luggage in the boot and she set off full of inner comfort at the start of her return to all those memories from that idyllic time. A few minutes brought her to the hotel and the taxi driver wheeled her luggage inside. They had a vacancy and registered her for a week, impressed by her address in Italy, to which she responded that Sandley had always been a place of happy memory.

The ambiance was that of a well-managed, comfortable hotel. The room was beautiful, the view was splendid. She could truly begin to relive those days that she had loved. But what a contrast with those times when both of them had been almost paupers! Days spent hand in hand just wandering about the prom and onto the pier; but they were happy days, days that had remained in her memory unblemished by time. Now, she could afford anything she wanted and chided herself at having hesitated so long to return. She was happier than she had ever been for over two decades and eager to view the town. The theatre she remembered from their days of penury was about to end one run and to start another the following week, which therefore offered the prospect of a visit on both occasions.

She stepped onto the pier and walked slowly to the end where she gazed at a view completely unchanged from the old days, the sea stretching to the horizon and the headland embracing the town. Her fears were unfounded. She remembered how it was she who had been embraced when she was last there. Words were not adequate to describe how happy they had been. It was so wonderful. But she reminded herself that that was over twenty years ago.

Where was he now? Probably slaving heroically away on some demanding office job, perhaps with a family to welcome him home. Her eyes watered and she pretended that it was the sea breeze that had blown across her face; but it was a sign that she had been so happy and perhaps could enjoy that time, again, in her mind, in this place and in another moment like those she had known before.

Acting upon a whim and almost without considering whether the play would be to her taste, she bought a ticket for the theatre performance that evening. She could have an early dinner and still have time to arrive before curtain up. They could not have done that when they were there twenty years before, but she had the freedom now to indulge an impulse without needing to consult a budget. Those days were over and she could sit back and enjoy the performance without the intrusion of economy. It was a farce with lots of doors opening and closing upon various lovers who somehow had become mixed up with the wrong partners. The audience were all holiday makers and inclined to merriment, but even Cordelia had to break out of her solemnity and abandon all constraint.

Both she and a woman in the adjacent seat left for the bar to spend the interval exchanging impressions of the first act over a glass of champagne that seemed the correct choice for adding even more bubbles to the laughter. The woman told Cordelia that she had lived locally since her retirement and had visited the theatre several times over the years. 'Always a lovely performance,' she said, 'and in winter they have concerts by visiting orchestras.'

Cordelia told her that this was her first visit for over twenty years, but much as she would like to return on future occasions, she lived in Italy and would probably not be able to come again.

'Plenty of opera in Italy, though,' the woman commented. 'But if you are ever in this country again, don't miss another visit.'

'I'm glad I came back. The town is wonderful and the views magnificent.'

'*I'm* glad that we have places to rival those in Italy. Too many people think that they must find contentment in some distant land when they have only to look for the glories around us.'

Cordelia knew that those words had been expressed in all innocence but, nonetheless, held a deeper meaning for her; she had returned from a far-flung land and could hold witness to that wisdom. The bell rang for the second act, and they took their seats for an even more uproarious procession of gaiety until, after numerous other complications of accusations and reconciliations, the happiest of endings was reached amid thunderous applause.

On walking back to the hotel, Cordelia could hardly cease smiling at the plot and subsequently sat at the bar twirling a cocktail glass, thinking how others lived lives of contentment either in retirement or in acting upon the stage. 'But what were their lives like when they were not upon the stage?' she wondered. 'Are we all actors, "*merely players with their exits and their entrances*"; or are we made of sterner stuff that can grapple all misfortune?'

Another thought struck her as she sipped her nightcap. She had profited from learning the opinion of the people with whom she had spoken in that each had added a shaft of wisdom to her life. To the recollection that one had told her that her ambitions had been 'very old fashioned', and another had told her that his granddaughter had been a 'huge consolation' to him, she could now add that, this evening, her theatre contact had told her to 'look for the glories around us'. No better confirmation could have been given that she had taken the wrong path all those years ago. She had become increasingly aware of her catastrophic error but, with the realisation that it was too late now, she went to her room, looked out over the sea to the darkening sky, sighed and prepared for bed.

Chapter 9

Bentley awoke with the sun and checked the time on the bedside clock. It was far too early to get up, he told himself, and he had nothing to do except to think of the day ahead. He lay back and drifted off for another forty minutes of being only half asleep, but he could not fight the sun that continued to stream into the room and he was finally compelled to throw back the duvet and to sit up, to get up and to dress up. He looked out of the window and over the sea. It was almost calm with a few white horses rolling into the bay. Even at this early hour, a few pedestrians were walking purposefully along the prom but, since they were not pausing to gaze out to sea, he concluded that they must be residents off to their daily grind. Or should that be their vocation, he wondered. He had never regarded his job as a grind, but whatever it would have been for this week, he was happy to have left it in Hector's capable hands. The day beckoned with a promise of excitement.

Breakfast was a counter self-selection, a big change from the old days when it was waitress service, but it enabled him to postpone making conversation with other guests until he had orientated himself into the new routine and enabled him to plan his day. But his mind was a blank. He had no plan, except to walk along the prom, perhaps, and to update himself on what changes had occurred since the last time he had visited the town.

Remembering what the old shops were proved a futile exercise. They all seemed to be new shops, and he was thrilled to find that one was a bicycle shop that hired bicycles for the day. Thoughts of eagerly exploring the countryside and emulating his boyhood adventures immediately engaged his attention and would be an appealing addition to his otherwise empty calendar. With this spark of excitement came action. He hired a trusty steed and set off to recapture those golden days of youth.

He spent the rest of the day riding over the hills thinking that he would explore the villages that he had known as a boy. He was out of practice but he had not forgotten how to keep his balance and he set himself a more leisurely pace than he had achieved nearly forty years before. He reached the crest and looked out to sea, wondering whether this was one of the places where he had stopped all those years ago, but it raised no remembrance of times past except that he felt himself happy and alone just as if he had never left his boyhood days.

'Happy? Yes, of course.' He had enjoyed his holidays when his mother had sent him off on one of his adventures. He recalled her voice, 'Be careful, don't get lost, come back in one piece.' Now, she lived very quietly in a village not too far from his house where she had plenty of people she could speak to. With his habitual shaft of pessimism, he thought that, in another thirty years, he would follow her example and live even more quietly than he did now. But not yet; the world was calling him.

He set off again slowly towards one of the villages he had known. The only difference was that, back in those schoolboy days, he had had no money, but, now, he could indulge himself at the Penley Arms if he wished. Attractive, old, with several tables and chairs set out in front, and only two people seated there. He dismounted and ordered a small beer, which he took outside, and sat at one of the tables, happy to stretch out and reflect on the first day of his holiday.

The sun shone down and drew a smile of satisfaction from him. He would have liked to have brought Heather here, he thought, but she would have had no interest in cycling or in stopping at a pub. She had wanted a more advanced existence, going to operas and viewing exhibitions. He would have accompanied her if he had not felt her waning interest in him and his consequent preference for the more mundane entertainments of walking through the parks, but he accepted that he had neglected her and understood why she had finally realised that he was stuck in a routine that knew no change.

Such were his considerations of how he had fallen into his now customary resort of enjoying his own company. Nobody since his first and only love had attained the heights of equality that he had so willingly welcomed. Still a treasured memory, she had left him with hardly a word and without a trace. His prospects were now of a life alone, but he had led that life ever since, even when Heather was with him. There would always be thoughts of what had been and of what might have been intruding into any new relationship he may have, but he doubted now that he would be able to sustain anybody's interest.

The two people at the other table rose and walked to their car, leaving him alone with the world. He would not have dreamed of interrupting their conversation, but their absence seemed to intensify the isolation, despite his knowing that several customers remained at the bar. He had always been reluctant to invade the privacy of others, but was pleased to respond to anybody who cared to engage him in conversation. Business was another matter. He had no hesitation then, because he knew that they would look to him for solutions and welcome his contribution and proposals for solving their predicament. But he was hardly likely to meet a cyclist with a background similar to his who would be satisfied with touring the villages. On top of the hills he was in a valley of his own.

He resumed his journey a little more leisurely but still enjoying the views and the gentle exercise. The country welcomed him and he was at peace until he realised that he still had the return journey to cover. But that appealed to him; a goal had been set and it was one that he achieved upon reaching the shop in good time before closure.

Bentley was tempted on the following day to resume his excursion but decided to defer that pleasure for a while. He ought to vary his activities, he thought, as he gazed abstractedly over the rail at the sea, happily observing two twelve-year-old children running over the beach. That brought back a few memories. 'They must be on holiday and looking for adventure, just as I did at their age' he thought. 'Were their parents concerned at letting them loose?' he wondered, but he knew the beach to be safe and perhaps their parents were also leaning on the rail watching them.

There were several people walking along the prom or looking out to sea and a few, either single or in pairs, leaning on the rail. Were they thinking of old times as well as he, he wondered. A couple, could they be the parents of the children he had seen? A young man, he must be a local because he wasn't dressed like a visitor. An old man with a walking stick, he must be a resident. A woman with a shopping bag, she must also be a resident. Further along the prom, a very smartly dressed woman with her back to him. She must be a holiday maker.

He strolled on, inevitably looking out to sea but also at the woman who seemed so addicted to the scene. As he approached her, she straightened up and turned to walk in his direction, still looking out to sea but then looking ahead not thirty feet from him. Each threw a casual glance at the other as they approached, and then halted in total astonishment. There had been no great change in either person to hinder immediate recognition of the other.

'Cordelia?' Bentley asked, somewhat startled at this astounding encounter.

'Bentley?' she responded. 'What on earth are you doing here?' she asked in a slight fluster at the unexpectedness of the meeting.

'I'm on holiday,' was all he could say. 'What are you doing here?'

'I'm on holiday, too,' she replied. 'I had no idea we would meet here.'

'It must be over twenty years,' Bentley said. 'Where have you been all that time?'

'Travelling mostly. I live in Italy now. But where have you been?'

'Working. I have a business in Hedderley, but I've just finished a big job and thought I'd take a week or so to relax.'

'I promised myself a little holiday, too. I haven't been back here since – the last time we were here,' she replied with a little hesitation.

'My partner told me to take a break, so I came here for a bit of sun – and to think,' he replied with equal resort to hesitation.

'Partner?' she queried. He must be spoken for by now, she thought.

'Hector. We are partners in the finance business that we founded together.'

She smiled. She did not deserve him anymore, but it was a relief to hear that her immediate assumption was unfounded – unless there was somebody else at home.

Bentley wanted to tell her that she looked as beautiful as ever, but he thought she might think him a little too forward and said instead, 'You are looking as splendid as you did back in the old days. The Italian fashions suit you.'

Cordelia smiled her response, having recovered from the shock of finding him there. 'Your business must have treated you well, too. I recognised you immediately. I thought I would visit the old haunts and fit in a trip to Sandley amongst all the other places I visited in the old days.'

Bentley had also overcome his shock and, seeking some new topic to extend the meeting, asked, 'Have you explored Freda's Tea Shop yet? If not, may I invite you to elevenses with a nice, morning tea?'

She admitted that she had marked it for her later acquaintance and accepted with a relief that would allow them to lead a more comfortable conversation. They sat at a table with sea view in, at that early hour, the little frequented tea shop. 'I came all the way from Italy to look at that view again,' she began, not admitting that she had actually come in order to relive the days of the past that she had particularly treasured.

'That's why I came,' Bentley replied. 'I haven't been back, either, since we were here last. I needed to relax and knew that this would be the place. Nice views – and memories,' he added. 'I hadn't expected to meet you, though.'

'Nor I you,' she responded. 'What are the chances of the two of us choosing the same time and place, I wonder?'

'It must be an alignment of the planets, circles of the mind, the sun touching the Heel Stone, but I'm happy to see you again. What have you done in the meantime?'

'I found a job in jet set photography and magazine interviews of business leaders, but after several years, I became disillusioned with it and bought a cottage in Italy. But I'm still uncertain of the future.'

Bentley volunteered a little about his job and how grateful he was to have sought a holiday. 'It was always challenging, very interesting, sometimes stressful, remunerative enough, but, like you, there came a time when I felt that revisiting the old days would have its attractions.'

'It's very relaxing here, but don't you get bored on your own?' she asked. She was also alone but anxious to ascertain whether he had formed a commitment to anyone whom he had left at home.

'Not yet,' he replied. 'I've found plenty to do, so far,' he told her, resorting to a little self-deception.

'Not married?' she asked directly.

'No. I had a girlfriend but she left after a few months. I was too quiet for her,' he confessed.

'Did that lead to your holiday decision?'

He hesitated, feeling a resurgence of resentment at Heather's motives for leaving, but only too aware of how she must have regarded his own deficiencies. 'Yes. I suppose it did,' he admitted. 'Life was the same as before I met her but everything seemed to have become a bit quieter after she had left.'

'But it will be quiet here, too, won't it?'

'Yes. But it offers a time to reflect and explore. After you left, I lived in a world of my own,' he told her. 'All I wanted was something that would provide some intensity of interest. I founded my business with Hector and I've done that for twenty years. I'm free to do more or less what I please, now. I've lived on my own, mostly, except for a few months. But she thought I was too reserved, didn't take her out enough. But I did; birthdays, weekends, but she thought the occasions too routine and unexciting. In the end she just said goodbye and I have never seen her again.'

Cordelia felt a pang of guilt at this familiar story. 'Did you want to?' she asked.

'Not really,' he admitted, realising that he seemed to be revealing his private thoughts quite freely to this sudden reappearance of his ideal partner, but Cordelia wondered whether he had thought the same of her. 'I sensed that she was always wanting to do things when all I wanted was—' he hesitated, but could not constrain the compulsion to admit, 'the old days that we had so enjoyed all those years ago.'

Cordelia was thrilled at hearing his confession and that his regrets were similar to hers. 'Home life has its advantages,' she replied. 'Most men are the same, I find. Very adventurous when single, exploring the world and its offers and wanting to impress, but they soon settle into some consuming hobby and inactivity when they become domesticated.'

'You make them sound like pet dogs.'

'That's what they are. Loyal to a fault, on guard at the slightest approach and always begging to be fed,' she teased him.

Bentley smiled. 'I suppose I was loyal,' he responded. 'And protective, or should that be complacent? But, then, nothing much intervened to lighten the routine and it was easy to descend into domesticity.'

'Descend rather than settle? But it sounds like an experience shared by most,' she responded, feeling that she had also descended into limbo. 'We struggle up the hills until we reach the summit of our achievement but, then, having feasted on the view, we coast slowly down again not quite to where we started but to find, whilst we were at the top, that the world has turned round beneath us. Only then do we realise that times have changed and we occupy a place in another era where a new order has developed and all about us have proved that they can survive without our intervention.'

'A new generation picking up the baton, struggling for recognition and elbowing out the weak and feeble remnants of the olden days,' Bentley responded with a sympathetic smile.

'I have joined the remnants, too, and become a shadow of my former self,' she continued, feeling that she needed finally to reveal her inner soul to somebody who would be a sympathetic listener. 'Simply taken for granted, no longer the object of pursuit nor yet of veneration but of being a piece of the furniture that has proved its use and has not yet been discarded. Not sought for advice or knowledge and not even being regarded as worthy of consideration,' she concluded, suddenly aware that she had slipped into confessional mode within minutes of meeting her old confidant, but also conscious that Bentley may think her too accusatory of their past relationship.

'That simply demonstrates how short sighted the world is around you,' Bentley responded. 'There is wisdom in that analysis but it has not yet been acknowledged.'

'No. Of course not. Nobody notices how intelligent or how wise a woman can be. We are half the world but we are invisible because people look straight through us,' she replied rather pensively. 'At best, we are the minions who carry out the bidding of others, at worst, trampled underfoot. Only occasionally do we rise to the top but then float away like a bubble reaching the air. Nonetheless, time marches on and I must fulfil whatever obligations the world has now destined for me,' she ended with a courageous optimism that belied a feeling that she had been defeated by life's adversities, and thinking that her destiny would contain very little of interest.

Bentley grasped her hand and looked at her sympathetically, which drew a little spark of gratitude from her. 'You have attributes that will attract great benefit from all who know you,' he told her comfortingly, and added, 'including me.' Holding her hand brought his memories flooding back into reality. A warm current seemed to be flowing through him, driving out all the doubts and uncertainties that had plagued him for years. She had come back, he had held her hand and she had not withdrawn it.

Cordelia felt that her visit to Sandley would be beneficial, after all. Bentley had miraculously reappeared, and the feelings of so long ago had stirred again. The old familiarity had been easily re-established and she could speak freely to him as if they had never parted.

They looked at each other, silently enjoying a moment of reflection on what might have been. Thoughts were unexpressed but, nonetheless, transmitted; speech was not required in order to convey regrets at those lost years. Bentley had been transformed from respected businessman to carefree youth full of hope and admiration for his former lover. Cordelia had experienced escape from years spent wandering almost without purpose through the complexities of a life misspent. It seemed that she had been raised on a cloud and lowered to the place where she had begun. The gods had not deserted her, after all.

Neither of them wished to break the silence, but Freda's Tea Shop had welcomed a few more customers, and the spell that had held them in their enchanted communication was broken. They awoke from their mutual exchange knowing that no further declaration was needed except to wander along the prom holding hands. Bentley was in heaven, the sun was shining and the view magnificent. For a short while, Cordelia revelled in escaping the maze in which she had been entrapped; but the world intruded into her mind. It had turned beneath her feet and she was reminded that her duties lay elsewhere. She was racked with indecision, and happiness remained a distant goal.

Chapter 10

In the gallery shop once more, Hedrick encountered a new assistant with a winning smile that drew him to her. He ascertained that she had been engaged the previous month having newly moved to the area. Her name was Astra, and she had taken the job in order to fund her existence whilst writing a doctoral thesis on the Dutch artists of the seventeenth century. Hedrick was impressed but hoped that, in explaining his own capabilities gained over the decade, he could attract a little admiration that might equal his for her. As the light illuminated her face, he felt as if she had stepped from the del Mano paintings that he so admired. The thoughts of the artist as he had first regarded his subject must have been those that now passed through his mind, also. But, even if he could not become an artist and create a portrait that would last for centuries, he felt that his admiration for this living creature standing before him would last for longer than he could ever wish. Astra felt that in her arrival in the midst of the greatest turmoil on the art scene that had occurred in decades, she was thrilled to have met one of the staff most closely connected to the painting.

They sat in the small staff dining area and exchanged views on art and on his background as well as hers. She had graduated in art history and was now engaged in writing a thesis on the seventeenth century Masters, and had been fortunate in having found a job at the gallery that would support her in the closing stage of her research.

Astra had wondered whether she could write a report on the theft but her thesis was almost complete and she needed to finish that first. Hedrick expressed his personal interest in the disappearance, not merely because he had framed the original but also because that was the painting that had awakened his interest in art. Now, he was totally bewildered at the loss and confessed his annoyance at having somehow been suspected as a participant in the theft. Astra could see that it was as if he had suffered the loss of a close relative. The painting had gone. Would it ever be found? she wondered. 'Let me know if anything new comes up,' she said, sympathetically.

Hedrick took her to the art for sale display and showed her the reproduction. 'What do you think of that?' he asked.

'Beautiful!' was her reply.

'It's a bit like you,' he told her and received a modest smile in response. 'The same shape of face and a little glow of light on the cheeks.'

He asked whether she played the harp but she told him that her talents lay elsewhere. 'A little piano, but nothing more.'

That evening, Astra added a few late thoughts to her thesis but was somewhat distracted by the mystery of the theft. 'The perfect crime,' she romanticised. 'Disappeared without trace despite all that security! No sign of entry or of damage, investigators baffled, the gallery the centre of attention and under siege by an unforgiving press.' The reproduction she had seen was certainly of a beautiful painting, even though printed in modern times by a lesser mortal. Hedrick had told her that it was his favourite painting and had also told her that it was a little like her. She remembered being held in his gaze as he had spoken. He did not seem to be one versed in flattering phrases but she felt the tremor of his praise flutter over her again as she checked her face in the mirror. She could not see a likeness but, as she turned her head, a glow of light fell across her cheek. It had not been flattery, after all, but a genuine compliment. Perhaps Hedrick had become her del Mano.

In his little house, Hedrick was looking idly out of the window wondering how he could arrange an evening with Astra. They could talk about the theft but they had already covered that subject. Perhaps they could just talk about themselves. 'Where did she come from?' he wondered. 'Not somebody local.' He could show her the several Dutch Masters in the collection but she had probably seen them already and that seemed a poor start to establishing a personal relationship.

Unfortunately, when she saw Hedrick again, Astra was in the middle of the task that had been allocated to her and another assistant of moving some of the products for sale to more accessible positions on the shelves. That took almost the whole morning with the consequence that she had to wait until midday in order to meet him accidentally on purpose. He detected her little deceit with an unexpressed pleasure and they sat in the restroom trying to think of news to exchange. Hedrick could only ask how she was getting on with her thesis, which thereby gave her the pretext to tell him that she needed to look once more at the Dutch room display. When Hedrick gallantly offered to show her the exhibits, she felt that her day would end in success.

The Dutch room exhibited only six paintings, not all of which had yet been reframed. 'I'm working on one at the moment,' Hedrick told her, hoping that he could claim an impressive familiarity with her subject. 'It's from the school of Vermeer,' he added hoping that he would not be questioned too deeply about it.

She quickly saw the opportunity to view the work in progress. 'What an interesting job!' she exclaimed. 'I'd really like to see the workroom.' Hedrick was overwhelmed with the possibility of displaying his skills to this gem of a girl, and immediately offered to lead her through security to his bench. 'It's a much bigger room than I had imagined,' she told him as she looked around at the array of equipment, framing squares, tools and numerous frame samples displayed in racks on the walls.

'Big enough for the two of us. Garrard is on pre-retirement leave. He's one of the craftsmen who taught me the trade. We met in the shop years ago when I was viewing the reproductions. He showed me the workroom and I was offered the job a few months later.'

'Working with Masters! You must feel their presence every day,' she responded.

'Yes. But not always the Dutch Masters. We also have French Impressionists, but only two del Mano now,' he ended sadly. 'The *Girl* was my favourite painting. Now it's gone and seems to be lost to the world,' he added in tones of great regret.

On leaving the workroom, they were passed by Spenser, who looked enquiringly at this stranger to the non-public area. 'This is Astra, the new shop assistant. I was just showing her the workroom. She's writing a doctoral thesis on Dutch Masters,' Hedrick told him proudly.

'An excellent subject,' Spenser replied, his interest stimulated by mention of an intellectual topic. 'If you need any information on our collection, do not hesitate to approach me, Miss – er,' he ended, thinking that first names would be a little too familiar.

'Tilson,' she informed him, at which he became more attentive.

'Tilson? Astra Tilson. Would your father be Walter Tilson, by any chance?'

'Yes. He's professor of art at Warton University. I'm doing my best to follow in his footsteps,' she replied with a smile.

'Astra! We have met before, although you won't remember. Nearly twenty years ago when your father and I were working on a television programme.'

'That must have been *Art on Display*. Dad told me about that but I didn't know you were part of it.'

'It was he who examined the del Mano reproductions. When all enquiries are over, I would very much like to meet him again to discuss old times.'

'I shall see him next month. I'm using him to criticise my thesis before I submit it to my panel,' she said with a wicked smile. 'I'll tell him that you'd like to renew contact.'

Hedrick stood by in astonishment that Astra should be so closely connected to the del Mano investigation, and was slightly disconcerted that he was a mere workshop assistant when she had a professor for a father. 'She wouldn't be interested in me, after all,' he concluded with disappointment.

'I didn't know it was your father who is the assessor in the del Mano theft,' he told her with a note of anxiety in his voice.

Astra could see that he had become a little apprehensive and rushed to assure him that she had no pretensions of grandeur, even if her father were a professor. 'I'll tell you all about the investigation this evening if you'd like to take me out for a hard-earned meal. Nowhere expensive, though, and we'll share the bill, of course,' she added encouragingly.

'How about *The Flying Swan*?' he suggested to her ready approval and returned to the workroom feeling slightly uncomfortable that this real-life *Girl with a Harp* was, by reason of background, just as distant as the painting, and that was hidden in some unknown corner of the world. Her situation was totally different from his, and they may as well be four hundred years apart.

Hedrick's evening wear differed only slightly from his daily uniform of shirt and jeans, but Astra had changed into a colourful new outfit, although one that had no conflict with his memory of the missing art. Her smile confirmed her as his lost ideal, despite having considered her to be beyond the gulf he had conjured between them, but as the evening progressed, he could not help but be overcome by thoughts of being unworthy of her.

She evidently detected his feelings of inferiority as she spoke of her background, her thesis and her ambitions, which, although somewhat imprecise, contained references to a career in history and art, or perhaps a teacher, perhaps an author. Hedrick gave a short account of how he had graduated from the stationery business to the gallery assisted by Garrard as friend and mentor. His thoughts tumbled out as he unveiled his secret ambition of possibly becoming self-employed, but of being apprehensive at the change from a fairly well-salaried position at the gallery.

Conversation inevitably turned to the whereabouts of Hedrick's favourite painting and the mystery of how it could have been stolen. He had taken it from the security of the workroom to the security of Spenser's office. The code had been verified when they had hung it next day in the presence of management, and the painting had been on exhibition for four months thereafter with no sign of tampering or of the security being switched off.

'Everybody is mystified,' Hedrick told her, 'including the Art Squad.'

They walked slowly back to her flat where they exchanged a few words about the night. She reached out to him in a silent entreaty for more but he was too inhibited and lost for words until she clasped him in her arms, and he finally responded to hold her in the closest encounter of his life. So that was what it was like to clasp the real *Girl with a Harp*. He was too bashful to stay, however, and she turned back to her empty flat, where she lay in bed drifting off to sleep with Dutch Masters competing with Italian Masters for her dreams.

Thoughts of Hedrick intervened as artists stroked the canvas with their brushes to depict her floating on the calmest sea towards the distant coast, the placid surface faintly ruffled by a zephyr breeze. She felt the gentle swell rising and falling to turn her thoughts to clouds racing across the waves as the quiet air became a wind that foretold a gathering storm. The billows rose in sympathy with the rushing torrent that paused and rushed again, driving her ever onwards as breakers thrashed the shore to cast her limp and exhausted on the sand beneath the towering cliffs. The glow of a starry sky bathed her cheek before Morpheus held her in his grasp.

It seemed but an instant before she awoke to a sun-filled room. Her recollections of the evening before gradually returned with the slight annoyance at her failed attempt to entice Hedrick to an indiscretion, evidently caused by a mixture of his bashfulness and her failure as a femme fatale. Perhaps he had reservations in a liaison with a professor's daughter, she reflected, or perhaps she should be a little more brazen. They could hardly avoid each other's company when they worked almost within earshot of each other, and she hoped that the outcome would be different on another occasion.

Suddenly, like a bolt of lightning, came the intuition of how the painting had been stolen. Certainly not by Hedrick. She was quite sure that his regret at the disappearance was genuine. But how could she convince anybody that her supposition was correct? They would usher her out with polite mockery if she were to tell them that she had received the information in a dream, and then collapse with laughter as soon as she had left. That would do nothing for her reputation except attach the label of dreamer to her work and damage any credibility she may have when submitting her thesis. Her theory was worth pursuing, surely, but how could she prove it?

Turning her attention to business, Astra sought an interview with Spenser which, owing to her close connection to Walter, was quickly granted. Her immediate conclusion from their meeting was that Spenser was no amateur. He seemed to know everything about the Dutch Masters in their possession that she wanted to know and even gave additional information, but she could hardly miss the opportunity to ask him about the del Mano. He answered all her questions as if the painting were a mere object of display rather than a four-centuries-old masterpiece, but he was an academic and not one controlled by emotions. Nonetheless, he confessed that he was greatly disturbed by the theft but had no hopes that the painting would ever be seen by the public again.

'That was the oldest and most valuable painting in our possession,' he told her. 'The theft is almost like losing one's eldest child. The painting has been kidnapped, but we have received no ransom demand. My assumption is that it is now hanging in a private gallery, somewhere. The thought that the thief may destroy the painting rather than be discovered with it in his possession is too painful to bear, but that may be a possible outcome,' he ended with a downcast look of distress.

'A likely person would be one who is artistic, has a love of art, is familiar with the period, possibly also of the artist,' he continued. 'Somebody who has a private gallery but very few visitors, perhaps lives in an inconspicuous place, but whether that would be in this neighbourhood or elsewhere, even abroad, is pure supposition.'

Astra commented that the oldest painting in the gallery was now *Lady in a Garden*, also by del Mano. Spenser could only reply that security could hardly be enhanced beyond the present routine, but he hoped that the thief would assume that safety measures had been intensified. They were, at least, patrolling the room more often, now.

On leaving the office, Astra was inevitably drawn to the workroom again, where a slightly gauche Hedrick welcomed her with an uncertain smile, thinking how childishly he had acted the evening before, but pleased that Astra had come to see him again.

He introduced Garrard, who had returned early from his week of pre-retirement leave, from whom she ascertained that he had spent his time thinking of how empty life would be without his customary routine. He had spent decades in the gallery, having started as a junior assistant creating a catalogue of the works on display together with all the information he could compile from his research about them.

Astra asked whether the catalogue included information on the Dutch Masters, and was rewarded with a copy of the rather compendious catalogue from his desk drawer. 'I spent a very interesting time creating that catalogue,' he told her. 'And then I undertook an apprenticeship with Gerald Stanley, now long since departed, in the art of framing. I've done that, and a few other things, ever since. Now, I'm about to leave for the pastured fields of the great outdoors,' he ended with a scarcely felt humour and the submission of somebody who had always known one world but would shortly be compelled to explore another.

It seemed to Astra that he would much prefer to stay within the confines of his present activities, but change was the ineluctable consequence of age. Her own prospect of an uncertain future bore down upon her as she listened. How could she advise a man of more than twice her age, if she couldn't even sort out her own life?

With an inviting glance at Hedrick she left with the catalogue and a determination to struggle through the vicissitudes of a beckoning future – a misty cloud of unknown content.

'Nice girl,' Garrard commented.

'Yes, but her father is a professor.'

'We are craftsmen and the equal of anybody,' Garrard replied, having noted Hedrick's hesitancy and suspecting an attachment. 'If it were not for craftsmen, the world would sink into ruin and desolation. Academics are commentators and not doers.'

Not for the first time, Hedrick was grateful to his mentor for a revelation that would lighten the road ahead.

Despite Hedrick's declaration that the Art Squad were as mystified as everybody else, Yardley and Forbes were determinedly continuing their investigations and had every intention of tracking down the insider whom they were convinced had carried out the theft. Having concluded that it was an inside job, they would interview all likely contenders and, in order to flush out the real culprit, had started by interviewing the least likely members of staff, which may cause the prey to break cover. They were the security staff, two men of impeccable record, the patrols, a team of three, only one of whom was long term, and the workroom staff consisting of three restorers and framers. There was also the management, which consisted of five directors, the administration being centred elsewhere.

A check on the directors had revealed no suspicions. One of them was even the founder's granddaughter. 'But surely she could not be an object of suspicion,' Forbes protested.

'Why not? Everybody is a suspect in this business,' Yardley responded. 'Perhaps the gallery is running into financial difficulties and insurance money could be a useful lifesaver.'

'But she's the sister of that industrialist, who could afford the occasional subvention.'

'Not the millions she might need, though,' was Yardley's gruff dismissal.

Chapter 11

Astra looked through the catalogue that Garrard had created nearly forty years previously. It was a thorough record of all the exhibits, including those in the Dutch room. The entries varied from a few brief details such as title, artist, date created and the location of town or landscape depicted. Other entries ran to several pages, which included names of sitters, interpretation of settings and comments on style. The Dutch paintings were fairly well documented. That would prove useful to her in her thesis, she thought, but she would need permission to quote from it by the copyrighter. She turned to the del Mano entries, noting that *Girl with a Harp* had gathered a long entry that seemed to be more a paean of praise as well as a list of facts. The studio had been in Florence where the artist had lived for most of his life. The painting had been acquired by Lewis Pelham in 1967 for less than fifty thousand. Quite apart from quality, four centuries of history would have added to its current worth, which she supposed must now be in the millions, but Spenser had given her his opinion that it would never be seen at auction again.

By the weekend, she had transcribed several details from the catalogue to her thesis and sat back looking out of the window into the wide-open world, wondering what she would do when she had achieved her doctorate. There would already be numerous candidates for whatever occupation she cared to follow but, with her speciality, any opening would probably be in some distant town. She would just have to start again in another place, she thought. Life was all a struggle. School, university, postgraduate work; and then she would have to find a job. That would be bad enough, but a career in which she could find fulfilment would be even more difficult. She sighed at life's hard road stretching out before her; but through what country did it lead? Was it straight or did it wind through hills and valleys and have signposts that pointed in the wrong direction? At least, her thesis was very nearly complete. She would give it to her father for a final review and then just submit it to the judgement of the panel and hope that they would welcome her to their number.

Another glance at the catalogue reminded her of the obligation to seek copyright approval for the notes she had extracted. She could be sure of Spenser's agreement, given her relationship to his old acquaintance, but, even if Garrard's permission was not strictly necessary, she would also like to obtain his consent. As the original author, he was the real hero who had compiled the work, no doubt with a loving regard for his pains. His house just outside the town was served by an hourly bus; she could be there and back before evening.

The notice board at the bus station gave the next arrival as another twenty minutes which gave her time, once more, to ponder life ahead. She could go back home and live rent free but, appealing though that might be, she enjoyed her solitude in the life she led, unexciting though it was. The alternative of returning home for any length of time would be to resume her childhood, but she had grown up now, and she preferred to continue her work at the shop until something came up.

She boarded the bus and alighted fifteen minutes later at the row of shops that suggested the centre of the locality and was directed to the road she wanted by a helpful lady with a child in a pushchair. The lady seemed very happy, she thought. A future of family feasts and celebrations seemed to have its charms. Perhaps a doctorate of arts may too, she hoped.

Garrard's home stood at the end of a row of three detached houses. She knocked and waited. She knocked again but nothing stirred. Only now did she realise that she should have arranged a time to see him before she had made the journey. No one was to be seen even when she walked round to the back of the house. He was quite obviously out. She turned to walk slowly back to the shops, thinking now foolish she had been. All she had achieved was an outing on the bus because she had not thought ahead.

On rounding the next corner, however, she saw Garrard walking towards her with two heavy shopping bags. She had never been so happy to meet somebody and smiled at him as he approached. 'I came on impulse to talk about your catalogue,' she told him, 'but you were not at home.'

'My stores were getting low,' he replied. 'And it's shopping day, today.'

She offered to help carry the bags but he declined politely and she turned to walk back with him. At his front door, he seemed to have a little reluctance to invite her in, but, polite as ever, decided that he must. 'It's a bit untidy,' he told her in explanation, although that was not at all evident to Astra, who told him that it was a lovely house and very nicely kept. He emptied the bags and began to store the contents, half turning to her wondering what she wanted to ask about the catalogue.

'I'd like to quote some material from it in my thesis and wanted to ask your permission as copyrighter.'

'I think copyright is held by the gallery,' he replied. 'But please quote any passages you like. I shall be pleased that anybody has ever read it.'

'It's full of useful notes. You must have invested a lot of time and study in its preparation.'

'Yes,' he replied, closing the cupboard on the last item and thinking back to his early time when he had devoted his life to creating the catalogue. 'Lovely days,' he sighed. 'Lovely days,' he repeated. Astra could see how moved he was at the recollection. 'The old general manager suggested I do it because the gallery was fairly new and he felt we should have a full list. I loved that job. It took me nearly three years to collect all the data, but I had to finish it sometime. All I got was a thank you but I didn't mind. I had the satisfaction that it had been printed and it was an absolute joy to have been able to do it.'

Astra wondered whether he was thinking of other things as well as the catalogue. 'Did you have anybody to help you with the research?' she asked.

He hesitated a little, but replied, 'There was somebody. Peri. But she left after a few years. Lovely days,' he added again. 'All gone now, though.'

'Except memories?' Astra added, perceptively.

Garrard turned to gaze out at his well-tended garden, having cast his mind back to his early years at the gallery. 'Yes. Except memories. Especially if they remain incomplete and never overtaken by events that should have followed,' he added in a slightly dismissive and self-critical tone. Astra saw that those memories flooding upon him were very dear to him and she could make a very accurate guess at what they were. She tactfully suggested they brew the tea.

The sitting room chairs were arranged in order to give a good view over the garden. 'My hobby,' he told her. 'It's not very big but it has been easy to manage since I laid it out nicely. Apart from gardening, all I have are my books, and music,' he added. 'A quiet life, but my own.'

'Now that retirement is approaching, you could travel a little or turn to writing about art, perhaps. You've cared for all the art at Pelham's for several decades and must know an awful lot about the paintings.'

'Yes. I have scanned every exhibit through a magnifying lens and have even seen how artists held their brush as if I were in their studio. I don't have the academic qualifications that

Spenser has but I take pride in practical accomplishment and leave the limelight to him. I've been happy in the workroom, and will be sorry to leave it, but I'm confident that Hedrick will be a worthy successor. I've compiled several papers on art since I completed the catalogue but never published them. I did it purely out of interest but I've always put off serious writing until I have more time. Perhaps that will be soon.'

'You could write a life of del Mano, perhaps. I noticed that your notes on *Girl with a Harp* are more extensive than on any other painting. Such a pity that it is no longer available for viewing,' she commented. 'Spenser told me that the Art Squad is interviewing everybody in the gallery. With your experience, you'll probably be able to help them.'

Garrard became silent for a while. 'They've interviewed me already, but I'm sure I haven't been able to contribute anything,' he replied in a rather downhearted but flustered tone.

'You could give them a few hints on the likely location. They know it's somewhere well-guarded, probably by somebody with a great love for that painting rather than for any other.'

'I have not been able to give them any information of interest. It could be hundreds of miles away by now for all I know.'

'I think you know a lot more about its whereabouts than you are admitting,' Astra ventured, cautiously.

'I have no idea where it is,' Garrard protested with some surprise.

'It is in a place not very far from here,' she continued.

'Where is that, then?' Garrard asked warily.

'Upstairs,' Astra replied.

Garrard sat stock still, looking shocked. 'Nonsense! Why do you say that?'

'You can rely on my discretion, Garrard. Your workplace is adjacent to Hedrick's. You framed a copy and swapped it with the real painting the evening before Hedrick took it to Spenser, thinking that it was the real one that he had just framed. I suggest you arrange a shipment to the gallery very soon. Anonymously and untraceably, of course.'

'If I had it, I would tell the gallery to pick it up,' he replied with some agitation.

'And face the consequences? We wouldn't want that. Would you like to show it to me,' she persevered.

'Certainly not. It's my house and not yours,' he told her, becoming slightly irritable as well as defensive.

'That response tells me a lot, Garrard. But I'll make a bargain with you. I came to ask for copyright permission and not to see the painting. I could run up the stairs very quickly even without your permission, but I won't. Hedrick described you as his mentor and I shan't do anything that detracts from his opinion of you. You hinted that Peri left you all those years ago, and you have been alone ever since. I don't want to be like that. Your part of the bargain is to tell Hedrick to say what you did not. That's all. But it's all a matter for you. I shan't tell anybody about your having the picture, in any event. Scouts honour!'

Garrard sat for what seemed a long time to both as he silently debated with himself what to do. With the boldness of youth, she had convinced herself that he had taken the painting and quite obviously wouldn't believe him if he denied having taken it; but he believed her when she said she would refrain from searching the house. She was a professor's daughter and one who believed in the essential goodness of mankind and in the solemnity of a promise. He had detected a nascent fondness for Hedrick whom he had mentored throughout the years and for whom he had a high regard not only for professionalism but also for integrity. She had been driven by an inability to address her feelings directly to him but he saw a parallel between them and his former self, when both he and Peri had been too inhibited to say what they really thought. That was also a time when he had very little money, but he had never forgotten Peri and, now, all these years later, Astra had appealed to him to speak out on her behalf. He had known that love was a powerful force that grips a person and never lets go but stays embedded for life. Perhaps he could address the omissions of his youth if he were to speak to Hedrick with the words he should have spoken to Peri.

Astra's voice reached him from what seemed a distant land. 'I shan't intrude upon your memory, Garrard. You have lived with the past for too long. Make up for it, now,' she said, with sensitivity but also with a note of pleading in her voice. 'Speak to Hedrick as if you were speaking to Peri.'

Garrard sat opposite her in silence thinking of Peri. Probably for the hundredth time, he wondered why he had not told her how much he had loved her. But she was a musician and he was just a junior employee in a provincial gallery with no prospects except to toil away in a lowly job until retirement. Now, Astra had seen into his soul and shared his grief. A grief and a guilt that, after all the years that had passed, he could not dismiss; but he might be able to alleviate the sorrows of two young people and redirect their lives into a channel that would lead on to the fulfilment that he had never achieved.

He returned to the present as if from a voyage round the world. He had known the conflicts of the spirit but had now seen a light in the darkness. 'All right,' he managed to say after a century of thought had elapsed. 'I'll do that. Hedrick still has great potential and will make your lives greater than mine.'

Astra gave him a wide smile of relief. 'I came to ask for permission to quote from your catalogue. I'm leaving with a life full of promise.'

'And a blessing,' Garrard added having substituted his innate feeling of goodwill for a momentary annoyance.

Astra walked back to the bus stop light of step and with a song in her heart. She was convinced that Garrard had taken the painting because it would remind him of a treasured episode in his life and be ever present in his retirement. He was also one of those rare people who readily put others before himself.

Garrard watched her go. She had jumped to a conclusion motivated by a frustration from which both he and Peri had suffered, but he was not one to believe ill of anyone. He would help if he could.

Astra rang her parents to tell them she would be coming home to Westerton the following week, a journey full of trains and buses. The house was nearly a mile from the station but taxis were a luxury on her salary. Her case was not too heavy and she could wheel it with only a little effort, but she was grateful that the road was partly along the flat. She contrasted her walk to Garrard's house the week before with the leafy lane along which she now passed. Had he done anything about the painting? Had he spoken to Hedrick about their meeting? She hoped he would do the sensible thing and be able to enter into a comfortable retirement. He was a lonely man, but a likeable man, and Hedrick thought highly of him. That was enough for her. He seemed to have few outlets for a man of his intelligence; perhaps retirement would prompt him to new experiences. She rested for a few minutes as she gained the top of a gentle slope where she looked around. Very pretty, very quiet, she thought, but she had heard nothing from Hedrick. He was very quiet, too.

She wheeled her case the last quarter mile, rang the bell and stepped into her home when her mother, Edith, opened the door with, 'Hello, dear. Welcome home. You should have called me and I could have fetched you in the car.'

'Hello, Mum,' she responded. 'I thought I should get a bit

of exercise. It's not too far and the walk was a pleasant change. Where's Dad?'

'Still at the college. He should be back within the hour.'

'I'll just take my case upstairs and unpack.'

Forty minutes later, the sound of a car turning into the drive and then the garage signalled the return of her father, whom she raced downstairs to greet. 'Hello, Dad. I'm back for a while. I've finished my thesis and I'm hoping that you can check it before I finally submit it to the panel.'

'I can if you can tell me all about that del Mano the art world is talking about. There's nothing like having a spy at the heart of the mystery.'

'Everybody is talking about it, except the Art Squad, who seem to be as puzzled as the rest of us. They are not getting very far with the investigation, so far as I know. No ransom notes, no idea of the method. The current theory is that it's hundreds of miles away in somebody's private gallery. They think it is an inside job, but they don't know who it could be. The staff whom I've met are all such nice people and all dedicated to art.'

'They should call in one of those fictional private detectives,' her father commented.

'The case of The Wandering Minstrel,' Astra suggested.

'More like the case of too many copies,' he replied.

Astra remembered Spenser's remark and told him of his desire to discuss the mystery with him. 'Could be another television programme, I suppose,' her father responded, 'but I've got your thesis to read first. I could start reading it over the weekend, if you like.'

'I thought you'd never ask, Dad,' Astra replied. 'Be as merciless as you like. I want it to pass muster when it's submitted.'

'What! And have a rival in the family for my job!' he joked.

'Don't worry, Dad. A girl's got more to think about than the grindstone.'

The same thought flashed across both parent's minds at the sudden implication that something was afoot in their daughter's life; that child of theirs had finally grown up – an adult about to become a doctor of arts. Could there be even a romance? But that was a private matter for later speculation.

The week passed with Astra waking to the sound of birdsong, helping her mother with the shopping and in the kitchen. Her father sat in his room engrossed in his daughter's thesis, but that required a thorough study and he tackled it in stages. They passed the next two weeks as a happy family, father off to college, mother and daughter spending valuable time together. Edith ventured to ask how Astra spent her days in Skelton but learned almost nothing of her social activities. 'No boyfriends?' she asked, tentatively, only to be assured that Astra spent most of her time on her thesis. 'All work and no play? No frantic debates about art with colleagues?'

'No. They have some really knowledgeable people there, very approachable but all tied up in their jobs; vocations, actually. Two of them are really devoted. Garrard created the gallery catalogue from which I extracted several facts for the thesis. He's worked there for decades, but his retirement date is looming and he's not looking forward to it. I hope they extend his employment because they haven't finished the huge security project they've embarked upon.'

'Nobody younger to follow in his footsteps?'

'Oh, yes. Hedrick. He's also a framer and very keen on the job, and he's fairly experienced, too.'

Her mother sensed a topic for further discussion.

On a Wednesday evening three weeks later as they were settling into their little relaxations, father with the thesis, mother with her knitting, Astra with her book casting a few glances at her father as he made notes in the margins, the telephone rang and Edith rose to answer it. 'Walter, it's the Art Squad for you.' Astra looked startled. Walter stepped to the phone, listened, asked a few questions and listened again before cradling the telephone. Turning to the intently questioning looks of the family, he announced, 'Guess what. The painting has been recovered. It's been delivered to the gallery, suddenly, with no prior warning. They want me to authenticate it. I hope it's not another copy.'

'Returned? By whom?' Astra asked.

'Anonymously, but they can trace the sender through the documentation, apparently. They said that the culprit must have become too nervous about the next round of questioning.'

Astra betrayed a never seen before look of wonder, nervousness and excitement at the news. 'She knows who it was,' her mother thought in a flash of premonition. 'That younger man, she hardly mentioned. A liaison she doesn't want to admit. Oh, goodness! Surely she's not mixed up with anything criminal.'

Astra's thoughts had, however, been riveted by the reference to documentation. Surely, Garrard could not have overlooked the necessity to mask his identity.

Edith drew Astra to her. 'Let's hope it passes off quietly,' she said, resolving to do anything required that would protect her.

Inspector Yardley had studied the paperwork that had accompanied the crate to the gallery. That would tell him the route. Delivered from a warehouse in Northington with no other instructions than to hold and deliver to schedule, but he had only to enquire how the crate had arrived at the warehouse in order easily to trace the source. Forbes drove both of them to the office of the warehouse manager who looked up the consignment details. 'Came from Storewell Logistics on Friday,' he was told. 'No further instructions. We loaded it on our scheduled vehicle a few days later and delivered on Tuesday.'

When visited, Storewell Logistics told them, 'Arrived three weeks ago, held according to instructions, loaded overnight on Thursday and despatched Friday. Delivery note signed, no fault.'

'Who delivered it to you?' Yardley asked.

'Depositor named as Brian Hampton. Probably a local resident or carter. We get all sorts of packages from all sorts of people. It was over three weeks ago, anyway. We must have had several hundred deliveries since then.'

Enquiries revealed a plumber named Brian Hampton in the locality but he had been in Tenerife on that date, and the given address was an old person's nursing home where the manager had no knowledge of the alleged sender.

Yardley and Forbes left the building with the too-familiar feeling of having drawn a blank. There may have been numerous people of that name further afield but they would not be able to associate any of them with the consignment. Their initial excitement dissipated into an annoying frustration until that gradually transformed into the consolation that their efforts had been the main factor in the painting's return.

Chapter 12

Bentley's relationship with Cordelia Harrington two decades before had been the most wonderful time of his life. It was springtime throughout the year, it was a time of sunshine even when the heavens were dark, a time that would last forever. But it was a time cut short by a thunder bolt. She had left him inexplicably; gone, never to return, he had thought. Until now. But that time they had spent together had been lodged in his mind ever since. The memory had never left him. That sunlit time was always present even if it had faded to the palest moonlight. Despite his being plunged into the depths of despair, he had resolved not to admit his distress to her with pleas for her to return but, for reasons of pride, had bitten back the pain of losing her. She did not want him, after all, and he was not going to demean himself by shouting into a wind that would not hear. He had been damaged and had buried himself in work with almost no affairs after that.

Now, more mature than in that blissful time when youth was still in bud, he had met her again, but, in these adult days of caution when he could express himself better, he feared the formality imposed by that long separation. How he regretted not having gained his current skills when he had first met her! She had meant the world to him at that time and he found her still fascinating despite the more than twenty years that had passed. She proved still to be very easy to talk to, a great receptor and exchanger of conversation. What might they have done! What might they have achieved together!

He told her of his business success but admitted being aware of not having attained total satisfaction. He had a nice house, furniture, a few friends but no domesticity. 'What about you?'

Cordelia told him of her work with a fashion magazine, of her photography, of her social round.

'A great advance on the activities we enjoyed all those years ago when neither of us had any money,' Bentley commented. 'Picnics and the cinema were all we could afford. Except that we did have some marvellous days here at the seaside. I still remember that time. A drive to the coast, walks on the prom and then onto the pier where we watched Punch and Judy among all those children. The week too soon over and, then, back to my flat and all the while saying we loved each other, and meaning it,' he continued. 'But then you disappeared. I'm not surprised. I could not give you the life you wanted. Not at that time, anyway. A few years later and it would have been a different story.'

'But I didn't want riches. We wouldn't have had poverty but we could have had just enough to survive. I remember those times, too. Beautiful, but ones that may not have lasted. I wanted to make my mark on the world, to do something, to be someone rather than to be part of the crowd. That was why I became a photographer, travelling around Europe mostly, but it was Italy I liked best. I've lived there for a little over a year overlooking the lake but, every day, I was reminded of our times spent on the prom and the pier.'

'We could have stayed together, though. It seems a long way for you to go just to get away. And why? Was I so bad?'

'No, of course not,' she hurriedly assured him. 'But I wanted more than life in a small flat. I wanted to make a future for myself. I got a job with a travel magazine and went on assignments photographing scenes that nobody else had captured or, at least, giving new perspectives on the old. I photographed fashion shows, beautiful houses and the lives of the glitterati, all of which were way beyond my resources, but then I found a little house in Italy. I bought it almost two years ago and renovated it. It was a bit lonely. I even thought of contacting you again but didn't know how to, and I foolishly dismissed the idea. I thought you would have an entirely different career and wouldn't want me anymore. I had walked out once and thought you would have somebody else by now.'

'I would have joined you without further thought. I suffered pangs of parting for years after you left.'

'If only I had known. We were both too undemonstrative and I needed more assurance than tongue-tied you could give me. I saw my cottage looking out over the lake and bought it in memory of—' She paused but then continued. 'In memory of days gone past – and this view over the bay. I had achieved an ambition, travelled, lived in the sun, but one is always drawn back home. I thought I would come back here just for old time's sake; and Sandley is as much home for me as anywhere.'

'They even have Punch and Judy on the pier, still.'

'Yes. I watched it again. It was exactly the same but it lacked the delight of the time we saw it. "*The stream remains; but the water changes*",' she quoted.

'I'm still the same old stick in the mud,' Bentley confessed, despite knowing that he had unwisely slipped back into his habitual self-denigration; but he quickly added, 'I formed a partnership with Hector that proved to be a huge success. I have a nice house in Handbury but I'm staying at the hotel for a week – also just for old time's sake. I came here as a boy with my mother. We came every year and it was good fun on a bike. But it was the days with you that I was remembering. You were the only girl I have ever really loved. First loves are always stronger, they say. True in my case, anyway. Nobody else ever matched you.'

Cordelia gave a quick smile, looking aside for an embarrassed moment. 'If only you knew my thoughts at that time. I was just as reticent as you to talk about the future, especially one that might endanger our relationship. But there's nothing like twenty years in order to think about things. Mostly all about the decisions one has taken and those that one has not taken, the things one has done and whether any of them was for the best. You are telling me a lot, now. I've never really thought my job was totally satisfying. Interesting for a while, remunerative, improving the world, or so I thought, but I was unsettled throughout. To be honest, I missed you over all those years, recollection fading a little as time passed but never forgotten. Now, it seems as if we had never parted. Time never seems to have lasted long when one looks back, but whilst it's passing, it is as if it would continue for ever.'

'We never had bad times. Not until after you left, anyway. I felt as if I had been cut in two and, even now, still feel the wounds.'

'I'm sorry. It was difficult for me, too. I was making a statement hoping that you would hear my prayer. But I was too naïve and ruined everything.'

They were silent for a few moments, each thinking of those stupidities of the past. Bentley placed his hand on hers and they smiled at each other. 'I feel the end of my booking fast approaching. I've registered for only one week,' he told her.

'Still the incarnation of modesty and correctness! Remember that the good times never end,' she said with a gently mocking smile. 'Extend the booking or find another place.'

Bentley felt the slight admonishment even if it had been lovingly meant. If only he could take her home with him, he thought, but he responded with 'Do you have a bicycle? We could go for a ride, somewhere.'

She laughed. 'Is that all you can think of? I don't have a bicycle, anyway.'

'We'll hire one from the shop at the end of the prom.'

'Now, you are being more positive. All right. We'll meet there tomorrow at ten o'clock.'

Bentley took her hand and they walked along the prom towards the bicycle shop, each remembering the time when they had walked along it over twenty years before. His previous mount was still available and they tested another for size, found it suitable and booked both for the following day. Wandering along the prom brought back memories of a life cut short, each silently thinking how foolish they had been.

'You were right to follow your ambition,' Bentley said at last. 'But we could still have been a perfectly ordinary couple just like all the others.'

'I didn't want ordinariness,' she replied. 'I wanted to be an achiever, but I didn't know what to achieve. I wanted to burst upon the world fully formed as some sort of expert rather than to spend years in gathering experience that would eventually be rewarded with a modest pay packet. But I was milling around in a sea of indecisiveness. Neither of us had any money. Yes, we could have joined the brigade of the have-nots but it would have led to stress and, finally, to breakup. In a way, I wanted to preserve our togetherness by leaving for something else, but it was not without huge regrets that I left. I've had my pangs of separation, too. I would always treasure the memory of what might have been but I left the might have been for a future of whatever would come.'

'We've both had our futures, now,' Bentley responded. 'Perhaps they have provided a little excitement in our lives even if we have cast our pasts adrift to float away on a sea of daydreams.'

'I had my boat, too,' she told him. 'We each drifted out of sight of each other but memories floated with us far over the horizon and have never drowned despite the billowing waves.'

They wandered down to the pier where the next performance of Punch and Judy was signalled to start in twenty minutes. Several children were already waiting and talking excitedly to one another. Over twenty years before, they had also been seated there among the children happily awaiting the show. They looked at each other, exchanging thoughts of the life that had passed and somehow aware of what they had missed; but a regretful gaze was all that could suffice to fill the yawning gap in an opportunity lost.

'This is the best day I've had since I got here,' Bentley told Cordelia. 'In fact, the best day since you left me all those years ago.'

She smiled wanly. 'I didn't leave you,' she said dreamily. 'I just melted away.'

'Melted into the future. But no explanation. I've always wondered why. I didn't think there was anybody else. You were too genuine for that. I hadn't made a career at that date and I don't blame you for leaving, but I wonder how we would have spent those years. May I tell you something?' he continued, and to her nodded response told her, 'I still love you. I hope you won't mind my telling you.'

'Of course not,' she responded, secretly pleased to have ascertained his feelings and wanting to respond in like manner. 'Do you want me to say I still love you?'

'Only if you mean it.'

She smiled graciously at him. 'All right. I'll tell you. I love you and I always have. What a shame I couldn't have taken you with me when I faded into the future.'

Bentley felt his sorrows fly away. 'Two happy people talking nonsense again,' he replied. 'But I meant what I said and I think you did, too.'

Cordelia felt herself sliding back into the days of roses. 'I hope we'll talk a lot more nonsense, now,' she replied. They were the same people as before, who had spoken no nonsense at all. They had spoken complete sense, meant every word and would have had their dreams to nourish them. Now, they felt the bonds of the past fastening about them in a reunion of souls.

'So, why did you disappear?'

'Somebody I had met at university introduced me to the magazine where they recruited me for property and fashion photography. They wanted somebody to fill a recent vacancy and sent me on an immediate assignment where I could help them out and they could assess whether I had the qualities they were seeking. I thought it might be a short job but it worked out well and they booked me as a freelance. I was lucky in finding the work and becoming one of the magazine's best contributors, but they never used the articles themselves. They told me that they syndicated them instead, but I never saw them published anywhere. They paid well so I didn't probe too deeply.

'I finally realised that constant travel was just a way to forget the past and to salve my conscience. After several years, I found the house in Italy and almost settled down but a neighbour persuaded me to take a last farewell of all that I had done.'

'Does that mean you are retired now or are you starting another life?'

'I first have to find out what the next life is, but fear of the unknown has pursued me – ever since I saw you last,' she added lamely. 'It hangs over me like a hovering cloud.'

'I could bring a little sunshine to your sky,' Bentley responded. 'If you'd let me,' he added cautiously.

Cordelia looked silently and longingly at him. 'Yes. He could,' she thought, rather troubled by the recent twist to her life. 'But I can't deny Frank, now.' Bravely resuming as much of a smile as she could, she replied sadly, 'There is not enough sunshine to dispel all the clouds, Bentley,' only too conscious that it was an ungracious response to a kindly meant offer. Bentley resolved to try again later.

At their dinner that evening, Cordelia felt that the day had dawned with little more than the prospect of reviewing the scenes she had treasured through the years, but they had blossomed again into the days she had lived before. The night was approaching and Bentley held her hand, looking meaningfully at her in silent appeal, but, full of conflict, she read his thoughts and told him that she must retire early that night in order to gather energy for the ride next day. Bentley swallowed his unspoken desire and must have betrayed his feelings to her somehow. 'Not yet, Bentley. It's too soon,' she added sympathetically, still trying to resolve her loyalties, and slipped away after promising to see him next day at the bicycle shop.

Once more in her room, she walked up and down, wringing her hands in an anguish of uncertainty and indecision. She had returned to Sandley to relive her memories, but she had had no idea that Bentley would also be there. That love of long ago had never died and had been fanned back into life, but too many threads of the past had now been so tightly wound about her that they could never be swept away.

The flame had been rekindled, but her obligations to Frank cast a shadow upon her mind. He would not let her slip from his grasp and would use any means to hold her back, and running away from him would destroy any possibility of the settled life she had been seeking for over twenty years.

Bentley had re-emerged from the past and she had felt a resurgence of the love that had remained dormant all those years. Was that merely a passing fancy, though, or had she come to another rebound from one episode in her life to another? Would she ever know peace of mind? Over twenty years of guilt rose up to overwhelm her. She had told Bentley that she did not want ordinariness, but now she realised how foolish she had been to have left him and had entered a maze of such complexity that she could never escape. She threw herself on the bed with thoughts racing through her mind until Morpheus intervened before she had come to a firm conclusion.

The sun rose upon a late awakening and Cordelia a little less troubled than in the evening before, but she had to hurry to meet Bentley at ten o'clock. The little physical movement in hurrying to the bicycle shop helped almost to dismiss the troubles she had felt, and the sight of him already waiting for her proved beneficial enough for her to raise a smile.

'Sorry I'm late,' she said. 'I overslept, but the day starts now.'

Bentley responded that she was worth waiting for, despite having had several minutes of despair thinking that she had fled again. They mounted the bicycles and rode slowly along the prom and up to the hills to turn into a lane that Bentley thought he remembered from those early episodes in his life when he had no cares. But now he had a greater pleasure; riding through memories with the woman who now meant even more to him than she had twenty years before. They rode abreast and looked at the sea view, and then at the view inland as well as at each other. His recollection of the roads was not perfect but they aimed for the higher land from where the sea was visible beyond the town, and the fields behind them stretched to the horizon with scattered villages nestled in the valleys.

Cordelia thought of her days at school and of the years in Italy where her favourite transport for short journeys had been a bicycle. Cars were not for her. Perhaps a bus, although only too often an aircraft for yet another assignment.

They dismounted at a deserted spot and sat on the grass. Here she was and here he was. She felt recovered from the turmoil of the previous evening, but the dilemma remained to be wrestled with later. 'I'm sorry about last night,' she told Bentley, thinking it better to forestall his questions. 'It's a long time since we last saw each other and I need to adjust.'

That would give her time to think and to avoid another embarrassment.

Bentley looked encouragingly at her. 'Don't worry. We need to get to know each other again,' he responded sympathetically, hinting at delights to come. But it was with a smile of disappointment that he spoke. He was bursting with love renewed and told himself that she had been taken by surprise and that he should be more patient. He must not alienate her now that he had found her again.

'I'm the same old indecisive being,' she confessed. 'It was ever so, and I'm still trying to straighten myself out.'

Bentley had detected the reserve beneath that polite exterior. 'I think you are no longer what you have been,' he said. 'You were looking for a solution, the key to existence. I hope you have found it now.'

'No. I have simply become just a bit older and what I am now – but not much wiser.'

'You must have learned a lot in your travels. Your job in the media business must have greatly enhanced your skills. You know how to gain insights into other people's lives, how to gain their confidence, how to acquire information, but still how to maintain good relations. Being a woman must help. No confrontation, no suspicion, no hostility.'

'That's your world, not mine. My neighbour is the richest and therefore the most powerful man in the neighbourhood,' she explained, but soon tore away her veil of restraint and continued, 'He's called Frank. The locals call him Franco but Svengali would be more appropriate. Everyone does his bidding not because he's too ruthless but because he supports most of the small business activities in the area. He's remorselessly persistent but also charming and deserves all the respect that he receives, even if it's only because of his money. The cottage was offered to me at a low price because it was run down but probably also because people might have thought that it was too close to his property.'

Bentley detected the note of regret in her voice. She sounded as if she were trapped by some mysterious spell. 'Not Svengali,' he responded. 'Rothbart sounds more appropriate.'

Cordelia's face contorted into an expression of despair. 'Yes. But there's no way out.'

'Love will find a way,' Bentley assured her, drawing her into his arms, but she remained unconvinced.

Chapter 13

Marcus called another board meeting in order to announce not only the return of the painting about which the whole building was buzzing with excitement, but also to inform the directors of all details that were currently known. He was unsurprisingly in a more confident mood than in his previous address to them when he had announced the theft, and was beaming widely at his colleagues, all of whom now shared his rather more jovial spirit. They had already spoken among themselves and exchanged opinions of what might have happened to the painting and were eager to learn the full story, such as was available, from Marcus.

'You will all be aware of the glorious news that *Girl with a Harp* has been returned to us in apparently undamaged condition,' he announced in confirmation of everybody's hopes. 'As a precaution, and in accordance with Art Squad instructions, we have shipped the painting to Professor Tilson for examination and identification. We don't want it be another copy that had been delivered, do we?' he joked, to the slight amusement of the now relaxed participants. 'According to our initial examination, however, it is the original and seems to have been well cared for. There are no obvious signs of damage,' he added.

Spenser noted that Marcus had not lost the capability of gathering to himself the announcement of good news and had omitted any reference to him for the initial examination or to his certainty that it was the original and undamaged painting. That had simply confirmed his contempt for the self-aggrandisement of the man whenever the opportunity arose.

'Is there any indication of where it has been during its absence, or of who may have returned it?' they asked.

'The painting seems to have taken a rather circuitous route via two warehouses and transport companies, but there is, unsurprisingly, no indication of sender. The original sender seems to have given a fictitious name and the Art Squad have reported that tracking him down will be a rather laborious process. Frankly, my impression is that it is unlikely they will be able to trace his whereabouts or true identity.'

'Have the Art Squad any pointers to the culprit?' was their inevitable next question.

'They are not revealing any details of their enquiries but have limited themselves to the suggestion that he was probably flushed out by their plan to interview everybody in the building.'

'It was presumably somebody with a respect for the painting and with the capability of carrying out the theft,' they contributed.

'That narrows the field but only by a slim margin. It could have been any one of the staff, including any one of us,' one of them added, smiling a little too accusingly for everybody's approval.

'Speak for yourself,' came the rather sharp and frosty response.

Marcus continued, 'The press are clamouring for an interview, now. I have scheduled it for tomorrow. I shall give what details I am able to impart and conclude with the statement that security has been enhanced and that further occurrences of this unfortunate matter are highly unlikely.'

The press conference was, nonetheless, somewhat more accusatory than Marcus had expected. The gentlemen of the press had been able to report on the biggest art theft of the decade, perhaps of the century, and were divided in thinking of the loss of an opportunity to criticise the management further but simultaneously of being able to prolong the story with speculation on the mystery of its restoration. There was also a sense of disappointment that no other sensational event was likely to appear in the near future in order to sustain their circulations by extending the excitement for a longer period. The thought that they could, once more, dredge up the original accusations of negligence, but now combine them with conjectures on the picture's fortuitous return, gave a malicious anticipation to them in prolonging the agony by continual reference to the identity of the unknown appropriator. They may even be able to accuse the gallery of a publicity stunt, perhaps with an invention that attendances were dwindling and income declining as a result.

An unsuspecting Marcus flanked by his directors opened the proceedings to the expectant representatives of both local and national press. Assuming his broadest smile he announced with a note of triumph that the Art Squad had achieved a stunning victory over the thief. They had enabled the return of the painting, the condition of which was currently being examined by the leading professor of art, Walter Tilson, who was confidently expected to confirm its identity.

The reporter from the local newspaper asked whether he had any clues to the identity of the perpetrator, to which Marcus replied cautiously that the Art Squad was diligently pursuing several leads, whereupon the national press asked how confident he was of unearthing the identity of the thief. Marcus pleaded the desirability of not divulging the latest state of the investigation without admitting his ignorance or that he was unaware whether the Art Squad was any nearer to detection of the perpetrator.

The reaction of the journalists was rather mocking and dismissive. The gallery had had three months to explore every possibility and they had not yet brought the matter to a conclusion. Marcus steeled himself to face a greater hostility from his questioners than he had anticipated and resorted to cautious platitudes in responding that investigations were at a very delicate stage and that he was eagerly awaiting an announcement. 'I cannot confirm whether the theft was attributable to a daring opportunist, or whether an international gang was involved,' he elaborated in an inspiration of the moment.

To another questioner asking whether any clues had been derived from the means of the return, Marcus replied with the practised capability of officialdom, telling his enquirer that it was inappropriate to reveal all information at the moment but gave his assurance that they could look forward to further revelations in due course. He had ensured that security measures had been increased and he was quite sure they were adequate to prevent any possibility of a recurrence.

The press filed out of the conference room not totally satisfied with the rather anodyne answers but already thinking of how to construct their reports given the paucity of information that had been conveyed.

Marcus breathed a sigh of relief and turned to Spenser, remarking, 'I think that went off well,' to which Spenser nodded polite agreement despite a little discomfort at the speculative component of international thieves, but he could be grateful that the latest hurdle had been crossed, although the finishing line was not yet visible.

Laura accompanied Spenser to his office in order to gain some assurance that he regarded the painting as genuine despite not having received the final report from Professor Tilson. 'Yes, I'm quite sure in my own mind that it is the genuine article. We examined it in the workshop and I have every confidence that Walter will also give the same verdict. My only concern is that the perpetrator is still unknown and we must live with the thought that he may strike again, unlikely though that may be. But apart from replacing the whole staff, an impossible undertaking given the skills that we would have to replace, we shall live forever in the shadow of the event and be constantly in fear of a repeat offence. We have never even had a case of petty theft, but one by some arch criminal, as Marcus seemed to imply, is so outrageous that we will never be at peace again.'

'The theory that the thief was one of the staff is merely an assumption.' Laura responded. 'Perhaps it *was* some international gang.'

'I doubt it. International gangsters are not known for their altruism. Furthermore, the painting was well packed and completely undamaged upon return. I can only presume that it was undoubtedly an inside job and only a few of our staff have the skills to have handled the painting so professionally.'

'Do you have anybody in mind?' Laura asked.

'Workroom staff, possibly,' he replied reluctantly, 'but I can't believe that any of them could have been even remotely involved. I may also be suspected by the Art Squad, since it was I who brought the painting to the rehanging ceremony. I am the only one who knows for certain that I wasn't the guilty party, but others may not believe me,' he replied. 'At least, the painting has been returned, but it's all very distressing,' he added, disconsolately. 'The *Girl* stolen and everybody a suspect.'

Laura walked away having learned little more than had already been announced, but she could, at least, update Frank on what had transpired so far. She had noted that despite the painting's return, Spenser was looking drawn, obviously still worried about how the theft had been accomplished and how safe the other exhibits were.

Astra joined her mother in a little shopping expedition in the town. She had heard nothing from Hedrick but perhaps that was because she had left no contact address. Her father had also given almost no comment on her thesis apart from a few non-committal remarks that she was unable to decipher as favourable or not, but she knew that his attention had also been diverted by the necessity to devote time both to his profession and to examination of the painting. Upon its receipt, he had judged it at a glance as the original but had sent it for DNA testing and was now awaiting sample tests on warehouse and workroom staff.

As they wheeled the trolley around the local supermarket, they ticked off their purchases on the list, but on approaching the checkout, Astra noticed the headline glaring from the *Banner*, a national newspaper of unrestrained speculation that gloried in the motto, '*Flag of Battle*'. Most readers would have expected an article on '*Girl Returned by International Thieves*' to be a salacious account of kidnap, but she knew instinctively that it must be the revelation of the painting's return. She added a copy to the purchases, hardly able to wait until she could read the report when they returned home.

The article was a lengthy account by their art and cultural editor of his 'current understanding'. It reiterated the story of the theft and the great mystery of how it could have occurred given the security methods employed by the gallery. The contrition of the management was understandable in its failure to protect the exhibit most revered by the public, and one that current assessments of value of the painting ranked highly in the world of art. The writer then suggested that important elements of conduct had been found inadequate to protect this remarkable legacy of the founder. The report continued by expressing the hope that current police investigations had revealed the possibility of an international crime element but stressed that no admission had been made of ransom money having been paid. The editor conjectured that a possible intervention by a little-known specialist in recovery negotiations may have secured the painting's return. Interest was gathering at the probability of an arrest in the near future.

Astra was left with a feeling of unease. The article was replete with guarded comments against management but almost devoid of hard facts. Was the reference to an arrest mere speculation by a press ignorant of the true position or had the net started to close upon that fabrication of an international gang which she knew was actually a lonely and gentle man of otherwise good conduct and generous disposition?

When her father returned home, she brandished the newspaper at him. 'Dad. Have you read this?' she asked.

'Yes. Not very informative, is it?' he replied dismissively. 'We should be able to eliminate most of the suspects soon. They'll be able to report real news then.'

'Have you been able to check DNA reports, yet?' she asked a little nervously.

'Yes. We can eliminate all handlers outside the gallery and have narrowed suspicion down to the workroom staff as well as to Spenser. He won't be too pleased if we question him, though,' her father joked. 'But it's practically certain that it is one of the workroom staff. Both of them have strong traces of DNA on the painting and particularly on the crate. We'll question both of them but my guess is that it must be the younger one,' he ended.

'I very much doubt it,' Astra responded, vehemently. 'I know him and I'm quite sure that he would not have been involved.' Edith could not help noticing the horrified expression on her daughter's face. She knew who it was, she remembered, and now she was defending him. 'Was she somehow involved herself?' she wondered. Her suspicions deepened as they sat at dinner that evening. Astra seemed unusually quiet, obviously thinking how to digest her father's revelation.

Professor Tilson had not lived with his wife for thirty years without being able to read her thoughts and her anxious glances at Astra. 'Who is your main suspect?' he asked Astra suddenly. 'We've ascertained that there are only three main possibilities, and I can't imagine Spenser can rank high in the list.'

'Dad, I know for an absolute certainty that it was not Hedrick. Call it intuition if you like. I also visited Garrard's house unexpectedly in order to get his approval for some of his copyright information but there was no sign of the painting there, either. Perhaps there is another candidate from among the less likely possibilities.'

'Have you also visited Hedrick's house, though?' he responded.

'No, I haven't. But I am quite sure that he is not the culprit, and probably not Spenser, either. What motive would he have, anyway?'

'Actually,' her father continued, 'If it were one of the three, we couldn't prove it even with the DNA evidence we have collected. The fact is they have all handled the painting over the years, so it is not surprising that they are implicated. But it was the workroom staff who opened the crate and took out the painting. No wonder their traces were the most prominent. Any barrister could easily get a charge dismissed given those facts.'

Astra visibly relaxed. They were all safe so long as they remained silent.

Walter wondered whether Astra had a stronger motive than intuition for her support of the staff. She had spent several weeks at the gallery and loyalty may have led her to draw a protective veil over the suspects. He was also debating in his mind how he could broach the topic with Spenser; it could hardly be avoided if a televised interview were to be held, and that prospect had begun to excite him. Talking about art was always stimulating, but the added enticement of discussing the biggest art theft since those of the Mona Lisa and the Duke of Wellington would surely offer the ultimate excitement.

Edith also relaxed as she noted Astra's obvious relief. But even if there was no absolute proof of this Hedrick's involvement, it did not mean that he was entirely innocent. Now, she sensed that Astra's relief was attributable to a liaison with this younger man, but what sort of man was it to whom she seemed to have become attached. An unprincipled master thief? Somebody who had oozed his charm on an innocent girl? A man who would stop at nothing to implicate their daughter in an international art conspiracy? Perhaps had recruited her into some inadmissible participation in the theft?

Next day, sitting opposite each other whilst sipping their morning coffee, she thought of a way to prise a little information from Astra by mentioning that she was considering plans for a new vegetable patch. 'A small selection of fresh vegetables, hopefully easy to tend and harvest. Back to the old days of a productive back garden.'

'Just buy them in the supermarket, Mum. Much less trouble and probably better quality, even if yours would be home grown.'

'Oh, I was just thinking of how to fill my time. I'm not really serious, but how do you fill your time? It can't all be devoted to your thesis, surely. Do you have any friends at that gallery of yours? Any boyfriends?'

'No. The girls in the shop are nice but there are not many men to choose from. They're either too old or all wrapped up in their paintings.'

'What about the workroom staff? They should be able to offer something.'

'There are only two of them and one is about to retire. The other one is frightened of his own shadow.'

'The one whom you are protecting for some reason. If he really was the thief, you're better off leaving him to fend for himself.'

'I don't have to protect him, Mum. He is not the thief. He wouldn't do anything like that.'

'But how do you know that?' she responded, reaching for her daughter's hand. 'You haven't done anything compromising, have you?' she pleaded.

'Certainly not. I just know as an absolute certainty that he had nothing to do with it.'

'Do you know who did it?'

'Oh, Mum, how could I know that, or even be able to tell you when I have no more proof than anybody else? Everybody is troubled by it, some more than others, especially Spenser. He seems to have aged several years in the last few months. I'm probably the least affected but it's very disturbing, nonetheless.'

Edith noted that Astra had not taken the opportunity to deny whether she knew who did it, which strengthened her conviction that she knew who it was. The sudden thought that the perpetrator must have been her daughter struck her like a thunderbolt. 'If you want to confide in me, you know you can trust us not to reveal anything incriminating.'

Astra was horrified that her own mother could even dream of her being involved in the theft, but how could she protest, knowing that she might be placing herself in danger of revealing the real perpetrator? 'It wasn't me, Mum, if that's what you're thinking. The fact is that I said something in company that may have led to the perpetrator having second thoughts. The painting was returned unharmed and will be rehung as soon as all the examinations have been completed. They are all nice people there and I wouldn't want to malign any of them, especially because everything will return to its previous state, and life will go on as if nothing had happened.'

Her mother was relieved at her daughter's declaration of innocence, but Astra's assumption of returning to normality seemed hopelessly naïve. 'Let's hope so,' she replied encouragingly, but then felt driven to a few well-meaning words of warning. 'The trouble is, once something has happened, it assumes its own momentum. Enquiries probably won't be concluded just because we wish them to be. Others will want to tie up all the loose ends, and that means the Art Squad, who probably won't want to leave the theft of the century unsolved.'

The words sank deep into Astra's heart. Her mother was right and she had deceived herself, probably not for the first time. Was she mistaken about Garrard? Could he and Hedrick have acted together? But she dismissed that as inconceivable even if she had been mistaken in thinking that she could have any attraction to Hedrick. He could have enquired her address but had not contacted her. That was proof enough.

From a life of study, reading and trawling through all the likely libraries in order to seek new observations on her subject, she had condensed two years of research into the several pages of a final document which, she now realised, would merely be read by a few scholars and then be placed upon a pile of neglected works lost in the farthest reaches of academe. That would gradually become submerged in other theses heaped upon it over the decades by other devoted students, all of whom, like her, would have laboured away in hope of fame and possibly, if not fortune, recognition. Here she was, wasting away sitting at home in her parents' house. What on earth was delaying her father in assessing her thesis? Perhaps she should just submit it and hope for the best. She had already left her job, but she would have to go back to the flat to collect her things and then ... find another job ... any job, anywhere.

Chapter 14

Since the gallery had resumed the normal tenor of its ways, a state of post-traumatic tranquillity had settled upon the premises, although the staff had not quite recovered from the shattering blow that the theft had delivered to its prestige. They could all take comfort from the fact that the painting had been returned, but it had been promptly whisked away for examination, the results of which were rumoured to be highly indicative of the 'modus operandi', as it was now called, by the semi-literate in matters of crime. The publicity had had a noticeable effect on gallery admissions, driven by the more curious of art lovers who were often found congregated around the blank space where the painting had been hung and was still adorned with the notice declaring that the painting had been withdrawn for examination.

Marcus employed his beaming exterior in the reassuring task of spreading calm and normality throughout the building, but, in the depths of his heart, he harboured grave misgivings at the thought that somebody in the building, either alone or with outside help, had so far successfully tested the security to destruction. Furthermore, he could not remain undisturbed by the press reports he had read that implied some sort of highly speculative suggestions of mismanagement. They were of a vaguely insinuating criticism claiming to represent the public interest whilst serving merely as a malicious opportunity to incite disquiet against which there would be no defence until the whole truth had been unearthed; and, even then, a bad smell of incompetence would linger throughout the building.

Spenser shared his misgivings, unable totally to relax, wondering who had committed the deed or why he or she had returned the painting without ransom demand or payment, or why no declaration by misguided protestors had been published or received. It was all very unsettling, but business would carry on as usual and he would have to contend with it. The thought occurred to him that he could write an account of the incident and publish it for sale in the gallery shop. He could also concentrate on the format of the desired television programme if it were to be scheduled and on what he could contribute to it. Both he and Walter had independently thought it improper to consult each other whilst the matter was not yet concluded, but he could look forward to a conversation with him soon.

Hedrick wondered whether it would be he who would reframe the painting if it were to be done in the workroom but he soon learned that the task would be undertaken by the National Gallery. That meant that everyone in the gallery was regarded as a suspect and he was annoyed at the aspersion not only on his character but also on that of all the staff. He had also noticed that Astra had left her job without any farewell. She obviously had no interest in him, but he resolved to dismiss her from his mind since a renewal of those few moments they had spent together would no longer be possible. But he was understandably a little depressed at his return to the days before she had gone.

Garrard had heard very little from Personnel about his impending retirement date. Could they be debating whether to ask him to stay for another year? He would be happy to do that but he had also wondered whether management would wish to continue the glazing project, given the subterfuge it had afforded the del Mano. They might even be wondering how many other paintings had been switched and whether the public would believe any of the exhibits to be genuine. That was a thought that troubled him. He had spent decades in the gallery and was familiar with every item, but he had framed many of the exhibits and was positive that all of his were genuine. He also had confidence that Hedrick's work was equally as reliable and as authentic as his.

He confided his fears to Hedrick, who attempted to console him with the thought that nobody, not even a whole gang of international art thieves, could have exchanged even a few of the exhibits for copies without the slightest indication of their activities being revealed. Garrard felt a little calmer. He was worrying about nothing, he admitted, except how he would occupy himself in retirement. He enjoyed friendly relations with his neighbours, he explained, but none of them had the same interests as he. Hedrick responded that perhaps he should interest himself in their activities, at which Garrard raised the slight trace of a smile.

'Yes. Do something. Everybody tells me that. That young lady to whom you introduced me, said something similar. "Write a book," she said. Perhaps I will. But I haven't seen her for a while. I suppose she's still around?'

'She's finished her thesis and gone back home, wherever that is,' Hedrick added, slightly dismissively.

'Westerton, I suppose. That's where Professor Tilson lives, anyway. But it's a pity she's gone. I liked her. Very polite and correct. She came to my house in order to ask for copyright permission. That wasn't necessary but it was nice of her to ask. We had a little talk, partly about you. She said you were a bit reticent, but aren't we all?'

'I'm not reticent. She's a professor's daughter, I'm just a workshop employee.'

'I got the impression that she was a little disappointed. Said she would have to get a job in some junior teaching post.'

'So much for private education and top universities. I could do a job such as that even though I started in a stationery factory.'

Garrard sensed a slight reluctance by Hedrick to enter into a deeper discussion of a topic that he detected as a sensitive issue and turned to another matter. 'How would you like to come to a little party at my house?' he asked. 'Call it my farewell party. Saturday evening. Just the two of us and I'll do the cooking.'

Hedrick was flattered after all these years to have been invited by his colleague and mentor to what would obviously be Garrard's only farewell to the gallery that he had served for decades. He could not refuse, nor did he want to refuse. His several evenings in his own company were occasionally relieved by visits to his mother or isolated reencounters with his old schoolmates but, knowing that Garrard was a man of few activities outside working hours, he felt greatly honoured by the invitation, and was unusually moved in stammering his acceptance.

Astra asked her father what he thought of her thesis and, having assumed that he had been too busy with the theft of the century, was pleased with his reply that he had read all of it and found a few inconsistencies. Her digression into del Mano was also a little unexpected but she protested that she would like to keep the reference by clarifying the contrast between Dutch and Italian Masters. Her father agreed that a reference to a contemporary of the period would not go amiss but that she should contrast the styles and period influences more clearly. Astra expressed her relief at his approval of Garrard's notes, which she mentioned had been collected by one of the workroom staff. Walter had already made a mental note, however, to summarise the passage in the television programme he was preparing.

Hedrick took the bus to Garrard's house, carefully carrying the bottle of wine he had purchased for the occasion. Garrard opened the door to him and, with beaming smiles, each greeted the other to the pleasant odour of something cooking. Hedrick felt immediately at home with this unusually convivial colleague in his comfortably furnished house. He brandished the wine with a salutation to a happy retirement. Garrard bustled about in the kitchen for a few minutes until he was ready to join Hedrick in the dining room.

'Welcome to my humble abode,' he said, and they poured the drinks in expectation of a glorious evening. 'I don't entertain much,' Garrard admitted. 'But this is a special occasion. My retirement. Possibly. But they haven't given me a final date, yet. And it's an opportunity to talk of all the things we have done together over the years.'

Hedrick raised his glass in expectation of a few reminiscences, chief among which would be his first encounter with Garrard all those years ago when he had been taken to the workroom for the first time. 'You'll be the main workroom man, now, I suppose,' Garrard continued. 'They'll have to replace me with a beginner just as they placed you.'

'I'm really glad to have encountered you in the shop. I might still be working in the stationery factory if we hadn't met,' Hedrick responded, and then congratulated Garrard on the garden.

'*An ill-favoured thing, sir, but mine own,*' Garrard replied. 'Astra said that as well when she was here. Nice girl that. She was a bit disappointed with you though.'

'I told you she was a cut above me.'

'She said she had almost finished her thesis and would get her father to check it before submission. There's nothing like having good connections. She'd be a good catch for you. Educated, arts background.'

'I doubt it. She's set on higher things.'

'Time for dinner,' Garrard announced. 'You can see my

copy of the painting upstairs whilst you're waiting if you like. It's in the small bedroom.'

Hedrick felt that he should follow Garrard's invitation and went upstairs. It was his first opportunity to view the picture in a domestic setting since his own copy had been taken for examination by the Art Squad. Looking at the painting again after several months, he was reminded of its likeness to Astra. 'Those cheeks! That golden glow!'

Garrard called that all was ready and he returned downstairs. 'Didn't the Art Squad take it for examination?' he asked.

'I didn't tell them about it. I've had it for years and knew that it was a copy, but perhaps you have your suspicions that it might be the real thing,' he laughed.

'No. It has the frame that was discontinued years ago, and we both know that the original has been returned unharmed.'

'Astra more or less accused me of the theft but promised never to tell anybody. But, like everybody else, you now know that the real one is elsewhere.'

'It's where it has been that I'm wondering about,' Hedrick replied, but Garrard simply shrugged at the mystery preferring to reminisce about his early days.

As they cleared the dishes, Hedrick told Garrard that he had no idea he was such a good cook. 'It's not too difficult when you try,' came the response. 'I managed on a limited variety at first until I resolved to do things properly.'

In the relaxed and congenial atmosphere of the evening, they settled back with another glass and Hedrick promised Garrard that he would try harder, too. Garrard responded, 'I wish I had tried harder with my relationships,' he mused aloud as he sought to fulfil his promise to Astra. 'I suspect we have the same feelings not just about the painting but what it means to us. I love that painting because it depicts a girl I knew who played the harp. If I had spoken up instead of burying everything I felt about her, she might be here now; but I was too tongue tied and she was a musician, whilst I was just a workroom apprentice thinking that she wouldn't want me. But through all these years, I've come to the conclusion that I could not have been more foolhardy. I'm sure she felt the same about me as I felt for her, but I ruined everything just because I was too restrained and said nothing; and in those days it was more or less expected that the initiative should come from the man. Perhaps that's still the case, but she went away somewhere and I've not seen her since.'

Garrard sank comfortingly back in his chair as the past enveloped him in a dreamy haze of distant days. 'I wonder whether she would have found somebody else or lived alone like me,' he mused, no longer burdened by his self-imposed reticence to reveal his private thoughts, and relaxed in the company of his friend and colleague. 'We might have had a family, perhaps become grandparents by now, but I lost the initiative and the girl. All I have now is – what? Retirement? Time to think? Emptiness, more like. But that's all in the past. It just shows that one can either make decisions that lead on to fortune or drift upon the current and be washed up on some distant shore. I've done the latter and, now, I'm on my own. I'll have to make do with tending the garden,' he ended with a wry smile.

Hedrick accepted another glass as they contemplated their futures in a meditative silence. He had very little knowledge of Garrard's early life except that he had shared the sort of youth that Hedrick had known, having been an assistant at the gallery since his early twenties, and had gradually developed the skills that had led to his present job. But Hedrick had not realised that he had had an unrequited love. 'History has a habit of repeating itself,' he thought.

His eye alighted on a tower cabinet crammed with CDs. 'I see you are not limited to books and paintings, Garrard. What sort of music do you like?'

'It's all classical. Anything from Bach to Bax and a bit later. I like to follow the text for Lieder and opera in order to understand them properly but I almost never visit performances.' He selected one that he thought Hedrick would like and they listened for a while, Garrard thinking intently whilst sunk in remembrance of the past, Hedrick thinking he should learn more about it.

He noticed the clock silently intruding upon the evening, and Garrard, seeing the direction of his glance, resignedly admitted that '*Time and Tide wait for no man*'. They parted with fraternal thanks and Hedrick walked thoughtfully away. Garrard thought that he had complied with his promise to Astra but he had also spent an enjoyable evening in this, for him, rare occurrence of a social occasion.

Whilst waiting several minutes for the bus, Hedrick marvelled at Garrard having revealed secrets from his past which indicated that he was no different from a million others and not at all a man without feelings but, rather, one who had experienced the same self-doubt as himself. He felt even closer to the man who had pulled him out of a crowd, which had thereby led to him being given the opportunity to develop a skill and to practise a trade. He was reminded that Garrard had expressed the conviction on a previous occasion that it was not merely a trade, but a craft that required as much knowledge and dedication as was required in any professional career. Hedrick had now learned that that was an insight that Garrard had formed by the reassessment of his life after he had lost the girl of his dreams. It was also one that he should adopt. He had acquired an expertise, he thought, and, reinforced by a new maturity, resolved to face the world with greater confidence.

Astra retraced her steps of over a month before but this time wheeling an almost empty case. She had updated her thesis and sent it to her invigilator and was now facing an interlude of little activity in which she would indulge herself in thinking idly of her future, a time of mists but perhaps not of mellow fruitfulness. 'Life has many turnings,' she thought as she reached the bus station, reciting to herself that some '*lead on to fortune*' and '*the paths of glory lead but to the grave*'. That led her to the conclusion that removing the rest of her belongings seemed symbolic. '*Ring out the old, ring in the new*. But what would that be?' she wondered.

The journey brought a sense of movement, perhaps of purpose, and, now that her thesis had set an end to her studies, a feeling that she was travelling to a land of discovery far beyond the days of youth into a new episode of opportunity. Her mood was reinforced when she reached her flat and looked out of the window onto the almost deserted street, thinking a little wistfully of the months she had spent there when finishing her thesis and working at the gallery. But that was all in the past and new ventures beckoned her into a world that held wide-open spaces where she could wend her way through all her future years.

She would have to terminate her lease soon, but she should also go back to the gallery shop and take a final farewell of the colleagues she had met and of the scenes she had known before. She would decide next day. Meanwhile, the few provisions she had brought with her sufficed for an evening meal after she had cleared all her remaining possessions and placed most of them in her case, intending to complete her packing next day. An early night was followed by a dreamless sleep.

Day broke to a dark sky which, together with the emptiness of her flat now that it was almost bare of possessions, seemed indicative of bleakness ahead. The past complete, the future unknown, life at a turning point, back to Westerton. Was that her future? Reliance on her parents for accommodation and on her father and his connections? The day brightened a little. 'Show some spirit, girl,' she told herself, and she set off for the gallery.

Her old friend, Viola, in the gallery shop greeted her with a smile expressing regret at losing her forever when told that Astra was moving on now that her thesis was finished. They snatched a brief respite in the rest room in order to catch up with the local gossip, but Viola quickly excused herself, telling Astra that she had to complete the shelf rearrangement before lunch time. Astra felt deflated at the thought that duty exceeded friendship, but understood that Viola had a family to nourish and she, herself, had only the vast expanse of an uncertain future that would never call but was simply waiting patiently for her to explore. They bade a hasty farewell and Astra resumed her seat to look idly out of the window, wondering how she could choose her destination or whether she should find a job at the gallery or even resume her work in the shop. University, masters, thesis were all stored away in the past; the evil day had arrived when she had to decide upon a career.

She turned her head at a slight movement behind her to find that it was Hedrick who had entered. Both were a little startled at unexpectedly meeting the other, but as Hedrick poured his coffee and brought it to her table, he ventured to say in an almost ungracious tone, 'Hello. I thought you had gone back home.'

'Yes. I had, but I had to return to collect the last of my belongings. I'll have to cancel the lease and then – do something. My thesis is finished and so am I,' she ended with mock hilarity.

Hedrick wanted to say that he would miss her, but thought that that would be too revealing. Gathering courage, he suggested, 'How would you like another meal at *The Flying Swan* this evening. A last chance to celebrate the end of your apprentice years.'

'And the start of a new era, a journey into the future,' she replied with a smile.

Hedrick noted an acceptance that seemed to carry a promise of things to come. He relaxed. 'Same place, same time,' he told her as he finished his coffee dissolved in smiles. The workroom was a happier place now.

Chapter 15

Astra remained in the rest room for several minutes after Hedrick had left, thinking still of her uncertain future. She was confident of her thesis but she would still have to find a welcoming greeting from an expectant employer. A great expanse of unknown territory spread before her and would have to be crossed before she could reach the promised land. She should adopt an active approach in preparation for the journey, but it was no world exploration she faced wherein she should pack a bag and book a ticket. No, it was a passage through moors and forests and over streams and stiles, along the paths and byways of experience, to a land that beckoned but was far away beyond the reaches of imagination.

Youth was full of ambition, but what was that? A lofty mountain capped with snow far away across the horizon and ringed with the foothills of exertion that she had to scale. But, somehow, in this quiet room, she was threading through the maze. The route had a dimly sighted goal and the start, a gate through which she had to pass in order to depart from the comfort of her home and seek her way through the wilderness of its surrounds.

She had benefited from a good education, loving parents and the guidance they had provided throughout her life. That must have brought her to the threshold of independence, surely. Now she must wend her way through the obstacles strewn before her. Or were they signposts that would point to a destination far away in a land of aspiration? All that devotion to art, her year writing a thesis that, now, she realised few would read, seemed merely to have cleared the preoccupations with pursuits of the past. Her endeavours had brought her to the topmost rung where she had achieved the state of knowing that it was time for a decision. From now on, she would take command, be positive and stride across the unknown region.

The thought that she should reward her friend for her company that morning drew her down to the gallery shop. Viola was reorganising the display in order to make room for the newly arrived exhibits. 'Can I help?' she asked. 'I'm free for the rest of the day.'

'All right. I could do with a little assistance,' her friend replied. 'I need to clear the old stock and replace it with the new products. They want to turn the great art theft into a business opportunity. We're seeing a few more visitors now that the painting has been rehung.'

Astra stepped into the breach, happy to participate in a refreshing activity in which she could occupy the few hours she would otherwise have spent in wandering through the town.

As they were working together, Spenser passed by and noticed her unexpected return. 'I thought you had left us forever,' he said. 'I hadn't realised you had returned.'

'Just unofficially,' she replied. 'It looks as if you will see a bit more trade.'

'Yes. *Girl with a Harp* has been rehung and is proving a great attraction. I have to give a lecture on it every afternoon, which is a big change for me from the somnolence of my normal days,' he joked. 'It will be useful practice for the television programme which your father and I will record tomorrow.'

'Oh! I hadn't realised it had been arranged already. I'll watch that with great interest.'

'They think a suitable transmission date would be Sunday,' he replied. 'But come to the lecture theatre this afternoon to hear a sample. Doors open at two thirty.'

'All right,' she responded. 'I'm free for the rest of the day.'

Viola congratulated her on the invitation as Spenser

returned to his office. Astra experienced a slight twinge of conscience that it had been her relationship that had attracted his attention to her and not to Viola, who had a family to support and was surely more deserving of notice. She could not but feel a little humbled at the thought that the invitation had been offered more for her connections rather than for her own efforts. Her determination to launch herself upon the world without the aura of parental fame was now redoubled.

The lecture was the first opportunity she had had of listening to Spenser, whose facility with words and subject were impeccable. He spoke fluently without notes on del Mano's background and the generosity of the gallery founder in bequeathing his collection. On turning to the painting now showing on screen, he informed his audience that it had been held by admirers for most of its existence, firstly by the well-to-do merchant who had commissioned it, but several decades later it had been sold into private hands as the family became reduced in fortune. Only in the early twentieth century had it appeared again when it had re-emerged at auction and, some sixty years later, been acquired by Lewis Pelham.

The subject, he continued, was an allegorical setting that depicted privilege in the midst of deprivation, denoted by the crowd displayed in the background seeking relief from their everyday tedium by admission to a celebration. The *Girl* was modelled by Risanta Ferra, a favourite of del Mano. Her features reflected the sun glinting through the window upon her rather serious demeanour and a harp that must have been costly to purchase and have taken many years of dedication to master. The scene thereby contrasted her riches and capabilities with the jollity of the throng pictured in the garden below. She had a privileged existence compared with that of the crowd, who were less fortunate but, nevertheless, happy at their probably rare day of relaxation. Spenser drew his audience's attention to the glowing features of the subject and contrasted them to the rather darker tones of the clothes worn by the crowd. 'A depiction of contentment amongst the humble strivings of the wider population,' he informed them.

A few questions were posed by the audience, to which Spenser replied that the model was almost certainly no harpist but that the music suggested by the harp had been captured and passed through the centuries as if to add intrigue and even more wonder to our admiration. 'If only we had a recording of her voice,' he continued, 'we might know whether she was also singing and what song it was. But we have only silence, although a silence that has sounded well beyond her time.'

The proceedings closed, followed by Spenser leading them to the floor below in order for them to view the original. He experienced a slight feeling of nervousness as he approached the del Mano room, wondering whether it would still be in position, but security staff were dutifully in attendance, and the Old Master was hanging in its rightful place. The visitors broke into new expressions of admiration bolstered by their knowledge so learnedly imparted only minutes before.

Astra looked at the painting with a new insight. An allegory of a little rich girl and a multitude of less privileged, quite ordinary people. The painting was four hundred years old but the world had not changed. She could not play the harp but she had been brought up in a well-situated family, had received a fine education and had spent over a year in researching and writing her thesis. Others, Viola, for instance, had not known those benefits, and had to work, admittedly, for not too many hours and, fortunately, in a benevolent institution, to help sustain her family.

Astra began to feel that same glow of sunshine that had been illuminating the *Girl's* face for centuries. 'Am I so different?'

she wondered. 'One who is also bathed in constant light, the beneficiary of another's labour that enables me to walk the world in an aura of self-gratification, and not even able to reward anybody with music unless it be my very limited repertoire on the piano?' There were numerous others in her position, but for the first time, she realised that there were obstacles, too, chief among which was that she might be regarded as occupying a position that might seem exalted to less favoured members of the human race to whom even the slightest differential in social standing could possibly pose a difficulty in making relationships. Hedrick, for example. 'That's why he was so reticent. What a fool I must have been not to have realised that.'

On the way out, she passed Hedrick in reception. 'See you later,' he said with an inviting smile, referring to their appointment at *The Flying Swan*.

'I'll be there,' she replied. 'I've just come from Spenser's lecture. Very interesting.'

'That will be two things we can talk about, then. Your thesis and the *Girl*.'

Astra wandered slowly back to her almost empty flat, where she sorted through her suitcase in order to extract a suitable change of clothing for the evening. Only another hour to wait, but one that seemed to last forever until she walked slowly past the shops idly gazing into the windows and slyly at her reflected image; but there was no glow of sunshine illuminating her cheeks, she noted thankfully as she passed, confident that there would be no remnant of inequality to disturb her enjoyment. She reached *The Flying Swan* only a few minutes early, happy to find that Hedrick had already arrived, which brought a genuine smile from both.

The atmosphere was much as it had been on their previous visit, warm with very quiet music and a low buzz of conversation from the few customers at the bar. In response to Hedrick's question, she replied over a glass of wine that tomorrow would be her last day, but added that she would miss her months at the gallery. 'Everything comes to an end some time,' she continued, sadly. 'Now, the world calls, but for what, I do not know.'

'You'll probably get a few offers,' he replied. 'I took a big gamble when I accepted an offer to work at the gallery but I've never regretted it. Once you've launched yourself into some sort of career, I'm sure you will make a success of it.'

'I suppose I'll have to spend a while at home again. I don't want to rely on connections, but I don't think the world is waiting expectantly for my big entrance. I'll have to apply for something and then persuade them how suited I am for the job before scaling the heights before me.'

'That sounds like the correct attitude to reach the altitude. "Onwards and upwards",' Hedrick responded. 'Ask Spenser whether he can suggest something. He knows an awful lot about art. Garrard and I attended his first lecture on *Girl with a Harp*, our favourite work of art. We both like it as a painting but Spenser told us a bit more about the artist. I framed it as well as a couple of copies, but the Art Squad pulled my copy to pieces. Garrard kept silent about his copy and didn't have to see his ruined by officialdom.'

Astra hesitated before asking whether Garrard still had his copy. 'I think it was upstairs when I visited him. Is it still there, do you know?'

'Yes. He's had it for years,' Hedrick replied. 'It reminds him of a girl he knew forty years ago, and he was very sentimental about it. I'm certain that he wouldn't part with it. I saw it when I spent an evening with him, recently, after the original had been returned. We had checked it upon arrival and verified that it was genuine. It was framed by the National, though, probably because we must have been the top suspects,' he laughed, 'and they didn't want it to be spirited away again.'

Astra was horrified at discovering that she had been totally wrong in accusing Garrard. But he had not protested his innocence. He was a man of infinite passivity and must have ranked her assumption as unworthy of retort.

'My dad told me that the painting had been examined for DNA traces and they found yours and Garrard's as well as Spenser's, but don't worry, he said that it wouldn't lead to anything because all of you were authorised personnel and had handled it several times in the past, but he wondered why no other traces were found. It's a complete mystery how it could have been removed but I told him that I was absolutely certain that it could not have been either you or Spenser,' she ended.

'Or Garrard?' Hedrick asked.

She confessed with great remorse, 'I've done a terrible thing, Hedrick. I accused Garrard of taking the picture. I was convinced that he had, but I was totally wrong. What must he have thought of me, a stupid little girl who just jumped to the wrong conclusion? I knew it couldn't be you or Spenser and therefore assumed that it must have been Garrard. I'll never be able to apologise profusely enough.'

'That's bad, but at least you have confessed to me. Since you are leaving the gallery now, you'll have to seek him out tomorrow and clear your conscience. Don't forget to tell your father that it wasn't him. That would be more persuasive than if any of us had to protest that we had nothing to do with it. But whoever it was chose the most valuable painting in the gallery which, in my view, indicates expert knowledge. My guess is that it was some sort of security test that would wake up everybody to the possibility of a theft. Otherwise, I can't understand why it should have been returned after a few months with no ransom and completely undamaged.'

'If that were the case, it would indicate somebody who was aware of how lax security might have been.'

'I'm not in security but I know that we do have the most effective monitoring system on the market. There must have been some great advance in technology that could circumvent it.'

'Something that the Art Squad have never heard of. They haven't made much progress.'

'The main thing is that the painting is back in its rightful place. Let's hope it stays there,' he ended. 'But what will you do now? More study, or face the dreadful day of looking for a job?'

'I'm finished with study. It's about time I stepped into the real world, but I have no idea what to do.'

'A difficult decision that we all have to face. I started in a stationery factory but I had a stroke of luck when Spenser picked me for an apprenticeship at the gallery. First jobs are a gamble because we don't know the world and have to gain experience by diving into an unknown ocean. But I hope you won't go somewhere too far away,' he told her, remembering Garrard's advice. 'When I first saw you, I thought you must have been the *Girl with a Harp*. You looked just like her with that same slightly studious expression and with the light falling on your face.'

'There must be some magic ingredient in that painting if you both had the same thought,' Astra responded. 'It's certainly a wonderful work of art. Garrard told me that it resembled a girl he once knew but she went away because he was too reserved to tell her his real feelings.'

'It has more magic than I had realised at the time,' Hedrick continued. 'I've loved that painting since I first saw it on a school trip and then was given the opportunity to frame a copy for myself and the real one for the gallery. We both, quite independently, selected the reproduction and framed our own copies, but mine was confiscated and broken up by the Art Squad.'

'Good thing it wasn't the real one,' she responded.

'Yes, but it made me think and to reach the conclusion that I had come of age and leaped into a maturity where I would be a lot less accepting of officialdom. If the Art Squad were to come again wanting to destroy another copy in my little display, I would show a bit more spirit in defying them. We were all devastated at the loss as if it were of a much-loved child, but despite his quiet modesty, Garrard showed his spirit in remaining silent about his copy and consequently did not have to suffer the invasion of privacy that I had. Now that you have come back, I am going to emulate him and frame another to keep as a remembrance of you.'

At the mention of reframing the picture, Astra was reminded of her obligation to Garrard. Leaving would be a wrench and the prospect of apologising to him filled her with a double dread. All she could say now was that she would have to leave again next day.

'That means that this is my last chance to tell you, firstly, that I shall miss you, and, secondly, that you ought to stay long enough for me to tell you how much.'

Astra smiled at the demonstration of his new assertiveness. 'Tell me now,' she replied in the hope that he would, at last, match his feelings to hers.

He looked at her for a moment, trying to collect the thoughts that would justify his new persona. 'I not only think that you are the embodiment of the *Girl* in the painting but also the most marvellous girl I've ever known: beauty and accomplishment that has stepped from the picture into the present. No wonder somebody stole it. I wouldn't mind keeping the real you in a private gallery playing the harp, but I wouldn't want to return you. Unless you wanted to be returned, of course,' he added.

Astra smiled at his declaration. 'I don't think I would want to be,' she responded. 'In breaking up your picture, the Art Squad have let a new spirit fly out from four hundred years of entrapment. *The Flying Swan*, perhaps.'

'Swans are very loyal and mate for life,' Hedrick told her. 'I'm a cob. You could be my pen.'

'That's being positive. You've broken out of the old and flown into the new.'

'I could have waited a bit longer to tell you. They say all will come in time but I would not want to wait as long as Garrard.'

'Certainly not,' Astra told him. 'Time is actually a destroyer of lives. All the cities and all the civilisations that have ever existed have been consumed by time, and everybody who has ever lived has been carried to the grave by his remorseless patrol. We may have known our grandparents but almost never our great grandparents. They and all their predecessors have worked throughout their lives in order to build a future not only for themselves, but also for their descendants. They have, nonetheless, been swept away by an unforgiving tyrant to join their ancestors beneath the sands of time, forgotten by those who come after, lost to history and to the world.'

'Quite right,' Hedrick agreed. 'We can live only in the present within the span that we are allotted and bequeath all our creation to the next in line when we retire into a land beyond recall. Time is the sand that runs through the glass to measure what has passed but also how little there is to come. That dwindling pile should warn us that we have but a single life in which to dig and delve or to spin and weave.'

'I've finished my thesis and, now, must embark on another journey,' Astra responded. 'If only I knew to what destination, but the first port of call is back home.'

'When you are at home looking across those stormy seas that you must encounter in your voyage to foreign lands, you will wish you had a pilot to stand with you on the bridge as you contemplate your future passage through the ocean waves.'

'That tyrant Time will still be with me. He could be in party mood and set me dancing, or, more probably, be the flag that flutters weakly in the breeze as I stand gazing at the wide horizon.'

'I'd rather hear you playing on the harp and singing of how the world is changing. How the future is always calling and how you are responding, set upon a steady course, perhaps, or joining with the crowd. You will survey a wider world, one that calls for exploration, and one that opens to a vista unknown until tomorrow. But if you stand upon the cliff and merely watch the sands as the tide encroaches, you will know that your decision to return was ill advised.'

'So what is your solution to my dilemma?'

'Stay with me and know that all your future is assured,' he replied.

'That's being positive, I suppose. But a girl has more to think about than you are obviously aware,' she smiled at him.

'I just thought that we could start as we mean to go on. There has to be a future for us, I hope. Remember Garrard and his lost love. I don't want to have the forty years of regrets that he has had.'

'I told him that I didn't want that either,' she admitted. 'I'll have to leave tomorrow, but you could visit next weekend if you'd like. Not to stay, though. My parents are already worried that you may be a bad influence on me.'

'They've never met me!' he exclaimed, somewhat aggrieved.

'It's only because I told them vehemently that I was absolutely positive that you were not the thief. They immediately thought the contrary and that I was protecting a master criminal. I am their only child, and they have high expectations of me.'

'You're not a child to me. Rather a desirable young woman and future partner when all the floods and ebbing tides will be washing over both our lives.'

'Come next Sunday, and put their minds at ease. Here's my address, you'll have to walk the last part, though.'

'All right. I'll go the extra mile.'

They left *The Flying Swan* hand in hand and walked back towards her apartment where they stopped to say goodnight. They embraced for several minutes before she broke away but, unlike the time before, a little more dishevelled and confirmed that he would be her future.

Chapter 16

Bentley was faced with the most difficult case that he had ever been called upon to negotiate. Throughout his career, all of his projects had demanded a minute examination of detail in preparation for achieving the goal that his clients wished him to reach; and, in the course through which he had to sail, he had succeeded in almost all his navigations of the Scyllas and Charybdises between which he had to steer. That was why he had obtained the results in his business for which he had been so handsomely remunerated, and why he had gained a high reputation within the profession. With figures at his fingertips and persuasive phrases on the tip of his tongue, and never overawed by majesty or outwitted by specious argument, his skills had been recognised as presenting a formidable challenge to any opponent. He had entered negotiations with confidence and had calmly and logically presented his client's position to an increasingly floundering opponent and thereby had won the day.

His present dilemma was of a far more personal nature, however. He had met her again and had rekindled the love that had lain dormant for over two decades. She had simply appeared out of the ether so unexpectedly, so astonishingly, that he had felt that the passage of time had not rolled by but that he had travelled back to the days that had been the happiest he had ever known. Even if he could count the little joys that had intervened in the meantime that seemed to have been wiped away by this reencounter, he had had no other episode to match that of knowing her.

Cordelia seemed to him less enamoured of those youthful days, and to have some reservation at restoring their previous relationship. The bond that had bound them so closely together had broken for reasons unknown to him at the time. She had simply disappeared with hardly any explanation and certainly not one that was anywhere near adequate, but he had been left to drift through his existence with the constant remembrance of magical times finally to conclude that they would never return. But she had come back! Meeting her in this town where they had spent those wonderful days so long ago was a coincidence of such incredible impossibility that he thought it must have been ordained by a higher authority. Neither of them had planned their meeting, and neither had returned until now, but after two decades, they had both chosen the date quite independently.

His anxiety rose as he felt the inadequacies of a life in the shadows returning. He had spent too many years wondering why and where she had gone and had finally and reluctantly accepted an existence without her. But they had met again and their pasts had leaped fully formed into the reality of the present. She appeared to be not as convinced as he was of the delights of their reencounter, but if she were about to disappear into the ether once more, he would be totally without hope that she would ever return but would waft through the air of a distant land, ever present in his mind but absent in body and invisible except in his dreams. His flight of ecstasy in the resumption of those halcyon days would crash to the ground on which he would be obliged to spend the rest of his life in an even more lonely existence than he had known hitherto.

The feeling of joyful anticipation that he had experienced over recent days at a more lasting reunion was now mixed with a little nervousness at any announcement she might make. She had a house in Italy, her life had changed from the constraints they had known before, she could afford the best hotel in town, she had not encouraged his advances of the evening before last and she had established a life without him.

He joined her as arranged on the prom, but as soon as they met, he regained the pure happiness of simply being near her. All trepidation fled, they smiled their greetings and leaned on the rail standing closely together and looking out to sea.

'Do you remember those days when we stood here all those years ago?' he said after a few moments of silence.

She certainly had remembered. This place had remained a sacred recollection to her because that week of absolute happiness had been unforgettable. Days filled with delight and nights locked in each other's arms. 'Of course I do,' she replied, turning her face to his. 'After all those places I've visited since then, this is the one that has given me the fondest memories. I hesitated to come back because I feared that the town may have changed in a way that would wipe aside the thoughts that I wanted to preserve forever.'

'I have not returned, either, until now. The business kept me in the office but that was probably a deliberate distraction to avoid reflecting too much on things past. This was the perfect place for a boyhood holiday, but it was visiting with you that made the memory so special. Now, it is we who have travelled back through time to live again untroubled by an uncertain future.'

'Yes. The future has passed and been stripped of all its secrets,' Cordelia replied a little sorrowfully. 'Mine gave me travel but also a growing distaste for wealth squandered on trivia.'

'Mine gave me the feeling that I was promoting not just wealth but also how industry could cope with a developing world. It was exciting, but I've relaxed a little, now, and my first thought was to come here for no other reason than to relive the old times and to think of you. I had not thought we would meet again, but this is as if film stars had stepped from the screen and become living creatures rather than to have remained trapped in celluloid.'

'It was a marvellous time in both our lives,' Cordelia replied. 'You said you loved me, once, but I wanted something in addition. We never advanced beyond expressions of mutual love but I concluded, probably wrongly, that you wanted me as a plaything, something that would fit into your life and be taken out of the toy box whenever you wished whilst I was always kept in some dark house waiting for the door to open and be given another chance to parade before you.

'There! That's why I left. I loved you, all right, but I could never persuade myself that you would love me forever in return. I sought the light, somewhere where I would be bathed in sunshine throughout the day and spend my nights alone to dream of what might have been. Now, I've had my nights, but loneliness finally lost its attraction and I took whatever came my way. No repeat of first love, but second helpings that got me through the years. Just enough to tell me that nothing would ever be the same and gradually I came to accept that my destiny was to follow the lonely path subjected to all the sympathetic glances at the girl on her own and to all the unwelcome propositions from the hopeful crowd.'

Bentley felt that no matter how deeply he had loved her, she had not returned his adoration in like measure, but had reproved and dismissed him with words like a stiletto plunging into his heart. His first inclination was to sink back into the defencelessness that was his customary refuge when his personal capacity was challenged, but Cordelia posed a quite different challenge; she was worth fighting for, and he had to rise to the occasion.

'I did not tell you once that I loved you,' he responded with a slight grammatical distortion of her words. 'I told you at least a thousand times and meant it.'

'I thought you did at the time, but you were too constrained. I wanted to believe you and I would have stayed if you had been more assertive. As it was, we were drifting in a bubble of time that floated through a world that changed around us. It seemed to me that we would never be anchored in reality but just be living a dream that would eventually float away.'

Bentley finally realised how foolish he had been. He should have spoken out; he had not been too inhibited to do so, but he had been too unconstructive about the future. 'Cordelia, I loved you even more deeply than I had words to tell you, but I thought I was too lucky even to have met you. You were the most precious person I had ever encountered. You were the most beautiful person I have ever known and I thought you could never love me forever and a day because I was so inadequate compared to you. But I was a fool. I was too anxious that I might do or say something we would regret and frighten you away. I wanted to keep you just as you were, but you're right. It was a bubble, and the bubble finally burst. It almost proved my point, but it was I and not you who should be blamed for being too fearful and too inarticulate.'

'If only you could have told me,' she replied, 'but I was also unable to reveal the depths of my soul. Two lovers who thought their love might be endangered by a misplaced word! The times were good but I thought they might not last, and uncertainty was not for me. I ran away and made a mark elsewhere. I was happy, almost, but after a few years, that also proved a delusion and I travelled around Europe until that, too, lost its allure. I finally bought the cottage and settled down, but I came back to this place because I recalled that it had been the best week that I had ever known. I had come with you and we had been the happiest of couples, but that time has gone. It will not come back.

"Man has no harbour, Time has no shore;
It flows, and we pass on!"

'I realised that, no matter how enticing memory may be, no repetition would recur,' she sighed.

Bentley was crushed. She did not want him, he concluded, and he could not fight the spectre that haunted her. They placed an arm about the other in a silent comfort but Cordelia was locked in indecision whilst Bentley feared that the moment would not last forever.

'Even without a shore, time can waft our memories to the skies and eventually be heard by those who know their language,' Bentley continued. 'One that is spoken by people living in the past with holes in their souls and waiting for words carried on the wind. I had too many conflicts then and too many inhibitions to confess my feelings for you in any persuasive way. No skills to convince you that, as an impecunious lover, I could offer you the comfort and security that you deserved.

'Now, I wait for the breeze that whispers the sounds of long ago when music played in the trees and sang the songs of love requited. Love that will never fade, a love that defeats all opponents who challenge the course of the flooding tide, love that remains throughout the magic of time where all the suffering has faded and flown away to leave the sparkle of life that was ours.'

They looked each other deeply in the eyes for a long, silent moment. They had exchanged words of the confessional and, now, a thousand recollections and a thousand possibilities thundered through chasms in their minds. Cordelia saw the life that she had wanted all those years ago but the ties that bound her now were prominently written on the giant screen displayed by the demons hidden in her brain. It was a barrier she could not cross.

Bentley saw the life that he had always wanted but had suppressed. '*Time flows, and we pass on!*' he resumed. 'But not without memories or regrets that could have been rectified by some appropriate word, a plea, an understanding. But that was beyond my powers,' he admitted. 'Even now, when I have greater self-confidence and a determination to plead, to persuade, I can't penetrate your defences. You are quite right. That new dawn you sought opened upon a path that would give you new experiences. But how different it would have been if only we had had the maturity we have now. We could have followed another path through the maze, a path with a companion, an admirer, a lover. But we were too young, too unworldly, thinking we could find a vision wider than we had known before. Now, the world has opened and we have seen the wide Pacific spread before us with all its enticing invitations, but no glimpse of harbour.

'Waves flood across our worlds and wash away everything we have known or seen,' he mused. 'Great cities bereft of everyone who has ever lived, replaced by those who must start again but, in turn, are lost. Generations come and generations perish having thought that they would last forever, but a remorseless tyrant sweeps them effortlessly away, and that tyrant's name is Time. Not such a tyrant that he has no generosity although that is strictly limited. He shares with us a part of time that we may use or waste according to our choice but are compelled to spend that gift in the span that he decrees.

'But it is our fortune to be inheritors of all the times before; of deeds that echo through the years, as well as the mistakes that were made. All is wrapped in silence but it is we who must unveil the past and correct the errors that it contains, thence, to sail the ocean upon our lease of time that has to us been granted and which we must, in turn, surrender to our legatees.'

He broke off knowing that he had lost her but could say no more. That empty world he had known before would also be his future.

Cordelia sank her eyes silently to the ground. Her Pacific had proved too wide to cross. She had sailed about in circles and come back to where she had started, burdened with a cargo of despair. She should have taken Bentley with her but she had sought a life alone and been consigned to drift upon the bobbing sea.

'I just have to think, Bentley,' she responded. 'Everything is too complicated at the moment. My mind is all confusion.'

Bentley was distressed that he was unable to fight the spectre that haunted her. Despite knowing how futile were his words, he told her, 'If I can help to unwrap the past, you know that I shall always be with you.' But neither could find the words to bring solace either to themselves or to the other. They nestled in silent comfort, reliving for one brief moment a fragment of their former joy, but Bentley feared that that moment would not last forever while Cordelia was racked with a guilt she dare not admit.

In a voice of broken sobs, she told her dearest friend that she had no alternative but to resume the life that she had now adopted and must, therefore, return to her seclusion. Bentley's pleas had been to no avail and, in his despair, he was unable to find more persuasive arguments. Having made her decision, she told him that she was called by a still, small voice to the conclusion that she would have to leave next day. Bentley was deeply wounded but the night had descended to wrap her mind in darkness. He could only promise that he would accompany her to the station.

A mood of absolute despair enveloped him in a misery deeper than he had felt after she had left him all those years ago. He had experienced a revival of a love that had lain untouched in the depths of his soul only to be rejected almost as soon as it had been reawakened.

Whilst staring expressionlessly over the bay after returning to his hotel, he felt that all argument had been exhausted and he could do no more. He could only hope that his last contact with Cordelia would be a parting without tears.

The following morning, he accordingly ensured that he was waiting in reception at The Grand only just able to manage a wan smile as she signed out of the hotel. In order to remain a part of her for a few more minutes, he suggested they walk along the prom, both of them knowing that it would be to their final point of departure. They held hands but they were bereft of words, knowing that she had decided her future and, she said, must now stick to her resolution. Bentley could hardly wish her well without his voice breaking but told her that he would love her to the end of his days, unable to think of any words more meaningful than those already uttered.

Both were incapable of speech as they gazed silently into each other's eyes, feeling the dread of parting. She weakened momentarily, but a remnant of the strength, perhaps of self-denial, or even of a misplaced determination that had sustained her through the years compelled her to board the train and wave resignedly, sorrowfully and expressionlessly to him as it departed. Bentley stood on the platform silent and despondent. He gave a last wave as the train pulled slowly away with its precious cargo, leaving him with a feeling of desperate loneliness. A huge feeling of emptiness filled his heart as he turned away after the train had rounded the bend in the distance. She had disappeared once more but, this time, he had had the chance to persuade her to stay – and he had failed.

Chapter 17

Bentley walked dejectedly away from his last glimpse of the woman whom he had loved even before they had spent that wonderful week over two decades ago. He passed through the exit as far as the prom where he slumped onto a bench looking out to sea and at his empty future stretching to the horizon. He had had no doubt that she had loved him too, but she had moved on from the life that they had shared in those times of cherished memory and found a place to breathe elsewhere. Only in the last few days she had told him again that she still loved him. She had sounded genuine and he had believed her, but she seemed to be compelled by some invisible force that drew her back to a world where she would neither receive nor give such a love that they had known. Theirs was a passion that could not fade, and he had thought that no force could part them; but the hand of fate had intervened and she had left so inexplicably. Not once, but twice, because she seemed to have fallen under a spell that had bound her with a power that could not be defeated, and he had no weapon that could free her from her bondage. Persuasion had failed and he was alone, but he could not be critical of her. She was the same person that he had met before but her persona had been modified by events that had intervened as if she had built a wall around herself. She had created a new life from within that stronghold and did not want to sally forth at the risk of further upheaval; and his skills were too inadequate to enable him to scale her defence and be readmitted to her world.

He sat on the bench dreaming of a past that had come so astoundingly to life so many years before. They had resolved to celebrate their togetherness in a holiday in the sun. They were young, they were in heaven, they were in love. His old Morris had fortunately ended the journey without mishap or breakdown and they had happily enjoyed the drive eagerly watching the countryside pass by as their approaching goal drew excited cries with every mile. In the unrestrained freedom of youth, they had shouted their delight at the first sight of the sea and he had stopped in order for them to admire it from a distance. They had hugged each other in a little dance, knowing that the week had truly started before they drove on to the cottage that had absorbed most of their cash. But they were there and they were happy. The sun had shone and they were lovers, impecunious but without a care. The prom was a land of freedom and the view from there was a glimpse of heaven, the pier was a walk through paradise. He remembered how delighted they were at a sight that had fulfilled all that they had wished and their joy at sitting among all those children watching the Punch and Judy and how they had laughed and enjoyed the show. They had almost no money but they were blessed and had walked the prom a dozen times, stopping to lean upon the rail, arms about each other and gazing silently out to sea. A photographer had pictured them standing so happily together and, next day, they had collected the picture that, apart from the memories they had stored, had proved their only souvenir.

But all too soon the week had ended and they had taken a fond farewell of the town. If only they could have stayed but they had barely enough money to replenish the tank and they had driven away from their dream so regretful at leaving. The journey led back to a life of routine instead of the keen anticipation of seeing the sea, but they vowed to return the following year to repeat that time of delight. Now, seated alone on the bench, Bentley reflected that it had not been until well over twenty years later that they had resumed at least a part of that wonderful week. Several months after returning from that holiday, he had been plunged from delight into despair when she had told him of her new job. She would be away for a few weeks, she had said, but she had not come back.

She had now confessed to him that she did not want ordinariness and he had to admit that he had been quite unremarkable at that time and too accepting of their circumstances. He had to concede that the contrast between the holiday and routine had weighed too heavily upon them.

The sun passed behind a cloud and Bentley felt the chill of the future embrace him, but there would be no comfort now. How long had he sat there sunk in despondency? Twenty minutes? He stood up and walked along the prom but only as far as the rail where he had reencountered her, thoughts racing but as incoherent as the reason for her loss.

He retraced his steps towards the station again but it no longer held the charm of meeting but the sadness of departure. He should have said more, been more persuasive, but inspiration had failed him. He stopped in the forecourt and stood remembering his last glimpse of the woman who meant more to him than anything he had ever known; more than the business he had built over all those years, more than the affluence he could now call his own, but also, more than the memories that flickered so full of meaning through his mind strengthened by a presence that had been renewed but now had fled.

A thought intruded into his despair. He walked briskly to the ticket machines and bought a ticket to Skettering. She might still be on the platform and he would tell her again. No! He would plead with her to stay. He would leave all reticence behind and pour out his love somehow hoping that the right words would come. He waited for the shuttle but it was not scheduled for another half hour. He walked impatiently up and down the platform, but he would have to wait. She was worth waiting for and he tried to summon up words that he would say to her. The shuttle finally arrived. He boarded it and asked the time of arrival, but the journey was frustratingly slow, seeming to take almost an hour rather than the twenty minutes he had been told. He alighted at the junction and was able to look hurriedly about, but it was an almost empty platform that greeted him. He was too late; the London train had departed and she would dissolve into the crowd at Waterloo to be seen no more.

She had re-entered his life but, once again, had torn herself away without adequate explanation, and, this time, he knew for certain that she would be gone forever. The last connection had been severed and would never be renewed. He was bereft, distraught, but the main line train had left, taking the meaning of existence with it. In a mood of deep despair, he passed through the exit barrier into the forecourt and the wider world outside, but despite the people passing by, it was into an emptiness that filled his soul, confirming what a fool he had been to let her leave all those years ago and, this time, he had been too weak to persuade her to stay. Now, he would have a future full of nothing, a house full of nothing, his mind in constant turmoil and full of self-recrimination.

A few steps sufficed for him to confirm his future. No greetings from those he passed, not even a casual glance. He was alone and there would be no relief from desolation. He walked slowly for several minutes along the street before he turned back to retrace his steps onto the platform. The shuttle had left and the station was almost as empty as his future. All the urgency of existence now belonged to those more fortunate others, but that meant nothing to him. Loneliness, your name is Bentley, he thought. The station café presented an equally dismal prospect; one with a future devoid of comfort but with an eternal dullness as unappealing as the grave. He walked slowly the length of the platform, stopped for a while, and then walked back noting that the clock had advanced only a pitiful few minutes. He turned about to recommence walking slowly through the perpetual apathy of dejection only to notice that the clock had not hastened its progress when he returned. He would be forever waiting, forever wanting. Perhaps the café could offer, hardly excitement, but some alleviation, somewhere he could sit and think of nothing. From now on that would be his ever-present companion.

The door opened upon several tables where only a few travellers were passing the time until their train arrived, one guarding a parcel, another couple talking quietly, no doubt waiting for the train to take them rapidly to their home and children. He looked around and stared in disbelief at a face of equal astonishment that met his own. For a moment, he could not believe that it was Cordelia sitting there. He slipped into the chair opposite her and both were silent at the shock of meeting so unexpectedly, but he felt his spirit flooding back into his soul.

'You missed the train,' he said, stating the obvious, as if waking from a long sleep. 'It had left before I arrived.'

Cordelia replied in a startled voice, 'I know. I had plenty of time and decided to wait for the next one.'

'I've had time to think,' Bentley said. 'Time to miss you even more deeply than I thought possible. I came to be near you again before you left. All the things I told you were true and sincere. I love you. Please stay. Don't leave me again. We'll be together for always, get married, live at my place, and Svengali will have no more power over you.'

Cordelia hesitated but, with the realisation that she could no longer hold back the truth, said regretfully, 'You're too late, Bentley. I'm engaged to marry him.'

Bentley's face crumpled as he absorbed the worst news that could ever have been expected. 'Engaged!' he breathed in a voice reflecting his deepest horror. That's why she had been so distant when they were so near. 'No,' he groaned in the realisation that she could never be his to hold for the rest of time. 'No. Tell me it's not true,' he pleaded.

'I wish it weren't,' she replied quietly and sorrowfully. 'But I can't. I promised Frank a month ago. I've never loved him but he offered me the comfort and security you spoke of, and I more or less accepted. But that was not what I wanted. I left you all those years ago and went abroad not only because of the job but to find happiness somewhere far away, not because of you, but the mediocrity of existence. It was a goal that proved more elusive than I had thought. I spent two decades searching for it until Frank finally asked me to share his life. I gave up the search for happiness hoping that I could, at least, act a part of my dreams, but I never cast out the thoughts that I had harboured through all those years. He had just as unfortunate memories as I and understood, but he lives alone and probably wanted me as a hostess at his occasional parties and never ceased trying to persuade me. I should have known that it was not worldly goods that I wanted, but I realised that I had consented in hope that my wanderings would end. Frank knew that the engagement was just another business contract, but he had got his way.

'I stayed on until I felt I must tear myself away. I told him that I had to think. He was generosity squared and was honourable towards me, and I had every intention of complying with the bargain even if I didn't want to. But I had no idea I would meet you again. I have never been able to negotiate my own path around the pin table, but I am perpetually bounced from one quandary to another and constantly shuttled between the two masters of wish and reality. It seems that I am fated to repeat the mistakes of the past.'

'All mistakes can be rectified,' Bentley responded, trying to put hope and persuasion into his plea. 'The fault was all mine. Break the cycle. Stay with me. You will make both of us happy.'

'I can't. I've promised that I will return like an ever-circling comet. He is used to getting his own way and won't give in easily.'

'Break your promise. Choose another life with happiness at last. I'm reasonably affluent enough to give you all the shelter you'll ever want.'

'No, Bentley. I chose another life and it did me no good,' she replied. 'I'm the Flying Dutchman doomed to sail the world, never to find domestic peace. Frank will not leave me alone. He has a compulsion to be the winner in everything he does. And I have my conscience too. Always hammering at me. Whatever I do is wrong.'

'But not meeting me,' Bentley insisted. 'I am the one who has done the wrong thing. Taking you for granted, not even trying to trace you, failing to express myself, even now,' he admitted, only too well aware of how poor was his power of speech when it mattered. He threw away all reserve and spoke at last from the depths of his soul. 'Love is more powerful than any magnetism exerted by bullying tyrants. My heart has felt your absence for too long but is large enough for both of us. Step inside and be embraced by a love as wide as the ocean. Whatever happens, we shall do it together and each be a comfort to the other.'

Cordelia felt lost in the tangled web of life. *Her* life. A life in which she had been so decisive in a career that had brought her wealth and recognition, but a life in which she had floundered from one crisis to the next, bounced from one corner to another, and all because of her wish to break away from the dreary life that all those years ago, she had supposed would be her lot. She had abandoned that existence and had sought another. It was a different life that she had gained from constant striving even if she could feel the old one pleading for her return.

The travellers at the other tables stood up to leave as the London train drew into the station. Cordelia hesitated, but in a voice that betrayed an agony of misery, she raised her eyes to him to speak the words she did not want to say. 'We can't relive those endless days when we passed the time as happy souls. They have faded and we have moved on. It's too late. I have to go back home, now.' She felt that she had made a decision, a decision that would enable her to live the life that she had chosen, but she also felt the wrench that had consigned that old existence to the waves.

Bentley felt the stiletto stab again. '*Home is where the heart is*,' he quoted, desperately trying to find more persuasive speech in these last moments together. He gathered his thoughts and continued, 'That time of happy souls has no end but has merely paused until we start again like a clock that has been newly mended. It has re-emerged to be examined from the perspective of a later age and found to be only slightly changed. We shall resume our place where we shall be as joyful as in our yesteryears, and all the intervals between will be forgotten. The travails of painful days shall be of short duration when they are cast aside by that recurrence of our former treasure when the sands still filled the glass. We shall recall the days of childhood, days of everlasting youth and days of blossomed fullness to be lived again throughout our years together.'

Cordelia heard the words that would have held her back if she had not clung so tenaciously to her conviction that those hopes had been abandoned. She rose slowly from her seat as if in a trance and wheeled her case silently and slowly towards the door, unable to fight her demons as Bentley followed devoid of power. The travellers had boarded the train and the platform was clear. The doors closed, the signal light changed from red to green and the train drew slowly away. She hung her head as if debating what to do. 'Another train, another sign,' she said quietly.

'The sign that a link to an existence without reward is broken,' Bentley responded. 'One that tells you to embrace that other life. A life with a love that will banish all your sorrows.'

Cordelia felt a light shining into her darkness. 'You are being a little more persuasive, now,' she said through her sadness but with the slightest hint of a smile, remembering their talk on the prom. 'Perhaps it is a sign that warns me to think again. I may as well go back now.'

'The shuttle will be here in a minute,' Bentley replied, grasping the straw that she had presented. 'Our journey starts now. I have the car at the hotel, and we shall be home soon. A home of peace and welcome,' he told her softly.

As the minute hand clicked on to the next part of her future, she felt that Bentley could unwrap her past and bring reform. 'A home and not a house', she thought. 'Yes. A home at last.'

Bentley picked up her case and they left the café to stand each with an arm around the other silently awaiting the train.

Chapter 18

Hector had returned to his office after Bentley's very modest party on the day before his holiday thinking that his partner spent too long at his desk and seldom took a holiday of any length. But, this time, it had been his own choice, albeit helped along by a little encouragement from Hector who hoped to welcome him back a renewed and happier man.

He stared into space, thinking of the camaraderie they still enjoyed but also what a puzzle Bentley was. Devoted to the business but no leisure pursuits. '*All work and no play makes Jack a dull boy,*' he thought. But that must be wrong. Despite his quiet demeanour, Bentley was also good company with a gift for conversation as well as being a hive of industry and the most capable negotiator he knew.

Throughout the years following Cordelia's disappearance, he had been aware of Bentley's depression and had done whatever he could to encourage him out of the lethargy that had been the unfortunate consequence. Their long-time friendship had intensified and Hector thought that, to some extent, he had been successful but modestly conceded that a more beneficial influence had probably been exercised by the passage of time. Bentley had found a cure for his misery by focussing on the tasks that clients had presented and had gradually learned to smile again.

They had had the good fortune in their early days of acting successfully in negotiating a very small business sale from which their partnership had developed into one ever more eagerly sought over the years by larger enterprises. Hector reflected upon a background that had enabled both partners to grow into highly regarded advisors. They had achieved success and had become affluent as well as respected members of the business community, but Hector hoped that Bentley would not enjoy his freedom from work too much. If he were to make a habit of taking holidays, or even to retire, he thought, he would find it very difficult to find a replacement for his old friend.

He assured himself that he would be capable of handling those intermittent periods of intense pressure that could unexpectedly arise. Perhaps he might have to turn down business but the prospect that that might leak out to competitors and thereby convey a corresponding loss of capability was an unwelcome thought. He would not like the assumption to be made that the business had been driven by Bentley's expertise rather than his; they had been equally as effective in the partnership and each valued the other's contribution. No, he did not want Bentley even to think of retirement. That would be a problem that he, Hector, might have to face in the fullness of time but it was hardly a probability that would occur in the near future. He was worrying unnecessarily. Bentley was extremely valuable to the partnership, but just because he had taken his first break for several years, unusual though that was, it did not mean that he would change his lifestyle overnight.

Next day, he met Fenton Barr, a long-standing contact who was a middle-ranking civil servant with some sort of unspecified connection to influential levers of power. Hector was never one to miss an occasion that might lead to a business proposition and joined him, as requested, at the club house. Conversation was limited to a few innocuous subjects until they were well into the course when Fenton asked totally out of the blue, 'Have you heard of a businessman named Norbert Grantley, Hector?'

Hector had, of course. He was the manager of the big engineering business that had, recently, been the latest of his partner's most successful negotiations.

'Yes. A very successful manager of Overdale Engineering with whom Bentley helped negotiate a merger with Lowfield and his installation as group MD. Why do you ask?'

'We're wondering whether he has a connection to a businessman named Franco Pelham.'

'Pelham!' Hector responded. 'He controls several European businesses but very much from the background. A good delegator by all accounts.'

'He's trying to regain management control of Lowfield.'

'Unhappy at being defeated, I suppose. He lost out because his representative had my partner as his opponent,' Hector responded with a touch of pride. 'But it's a good business and the new group is even stronger now, which means it will be even more expensive to acquire.'

'Pelham is keen to take control of Softlyn, the software component of the former Lowfield, which would enable Grantley to sell that off to recoup some of his investment.'

'But for Pelham to risk millions on acquiring the group? It would be better to make a direct offer to buy out the software company.'

'Control of the group would attract admiration and respect and not draw attention to his main target. We believe that he does not wish to identify himself openly with Softlyn. I wonder whether he would appoint Bentley to act directly on his behalf this time.'

'Probably not. Bentley is on holiday at the moment. But if Pelham approaches us, I could take over. I know the background and I could consult Bentley on any details, if necessary. But why are you wondering about Grantley? The group has a good reputation but has nothing that could be of interest to the civil service, surely.'

'Softlyn has government contracts that we would like to keep confidential. We think it likely that Pelham will approach

Grantley with a proposal. Given your recent contact with him, it's possible that he might approach you for advice. If he does, please let me know what happens.'

Hector promised with the proviso that any business discussions should remain confidential. Fenton replied, 'You may be sure that all details would be treated with the utmost secrecy,' which Hector thought was a little presumptuous but, not for the first time, wondered not only whether Fenton really was the middle-ranking figure he had once admitted to being, but also why he should express interest in a minor constituent of a substantial engineering group.

'What sort of government connection does Softlyn have?' he asked, his curiosity having been piqued.

'Let's say it's defence orientated. It would be unwise of me to say more at this stage.'

Hector understood, more than ever convinced that Fenton was not the moderately senior civil servant that he claimed to be. They resumed their round and parted at the club house after polite exchanges of little concern, but Hector soon dismissed the conversation on the course in favour of the more pressing matter of preparing his family for their annual holiday. They would not leave for two weeks but business was very slack and he wished it were earlier.

Fenton was not one who ever tended to reveal many personal details and had always been a little mysterious in releasing any account of his true role in his professional activities. It was also second nature to apply his reticence on security matters to his domestic circumstances. That was a slightly embarrassing matter that he wished not to discuss, but he was used to telling half-truths and had easily escaped close scrutiny. He had been living alone for three years since his long-term partner had announced that she must go back to her mother's home in order to look after her in her declining years. After six months she had telephoned to say that she would not be coming back. She had thought about the decision for a long time and finally concluded that their lives had become routine and no magic was left.

It was disappointing to him that she thought their relationship had declined into routine when he had thought that they were coasting along nicely, but he was more than upset when Jessica reminded him of her investment in the house and enquired tentatively whether he could sell up and return her share. Being the upright citizen that he was, he had swallowed hard but promised to place it on the market. It had been snapped up and he had moved into a two-bedroom, two-bathroom bungalow having ensured that the agreed figure had been remitted to her account. But he comforted himself that his new residence had some advantages of being more easily maintained, less cumbersome and more suitable for a single man.

As Hector's holiday date drew nearer, there was little for him to do except to peruse a few papers and leave for home halfway through the afternoon. The telephone rang at last. 'It must be Bentley wanting his job back,' he hoped, but it was a most unexpected call from Norbert Grantley, about whom Fenton had spoken the previous week. Surely, that could not be a coincidence, he thought, and made an appointment for the following day.

Grantley entered full of smiles expressing his disappointment on hearing that Bentley had taken a holiday. 'Only a short one, I hope,' Hector added. 'It's always a slacker time in summer and he's taken a few weeks' badly needed leave.'

'He was very useful in our recent amalgamation. Now something else has come up in which his negotiation skills might be of further assistance.'

Hector smiled and responded, 'Could it have anything to do with Softlyn?'

'How on earth could you possibly have known that?' Grantley replied in astonishment.

'We make it our business to keep up to date with business trends,' Hector told him with a straight face, to which Grantley replied that the matter had been broached in total confidence.

'I suspect that you've been approached by Frank Pelham, who has offered to buy the company,' Hector continued hoping to impress Grantley even further.

'That's right. But how did you know that? The subject has been discussed not merely in strict confidence but in conditions of total secrecy. Somehow, it seems that it is known to the whole world! So much for our precautions!' he ended with a note of exasperation.

'Not the whole world. In this business, I find it useful to keep my ear to the ground for any tremors of distant earthquakes and, now, you have confirmed my assumption. How can we help?'

Grantley gave Hector a look of incomprehension mixed with a feeling that Railton Barratt Consultants must have access to information garnered from fields unknown to ordinary mortals. Wondering whether he was adding more layers to that mysterious source, he continued, 'When I assumed control of Lowfield, I found that the main business was functioning splendidly and was well managed, but there were several small units, some of which generated reasonable if not spectacular profits, but others which had no connection to the core business and were just a total distraction to management. I've proposed divesting some of them, including Softlyn, not a poor performer but one that is totally outside our main expertise. Thanks to you, Pelham lost out in his attempt to gain control of Lowfield but he has now expressed an interest in adding Softlyn to his software division. Bentley did a great job for me and I thought he would be a good man to negotiate a decent price.'

'Price is as much driven by a desire to acquire a business as it is by arithmetic. You'll have to give me every scrap of information: turnover, profits, products, projects, plans, staff details, et cetera in order for me or Bentley to speak with any persuasion on your behalf. I have booked a holiday for the family from the end of next week but I could be fully at your service when I return.'

Grantley opened his attaché case and withdrew a full volume of papers. 'Is this enough to start with?' he asked with a little amusement and pleased at his own foresight. Hector matched his smile, flicked through the file and responded that he would need a few days to study the contents. 'I'll keep this in the safe. I know you'll want to preserve total secrecy,' he added with a reassuring smile.

For want of other business, Hector began his perusal of the file immediately after Grantley had left, but he was also conscious of having to learn as much about the vaguely known Pelham as about Softlyn. After an intense few hours of familiarisation, he closed the file, locked it in the safe and went home early, wondering how he could open discussions with Pelham, about whom he knew almost nothing.

Another day passed almost uneventfully. 'It is not only I who is closing down for holidays but the whole business community, it seems,' he reflected in late morning. 'I suppose that will give me time to absorb the new project.' The afternoon passed in similar fashion until, just as thoughts of another early departure intruded into his thoughts, the telephone rang for only the second time that day.

'Hello Hector,' Bentley's unforgettable voice greeted him. 'I've been back for a few days and thought I should announce my return, and,' he added mysteriously, 'I have some good news for you.'

Hector welcomed the interruption to his studies and brightened up at the unaccustomed radiant tone of Bentley's voice. 'I hope you enjoyed your holiday, Bentley. Welcome back. You sound as if you have made good use of the interval.'

'Very good use. I had the great good fortune of meeting Cordelia, again, whom you will remember from twenty years ago, and I'm bursting to reintroduce you to her. I'd like to invite you for a little celebration tomorrow.'

'I'd be delighted to meet her, again,' Hector responded somewhat astonished at Bentley's announcement but, nonetheless, experiencing a feeling of unease. He had known that Bentley's depression had been caused by Cordelia's disappearance but he had seldom heard this new degree of cheerfulness since well into formation of their partnership. She must have meant even more than he had realised; but what was *her* situation after twenty or more years had elapsed?

Hector spent the next morning hardly able to concentrate on his papers. The thought of a warm wind blowing through the partnership was as unexpected as it was exciting. It would mean either a new Bentley having completed his journey to recovery or the resumption of the old despair if Cordelia were to prove but a passing liner sailing by. Had Bentley become oblivious to a reality that he refused to recognise, or had they both reached a harbour that would be their mooring until the end of their days? Hector had known her in the old days, at which time none of them had any prospect of success, but he knew her to be highly intelligent and of stable temperament and thought her a worthy addition to their circle; but why she had disappeared was a mystery to him, and as the prospect of renewing their acquaintance drew near, his only fear was whether she would disappear again.

He left the office early enough to collect his wife, Hermione, the children being old enough to look after themselves, and then to drive on to the re-awakening of their carefree youth.

The door was flung wide as they approached and both Bentley and Cordelia greeted them with fulsome smiles. Cordelia looked even more stunning than Hector could recall, hardly changed but so better dressed than in those far-off times. 'You are a very lucky man, Bentley,' he said as they shook hands and, quickly turning to Cordelia, added, 'And may I extend a great welcome to a lady who, once more, has brought sunshine into all our lives. It is so lovely to see you again, Cordelia.'

Cordelia replied that she was so happy to have returned at last and to have reacquainted herself with her old friends. Hermione was less formal and merely greeted her with a relaxing smile and words full of heartfelt welcome that sufficed immediately to rekindle their old friendship.

Whilst Bentley poured the drinks, Hermione admired the obviously happy couple, judging their smiles to have no shadow of reserve, and, later, was particularly pleased to notice that they were holding hands. She needed no better evidence to convey to her that Cordelia had come to stay.

Bentley told Hector that they would spend several more days together before he would think of returning to work. 'There would be nothing to do if you were to return,' Hector responded. 'It's summer holidays for everyone, now. I had only two telephone calls yesterday, and today I had none.'

Hermione wandered off a little with Cordelia only too keen to learn what she had done since they had last met. Her polite expressions of envy at Cordelia's activities were met with the retort that the world of the glitterati had repelled rather than attracted her. She had eventually become disillusioned and had retired to a small house overlooking a lake. 'It is very scenic there but my only positive achievement has been to gather a reasonable fluency in Italian. I shouldn't have gone,' she confessed. 'I've missed a lot, a career, a family and old friends, of course. Fortunately, before I could accept an offer from my neighbour, I decided to revisit the old days, my university digs and a theatre but, best of all, Sandley, where both Bentley and I met again totally unexpectedly. I suddenly realised that I had been following the wrong track for years and had got into a complete muddle until Bentley showed me the way home.'

'But what sort of offer did your neighbour make?' Hermione asked curious at the rather formal expression.

'I was far too much distracted at the time and didn't pay too much attention. Afterwards, I thought it might have been a proposal of marriage. It sounds absolutely extraordinary but my mind was living in another world at the time and I can hardly recall whether I accepted or declined. I was dreaming of coming back and couldn't think straight. But, against all odds, and with an amazing stroke of luck, I've got Bentley now – and perhaps a conscience about letting Frank down. I'll sell the house or rent it to holiday makers, but I'm finished with Italy. The wanderer returns and Handbury will be enough for me, now.'

When Hermione mentioned that they were about to leave for their holiday in Bologna, Cordelia told them that her house overlooked Lago di Suviana not far from there, and offered her key should they wish to stay. 'It's in a little village and you might find my neighbour, Frank, good company, Hector. He lives alone, mostly, but somehow manages a big industrial group.'

'Frank?' Hector queried. 'Not Frank Pelham?'

'Yes. That's him. Have you heard of him?

'I certainly have. I wouldn't mind meeting him.'

'Make the most of the holiday, then. This is the address of my little house, *Vista Lago,*' she told him as she offered her visiting card. 'Frank's house is the big one next to mine.'

Hector felt a degree of uncertainty at the news. He had not been instructed by Grantley on the price he wanted for Softlyn, nor had Fenton given any indication of what the relevance of the company was either to Pelham or to the government. Fenton was a civil servant and not an industrialist, but the contractual relationship of the company to the government had been hinted at as something of importance to the defence of the realm and he was reminded of his undertaking to keep him informed of events. Perhaps he should seek guidance from him even if no contact with Pelham had yet taken place or been proposed, but the opportunity to meet Pelham was one that could not be ignored.

That was business, however, and the evening was one to be spent in welcome and congratulations all round. Bentley was more relaxed than Hector could remember while Cordelia was as happy and pleasant as a woman could be who had finally found that destiny had prepared a sanctuary of calm in place of a whirlwind of conflicting emotions.

On their way home that evening, Hermione revealed that Cordelia had received an offer. 'What of?' Hector replied, 'I hope it was marriage. It's about time Bentley had an anchor in his life.'

'It was marriage, but not from Bentley. Guess whom it was from.'

Hector's assumption that Bentley and Cordelia had now become a permanent fixture dissolved in a flash. 'If not from Bentley, from whom could it be?' he wondered. 'I've no idea,' he replied with a feeling of trepidation.

'She said it was from Frank Pelham.'

'What! He's a billionaire industrialist!' he exclaimed, his immediate reaction being that that would certainly outclass Bentley.

'Bentley must have something more than millions,' Hermione smiled back. 'It's over twenty years since she left and she must have met numerous prospects in the sort of career she has followed, but it's Bentley whom she prefers, it seems. She told me that she had been bounced around from one uncertainty to another but, now, she has regained the happiness she had been seeking for years, so I think it's probably permanent.'

'If only she had not thrown it away twenty years ago,' Hector commented drily but, as he turned into their drive, he could not help thinking that it might be just one last fling for her before she gained access to a share of unlimited wealth. Bentley was well situated financially but he was not a billionaire. If she left him again, Bentley would be cast from the heights of this joyful reunion into yet another pit of despair even deeper than before. 'What would be the consequence of that?' Hector could not help wondering. After a splendid evening with the newly reunited couple, a doubt had intervened to leave him with a troubled mind.

Chapter 19

Hector and family arrived in Bologna after an uneventful flight, retrieved their baggage and took a taxi to the hotel. After a brief moment spent settling into their rooms, their first outing was a stroll through the old city spent in the warmth of the late afternoon sun, but the colonnaded porticos provided a delightful protection against the heat and would have served as storm protection in another season. Upon seeing the towers, fourteen-year-old Tim exclaimed, 'I thought it was Pisa that had the leaning tower.' Hector was also surprised but could only comment that Italians must have been more interested in building ever higher than their rivals and had given too little consideration to the foundations.

At dinner that evening, he suggested they could not miss a visit to Villa Marconi now that they were so near. Next morning, thirteen-year-old Juliet accordingly approached the desk with a brave 'Buongiorno', but then stood back for her father to continue. He managed quite well in his native language but all the while feeling totally inadequate and humbled as the receptionist responded in impeccable English. They would have to visit with a group next day and probably take the bus to the destination, she informed him. But, turning to the family, he told them that that would add interest to the day as, indeed it did, although the children had mixed feelings that the villa was nowhere near a beach.

Hector was thereby reminded that Cordelia had mentioned a lake and suggested they hire a car in order to visit the area on the following day. Tim was entrusted with navigation aided by Juliet's criticism of his inadequacy. To great excitement, they reached the destination but not quite sure of the whereabouts of *Vista Lago*. A man whom they passed in the village appeared ignorant of its location, whereupon Hector ventured the name of 'Frank Pelham'. 'Ah, si, si. Franco,' he answered and pointed out the direction to the location not very far away. They expressed their thanks as best they could with frequent repetitions of 'Grazie' and drove on for barely a mile where two small houses appeared with a mansion nearby and beautiful views over the lake opening up behind them. 'That's it,' called Juliet. '*Vista Lago*. We've found it.'

They pulled up outside and admired the cottage and gardens from the road. It was inevitably unoccupied, but Hector had the key and permission. They entered a remarkably cool house that offered comfort and quiet with views over the lake. 'So this is where she had ended up,' thought Hector. 'A very nice location to retire to.'

They went into the garden behind and admired the display, compact though it was, and inevitably casting their eyes around with particular attention to the well-presented mansion a short distance away. 'Look at that house,' Hermione said. 'It must be owned by a film star.'

'Or a millionaire,' Tim added.

'Both, probably,' Juliet said not to be outdone.

But the unexpected presence of an entire family had inevitably been observed by the occupant, whose attention had been attracted by distant voices carried faintly through his study window. Frank stood up, wondering who these people were and what they were doing. He had heard nothing from Cordelia since she had left five weeks before and was inevitably curious why a complete family seemed to have taken possession of the cottage. He would have been informed if it were for sale but he had heard nothing, despite being well connected with all the local businesses. His curiosity transformed him from a businessman to a mere member of society that brought him out of the house and into the garden to stare at the people wandering about as if they were assessing a purchase. The father turned towards him and from a distance of a hundred metres gave an uncertain wave of greeting as if he had taken possession and wanted to meet his new neighbour.

Despite having been compelled to pause the perusal of his latest strategy papers, Frank was not averse to an opportunity of ascertaining the reason for this sudden and unexpected appearance of a complete family roaming about the garden next door and from whom he heard a few comments in English. They must be friends of Cordelia, he assumed, and, in order to satisfy his curiosity, walked towards the man, which encouraged Hector also to approach and to introduce himself and his family, explaining that they had met the cottage owner at a party. She had encouraged a short visit whilst they were on holiday in Bologna, to which Frank replied that he expected her to return soon, but Hector responded that he thought her return would be a little delayed because she was meeting old friends and was likely to stay awhile.

In meeting the visitors, Frank had been presented with an unheralded opportunity to update himself on Cordelia's activities and invited the family into his house. He noted their approving glances at the furnishings and ambiance of the interior. 'It's a bit big for me,' he explained with an apologetic attempt at modesty, whilst pouring a few welcome drinks and tomato juices for the children. 'But I have the family from time to time and a few business colleagues or neighbours, and I spend a lot of my day on the telephone just checking up on progress. That keeps me busy enough.'

Despite Hector being vaguely aware of the business, he could not help seeking more information explaining that he was a partner in a business consultancy. Frank gave the name of Coral Ital, at which Hector expressed mild interest. His consultancy dealt mostly in UK business, he replied, and prompted by Frank, gave the name of Railton Barratt Consultants. 'Railton!' Frank exclaimed. 'You acted for Overdale Engineering recently.'

'Yes. That was handled by my partner, though. How did you know about that?' Hector replied, hoping that Frank would be drawn into discussion.

'Whoever your partner is, he did a good job in completing the deal. One of my companies was on the losing side.'

'Bentley likes the intensity of negotiations but it's summer now and there's never any pressure at this time of year. He has just returned from his much-deserved holiday which seems to have done him a lot of good. He has even decided to get married, at last.'

'That's good. I'm getting married soon, as well.'

'Congratulations!' Hector responded, whilst managing to suppress the revelation that Cordelia was now promised to another. They were on holiday and this was not the moment for unauthorised counselling. 'Everybody is settling down,' he added.

'Yes. I've put it off for too long,' Frank concluded, wondering whether Hector's credentials could be of interest to him. He was worth cultivating and Frank could afford a slight deviation from his timetable, but he had noticed his audience showing polite disquiet at business talk and resumed a more acceptable topic. 'But you are on holiday. Let me introduce you to the delights of Buenterra,' he ventured in an attempt to extend his contact with Hector. 'You will find the lake offers boat trips and boat hire, or safe bathing places, if that's what you are looking for.'

He noted the looks of appreciation on the faces of his audience and, in a further effort to sustain their interest, asked whether, if they cared to stay a little longer, they would like to accept an invitation to the local restaurant that evening.

'You will be doing me a favour. I live alone and have nothing scheduled. It would be a pleasure to entertain an English family.'

Hector looked enquiringly at Hermione, who, with a glance at the children, overcame her initial instinct against placing a burden upon a complete stranger which she felt she should politely decline. 'If it is no inconvenience,' she replied and, to smiles all round, added, 'we would be honoured to accept your offer.'

'No inconvenience, at all,' Franco assured them. 'It will be a treat for me and you will be my guests. I assume you will be staying at the cottage. I shall take you all in my car and also bring you back. Now, I suggest you go down to the boatyard. You will find it of great interest. We shall meet again at seven.'

Hector and family left with a feeling that they would be experiencing an unexpected delight in having so quickly established relations with an influential resident. They found their way easily to the boatyard, walked around to view the scene and, having noticed a small group boarding a boat, joined them on a sight-seeing trip around the lake.

They had no understanding of the commentary presented by a woman who, presumably, was the boatman's wife, but when the group turned their heads towards the sight that was the current topic, they turned theirs. They showed particular interest when she mentioned the name Franco Pelham whilst pointing out the house they had just left and caught the general sense of her words, among which they understood industry, philanthropy and art. 'That's the house we were at,' Tim remarked excitedly to the awareness of the group to English people aboard.

As the boat continued round the lake, other prosperous looking, large houses appeared between small hamlets, which, they concluded, clearly offered an area favoured by millionaires. Hector had a recurrence of doubt that Cordelia would wish to leave this beautiful area, but his next thought that Bentley might wish to retire to this place with Cordelia horrified him. The partnership would not be the same.

The children delighted in sighting a beach that would have attractions not offered by cities, however historic they may be. Juliet voted for the next day to be spent messing about on the water and Tim agreed, but with a suggestion to follow the footpath around the water's edge the following day. Their parents were happy at that. Hermione could spend the day in a deckchair and Hector might be able to continue his conversation with Frank.

They left the boat at the landing stage where they had boarded and wandered about once more. The group they had encountered on the boat dispersed and a stillness pervaded the late afternoon to remind them of the invitation they had received from the neighbour. Hermione was a little embarrassed that they had no fresh clothes to change into but Hector persuaded them that the evening would surely be very informal.

Frank dutifully appeared in his big car a few minutes before the appointed time. He was all smiles, befitting a man who had been presented not only with the opportunity to entertain and to be entertained by a family but also with the possibility of establishing a relationship with a useful business consultant. Hector reminded Hermione that, in order not to provoke an awkward situation, she should not mention Cordelia's relationship with Bentley. 'Of course I'm not going to do that,' she protested. 'I'm sure Cordelia will be able to sort out her own affairs.' Hector thought that the word was unfortunate. It suggested a temporary escapade that would eventually lead to Bentley having to face another calamity and lose all faith in a bounteous world.

They clambered into the car and drove to the local restaurant where Franco had booked a table and was greeted by the owner himself, who gushed his warmest welcome at the lady and children, but was especially welcoming to Franco, who was an infrequent visitor but well known as a particularly generous one.

Menus were flourished and wine lists produced. Frank settled back in the role of counsellor to those uninitiated in the Italian language. He evidently enjoyed an occasion to demonstrate his skills at interpreting and imparting advice. This was his usual function but, in this place remote from the boardrooms that he had almost left behind, one that he had not had to exercise as often as he would have liked. He curbed his enthusiasm upon noting the expectant but blank faces of his audience and assumed a more direct activity of recommending a suitable dish to all with particular attention to the children, who brightened up at the prospect of tasting Italian cuisine. Wine was produced with fruit juice for the children, menus were whisked politely away and conversation was undertaken to the accompaniment of some preliminary nibbles.

'We have little opportunity to dine at a genuine Italian restaurant,' Hermione began with an appreciative smile. 'It's a lovely ambiance and so nice of you to invite us.'

'It is a great pleasure for me,' Frank replied. 'I much prefer dining in company, but I seldom have guests whom I can entertain.'

'You spoke of family, though,' Hector intervened. 'You should invite them more often.'

'My sister's family, with a nephew and niece. But they visit only two or three times a year. Otherwise, I have only my business colleagues to invite, and that tends to be somewhat more formal.'

'But you said you were getting married, soon,' Hermione continued. 'You have obviously come to a much-considered decision.'

'Yes. I have known Rosa for most of my life. She has

certainly passed the test of loyalty and has demonstrated a considerable amount of patience that I do not deserve. I have buried myself in business for years and only recently have I emerged into the outside world.'

Hector exchanged glances with Hermione at the mention of Rosa. They had each assumed that it was Cordelia whom he had had in mind but they remained silent on that topic.

'Well! It's about time you tied the knot,' Hector remarked.

'And we wish you every happiness for the future,' Hermione added.

But both Tim and Juliet had repressed their enthusiasm enough. 'We are going to the beach tomorrow. We saw it from the boat,' Tim told Frank, and Juliet added, 'And we shall walk around the lake.'

'I've never done that,' he responded. 'But I have friends along the route who tell me that it is a very pleasant walk. And there is a bird sanctuary about halfway.'

Tim turned to a waiter and, smiling smugly to the others, said, 'Un altro succo di frutta per favor.' The family blinked in astonishment.

'I didn't know you could speak Italian,' his mother said.

Tim shrugged his shoulders. 'Just something I picked up,' he replied modestly with a sly smile at Juliet, who felt that she should have known just as much and wondered whether she could pick up a few words, too.

'Bravo,' Frank said. 'We'll have you fluent in a few days.' Turning to Hector, he said with a smile, 'Children can learn anything when there is no compulsion.' He seized the opportunity to add, 'If you have an hour or two to spare, we could pass the time in exchanging our reminiscences. It would be a pity to omit the chance of a friendly discussion.'

Hector felt unable to decline the offer since Frank had shown great generosity in entertaining a family of casual visitors to the cottage, and therefore replied that he would not like to miss the opportunity of conducting a relaxed talk about their careers. Frank felt that his strategy to gather information about the former Lowfield in this completely unexpected but fortunate encounter was promising to deliver a useful development.

They continued to enjoy the evening until Hermione cautiously suggested that the children had had a tiring day and that they should retire soon. 'Of course,' Franco conceded. 'It would be wrong of me to insist on prolonging this most enjoyable occasion at the expense of overtiring the children.'

He signalled for the bill, which was soon presented and paid without scrutiny. They left with fond memories of a perfect evening and were driven back to the cottage. The only note of dissent came from Hermione, who told Hector when they were safely inside that she thought losing him to a business talk was surely an unnecessary sacrifice when they were supposed to be on holiday. He simply responded that they could not be so ill mannered as not to reward Frank with a little company. 'He's been very generous, and it would be best if we did not delay too long in returning the compliment. He lives all alone and I would not like to forgo the opportunity to speak to a leading industrialist, anyway. We'll take the children to the beach and, after an hour or two, I'll come back and go over to the house.'

Tim volunteered to sleep on the sofa partly as an adventure but also because he would be captain in charge of the ship whilst his passengers were asleep in their bunks. But hardly before he had considered his course for the following day, the night closed upon him until well after dawn.

Daylight wandered uninvited into the room but was, nonetheless, welcome. It promised action, activity and adventure. 'Let's go to the beach, today,' he suggested, to Juliet's support and Hector's ready acceptance.

'I'll take you all to the beach but I have arranged to spend some time with Frank. He seems in need of occupation and, after last night's entertainment, I can hardly leave him to the enjoyment of his own company.'

'That's all right, Dad,' Tim replied, happy to take charge by giving a decisive opinion. 'We'll be able to manage on our own.'

Hector transmitted a smile to Hermione that yielded submission to Tim's approaching sense of command, as well as to the thought that his son may, after all, be benefitting from his rather expensive education.

They loaded all they were likely to need into the car and set off to the beach where Hector felt obliged to remain for an hour before Tim reminded him that he owed a duty visit to Frank. 'Oh, yes,' Hector replied. 'I almost forgot.' But he was only too anxious to conclude his family duty and to exchange the ball games he thought his children wanted for the more mature delights that Frank could offer. With a brief apology to Hermione he drove slowly away. She adjusted her sunglasses whilst Tim and Juliet were thankful, at last, to share their ball with the other children on the beach.

Chapter 20

Hector drove to the big house to be greeted by the watchful Frank, to whom he confessed with a smile of relief that his paternal duties were now reluctantly in abeyance for the day. Frank responded with equal pretence that he must have been happy to enjoy an hour within the bosom of his family. 'But, now, I shall teach you how to make a cup of Italian coffee, and perhaps we can exchange a few topics more amenable to our adult tastes.

'Very few tourists come this way,' he continued as they sat in his rather large sitting room. 'Most are mainly interested in historic buildings and museums or spend their time at the coast. But your presence is very welcome and a pleasant distraction for me. Otherwise, I would have to invite some of the other residents whom I know around the shore. Or they might take pity on me and invite me to one of their frequent parties.'

'The view from here is very beautiful,' Hector responded, 'but I suppose it lacks the sort of satisfaction that one can obtain in human relationships. I wonder that you did not consider marriage a little earlier in life. None of us can resist Time's remorseless onslaught and we may as well spend our lives productively whilst we are able.'

'I chose to fight time by contending with business and its problems. It is only recently that I have come to the realisation that the success and rewards that it brings is not as satisfying as I had once thought, and they can't buy back the time that I spent in their pursuit. I envy you in having contended with business but also to have blended a family with it, and even have children to be proud of, whereas my reward is a rather barren prosperity.'

'That's similar to my partner's history. He made a success of business but his motivation was to blot out the feeling of loss when his great love disappeared. It's taken him decades to overcome it.'

'Even more of a coincidence. My fiancé died many years ago in a climbing accident,' he confided. 'I've always blamed myself for not being able to pull her back. Now, I blame myself for being too obsessed with the tragedy and visiting the consequences on others. I must have been a huge burden to them but everybody rallied round and I'm conscious of never having rewarded them adequately. I even emigrated here in order to get away from it all, but I can't escape the memories that stay to plague me. My sister brings her family thinking they would provide some sort of compensation but I've only just realised that I have to make some effort myself.'

'It sounds as if all will end happily both for you and for Bentley. I suspect that your sister will feel as much relief at your marriage as I shall when Bentley marries his long-lost Cordelia.'

'Cordelia!' Frank exclaimed. 'Do you mean the Cordelia who owns the cottage?'

'Yes. We met her at a party when Bentley returned from holiday. We told her we were booked for Bologna and she offered her cottage should we wish to use it.'

'She hasn't contacted me since the day she arrived in London over a month ago. Not that she had to, but I thought she would have told me the news herself. We have been close neighbours for nearly a year, after all.'

'I don't know whether she will return, but Bentley has a nice house already where I suspect they will remain and I suppose she will have to sell or let the cottage.'

'That puts a new perspective on matters. I even thought that Cordelia might want to consider me as her partner until Rosa told me, in no uncertain terms, not to risk a relationship with an almost complete stranger. I realised that she, at least, was speaking the sense that I was ignoring, even if there was an element of self-interest in her advice. I don't know how to contact Cordelia to congratulate her on her good fortune. She was a rather puzzling, mysterious personality and now, thanks to you, I know why. I'm happy that she has finally found her place in the world. Please give her my good wishes and,' he said reaching for a card, 'this invitation to our wedding.'

'Certainly. I think that will lift the last veil of doubt at her decision and complete her restoration to a full life with Bentley.'

'I wonder whether you could also negotiate a little agreement with him on my behalf,' Frank continued a little uncertainly. 'I may be getting married but I haven't entirely lost my interest in business.'

'What agreement would you wish to suggest to him?' Hector asked, half suspecting the topic.

'He has demonstrated the sort of negotiation skills that I suspect will be necessary to achieve the result I want,' Frank responded. 'Have you heard of a company called Softlyn?' he asked, immediately confirming Hector's assumption.

'Yes. It's a small business in the Lowfield Engineering group that has now, thanks to Bentley, been absorbed by Overdale which we, or rather Bentley, represented recently. It's a software business, but what interest can you have in that? I don't know much about your group, but it's all engineering as far as I know.'

'It is. But Softlyn has a very interesting product line that could have wider implications in security.'

'Security! That might raise problems if it has anything to do with defence. It would be subject to the national interest and invite government regulation. And then there might be a possible vulnerability to cyber theft.'

'It has very little to do with defence. Those parts could be cut out and reassigned elsewhere. I am interested in its electronic safety capabilities, that is to say, electronic security systems.'

Hector's immediate assumption was of intruder alarms, which seemed a very ordinary product line that would tempt Frank to any interest. 'What sort of security?' he asked. 'Nothing subversive, I hope. We couldn't under any circumstances represent you in anything remotely criminal.'

'Don't worry. I have the most innocent of motives. It is protection from unwarranted intrusions that I have in mind. Softlyn not only has the technology to commit whatever breaches of security it cares to, but also the capability of restoring the breach to normality. Thefts from locked rooms or safes or any other electronically controlled space: unlock, extract and relock. No trace of entry, no trace of exit, but the goods mysteriously removed; or possibly replaced with a substitute, and nobody the wiser.'

'How do you know that?' Hector asked, somewhat puzzled at having no recollection of such a product in the papers he had been given.

'I'm sure that you are often privy to undisclosed secrets in your business. I have a wide range of interests and discover sometimes by accident, sometimes by intermediaries, propositions from which I might prosper as well as others from which I might suffer. It is from the latter that I wish to protect myself and my businesses.'

'So how many safes do you want to protect?' Hector asked.

'None. At least, none of the sort that store the valuables and papers that you may link with office security.'

'What then?'

'Art galleries.'

'Art galleries!' Hector exclaimed.

'Yes. Art galleries. You must have heard about the recent theft of a valuable Old Master in the Pelham Gallery in Skelton.'

'Only the vaguest of vaguely. Pelham Gallery! Is that your gallery? I don't have much interest in old paintings even if they are Old Masters, and I hadn't connected you to galleries, either.'

'I confess that I, also, have very little interest in them. I prefer the present and not the past, but it was my grandfather who founded the gallery and I am nominally the major trustee. My sister serves as my representative on the board.

'Nearly a year ago, one of my contacts informed me that Lowfield Engineering may be threatened by an unwelcome merger approach. I thought the opportunity worth following up and I accordingly arranged a meeting with the then managing director, who seemed amenable to an alternative proposition. My interest lay in acquiring the group but I follow many companies that might prove of value. Softlyn also belonged to the group, and would have been of little interest to me if it had not been founded by a man I once knew who could possibly have proved antagonistic towards me.

'I base that opinion on knowing that Softlyn had conducted a remarkably effective vulnerability test of security at a museum with which I have a family connection. I attempted to contact the MD, again, but, by then, as a result of your partner's negotiating skills, he had taken gardening leave and control had been transferred to the rival group.'

'But if you want to purchase Softlyn and close it down or at least control the product release,' Hector responded, 'the technology will still exist to be marketed clandestinely to anybody who cares to pay.'

'I was primarily concerned with contacting my former acquaintance in Softlyn, but shortly before I had first spoken to the MD, I was contacted by, let us say, a man of determined disposition. He attracted my interest because he mentioned the use of Softlyn technology in national security. I was not particularly concerned about national security but the mention of Softlyn was enough for me to agree to his request for him to visit me.

'I was concerned that he had discovered my confidential telephone number, and I therefore asked my representative in London to make a routine check. He traced the call to a resident of a small hotel in London who had arrived late one night but left after making the call the following morning. He made enquiries but the guest book revealed a quite innocuous name for that room, probably false anyway, and the caller could not be traced. The call was not recorded and no suspicious circumstances could be attached to a guest who was no different from thousands of other hotel residents who book a single night in a major city. Little could be obtained from the receptionist who had had no reason to suppose anything being untoward. He could give only a very general description from among several leavers that morning: adult male, average appearance. The only unusual feature was that he settled the bill in cash.'

'Which leaves no trace,' Hector commented. 'Did the caller have any identifying characteristics? Accent, technical fluency, colloquial or slang expressions, for example.'

'He was well spoken, well educated, confident with no hesitations. Somebody used to a senior position, and I know that he was English because he verified his credentials when he visited a week later, but I agreed not to reveal his identity when he gave a convincing reason for him to conduct a security test on the gallery.'

Hector thought that there would be thousands of English people whose speech could be described in the terms that Frank had used; but he just happened to know one such who also had an interest in Softlyn. 'May I venture the name of Fenton Barr?' he asked.

Frank was a little taken aback by Hector's knowledgeable response. 'I am obligated not to reveal the name but that is one that I shall not deny,' he replied after a moment of hesitation.

Hector nodded his appreciation of the diplomatic confirmation. 'We know him from our occasional dealings with government agencies,' he responded and drew the conversation back to the current topic. 'You can be sure that Bentley had no insider knowledge of Softlyn's product range. He had no reason to select that company out of all the others and based his arguments mainly on the management skills of the group. They were fairly evenly matched, I believe, but it would have been pure logic and persuasion that clinched the deal.'

'Your Bentley should have worked for me. He has not only won the argument but has also won the girl. Obviously a formidable opponent,' Frank concluded with a smile.

Hector was cautious about revealing to Frank that he had plentiful information on Softlyn locked in his safe but, since that was mechanically rather than electronically secured, he hoped that it would remain undisturbed until his return. He was also conscious of Fenton's recent declaration of interest and therefore hesitated to offer his services despite the attraction of a possibly lucrative contract about to be offered to him. He adopted a response that would offer a pause for consideration.

'You said you wanted to negotiate a little agreement with Bentley. He is back from holiday now and therefore available. I could ask him for his opinion when I return, but he is bound to want another challenge, or we could also work together on the project.'

'That would be helpful. Everybody at the gallery is very nervous of another occurrence. They are completely mystified at how or why an Old Master was stolen. No ransom note was received and contrary to all expectations, the painting was returned undamaged three months later. Nobody, except me and, now, you, has any idea who was responsible, but the fact remains that the gallery and all the others now exist with the threat of another theft being undertaken. They have night patrols now but the danger is ever present. The sooner I, or rather we, can negotiate a satisfactory conclusion, the safer I shall feel. If it had not been for your partner, I would have control of Softlyn by now and have been able to search out and repurpose the equipment they used.

'It's possible that other galleries have been approached and kept it quiet, perhaps even paying a ransom. But I think that very unlikely. My assumption is that the art theft is merely an indicator that no business, including mine, would be immune from a similar attack. I shan't feel safe until your negotiating skills persuade the perpetrator to sell the product to me, or, even better, to place it into safe custody.'

Over a relaxing glass of vino they attempted to spot Hector's family cavorting about at the bathing place but that was too far away to distinguish individuals. Hector wondered whether he and Bentley could handle the project just posed by Frank. All they had to do was to make an offer that would satisfy the perpetrator; but what was his motive? Frank had pleaded a sensitive matter that may have contributed to the antagonism to which Frank had referred, but was there substance to a threat that Frank considered might endanger the gallery – or his business? But this was Italy. He probably had procedures to contend with threatening approaches, but mud would surely stick if ever it were breathed abroad. Hector was wallowing in uncertainty but recollected that he had had only Frank's version. Could there be another?

'I'll have to discuss the matter with my partner, Frank. His experience in the Overdale negotiations might prove of assistance before we formally arrange a contract.'

Frank agreed that he should do so. He had at least had an opportunity to discuss the matter with a knowledgeable contact. It might lead to nothing, but there was no other person to whom he could broach the matter. Whatever Railton could contribute to his peace of mind would be advantageous, but he regretted having had to give any rendition of his encounter with The Department. He had woven a fairly persuasive tale about his meeting with Fenton, who had actually visited him specifically to discuss a field test of the Softlyn product, but that had given him cause to believe that Bamber still retained adverse feelings against him.

Contrary to his normal directness, he was at a loss how best to approach him. The talk with Hector had given him an opportunity to explore the topic with a potential ally but he wanted results and not procrastination. His indecision suddenly cleared. He would undertake discussions with Overdale about an offer for Softlyn. That would force a meeting with Bamber that might possibly clear both their minds.

Hector drove to the beach again to find his family well ensconced with the locals and exchanging broken Italian for broken English. He was suddenly transformed from a man of business discussing top level, delicate issues into a man floundering in a sea of ignorance and subject to the mockery of his own children.

Hermione greeted him with a mood halfway between relief and admonishment. 'I hope you had a nice time up there,' she said. 'I've been struggling to keep up with events. Ball games, ice cream purchases and attempts to communicate, more by sign language than speech, but it seems that the children have been speaking Italian almost since they were born. They're certainly doing a lot better than I am.'

Hector attempted to join the party but he could not decide whether it was beneficial for English to be the international language for the whole world. It seemed that everybody insisted to his embarrassment on exercising their very limited vocabulary on him, which drove him willingly to become the ice cream purchaser of choice and thereby to seek at least a modicum of importance rather than a man of ignorant pretensions; but he was also driven to the opinion that languages should be taught more often in schools.

What a relief it was to arrive, once more, at the cottage and to relax in the freedom of a language he understood! Hermione insisted on a little siesta for the children and suggested they visit the same restaurant to which they had been invited the previous evening. Hector used the time to email Bentley in order to give him a summary of the project that Frank had in mind. 'If you are back in the office,' he told him, 'look in the safe and study the Softlyn details. Keep them well locked up. Security is a pre-requisite,' he added pointedly.

It was not until the following day that Bentley replied. 'I'm still taking things easy. We have days out and spend the evenings with the neighbours and visiting a local art club. I have responsibilities now, but I'll get back to the grindstone soon.'

Hector sighed, partly in disappointment that the project was not being progressed, but also happily in recognition that Bentley was now pursuing the path he should have taken years before.

Chapter 21

Bentley and Cordelia greeted Hector and family upon their return from holiday, the children still in excellent mood although both Hector and Hermione looked rather weary. 'We're worn out, Bentley. We didn't know how tiring a holiday could be, and, frankly, we're glad to be back.'

'We are going to learn Italian, when we get back to school,' Juliet announced, gleefully.

'We've learned nearly everything about it, already,' Tim added confidently. 'I suppose we'll have to take exams, though, but it's dead easy, so we won't have any problems.'

'Your Franco said that children had no difficulty with languages when they were not compulsory,' Hector explained to Cordelia, 'but I have to admit that English made our lives easier. They all wanted to speak Italian but dropped into English when we were floundering.'

'And he's not your Franco, Cordelia,' Hermione told her, correcting Hector's careless speech. 'He has a fiancée now. Rosa. He said that he has known her for years.'

Cordelia had been momentarily startled by Hector's announcement but quickly recovered as the latest news was imparted. 'Rosa! Yes. She's been a long-time friend of his and now she can shake off any fear that I might just jump into her, no doubt, long desired rightful place. I have no idea why they hadn't married years ago, but she visited quite often; and I'm very glad to hear the news.' Not only was she very glad, but also highly relieved that her confusion had finally been resolved as the last vestige of her burden fell away, thereby enabling her truly to relax at last.

When they next met in order to share their holiday memories, it seemed as if their circle was complete. No closer attachment needed to be formed by Hector and Bentley, who had known each other for nearly thirty years, but their friendship had now been enhanced by the presence of the two ladies who were linked again in matters quite apart from the business talk that interested their partners. Old times were always a matter of interest, recent times a matter of discussion, and the times between a topic respectively of admiration and dismissal. But whatever their subject, it was always an aid to bonding. Hermione had her friends but Cordelia had always been special and their former closeness had been quickly re-established.

'You know, Hermione, I'm really glad to wash Franco right out of my hair. He will be better off with Rosa anyway. I half suspected that they were more than good friends and maybe they would have continued to be so, no matter what, but that wouldn't have been the sort of marriage that would have suited me. She would have become completely hostile to me, we would have been perpetually at daggers drawn, and I don't suppose Franco would have done much to intervene.

'The last few weeks with Bentley have been more than satisfying, in all sorts of ways,' she smiled meaningfully to Hermione's immediate comprehension. 'My truant past just wiped away, and every day a joy. It's a miracle that Bentley could have stayed single for all that time.'

'You did, too, but that was because neither of you could find a better match. He has bottled up all his frustration and disappointment in an almost monastic existence and applied all his attention to the business. I suspect you will have the longest honeymoon in history, but I hope you'll leave him enough energy to take on other projects.'

'Don't worry. I'll make sure he performs to the best of his ability,' Cordelia assured her.

Hector was meanwhile talking business already. 'Frank gave me an astonishing piece of news about Softlyn, Bentley. He told me that it belonged to the group that you ensured was merged into Overdale. It has a world-beating product in security and, now, he wants to buy it.'

'I've read the papers you left in the safe,' Bentley replied. 'It's a moderately sized business but would need a lot more capital if it is to market a product to take on the big companies. But I have no appetite for anything to do with aiding Franco, a man who almost snatched Cordelia away for ever.'

'You triumphed over him in one regard. You've won the girl, now you can take the spoils.'

'The girl is enough. If I were to act for him, Cordelia would never believe that she could be free of his influence. No. I'll wait for another project to turn up.'

That was a refusal decisive enough for Hector. He had not committed himself to any course of action and would not pressurise Bentley, a long-time friend and partner. Nor would he jeopardise their relationship or the very welcome reappearance of Cordelia, but would tell Fenton what had transpired and forgo any possibility of acting for Frank.

Two days later, whilst the menfolk joined Fenton to indulge themselves on the golf course, Cordelia accepted a suggestion from Hermione to visit a matinee performance of the latest musical. Neither wanted to spend the day alone, and the opportunity to exchange anecdotes of the past need no longer be postponed.

Their first task was to secure their seats for the afternoon but then to indulge themselves in window shopping with elevenses in between. Cordelia conceded diplomatically that the fashions were quite acceptable but more for the mass market than she had been used to. They enjoyed a small lunch well before admission time, at which Cordelia claimed that she was an expert on theatres now. 'I visited the show at the Taggard along the street while I was trying to sort myself out by visiting my old haunts as a student. I needed a change from the routine that was giving me too much time to think. But how I thank my lucky stars that Bentley's path crossed mine at Sandley! It's curtain up on a new act, now.'

Hermione congratulated her on taking the right turn away from the path that wandered aimlessly through the landscape of rivalry and squander so ably illustrated by Cordelia's tales of the wealthy lives she had observed and her disgust at the profligate lifestyle of the super-rich.

She sensed a slight dismissal in Cordelia's response to her question about Franco. 'He lived a very quiet existence despite the riches that he obviously earned; the biggest house in the neighbourhood, friendly disposition, only a few visitors but an enormous reticence about his past. He always said that he was married to his job but I think there must have been a big crisis in his early life.'

'A business failure, a death in the family, a thwarted love?' Hermione suggested.

'I doubt whether it was a business failure. He seemed to have a magic touch so far as that was concerned. Nobody spoke of the past, though, but I suppose we are all creatures of our early days. Look at me. I have spent my time trying to escape the consequences of poor decisions. I've spent decades on the wrong path and only just found the way out of despondency. I should have stayed with Bentley and had a family, just like you. But, at least, I've got my sanity back.'

'Families have their difficulties,' Hermione replied, 'but I'm glad that, now, all we need do is wonder about their future.'

She noticed a slight smile from Cordelia that seemed to portend disclosure of a little secret. 'I have made a huge decision that should secure an absolutely firm future for both of us,' Cordelia told her. 'Bentley said we would get married when we had returned to civilisation. I did not need much persuading and, last week, we agreed a date. You are invited of course and we shall spend a honeymoon at my cottage.'

Hermione was delighted. That would ensure stability, at last, safety from any rivals and was news that Hector would welcome.

After the sun soaked and densely populated beaches of the Adriatic, Hector welcomed the well-tended greens of the course whilst Bentley greeted the opportunity to update himself on whatever small news his partner had encountered, unsurprised to learn that it amounted to very little apart from Pelham's interest in Softlyn.

Fenton chose the almost deserted spot well away from the fairway where he had spoken to Hector before. He turned towards them to congratulate Bentley on his finding the beautiful partner whom he had brought home from his holidays. 'And I don't mean Hector,' he added with a smile. He received the answer that one did not always have to go abroad to find beauty; he had been able to relive his early memories and to be rewarded with an unexpected prize.

'And how did you like *your* holiday?' Fenton continued, turning towards Hector to which he received the reply that he had enjoyed almost everything except the fatigue of being a tourist.

'The office has its compensations,' Hector continued, suggesting to his listeners that his experience had been less than refreshing. 'No more distractions until we are compelled to repeat our frolics in a future year. Relaxing at home every evening with intellects poised for challenges ahead, if there are any, will make a welcome change,' he added with a smile.

'That brings me nicely to the point we discussed before you left. Did you manage to meet Frank Pelham?'

'Yes. He was amazingly hospitable. Treated the family to an evening at the local restaurant and I felt compelled to spend half a day with him talking business. He did mention Softlyn, but Bentley has personal reasons for declining to act and I'm fully in support of him.'

Bentley gave the explanation that they could not assist him in the matter, because his fiancée had no wish to be continually reminded of her neighbour, whom she regarded as a controller of souls. 'Sorry, Fenton. She has had enough uncertainty in her life and, now that she has found a haven with me, all thought of her Svengali must be driven from her mind. And I don't want any intrusion from him, either,' he added. 'He would just be a continual disturbance and unsettle both of us.'

'That sounds conclusive,' Fenton replied, with a note of despair. He had had great hopes of recruiting Railton Barratt but they had been dashed as quickly as they had arisen. 'But it's a huge disappointment for me,' he continued, hoping to gather a few persuasive words that would implant some thought of reconsideration. 'Softlyn has valuable links to defence and we like to keep in touch with developments. I'll just have to accept your decision, I suppose. Unfortunately, it means that we are back to the risk that the technology may fall into the wrong hands, and that will pose huge problems for the realm. Grantley is examining the portfolio of companies in the newly acquired Lowfield group and will obviously seek a purchaser for Softlyn, since its business is not that of engineering.'

Hector glanced at Bentley and received his nod of agreement to his unspoken request. 'They have already consulted us on that matter,' he revealed. 'We could assist them, as long as it does not involve Pelham.'

'Now you tell me!' Fenton exclaimed. 'Your reputation

for confidentiality is well deserved! At least, it confirms our assumption that Grantley wants to sell the company.'

'We have full details of the business and have reached a wide range of preliminary valuations, but there is no mention in the papers he gave us of any product that causes you so much concern. I suspect that Grantley has no idea of the value you imply is locked in the company, simply because the expanded group has numerous other matters with which he needs to grapple. But, now that holidays are over, we can contact him and take his instruction.'

'I wonder whether you could turn your efforts to steering the company into a more secure destination. Keep them in the family, so to speak. Make sure they don't go astray.'

'But they will still be an object of prey wherever they go,' Bentley responded. 'Pelham could simply make another offer to whomever becomes the new owner.'

Hector did not want to betray Pelham's admission of Fenton's identity but simply added, 'Pelham told me that he had received a call from somebody who threatened to expose a dark secret from his younger days. He said he had methods of dealing with threats. I advise you not to encourage them, Fenton.'

That brought a brief hesitation lasting for just a fraction of a moment, but followed by the defensive response, 'You are jumping to conclusions, Hector. How would I know anything about his younger days?'

'It's quite obvious. You have already revealed your connection to Softlyn. They are in security and probably have their methods of enquiry and surveillance. You referred to them having a defence orientation. You must have got that information from them and I'm pretty sure that you work for The Department, which is always anxious about leaks.'

Fenton had to admit that he had been a little too lax in his language. 'Quite right,' he responded. 'I am currently working on an international money-laundering project and the Softlyn equipment offers the prospect of tapping into the most secure systems we know. Having told you that, I must entreat you never to reveal our discussions or to make any reference to Softlyn outside of this little circle. They may also have information on you, or me, perhaps,' he added in supplication and an indication of surrender.

'Don't worry, Fenton. Our business runs on a high level of trust and we always observe client confidentiality and secrecy,' Bentley assured him.

'Pelham doubted that any other gallery had been the target of a similar theft, and the painting was returned undamaged three months later,' Hector continued. 'That suggests to me that the theft was merely a demonstration of capability, and one not necessarily directed solely at Pelham. It could have been merely a field trial intended to confirm the effectiveness of the equipment.'

'I thought you were business specialists,' Fenton responded. 'But I see that you think in a wider spectrum than I had supposed. Yes, you are right in your deductions. You should take the opportunity to consult the main actor in the business, Bamber Stapleton. He's the brains behind the project in which we are interested.'

Rather than continue their game, they walked the rest of the course in an almost cloistered silence until they parted upon reaching the car park, but not before Fenton had reminded them of the necessity to guard the secret with their lives. 'This is a matter of national importance,' he told them.

Arriving at the office again next day, both Hector and Bentley recalled the freshness of a new term at school when summer holidays were over and they were faced with a new curriculum. In contrast to those happy days of youth before the trials of adulthood had intruded into their lives, their roles had now transformed into shaping the world.

Their focus was inevitably upon Grantley, but he was one already well versed in the challenges of industry, even if he was inexperienced in disposals. He had achieved an elevated position in management of the larger group from which he would demand an additional accretion of prosperity rather than an extension to knowledge.

Fenton's injunction to secrecy resonated in their minds as they discussed the limitations that it would impose on their actions. 'We still have to give Grantley an answer whether we can act for him, or not. I told him that I would do so after studying the papers and we had each returned from holiday,' Hector said.

Bentley nodded his agreement, 'We need not reveal the national security implications yet. We may not need to if we don't take on the project, and I have great reservations about having to deal with Pelham, anyway. I'm not going to jeopardise my association with Cordelia for anybody or for any financial inducement no matter how alluring it may be.'

A few minutes consideration followed in an attempt to rationalise their role in what seemed to be a matter of national importance. If not them, Grantley would choose somebody else to undertake the negotiations. They could simply walk away, but security would not be compromised by their gathering additional information, they thought. Hector rang Grantley, therefore, who, still anxious to preserve the confidentiality of discussions so far, suggested an appointment for the following day at the Railton offices.

Upon his arrival, the partners greeted him with an exchange of a few sentences that sufficed to dismiss the holiday period with brief allusions to happy days, but also to the consequent rejuvenation that would promote eagerness for tackling the tasks ahead. They were all well briefed by the Softlyn papers and entered quickly into discussion.

Hector stressed that they had as yet no contract that would have directed their efforts but he had, nonetheless, taken the opportunity of meeting Frank Pelham to engage him in a general discussion in which his interest in Softlyn had been revealed. Bentley intervened to express his understanding of Grantley's wish to dispose of a company because its expertise lay outside the normal scope of group operations, but also to mention his puzzlement that Pelham, with an almost identical group, wished to acquire it. Furthermore, it was not a large company, although the expertise of its employees had achieved a reasonably acceptable profitability.

Grantley suggested that they should not look at gift horses too intently; he was keen to divest the company and Pelham could have it if he cared to buy it. Bentley responded that Pelham must have some hidden motive and suspected that a deeper investigation might lead to gaining a more profitable sale. 'It would be advisable for us to speak to the management of the business before proceeding to contract,' he suggested.

'Our Mr Stapleton can give you all the details you need. He is the one most familiar with the products,' Grantley responded.

'Please do not mention Pelham before we have gained a better insight from him,' Bentley continued. 'We can raise that name at a later date, if appropriate.'

On the assumption that Fenton had already been in contact, possibly complicit, with Stapleton, they requested as a precaution against too wide a revelation that the venue should be the Railton office. It would also be advisable for the meeting to be attended only by Stapleton, who would therefore be less inhibited in whatever revelations he cared to make, if any. Consequently, they very politely requested that

Grantley should forgo the experience; the fewer people there were in the discussion would allow greater freedom of speech, they told him, at which he, with only a general knowledge of the business, was happy to bow out gracefully and leave the technicalities to those who seemed to have a more precise understanding of such matters.

Hector had a feeling that the meeting would not be as productive as they had hoped. Stapleton was apparently unaware of the negotiations to divest his company from the group and to sell it off to Pelham. He would be taken by surprise and react against a proposal that might impose great changes upon his life. Hector therefore invited Fenton to the meeting for him to brief Stapleton on the action and the *bona fides* of Railton.

Chapter 22

Bamber Stapleton arrived two days later and was met by Fenton with a few quiet words of recommendation and explanation before he introduced him to the partners. They met in the meeting room, which had a rather more inviting ambiance than the main office, by which means they hoped to ease discussion of a sensitive nature.

Despite the well-meant words of greeting intended to gain their visitor's goodwill, Bamber maintained a resolute and distant response. He evidently had no relish for discussing the intention to sell off the business he had nurtured for several years and was particularly annoyed that he had not been consulted on the matter until recent days despite his being the key man and highly successful in directing product development.

Bentley suggested that the sale would be highly beneficial to him both financially and professionally. He would be recognised as a leading figure in the industry and become a much sought-after talent who could almost name his own price.

The proposition was immediately rejected. 'I am the one who has built it from nothing and I'm not going to have it sold off over my head and without my consent. I have my own reasons for wanting the company to remain with Lowfield, or better still for me to control outright,' he replied.

Hector expressed his understanding of that view by offering the sympathetic thought that he would also not wish to part with his own business that he had helped build over the course of twenty years. Now that Bamber had revealed the possibility of independence, however, he suggested that they would be able to assist in attaining that objective rather than to sell the company to some remote and uncaring owner.

'A pleasant thought,' he replied, 'but I don't have the finance that would match anybody else's offer. The only reason why we were happy to enter the Lowfield group was merely to obtain funds for company development. Now I realise that we are just going to be sold off like an old toy no longer wanted.'

'We meet numerous business creators who say the same thing. They understandably have proprietorial feelings for their company, but it is our business to arrange buy outs and to negotiate a supply of cash to do so. We could do that for you if that's what you want.'

'It's probably worth a few millions. I couldn't finance that no matter what financial proposition you could arrange,' Bamber responded in exasperation.

'We have studied all the papers that Grantley has supplied and established a likely range of values. But we suspect that the dynamics of the company could tempt a buyer to a price far beyond what we consider to be fair value.'

'Which would simply raise the buyout price even further,' Bamber responded dismissively.

'Only if they know what we know,' Bentley intervened.

Fenton chose this moment to break his silence. 'I've told them about Ballantyne,' he explained. 'Pelham is the only person outside this room who has any knowledge of what that can do, but for strategic reasons, we cannot permit any release to any other party; and that includes Grantley,' he concluded.

Bamber thought that Fenton was being a little too authoritative, but responded, 'I have no intention of disclosing it to anybody,' he replied. 'It was you who wanted a field demonstration, and I was only too happy to select the target.'

'But why Pelham?' Hector asked with a touch of bewilderment.

'Because he now knows how effective Ballantyne is and how

vulnerable he is to repeated attacks,' Bamber told them with more than a note of disdain in his voice.

'But an art gallery!' Hector exclaimed.

'No. An all-out attack on his business. One that will bring him cringing and pleading to a confession,' Bamber responded in a dismissive display of contempt. 'And then the world will know him as he truly is.'

'And what must the world know about him, other than that he is a successful businessman? Perhaps he has been guilty of a few venal acts or of unpalatable treatment of personnel, but business is a tough world and demands tough decisions, sometimes.'

'Venal is not the word. Try criminal.'

'Criminal! What criminality is he guilty of? He would have been prosecuted by now if there were any evidence.'

'There is no evidence strong enough for a conviction; but I know what happened.'

His hearers waited expectantly in anticipation of further comment, but he remained silent. After several seconds, Bentley prompted, 'What did happen?'

Bamber paused, obviously debating what information to release. After a while, he resumed. 'Twenty years ago I won a scholarship to a prestigious university in the US where for five years I majored in electronics and computer science. After that, I undertook research in the laboratory of an international electronics company. Through most of that time, I was consumed with revulsion at Pelham's dismissal of liability, but I could do nothing until I thought of a way to destroy him, that is to say, his reputation, so that he would live with the disgrace that he deserved and everybody knowing that he was living a lie.

'After a few years, I developed the method that would undermine him and all his swagger and denial. It took me several years to develop my ideas and to bring them into practical form, but with the consent of the local museum in Skelton, I tested it on their security system. It worked, of course, and they commissioned Softlyn to provide a defence mechanism. I have a solution to that already, but it will not be marketed to Pelham.'

Fenton interrupted in order to add, 'The museum contacted us before their acceptance but the capability was new to us. They referred us to Softlyn and we worked with Bamber on the test. He then suggested another demonstration, but without the target's knowledge or consent. He chose the Pelham Gallery, a much unexpected target, but, with a specialist penetration unit that we supplied, he achieved the theft of the century and enormous criticism by the art world of gallery security.'

'Yes. That is quite clear,' Bentley responded. 'But why Pelham?'

'Because he is a criminal beyond forgiveness.'

'But what criminality?' Bentley asked in exasperation.

'Until I receive exact proposals for your selling off my company, I shall retain that knowledge as totally confidential.'

Bentley was used to annoyingly non-informative answers such as that. 'Give us a clue,' he pleaded without expecting an answer, but Bamber replied with the puzzling, '*A Tale of the Pacific Ocean.*'

They realised that they would get no further. Bamber had not been consulted early enough and had adopted an obdurate attitude, conscious that it was he who held the knowledge anyone would seek in a takeover.

'We'll have to consider our position, Bamber. Strictly speaking, our relationship should be with Grantley, but we have no formal contract with him yet, and, in sensitive matters such as this, we would not proceed without the consent of the key people in the company of whom you rank as the most important.'

'Not just the most important. It probably hasn't escaped your notice that it is only I who has a thorough knowledge of the system. Without me, the company would be nothing. And don't think that the devices will be of any advantage to the buyer,' he added. 'I have not only sole custody of the activation codes but also the capability to resume development elsewhere. With Lowfield funding, I have brought Softlyn far beyond its small beginnings, but if I walked away to a rival or started another business, it would be almost worthless. You help me and I'll help you,' he replied.

'What help would you need?'

'Get Pelham,' was the curt reply.

The meeting ended inconclusively. Bamber felt that he had gained a victory in stressing his importance, Fenton was almost apologetic at the lack of progress and the partners were left in a state of ignorance. Not a good start to the new term!

Bamber walked away thinking that he had made it clear that it was his invention, the details of which he would be wise not to reveal to anybody. The mention of the company about to be sold off without consulting him was an insult. After all those years, he was being thrown out as if his efforts counted for nothing. Not even Fenton, who had previously shown some interest, had made any attempt to support him.

Instead of returning to the company, he went back home and reported to his wife, Lois, that the company was up for sale and his contribution to its success had been totally ignored. 'Any buyer would have to have my approval, even if I'm a minority shareholder,' he told her, although he knew in his soul that he could always be replaced by somebody with similar expertise to his while he would be compelled to leave with, at best, a golden handshake or, at worst, a mere thank you. 'But they wouldn't know anything about Ballantyne,' he thought.

'All that knowledge resides with me, and I'll make sure they won't even know about it.'

His wife of several years could only offer sympathy. She knew nothing of the business or how she could intervene to halt the sale. 'With your experience, you'll get another job easily enough. You might get a promotion into a bigger group, though, or possibly receive a pay-off that might be enough to start another company,' was all she could contribute.

Bamber reluctantly agreed, but another job would probably mean moving house, taking on another mortgage, and possibly a change of school for his daughters. He did not have many options, but he would have to think hard about his future. He had nursed his grievance for over twenty years and had no intention of relenting. Pelham deserved to reap the consequences of causing Cora's death, or, at the very least, of not having prevented it. He remembered Pelham's testimony at the inquest delivered in a subdued monotone that did not seem as if it could have emanated from the tragic experience of a forlorn lover; and, afterwards, he had maintained a formality with the family incompatible with a broken heart, but, rather, an unemotional portrayal of a final ending, a few words of consolation and, then, nothing. No tearful farewell, no last words of commiseration. Laura had told him that Frank was truly devastated but Bamber was unconvinced. He knew where he lived and had watched his business bloom over the years. Obviously, a man who had the energy and ambition to succeed, but one without a heart!

Fenton returned to his office thinking that Bamber had done nothing to help himself out of his position, neither had he said anything that would aid Railton or The Department. The company could be sold on without him, but he could retain possession and control of the device without anybody outside the quartet that had just dispersed knowing anything about it. Grantley would be only too happy to dispose of the business to any buyer and even a low price would be an addition to the group bank account. But Bamber had total control of the product, whether or not the company was divested, and would be able to market it as a sole contractor, perhaps not to a party with malevolent intent, but his actions would forever remain a source of uncertainty; and that was a word that made The Department uneasy. Even if he, Fenton, could persuade the authorities to purchase the business, the mere knowledge could never be erased and would pose an ever-present danger to the state.

Hector and Bentley sat slumped in their chairs thinking that the morning had achieved very little. 'Grantley will contact us if we don't update him soon,' Hector said. 'He's bound to want a word about progress.'

'We have no contractual obligation with anyone at the moment,' Bentley replied. 'Either we plead for more time or tell him we are unable to proceed.'

'I don't like to admit that we are getting nowhere, but I can't see much prospect of advancement if we have to serve three masters: Pelham, Fenton and Grantley. We either give up the whole thing or choose one of them as a contractual partner.'

'Or just possibly, Stapleton,' Bentley added.

'I wonder what crime it is that he alleges against Pelham. It must be something serious in order to have rankled with him for twenty years.'

They examined the internet for the quotation Bamber had given. *The Coral Island* by R M Ballantyne, but that meant nothing to them. Fenton could only say that either '*Coral*' or '*Island*' held the clue.

'Or the two together,' Hector added.

'Or nothing at all. Perhaps it's a false trail,' Bentley contributed. 'But wait – "Coral Ital". That's Pelham's company.'

The partners left for their respective homes, Hector wondering how, or whether, to report back to Frank when little progress had been made, Bentley dismissing an episode of near futility, but unusually now able to look forward in compensation to a greeting from Cordelia.

He was disappointed on arriving home that she had not yet returned from her outing with Hermione and only momentarily suffered a flashback to the desultory interval before he had found her again, but he was confident that she would return shortly. They had renewed the days of old and had resumed their youth from the moment when it had been interrupted. He was, nonetheless, relieved when he heard the key turn in the lock and to find her contented smile in her appreciative glance at the interior, a signal that she was happy to be home.

'What a lovely day,' she said as he welcomed her with a slight embrace. 'Something to occupy my days that formerly I spent alone; and plenty to talk about with Hermione. The theatre was a delight too. Two lovers parted by circumstance until reunification. Just like us,' she concluded with a smile.

'I also used to spend most of my days alone, but I could hardly wait for your return after my very inconclusive day at the office. Now, we shall be that ordinary couple that you once thought would be a future unfulfilled.'

'Yes. Ordinary. That's the word. Once disdained, but now a welcome label, and every day a joy. So far, at least,' she teased him.

'Days for joy, nights for love,' he responded.

Cordelia gave a mock smile of admonishment, although his analysis was also hers. 'What was inconclusive about your day?' she asked. 'You were only too keen to get back to the grindstone, I thought.'

'When Hector met that famous neighbour of yours whilst he was on holiday in Bologna, he discovered that he wants to launch a takeover prospect of a UK group that seems would involve government security.'

'You mean Frank Pelham?' she replied with a touch of concern. 'My advice is don't touch him with a bargepole. He's extremely polite but very persistent and you won't be able to shake him off.'

'We don't have a contract with him. We have reservations about taking on the job with any of the parties concerned; and I don't want to get involved with anybody of whom you would disapprove,' he concluded to her relief.

Bentley reported to Hector next day that, in order not to prejudice relations with Cordelia, he was confirmed in his opinion that they should ignore the temptations of acting. Hector had his loyalty to Bentley to consider and immediately decided to forgo all connection with the matter. He rang Grantley to inform him of their decision but was much surprised to hear that he had just been approached by Pelham about Softlyn and they had arranged a preliminary discussion for the following week.

The partners had not yet told Fenton, and therefore rang to tell him that they had no interest in acting on the project, but also of the news of the meeting between the industrialists. On hearing that, Fenton began to feel great discomfort, but his alarm did not match that of Bamber, who was horrified that his company was not only about to be sold off but also that he would be present at the discussion. He wondered whether Frank realised whom he would be meeting. It would no doubt be a strain for both of them, but even if they had not met for twenty years, the embarrassment of their meeting would make discussions fraught with antagonism.

He reviewed all activity relating to the creation of Ballantyne, collected whatever papers there were, and took custody of the device and all testbed remnants that could possibly be connected with it. He also carried his computer to the car in order to ensure that all designs and construction details would no longer be in danger of expropriation, drove home and switched it with an old model that he occasionally used for personal data storage, explaining to Lois that he would need access to the data before the meeting. He then returned to the office in order to attend a preliminary discussion that afternoon with Grantley.

The meeting was held in the board room and several managers attended. The atmosphere was one of good-natured camaraderie in which the participants began with anecdotes of their holidays and of the old days when they had joined the group. They relaxed at the news that their group had attracted the attention of a well-known industrialist, all except Bamber rejoicing that they had been the focus of international recognition, although each was pleased that it was not their own company that had been targeted. They congratulated Bamber on his success at building the business to a desirable object of scrutiny, commenting on the slightly unusual product lines Softlyn possessed compared with the engineering expertise of the group.

Grantley called the meeting to order, explaining that Pelham had contacted him with the suggestion to explore the possibility of bidding for Softlyn because he had noted its success but appeared to lack integration into the Overdale core businesses which might, therefore, hinder its future development. He had continued that it may lack management attention within the engineering ethos of the group whereas his own software division could apply a more appropriate focus that would give greater encouragement to new products.

Bamber reminded the meeting of previous congratulations on his having led the growth of his company and ventured to add that he could bring it to even greater performance. He gave his opinion that Pelham would simply break up the company and disperse the staff, whose expertise had built the business. Furthermore, he was likely to undervalue the company with what he presumed would be a sum well below what its future prospects would attract.

His audience had only slight loyalty to a business so different from theirs and they rejected as implausible the argument that Pelham would steer the company into extinction after paying good money for it, particularly if Grantley could drive up the sale price on the prospect of future growth. They also expressed the opinion that whatever Pelham did with Softlyn would be of no interest to them.

Much to Bamber's annoyance, the meeting resolved that the group should enter discussions for sale. The managers broke up with a few consolatory words to Bamber accompanied by encouragement for future prosperity. But, whatever the sentiments, the company was up for sale.

Chapter 23

Spenser looked idly out of the train window as he travelled to the television centre in order to take part in the third of the programmes in which he had participated for the 'Art on Display' lectures. The first had been featured many years before when the series had been aired for several episodes and had attracted moderate audiences. It had been an opportunity for him to mingle with others in his profession who proved to be not only academics of high standing but also those with whom he could participate in the learned conversations about art that he enjoyed.

The series that had followed the first after a short break, had, he thought, given way to a less satisfactory presentation of what seemed to be more like travel programmes about the major cities in which the art could be viewed but which featured less prominently than its title suggested. Now, as art director of the most talked about gallery of the time, he had been approached by the broadcaster to take part in a special programme about the most audacious art theft in many decades. He had been assured that the old format would be restored under the former presenter and that he would have another opportunity to meet Walter Tilson, with whom he had enjoyed not only their previous debate but also the personal contact with a man of unrivalled knowledge in his field.

Upon arrival some two hours before start of recording, he was greeted by the programme presenter, Bernard Marston, a man of broad smiles and generator of comforting conversation designed to place participants at their ease. Walter Tilson had also just arrived and been recipient of an equally calming welcome.

In order to familiarise his guests with the studio ambiance and to re-establish their personal relationships, Bernard had ensured that the two participants could greet each other in good time. Amid deep-felt mutual expressions of goodwill leading to fond recollections of their old programme, they quickly rebuilt the atmosphere so conducive to lively exchanges of constructive opinions. Spenser mentioned his surprise at meeting Astra again after so many years when he had last seen her as a small child. Walter replied that she had submitted her thesis and was sure that a doctorate would be conferred within three months. 'She said she had gained a lot of insight whilst working at the gallery, as well as meeting you and the people behind the scenes,' Walter continued. 'That, with a few improvements that I suggested, has enabled her to incorporate a lot more argument in her thesis which I think will easily surpass the standard of scholarship that the board will require.'

Bernard explained the format of the three-quarter hour programme so that the two experts would feel comfortable together and be quite familiar with the intended course he wished to follow. He would be the moderator, introducing the topics and calling upon them in turn in order for them to express their views, for which he assured them of adequate time to answer before he would grant the opportunity for the other to add further comment.

They entered the studio, which was staffed by several technicians and cameramen on one side but on the other a mock-up of a comfortable sitting room with three armchairs for the participants. A make-up artist stepped forward to ensure that they were well presented with hair combed and faces slightly tanned. Bernard asked for a brief microphone test and put a question to each in order to settle them into a comfortable routine and level of speech.

As the time scheduled for the recording approached, Bernard appeared to be the only one who seemed to be perfectly relaxed and even full of smiles, together with a few calming remarks, whilst a very slight and almost imperceptible nervousness was felt by the guests, who each gave a shrug at resuming the daunting prospect before them, but not without practising a brave smile to the other. The controller spoke clearly over the internal speaker to announce that the recording had started. Numerous Old Masters would float for several seconds across the screen as music played to introduce the programme to the viewers. As the last notes of introduction sounded, the title would appear as *Art on Display* in a well-remembered reference to the several predecessors of the current edition.

At the red-light signal, Bernard spoke to camera with his practised capability recognisable to all as one who was well known for his presentational skills. 'Welcome to this special edition of *Art on Display*,' he said by way of introduction. 'We bring again a discussion programme on current topics of art that have interested those in galleries and audiences around the globe. Few people can be ignorant of the most recent and startling phenomenon in the world of art. I speak, of course, about the greatest art theft in centuries following those of the Mona Lisa from the Louvre and the Duke of Wellington from our own National Gallery. The art world has recently experienced an enormous shock in learning of the disappearance of the much-loved seventeenth century work by Batista del Mano of the Old Master, *Girl with a Harp*.

'In order to discuss this audacious theft, we have invited the two foremost experts on the period and, in particular, of del Mano and his works.'

The camera drew back to focus upon the two participants sitting in comfortable chairs on either side of the presenter, before the cameras cut to the individual experts as they were introduced.

'From the Pelham Gallery, we have the art director, Spenser Ferndale, who has suffered the most appalling incident that any gallery manager could imagine. We also have the foremost expert in this art form of the period, Professor Walter Tilson, who conducted an assessment of the theft and the possible motives for it.'

He turned towards Spenser, to whom he addressed the opening question that he had rehearsed just a few minutes before. 'Spenser Ferndale, *Girl with a Harp* has been in the custody of the Pelham Gallery for several decades. How do you think it ranks among the great works of art that have descended to us through the centuries and that we have been privileged to view?'

Spenser replied with complete assurance that the painting ranked among the greatest in the history of art. They were extremely honoured to have been the recipients of the Lewis Pelham collection and had guarded *Girl with a Harp* with the knowledge that it was their most prized possession. It was almost four hundred years old but had spent most of its existence in the seclusion of private collections until acquisition by their founder, who had included it in his bequest.

Bernard turned to his other guest to ask whether the painting stood proudly among the ranks of the great names of that period, to which Walter conceded that it had an exalted place in the history of art and added that del Mano was a lesser-known artist merely because he had lived a rather sequestered existence and had accordingly never received the focus that his contemporaries had experienced. 'That is not to overlook his considerable talents that simply had not been known to a wider public,' he added.

Spenser contributed the information that del Mano had lived and died mostly in Florence and was not well known further abroad. His induction into the world of art was obscure but he was thought to have gained his artistry as a junior assistant in the workplace of a minor master and learned as much about painting by observation as by instruction. His skills were those of one capable of depicting crowd scenes where facial details were realistic but drawn from imagination rather than faithful depictions of a subject.

'Yes,' Walter agreed. 'And that was the most useful introduction to the important skill of rendering a true likeness of his main subject. We cannot know how accurate his depictions were because he did not move in the circles of the wealthy elite and therefore was not an artist whose works could be judged alongside those by other masters from which we might have been able to obtain a comparison. His subjects served mainly allegorical purposes, for which he used almost unknown models drawn from his domestic circle rather than persons of note whose portraits were commissioned by the leading citizens of the day.'

Spenser followed with the comment, 'But the quality of the paintings that we have indicates a masterly facility in depicting the female face. *Girl with a Harp* is proof of his artistry and, even if we had no other portraits, one can admire his capability in the beatific expression he has depicted on her face. We do know that his model was Risanta Ferra and that she appeared again in *Lady with Flowers*, also exhibited in our gallery,' he added, proudly, 'And that also exhibits his capability in depicting light illuminating the face.'

Having obtained a little information about the artist and his career, Bernard directed further attention to Spenser. 'We should now turn to a discussion of the most remarkable event in the world of art that ranks with the most audacious of the century. I refer, of course, to the theft of one of the most treasured works in your gallery. Or perhaps I should say substitution, because it was not until a routine check detected that the art on display was, in fact, a copy. What was it that drew your attention to that startling discovery?'

'I knew that the genuine painting had been displayed from several months before because it had been locked securely overnight in my office and I had hung it myself in the del Mano room in the presence of several other gallery staff. All works carry a distinctive code which is verified at time of hanging and in periodic inspections. Much to our great consternation, I was informed after one inspection that the code was missing, which triggered an examination and revealed that an exchange must presumably have taken place at some time in the previous several weeks. You can imagine our alarm and our distress. Despite the painting having been disconnected and removed and a copy hung and reconnected in its place, our electronically generated security records found that no interruption had occurred. The equipment was checked and found to be in order, the premises were thoroughly searched but there was no sign of the genuine item. We then alerted the Art Squad, who conducted interviews with all the staff, including me, but came to no definite conclusion.'

Walter intervened to say, 'Several copies of the *Girl* also existed. Visitors were able to obtain them from the gallery shop but some had been expertly framed by workshop staff. The Art Squad was obliged to examine them but they all proved quite legitimately to have been purchased and held in private houses, but the genuine one had, somehow, been spirited away without trace. Unusually, no ransom had been demanded and the assumption was that it had been stolen, perhaps to order, by a private collector.'

'That would at least give some comfort that it would remain in good condition,' Spenser added, 'but there was also the worry that it may even have been destroyed if the culprit were to realise that the pursuit had become more intense.'

Bernard commented, much to Spenser's disquiet, that the gallery must have suffered a severe setback in its reputation for safe keeping, to which he responded as imperturbably as possible, 'The disappearance was certainly a huge blow to us because we have guarded our exhibits with the utmost care throughout our history. We updated our security only a few years ago when we installed the latest and allegedly the most tamper-proof update. We tested it thoroughly upon installation and have also tested it daily. But it seems that whatever precautions one may take, the criminal world is not far behind.'

'Whatever method was utilised to remove the painting,' Walter added with a slight note of sympathy in his voice, 'the capability of the underworld cannot be underestimated. But,' he continued, 'the most astonishing aspect of the removal was the fact that the painting was returned without trace of origin, but undamaged, only a few months later. That suggests to me and all who were concerned in the matter that the removal was more in the nature of a security test rather than a theft. I am quite sure that the Art Squad had considered the cooperation of the board in a test, a most unlikely possibility, but all investigations came to no firm conclusion.'

Spenser quickly added, 'The Art Squad had commendably interviewed each member of the board including me. Our first thought was that the removal must have been an inside job, but the electronic evidence, in particular, was unassailable. Neither an inside nor an outside job had been detected. But that faced us with a conundrum, namely, whether an inside or an outside job, how could it have been accomplished and who could have been the perpetrator?'

'And I believe you were then contacted by a most unexpected source,' Bernard continued.

'Yes, and quite astoundingly, from a most astonishing quarter,' Walter responded.

'This is beginning to sound most intriguing,' Bernard added with a knowing smile in expectation of the forthcoming revelation.

Spenser spoke up to inform his audience of the gallery origin. 'It was established with a legacy from our now departed founder, Lewis Pelham, an industrialist who had created a private collection over many years, which he most generously bequeathed to a trust managed by the present board. His grandson, Frank Pelham, is the main trustee but has lived in Italy for many years and bears great responsibility for managing the performance of a rather large engineering group, which one can imagine must demand a great deal of his time. He consequently delegates all management activity to the board, on which he is represented by his sister.

'Quite apart from the fact that he lives in Italy, a world away from the gallery in Skelton, he has little to do with the gallery management, and, although the removal of the painting from its place of display has created enormous comment in the art world, he has remained, until fairly recently, totally unaware of the turmoil that has followed.'

'But one presumes that he was informed of the theft,' Bernard prompted.

'Yes, of course. His sister undertook to report the event to him and also the fact that the matter was being investigated by the Art Squad, which, we had assumed, would have provided some comfort that the experts had control.'

'As we know,' Walter continued, 'little progress had been made beyond eliminating all likely possibilities. The investigation was enlivened with the return of the painting, but, apart from that of authorised handlers, no DNA traces were found and it is probable that the painting had not even been removed from its crate, which strengthened my suspicion that the removal was a mere test of security.'

'But what was this astonishing quarter you mentioned?' Bernard asked with the slightest of smiles and feigning a little ignorance at the forthcoming answer.

Walter responded, 'The astonishing quarter was located at the house of the main trustee to whom the knowledge that the art world was in uproar had, at last, penetrated. Frank Pelham hastened to announce to the board that the removal had been instigated by government representatives who were conducting field tests on top secret electronic equipment. He was the main trustee and they had chosen to seek his consent rather than that of the board in order to minimise the risk of any leak of information if the board as a whole were to be approached.'

Spenser added that, 'None of us had been informed of the test, which led inevitably to all of us suffering greatly as a consequence, not to mention our chairman, whose task it was to announce the matter to the press. I felt very deeply indeed the anguish of losing a masterpiece perhaps to another few centuries of obscurity in some collection unknown to the world – and,' he added with some emotion, 'I would never know whether that beautiful painting had even been destroyed,' he ended to a short pause with the sympathy of his listeners.

'The media interest was very intense at the outset,' he continued after a moment, 'but just a few months later grew to even greater frenzy at the return of the painting. We were greatly relieved at its recovery but, nonetheless, totally mystified. We thought that the thief had recalled that both the Mona Lisa and the Duke of Wellington had been recovered and that he should also act accordingly, having achieved some sort of triumph; and, may I add, totally defeated the investigative authorities.'

Bernard turned again to camera, concluding the programme with some explanatory and comforting words. 'The greatest art theft of the century has now been revealed as one undertaken as a test of electronics authorised by the main trustee and carried out by a government department but without the knowledge of the gallery personnel. One can only hope that the security measures in all our galleries can be relied upon to hinder another astounding theft. May I thank Professor Walter Tilson and Art Director Spenser Ferndale, for their insightful revelations and to you, our audience, wish an untroubled viewing of – *Art on Display*.'

Having completed the recording, the director would ensure that the closing credits would begin to roll and viewers be able to see the participants in silent conversation until the familiar music sounded no more. The nation would, then, either switch off or remain seated in order to view the following transmission.

The studio participants rose from their seats with congratulations all round as the technical staff cleared the studio. Bernard thanked his guests for the professionalism they had demonstrated and Walter commiserated with Spenser at the distress that he had suffered. 'Your reaction to the theft was understandably more deeply felt than mine. To me, it was an opportunity to undertake a study of what I had hoped with each examination would be the discovery of the century, but that was postponed until the last when the painting had been returned rather than discovered.'

Spenser replied that he felt so relieved at its return in good condition that he had almost sobbed. Walter felt obliged, as they left the studio, to offer more than a hand of comfort and friendship to this sensitive man by inviting him to a little celebration at home, which Spenser accepted in the hope that he could exchange not only erudite conversation but also experience a period of rehabilitation from the stress and worry of the previous months so stoically borne.

He returned to the terminus, boarded the commuter train to his local station and drove carefully home through the early evening, relieved not only that the programme had been concluded, but also that the next day's dawn would bring new light. Back to routine? Probably not. The press would, no doubt, be clamouring for more and be sure to treat all responses as further material for criticism.

On reaching home just after eight, the door was opened by his long-time partner, Mariol, who hugged him briefly, detecting that Spenser was not entirely his old self. They had met fifteen years previously in a crowd listening to the guide at Amboise and each had immediately found an ideal. She admired Spenser for his knowledge of art and he admired her for her intelligence, professionalism and caring personality. 'I hope all went well,' she said, to which Spenser replied with a feeling of catharsis in having survived a tragic event, and now being able to relax once more at home in company with his intellectual equal. 'It will be transmitted on Sunday evening. The director told us that he was very happy with it.'

'We'll watch it together. It should be a very interesting programme and I am sure that both of you will be most informative,' Mariol assured him.

'I'm not looking forward to the inquest that will follow, though. I fear we will be pilloried by those ignorant people of the press, not to speak of that old fool, Marcus. He's bound to imply that the fault was all mine.'

'He's chairman of the board and should shoulder all the responsibility, Spenser. But you're tired and need a little rest. I've cooked a light meal for both of us. A glass of wine and then bed time. Don't forget our little holiday is approaching, shortly. We'll relax at the apartment over there and leave all the stress to the others.'

Spenser realised how tired he was but so thankful that his comforter of several years was always there for him. He began to look forward to viewing the art and sculpture they would see. Perhaps they could indulge themselves in, yet again, attempting to trace the site of del Mano's studio.

Chapter 24

The day after leaving Hedrick, Astra was faced with the unwelcome task of apologising to Garrard. He would be at the gallery all day but she dreaded the prospect of encountering him in the company of others. She waited until evening in order to visit him at home once more in order to ensure that they would be alone. After postponing her journey for another half hour at the bus station, she boarded the bus to his house, hoping that he would not refuse her admission but also half wishing that he would not even be there.

She rang the bell in an agony of uncertainty at her reception. He opened the door and broke into a welcoming smile at sight of her. 'Astra! A pleasant surprise. To what do I owe the honour of seeing you this time?'

Astra took an uncertain step inside and blurted out the excuse that she was leaving next day and wanted to say goodbye. 'You needn't have come all this way,' he replied. 'I've been at the gallery all day.'

'Actually, I've come for something else,' she stammered. 'It's about what I said when I was here last.'

Garrard looked puzzled. 'If it's about Hedrick, I've had a little talk with him, like you asked.'

'Yes, I know, but that's not it,' but then she suddenly burst out, 'I'm terribly sorry about what I said. I shouldn't have been so stupid. I thought I had sorted things out in my head but it was all wrong.'

She saw that Garrard had greeted her announcement with disappointment but she could think of nothing more to add. 'Well. Goodbye then. I'm going home tomorrow.'

'I'm sorry you are leaving. It was a great pleasure to have

met you,' Garrard responded. 'I'm sorry I couldn't do more for you. I thought you were both very well suited to each other.'

He had misunderstood, Astra realised. 'No, that's not what I meant. We are getting on nicely. I just came to – apologise,' she finally blurted out. 'For those stupid things I said – about the painting.'

'Oh! You mean that nonsense. I thought for a moment you were splitting up with Hedrick. Thank goodness it was only the picture. I knew you couldn't mean it but my experience with ladies is very limited and I just thought it was said to cover any embarrassment you may have felt.'

She felt humbled at his obvious lack of resentment but she had apologised and turned to go. 'I wish you well for your future, whatever it may be,' were his parting words. Astra gave a thankful smile in return and walked away.

Having surrendered her key to the flat, Astra arrived home on Saturday happy to be greeted by family again but immediately faced with the emptiness of her future; no more study, no more thesis, no more helping out at the gallery shop. Now she was on a cliff gazing at the ocean as if '*a girl aloft there scans the scene with none but wind attending*'.

Almost the first question was to ask her father how the recording had gone, to which he replied that it had passed off very well and had been ably presented by the moderator, whom he had known from previous transmissions. 'The broadcast is tomorrow so you can judge for yourself. Spenser was also good and a pleasure to meet again. And I've invited him for dinner next Sunday.'

'Oh!' Astra said, 'I've invited somebody too. From the gallery workshop. Hedrick. He does framing, mainly. They have a big job reframing all their exhibits for the new safety precautions.'

Her mother jumped immediately to the suspicion she had formed before when Astra had indicated, almost hinted, that this was the man who had led her daughter into some nefarious activity. 'Well, dear! I'm sure we can fit him in,' she said politely but not without some alarm that he had now worked his way into her daughter's affections, and privately thinking that his attentions must be discouraged.

The following evening, they gathered in front of the television just as they had in the days when Astra had sat between her parents revelling in the entertainment that it had then offered, but she had grown up now and Walter chose to sit in the easy chair in order to allow more room on the sofa. The last few minutes of the previous programme drew slowly to a close as excitement mounted in the Tilson family. An announcer spoke enthusiastically about a programme scheduled for mid-week but finally moved to the present and scenes of art floating across the screen. 'Here we go,' Walter commented as Bernard Marston appeared. 'Oh, gosh,' Walter said as the participants were revealed. 'Don't I look awful,' but he was hushed into silence by his wife.

Spenser appeared with a confident response to Bernard's question, followed by Walter to the excitement of his family. The revelation of government intervention came as a surprise to both Astra and Edith, because the warning that the mention of it may be inappropriate until permission had been obtained had only recently been withdrawn.

At the Spenser household, Mariol poured a celebratory drink when they had viewed the programme. 'That was a splendid programme, Spenser, and I'm so proud to be living with our new television personality,' she said. 'But I'm always proud to be living with you. Here's to even more of a happy future,' she said as she saluted him.

'I could have said more,' he responded, 'but I think it was reasonably good.'

Mariol assured him that it was more than reasonably good. 'I haven't seen those first programmes in which you appeared, but this one was no less than I had expected of you; a masterful performance. I wonder what the Tilsons would have thought.'

'We'll find out next Sunday. I'm looking forward to meeting him again outside the studio. I visited them twenty years ago and have enjoyed the memory ever since. Very intelligent and extremely knowledgeable about art, and a daughter who will probably be awarded a doctorate soon.'

'We shall enjoy the outing, Spenser. There are too few opportunities for us to meet good company,' she replied with an appreciative smile. 'I wonder what I would have done if we had never met,' she mused. 'A thousand to one chance brought us into contact in that crowd and we have never outlasted our pleasure at the encounter.'

'I hope you will understand that I have used up all my expressions of thanks and admiration for my beautiful and intelligent partner. Before I met you, I had never thought I would ever have such loving feelings for another as I have for you. Somebody who has loved me in return and carried me through all adversity.'

'I shall always be here for you, Spenser. You are not only my lover and my delight but also my guide and mentor.'

'You don't need a mentor and you have guided and advised me just as much as I have ever guided you.'

Hedrick watched the programme with just a little trepidation that he would in a few days meet not only so respected a man as a professor but also, he hoped, his future father-in-law. Spenser had been his usual confident self and the two participants struck him as experts of equal standing. Garrard had probably watched the programme, too. They would, no doubt, exchange opinions, and, if he met Spenser, he could congratulate him the next day upon his performance.

The house seemed incomplete now that the programme had brought to a conclusion his period of contact with Astra; and emptier than he had ever realised. He suffered a brief return to his old inferiority complex in which he experienced a vision of Astra held by a force exerted by her nearest and dearest trapped forever in her turret, but he quickly reasserted himself. He loved her and he was sure that she loved him. That would be a power greater than any obstacle he might face. He would assert himself against all the forces directed against him, if they ever were, and face any difficulties with Astra beside him. Now, he could imagine himself riding to her house and swinging her onto the saddle before they both rode off into the sunset.

Bamber also watched the programme, wondering how the participants would explain the return of the painting. He felt gratified at the brevity of the explanation; not he but the government had undertaken the field test. Fenton must have liaised with Frank who, he now learned, had not accounted to the board for his acquiescence to the theft. But that was a concern that ranked far below his fear of losing the company. He remained disturbed at the possibility of a sale to some international electronics company who would probably be able to do without his experience despite how impressive his credentials were. He would have to contact Railton for guidance.

Edith looked out for the tenth time on the following Sunday but the expected guest seemed tantalisingly not yet in sight.

As she turned away she heard a car approaching a little uncertainly obviously checking that they had come to the correct house. As it turned into the drive, she called out to the household hidden in their respective studies, 'He's arrived.' But as they emerged from their lairs, she noticed with surprise that Spenser, whom she recognised from the broadcast, had arrived but unexpectedly with a lady. She was a slim woman of neat, slightly continental appearance who looked approvingly at the house and advanced with Spenser to the door. 'Walter, you didn't tell me that he was married,' she told him in an undercurrent as they rang the bell.

'No, he's not. Who is she, I wonder?' he said in a low voice as he reached the door.

He was greeted by the smiling couple, whom he ushered inside, Spenser apologising that they were a little late. 'I don't think you have met my partner,' he said. 'This is Mariol, my young lady and companion of many years. And an excellent navigator,' he added.

'You are most welcome,' Edith told them in her most polite manner but a little puzzled at this unexpected visitor.

'We are so pleased at your invitation, Madame Tilson,' Mariol replied with the slightest trace of a Gallic accent. 'It is very generous of you. Spenser and I have very few opportunities for social occasions together, but he assures me that we shall be among the most delightful company.'

Edith hastened to inform her that they had long desired their presence, at which moment, Astra entered to be greeted with similar effusions of friendship. 'I was hoping to meet Astra again and to introduce her to Mariol,' Spenser gleamed. 'My dear, this is the young lady I told you of. A valuable addition to the Tilson family and one who is about to reach an even higher status when her doctorate is awarded.'

'I am so delighted to meet you,' Mariol responded with a

huge smile. Astra replied that she was most welcome and that it was a great pleasure to see her.

'We shall have much to talk about,' she concluded, quickly adjusting her assumptions about Spenser's inclinations.

'We are expecting another visitor soon,' Walter continued. 'A friend of Astra. So we shall be a big, happy family.'

'Hedrick Tarrant from the workshop,' Astra intervened.

'Oh, yes. Our picture framer,' Spenser told his companion. 'It was I who spotted his aptitude and snapped him up for the gallery, and a very good recruit he turned out to be. His work adds a certain resonance to all the paintings he frames,' he said, having recalled that poetic expression, but he also realised that Hedrick must have more than a casual acquaintance with Astra.

Mariol registered the some thought as if it had been transmitted by osmosis. 'Then we shall not be too much biased towards the elderly if there is an infusion of young people in our midst.'

Astra felt that she was an imbalance amongst the two couples before her and wished that Hedrick were already there. His arrival would help to balance the party, and she had missed his embrace for over a week.

Hedrick was meanwhile standing outside the station looking around for a taxi but none was in sight and he had no idea when, or if, one would arrive soon. He set out along the road that the station inspector had pointed out as the one leading to his destination. Fortunately, the weather was fine and the route scenic. The first half mile was only slightly uphill before levelling off. Another ten minutes brought him to the house where a car stood in the drive. 'Here goes,' he said to himself as he rang the bell, but the door opened almost instantly and Astra almost dragged him inside. 'I saw you coming. Dad invited Spenser and he's just arrived. With his "young lady",' she told him in an excited whisper.

'Hedrick has arrived,' she told everybody, triumphantly. 'These are my parents, you know Spenser, and this is Mariol, Spenser's companion.'

Edith saw a young man of an unexpectedly well-dressed appearance. 'Was this the man who had captivated her daughter,' she wondered, but smiled an uncertain greeting. Her father shook his hand, expressing a brief welcome whilst assessing the character of this man of mystery. Spenser followed suit with an awkward joke that he had been tracked down, but Mariol remained the epitome of politeness. 'Such a pity that we had not been able to bring you from the station. I hope the walk was not too strenuous.'

He assured her that it was an easy walk through very pleasant countryside but was, now, pleased to make everybody's acquaintance. Astra smiled her delight at his reception. 'Not too bad,' but she had noticed a little reservation in her parents. 'They're wondering about us,' she thought with amusement. 'They can't still think him an arch criminal after that revelation of government involvement.' Then, she knew that they were horrified at the thought of an impecunious young man carrying her off to a life of impoverishment. She almost collapsed with laughter, but she was also confident that he had not made the journey without a purpose.

Hedrick congratulated both Walter and Spenser on their television programme and the revelation of government intervention. He also expressed his delight that the painting had been returned intact. 'That was the one that fascinated me from my first visit to the gallery and has continued to do so. I had the great honour of framing the original and my own copy and had felt myself to be almost an owner of such an exquisite work of art before the Art Squad commandeered it.'

'Our oldest and perhaps most revered of all our exhibits,' Spenser contributed. 'You will understand my relief at seeing it restored, unharmed, to its rightful place.'

'But I still don't understand how even government could have circumvented the security,' Walter added. 'Your records show no sign of interference.'

'Frank Pelham might know. If he doesn't reveal his contacts, I shall ask him directly when we are over there in a few weeks,' Spenser responded.

'We are going to relax at our apartment for two weeks and leave all the stress behind,' Mariol revealed. 'Spenser needs a little rest from all the pressures he has had recently. But, Spenser, I shall not allow you to be too agitated when you meet Monsieur Pelham. We are going in order to calm down and not to get too excited.'

They all noted how caring she was and Spenser felt even more devoted to Mariol for her consideration. Another proof of how indebted he was to her.

Hedrick and Astra wandered into the rear of the house and looked out at the garden. They held hands at last and enjoyed an embrace in the privacy of the terrace room. 'They're wondering about us,' Astra told him.

'It can't be whether I'm an arch criminal,' Hedrick replied. 'They're wondering whether I might run off with you and drag you into the depths of depravity, but I have to admit that I couldn't support you in the way to which you are accustomed.'

'What does that matter? You haven't seen my old flat. It's pretty basic but I've put up with it for several months.'

'My house is a bit bigger. Move in with me and get another job at the gallery.'

'So you *are* going to drag me off into a world of iniquity,' she teased.

'I mean that we could get married and then you could move in.'

'That sounds better. Reputations preserved and relations retained. All right, let's do it and I'll be another Mariol. Did you notice how close they are? Something that I would never have suspected.'

'There will be no limit to our devotion, either,' he told her as they indulged in a deeper embrace, both thinking of their lives together.

Walter and Edith had noticed the absence of the two youngsters, but Spenser had also noted their concern. 'That Hedrick is an excellent framer of our exhibits and we are in the process of adding UV protection to all of them. The project will take almost a year in total and then he would take over all responsibility from Garrard Portman, who will retire when the project is concluded. He has the very stable temperament and patience for a very important job. We only hope that he will remain with us for several years.'

Mariol gave her opinion that he would not have come just to meet Astra's parents. 'You may be sure that he has quite another reason. I do not know either of them but I have my suspicions that something is afoot. He seems a nice person, and Spenser has not only known him for several years but is also impressed by him. I suggest you let the garden grow and flowers will bloom for you throughout the years.'

Edith was only partially persuaded. Astra had always been with them, except when at university or those few weeks on study tour or at the gallery, perhaps. But a permanent absence now seemed in prospect. Would he look after her as much as they had protected her? Walter was also not without concern. His only child, his lovely daughter, torn away. She had been away before. But not forever!

Hedrick and Astra indulged in another hug before Astra said that her parents would be getting anxious. They returned to the living room, Hedrick slightly bashful, Astra beaming her most appealing smile. Mariol needed no more than a glimpse to confirm her opinion and nodded knowingly at the others. She smiled her greeting at Astra, who realised that their little secret had been broadcast to the world but maintained her silence.

Hedrick grasped her hand and, with a nod of agreement from Astra, announced to an expectant audience, 'Only a few minutes ago, a transformation has happened in the fortunes of the Tarrant and Tilson families. A matter of the utmost importance has been discussed and decided. Now it can be proclaimed to all the world that,' he paused for effect, 'Astra and I are now engaged.'

Mariol beamed with pleasure and burst into applause. Spenser broke into a broad smile of support. 'We wondered what was happening,' he said.

Walter and Edith threw their doubts into the clouds and hugged their lovely daughter amid the joyful response of the others. 'Time for a celebration,' Walter announced, filling the glasses. 'Congratulations to the loveliest couple I know,' he said, but not without a sense of the loss to come.

Mariol declared that Astra had attained the highest state of being. 'May you be as happy as we are. We wish you every delight throughout all the years to come.'

Spenser felt obliged to inform Walter that he had not lost a daughter but had gained a son, at which Walter looked again at Hedrick with new light and thought he might, after all, be the ideal partner for his daughter. Edith hugged Astra with tears in her eyes. 'Be happy, my dear. You deserve it.' Whatever doubts she had had were now exchanged for great expectations.

The afternoon drew slowly to a close filled with questions of where would they live, what would Astra do now, when would they set a date? Dinner provided a brief pause to their questions and suggestions but after another pause for relaxation, Mariol reminded Spenser of the time and forbade him another drink. They made their farewells and drove off after the happiest of days for several years.

The newly engaged couple walked together to the station in order to postpone their parting for as long as possible. They waited for the train and hugged their farewell, but not without the promise to meet again soon. Hedrick waved goodbye to his fiancée sadly disappearing from sight as the train drew out of the station, already wondering how long their parting would be. He would meet Garrard next day and enjoy telling him of his engagement, but also be able to take the opportunity to thank him for his advice.

Astra walked slowly back home thinking that all had changed. She would stay with her parents for a while longer but not too long. Her future beckoned with the promise of greater times ahead than she had experienced till now. Even if her horizons were less widely defined, they were now replete with possibilities.

Among the topics that Walter and Edith were meanwhile reflecting upon was the minor one of Walter's surprise at Spenser, a man who had not mentioned his companion when they had met at the studio. He knew him to be living alone when they had met at their previous debate, but that was twenty years ago, and he concluded that there had been no reason for him to declare his change of status.

But the main subject on which they were focussing with just a little reservation at her choice was the happiness of their daughter. She was a talented girl who could have had the pick of anybody she met whereas Hedrick, polite and suitable though he may be, was not the academic type they had visualised for her. But they were encouraged by the endorsement of fulsome praise that Hedrick had received from Spenser, who had known him for years as a man of stable temperament. A good recommendation but an unexpected candidate for her affections, they thought, although they were undoubtedly on display and had been easily transmitted to Mariol, a very intelligent woman and, as an independent witness, one who lacked the bias that protective parents might feel.

'It had to happen sometime, Walter. Let us wish them every happiness.' And, remembering Mariol's words, Edith added, 'Flowers may soon be blooming.'

Chapter 25

Bamber passed the next few days with the uncomfortable prospect before him of losing his existence of several years at Softlyn, but also with the anticipation of meeting Pelham face to face. Events had taken a path that he had thought unlikely to have occurred at this stage of his plan to unmask him, but the moment had now arrived unprompted and a little earlier than he had imagined. Perhaps it was for the best, he reasoned. If it's going to happen, it might as well be now. All uncertainty would be resolved, any unpleasantness would pass away and the future be free of any distaste to come. But he allowed no dark thoughts to shadow his mind, confident that he held the trump card and could stand his ground when faced with the forthcoming challenge.

The weekend was spent in a relaxing outing with the family to the local pageant of the 'Days of Old', a celebration presented by the inhabitants of the neighbouring village in memory of centuries past. The girls enjoyed the atmosphere, flag waving, dancing, horses and traction engines, and Bamber enjoyed the fact that he was spending a day of unusual activity in the company of Lois and children, shepherding his family from one event to another.

At the museum exhibit, they were invited by an informative lady to view old photographs of nineteenth-century life, mostly of farming and crafts but also of ladies' fashions. The manager, Maddox Byrne, was also at the show and pleased to resume contact with Bamber, with whom he reminisced about their previous collaboration on security, but the girls were keen to move on to the more animated exhibits and drew him away too early. Despite that, he could experience a time of relaxation ushering them about and able to cast aside all trepidation that had arisen from the portents of the following week. For all the inventions and innovations he had contributed to the world, nothing could equal the sight of his family, no longer babes in arms but lively girls growing into maturity. They could leave the scenes that history had presented and return home with thoughts of how the society of a hundred or more years before could have changed to that of the present day and wondering whether it had always been so colourful. They decided that, however charming those lives had seemed, the wonders of the electronic age could not easily be dispensed with. Even Bamber had had a few hours of relief and felt fully prepared to face what he felt could be a difficult time at the forthcoming meeting.

Grantley told him on Tuesday that he was familiar with such meetings and did not expect this one to raise any difficulties. They would come at a later date, he assured Bamber, when the real negotiations would take place with audits, proposals, rebuttals and final agreements. Bamber knew of another cause for argument but did not mention it.

The day dawned and Pelham arrived at late morning accompanied by Angelo Sarandon, his specialist advisor and one whose analyses he valued. Grantley greeted them with welcoming smiles. Bamber looked at Pelham as they were introducing themselves and saw a confident man of business who had no hesitations at the task ahead. He offered his hand whilst holding Pelham in a steady gaze. 'Hello, Frank,' he said calmly. 'It's been a long time.'

'I'm happy to meet you again, Bamber. Yes. Twenty-five years is quite a time.'

'Do you two know each other?' Grantley gasped in surprise at this totally unexpected turn of events.

'We met at various family functions,' Bamber explained without any deeper enlightenment. They had often met, mostly on happy occasions, but their last meetings had been at the saddest of times and nobody outside their circle need know further details.

'I remember them well. Yes, mostly happy times. Very happy times,' Pelham responded, knowing that later occasions had been darker than he cared to enumerate.

'Well, we can at least start on a happy note,' Grantley said with a beaming smile. 'A good omen for our discussions,' he added with a puzzled look at Bamber and wondering why he had not already volunteered his knowing Pelham.

They settled into the generalities of business in the current political and economic climate in which both parties expressed no particular opinion either for or against the virtues of their respective countries. Pelham explained to a still slightly puzzled Grantley, and with a conspiratorial glance at Bamber, that he had moved to Italy many years before more to enjoy the Italian sunshine rather than the gloom of the British weather. Bamber nodded his silent understanding of the subterfuge. Both of them knew the real reason but that did not need disclosure. Neither had any idea of the suffering the other had experienced, having simply assumed that each had harboured only a modicum of sorrow and unaware of the painful depths of anguish buried in their hearts.

Business intervened, discussions were friendly and productive, prices were mentioned but deliberately set somewhat lower than would be agreed in a final deal to be held after further negotiation. Grantley suggested they meet that evening for a celebratory dinner, but Pelham declined on account of an early return flight and countered with the suggestion they break up for informal talks.

Grantley conducted Sarandon around the office, unaware

that he was yielding useful information to a possible bidder. Pelham sought Bamber's company in the privacy of the empty dining hall.

'I was aware of your position in Lowfield,' Pelham began in explanatory mode. 'There can't be many Bamber Stapletons with a doctorate in electronics,' he said, 'and it was easy to follow your progress, but this meeting gives us both the chance to update each other on our backgrounds.'

'I've also followed your career over the years,' Bamber replied. 'When we first became acquainted all that time ago, neither of us would have dreamed how each of our lives would have developed.'

Pelham resumed a more serious tone as he replied. 'I've experienced huge withdrawal symptoms through all those years but I have finally come to the conclusion that I have grieved long enough. I wanted to tell you about my decision to get married at last, but I hope you will not think me unfeeling. I have never forgotten Cora. She was the loveliest girl I have ever known, but she was snatched away and left both of us devastated.'

'It was an accident that you could have prevented,' Bamber replied, descending, at last, into an accusatory tone and, to Pelham's horror, added, 'It was your fault for taking her there. You let her stand too close to the edge and did nothing to stop her fall. You could have saved her, and you didn't,' he sneered.

'Is that what you have thought throughout all this time?' Pelham responded. 'Don't you think I tried? I rushed towards her but she was already falling. All I had was an uncertain grip with one hand on her coat and I couldn't hold her. She just slipped from my grasp, and it was the last time I held her,' he said with an emotional relapse into past agonies and obviously unfeigned remorse. 'But you're right,' he said as he recovered from a momentary loss of control. 'It was my fault for taking her there. I should have saved her. The fact that I failed has plagued me with self-recrimination for a lifetime. If I had been able to reach her even just one second earlier, she might still have been with us – and I have had nightmares about it ever since.'

Bamber remained silent for a few seconds. He had learned a little more about his sister's last moments. It sounded genuine but nothing would bring her back. In his accusation, he had released the anguish he had felt for years and had reached a catharsis followed by a draining of pointless rancour. 'You've had your regrets and I've had mine,' he said softly, but at least he had heard a sort of apology. Totally inadequate, of course, but something; and, on reflection, an admission that would suffice to allay his animosity. He felt that the truth had been confessed in a revelation that he could believe. His sister had died well over twenty years before and would never return to the land of the living, but he had prompted an explanation and received one that sounded plausible, however inadequate, and one that he had to accept. He could do no more.

Both remained silent for a long moment swept by thoughts of the past merging slowly into the present. Pelham saw again the scene that had so often haunted him but, now, feeling that the image of Cora was dissolving rather than falling. He became aware of Bamber's voice intruding into his reverie. 'Of course you should get married,' Bamber was telling him in unexpectedly forgiving tones. 'I did and have never regretted it,' he continued, in a sign that he had accepted the explanation.

Pelham sighed an inward sigh of relief. He felt that this was the nearest to absolution that he could have hoped for. 'Any children?' he asked.

'Yes. Two girls,' Bamber replied, reaching for his wallet and extracting a photograph of the family. 'The nine-year-old is Louisa, and the eleven-year-old is – Cora.'

Pelham gazed silently at the picture. 'Cora!' he sighed. 'A living remembrance and a near likeness.' Raising his face in a sincere reverence near to tears, he added, 'She will live again,' convincing Bamber that his sorrow was no mere charade. Perhaps it had been impossible to save her, after all.

They both spent several seconds in a silent pause of recovery, in which they remembered all that had happened, the years of regret that had followed and the reincarnation of a girl lost to the world. Pelham broke the silence and, with a difficult emergence from the past, returned to current affairs.

'Just in case you were wondering, Bamber, I know you were responsible for the mysterious disappearance of the painting. No doubt a trial of some secret weapon of yours, but I am merely the trustee of the gallery and have no interest in art, neither do I take part in its management, with the consequence that I have not been so affected by the theft as everybody else has been. But I congratulate you on achieving the theft of the century,' he said with an awkward smile, whilst Bamber remained impassive but without denial.

'My assumption is that there will be no recurrence,' he continued. 'I reason from the fact that the painting was returned undamaged, indicating no malevolent motive and that no other theft has been reported by any other gallery. The theft was also preceded by a rather amateurish telephone call that I traced from somebody in London threatening untold danger. It was easy to conclude that he must have been unfamiliar with the more sophisticated approaches I sometimes receive, and unaware that they never emanate from London. A week later he rang again and invited himself to a meeting at which I dismissed his threat as a pure fabrication, but he produced proof of his being from The Department and told me about Ballantyne. My interest was aroused immediately he mentioned Softlyn.

'I gathered from the meeting we had this morning,' he continued, 'that you are not keen on selling the company to my group, probably because you think I may get control of your invention. But I have quite other intentions. Quite confidentially, I am not interested in buying it. It would fit into my group as little as it fits into Overdale, but all I wanted was merely to create a guaranteed opportunity of seeing you and not simply to inform you of my proposed marriage but rather to receive your blessing upon it. I have been ravaged for years by thoughts of betraying Cora's memory if I were to consider another partner, but I suppose I have fallen under the spell of Italian religiosity and you would do me a huge favour, as an almost brother-in-law, to give your consent. It's too late for me to emulate you as a family man, but at least I shan't be living alone anymore.'

Bamber had another moment of transformation. Of course, he would not withhold consent or a blessing and expressed himself accordingly when he confessed that he had held to the wrong opinion of him all this time and wished him a happy marriage. 'You won't regret it, Frank,' he added, addressing him by his first name for only the second time that morning.

'You are correct in your deductions. I have no cause to use my creation now that I understand you and your remorse. Your explanation sets everything in a new light that tells me that I've held to the wrong opinion for years. I'll transfer all my specifications to official custody, now, and go back to business without the distraction of plotting for your exposure.'

'And I'll reveal to the authorities, if asked,' Frank responded, 'my written acceptance to The Department for them to spirit the painting away from the gallery in order to test its security, but subsequently to return the painting undamaged. Laura kept me informed of proceedings but I was, nonetheless, unaware of the commotion that its absence had caused. Living in Italy and having no interest in the gallery, I concentrated on business confident that it would be returned as agreed. But I must admit that I had not realised the impact that the disappearance would have had on the gallery. Unfortunately, The Department had insisted that my acceptance also include the proviso that the parties would adopt a strict non-disclosure policy.'

Bamber merely nodded at the explanation, somewhat relieved that his participation need never be revealed. Neither he nor Frank would be implicated and The Department would bear all responsibility. They rose from the table to re-join the others in Grantley's office.

'Here they are, at last,' Grantley beamed, assuming that business had been thoroughly and persuasively discussed. 'I hope you have ascertained all you need to know, Mr Pelham. Your colleague and I have had a most interesting conversation and we hope to enter into plenary talks in the near future.'

'Yes. We have had a very detailed discussion and come to a clear understanding on our future action,' Pelham replied. 'Old times, future collaboration and business relationships.'

'Excellent,' Grantley responded. 'We shall be in touch again, shortly, I hope.'

'We shall each consider the matter in the privacy of our respective offices and contact each other in due course,' Pelham replied. 'But I think time is drawing on and we have a rather long journey to complete – Gatwick, you know. We'd better start now. Thank you for the opportunity you have presented for preliminary discussions, but we must take our leave.'

They called the driver and moved to the car where farewells were taken before they parted with expressions of goodwill on both sides. The car drew away, Frank feeling that he had left his burden behind and Bamber converting thoughts of revenge into good intentions.

'Well!' Grantley beamed as he and Bamber returned to his office. 'That could hardly have gone better. Pelham has a very good reputation and it seems that you had a profitable talk. Did you detect any doubts or hesitations on his part?'

'A slightly awkward start on both sides, but we were soon able to gain confidence in the other. I think the outcome will be most satisfactory.'

'Well done. He will be in touch again, soon, and no doubt with an interesting proposal.'

Bamber felt a mixture of relief, deflation and weariness at the conclusion of an episode that had scarred his life over more than twenty years. The dedication that he had shown to his Ballantyne project would now be laid aside and his energies turned to other developments. 'He said he would consider the matter, but I wonder what "in due course" means,' he replied.

'He will investigate, plan and prepare for another session within a month,' Grantley replied knowingly. 'He seems keen on the acquisition,' he continued with a self-satisfied smile.

'We can only wait for his proposal,' Bamber responded, knowing precisely what it would be, but without admitting that he knew already. 'But the excitement is over for now. I'm going back to routine.'

But it was not routine to which he returned. He felt drained. The strain he had expected from a confrontation with Pelham had been short lived but he felt empty. He had no inner fury any longer, his invention would not be used in anger and probably not be marketed at all. He felt that he had done his duty towards Cora as he had seen it over the years. That had now closed, but while thinking of his sister, his thoughts turned to his daughter and the role that her picture had played in revealing Pelham's true feelings in his assurance that he was as regretful as himself. 'Cora would live again,' Pelham had said. 'Yes', Bamber had agreed. 'She would live on in her younger self and become an even greater joy than she is already.'

He returned to the familiarity of his office where he found a comforting silence and time to think. The future was clearer, he was no longer oppressed by thoughts of how and where to deploy Ballantyne. On the contrary, he now had a view of the path ahead even if one that led to unknown territory, but that was a land that would open to new vistas where he could devote his energies without the diversions that had, hitherto, cast such a blight on his mind.

On consideration, he felt that Frank had proved to be a man not dissimilar to him, one who had retained and treasured the memory of Cora and who had been haunted by a feeling of guilt for twenty-five years but one who had lived alone that whole time in which he had turned his energies to business probably as a penance and in order to drive his demons away. He, Bamber, in contrast, had been driven by thoughts of revenge. He had not suffered the depths of misery that Frank had evidently endured but neither had he forgotten his sister throughout that time. He had married and they had been blessed with two children both of whom had become a delight but also one who, by merely existing, had unknowingly proved a salvation for both Frank and himself.

With those thoughts of family, he turned to the future and how he would follow the path that had been set before him into the enlightenment that had now opened. He wondered how to contact that mysterious Fenton, who appeared to have some sort of official status but had never been keen to reveal much detail of his whereabouts. Railton would know. They seemed to know everybody. They might even prove useful in directing his next move.

The afternoon wore on as Bamber tried to think through his options: do nothing and wait for another buyer to arrive, but one who would probably be keen for a bargain; resign from the company and retire, but he was too young for that;

start another company, but that would mean losing all his development so far; offer Grantley a buyout possibility, but that would entail a huge investment with borrowed money. He was already half persuaded to consult Railton in order to contact Fenton. He ought to do something, but what?

He was tempted to let fortune lead him through the labyrinth, but knew that lack of decisiveness would merely cause the wind to blow him first one way and then another, neither would walking up and down in thought be of assistance. Railton had the sort of experience he needed and would be glad of another contract, after free initial consultation, of course.

He reached for the telephone.

Chapter 26

Hector and Bentley had returned to the office after the holidays only to endure rather than to enjoy the inactivity with which they were presented. Time dragged out its weary way until an early end of the day could impose a welcome interruption.

On the Wednesday on which Pelham was deep in negotiations with Grantley, Hector wandered into Bentley's office and seated himself opposite his colleague who was in a similar meditative mood. Bentley sighed at the lack of any interruption to the somnolence of the day. 'You said that business would pick up after the holidays, Hector, but I'm wondering, now, whether there is anybody out there who has an entrepreneurial spirit that would prompt us into action.'

'So am I,' Hector responded. 'Business has never had this long a pause in the whole of our glorious history. What are people doing if they aren't plotting takeovers or restructuring their companies?'

Before Bentley could reply, they were startled to hear Hector's telephone ring in the adjacent office who, with a glance of wonder at Bentley, rushed in to answer the call. He switched on the speaker for both to listen. Bamber's steady voice enquired whether he could come next day in order to update him on that day's encounter with Pelham. The partners were eager to hear the news, particularly if it were to announce some welcome activity at last. They could look forward to the morning with more than a little excitement.

Bamber arrived with a more cooperative intention than that he had had on the previous occasion, and was greeted by the partners with handshakes and an eager welcome. He took the proffered seat and told them that the meeting had gone according to schedule and in a good spirit that promised future cooperation. 'Grantley was in his element assuring me that he was confident of a happy outcome.'

The partners greeted his words with smiles of satisfaction. 'But are *you* assured of a happy outcome?' Hector asked.

'I had expected a quite different approach from the one that Pelham adopted, but he was pure reasonableness. We agreed a mutually acceptable procedure which would preserve the group in its existing entirety. Softlyn will remain in the group and Pelham have no managerial authority within it.'

The partners were somewhat confused at this explanation of business diplomacy. 'But Pelham wanted to launch a takeover of Softlyn. Are you saying that he has adopted some other course?' Bentley asked, thinking that the target had now become the group as a whole.

'Yes. He told me expressly that he had no interest in any part of the group.'

'So why is Grantley confident of a happy outcome?' Hector asked. 'Somebody must have spoken extremely persuasively to dissuade a man like Pelham to give up so quickly.'

'Grantley is happy because he expects an offer within a month,' Bamber continued to the puzzlement of his listeners who were finding difficulty in reconciling what seemed to be totally conflicting statements.

'You said that Pelham has withdrawn his interest in both the company and the group and yet Grantley is awaiting some sort of offer within a month. That seems a curious contradiction.'

'Grantley does not know what I know,' Bamber said in an echo of Bentley's words of the previous week. 'Pelham and I have reached an agreement on the deployment of Ballantyne. I will not use it against Coral and he will not bid for the company. Grantley does not even know that Ballantyne exists, and conscious of Fenton's cautionary words, I do not want to tell him about it. I expect Pelham to write soon in order to inform him that, upon further consideration, he no longer has any interest in his former proposal.'

'This is all very enlightening. I wonder how Grantley will react when he receives the verdict,' Bentley commented. 'My guess is that he will be furious at the sudden withdrawal of interest but, then, will actively seek a purchaser from the wider market.'

'Quite likely! That is why I have been thinking of the services you mentioned at our last meeting. I have a minority investment in the company originating from the days when I operated it as a start-up venture. I wonder whether you could suggest an affordable means for me to acquire the whole.'

The partners were once more alert to the unexpected return to business. 'Once the deal is complete, you could surrender your intellectual property in Ballantyne to The Department. Fenton would, no doubt, be delighted to negotiate a purchase,' Bentley suggested.

'That offers a good solution,' Bamber replied. 'Please proceed on my behalf but the deal must, presumably, be big enough to match or exceed the prices mentioned by Pelham at the meeting. But there is, also, another little deal you would need to oversee in parallel,' he continued, tentatively, to the sudden curiosity of the partners.

'As you know, Fenton authorised the security test at the Pelham Gallery and subsequently provided the access team that enabled me to prove the efficacy of Ballantyne and led to the biggest art scoop of the century. But, as agreed, they returned the Old Master unhandled and undamaged within a few months. Fenton was delighted at the success even if it sent the art world into turmoil. I previously told you that my intention was to warn Pelham that further intrusions were probable, but before I could even broach the subject in our meeting, yesterday, Pelham made a highly persuasive revelation of a personal nature that persuaded me not to pursue that course. Furthermore, as main trustee of the gallery, he has assured me that he had provided written permission to conduct the test of the gallery security. I am fairly sure that he has given that authority to Fenton, but I ask you, now, to ensure that he has.'

'But the crimes of entry and theft are matters for which he would lack the capacity of absolution. They would become a matter for officials to investigate and it would be they who would determine the consequence,' Bentley responded.

'That is why I seek your assistance. Pelham is based in Italy and takes no interest in the gallery. He delegates everything to the board whilst he spends all his time managing a big industrial group and could quite plausibly claim that he was merely assessing the competence of his gallery managers by testing their security.'

'I suppose it could be argued that he lived in an entirely different world. We recently spent a holiday in Bologna and met him almost by chance,' Hector intervened. 'His neighbours are all from backgrounds similar to his, I believe, and he has few outside interests other than competing with them for having a better garden. But being entirely ignorant of the event seems hardly likely if he has commissioned it.'

'Approaching Grantley with an offer to buy Softlyn also suggests prior contact or, at least, knowing the effectiveness of Ballantyne and a desire to remove the threat to his business,' Bentley contributed.

'He had no contact with me until yesterday, though,' Bamber reminded them. 'We split into pairs in order to talk about details, but he revealed to me that he had no interest in purchasing the company or the group.'

The partners experienced another unexpected twist to this ever more bizarre situation. 'That's an astonishing admission,'

Hector expostulated. 'Why has he undertaken negotiations to buy the company if he doesn't want it?'

'I told you before that I knew Pelham from the old days. We met fairly often when he was engaged to my sister but she was killed in an accident twenty-five years ago and a few years later he moved to Italy, presumably in order to bury his woes in building a business. He has remained single ever since but he now wants to marry somebody else and wanted my blessing on his decision.'

'I hope you gave it,' Bentley responded. 'But it's an extraordinarily expensive way to ask for your blessing.'

'We haven't met since he emigrated, and our relationship was not cordial before that. He couldn't just telephone me out of the blue on such a personal matter and his proposal ensured that he would be able to meet me face to face. But he also wanted to admit that he had prior knowledge about the gallery theft. His manner was very convincing and he knew that it was a Softlyn product. It was obviously Fenton who told him. He was complicit in the successful attempt on the museum and was undoubtedly the source of the telephone call to Pelham.'

'We have only Pelham's version of the call,' Hector contributed. 'He also said that Fenton had contacted him, later, in order to gain authority for a field test on the gallery.'

'But why would he consent to a raid just because he was contacted by a stranger on the telephone?' Bamber asked.

Only a short silence was required for Hector to divine the reason for Pelham's consent to the art theft as well as to the relevance of his visit to Bamber. 'He consented because he wanted to know whether Ballantyne was as effective as you have claimed. After the museum and gallery raids had revealed his vulnerability, he adopted any policy, regardless of the cost, to call a truce with you.'

'Of course! That's it,' Bamber exclaimed. 'He probably thought that I would have rejected every approach from him, but one to take over the company would have compelled a meeting, especially when group management favoured a deal. He wanted my blessing on his forthcoming marriage and a chance to absolve himself from my sister's death.' After the slightest of pauses, he added with a slight note of admiration, 'He also knows how to divert a threat,' before continuing, 'But, now that it's all over, I can only say that I'm glad that he took that initiative that has laid twenty years of antagonism to rest.

'Fenton would probably have been given his telephone number by the Skelton Museum. It has no connection to the gallery but they were funded in the early days by Lewis Pelham. Their manager, Maddox Byrne, may have known Frank's number and given it to Fenton when they were negotiating the Ballantyne test on the museum. I was keen for the gallery to be the target of a surprise field test and Fenton could have opened discussions about it with Frank. It's a pity I didn't need to know at the weekend. Maddox was active on the local pageant that we visited then. I could contact him to ask about security and work in a question about Pelham.'

'All right. Meanwhile, we can think of an approach to Fenton and whether he could arrange a deal. If so, we can then negotiate with Grantley.'

Whilst the deliberations on how to approach Grantley were proceeding, Fenton was engaged in a revue with Harold Westcott, a colleague working with him on the money-laundering project. A first-floor window of an office block several miles away from the Railton office flashed sunlight to the outside world of Hyde Park as Harold closed the opening to dull the noise of traffic outside.

'"*Once more, we stop the mighty roar of London's traffic*",' he quoted from his father's recollection of an old radio programme, and turned to Fenton in order to continue their information exchange, he on his money-laundering investigation, Fenton on his security project.

Their monthly conference discussing their progress, or, more often, lack of progress, seemed to be emulating those of all prior months. Harold expressed the thought that they were both in jobs that guaranteed their turning grey with frustration if no achievements could be registered. 'We are not making much progress on pinning down the driving force behind the biggest laundering activity of the century,' he sighed. 'Not surprisingly, top brass are enquiring and getting more than a little impatient upon discovering that we have very little to show for our efforts. We'll have to scrape up some information, somehow, or we'll be branded as complete amateurs.'

At risk of telling Harold how to do his job, Fenton could, at least, tell him that bank transfers would be the only way to move money in large scale from one jurisdiction to another. 'It could then be used in property purchase,' he continued, 'but that would be exchanging a liquid asset for an immobile one. A better use would be either a loan to a company for the purpose of supplying capital for a proposed investment project or, better still, actually purchasing the share capital and thereby retaining an investment which could be acquired by a competitor with clean funds. That could then be transferred legitimately to the final destination or into another investment that would repeat the process.'

Harold's reaction was simply one of a rather dismissive grunt that he knew all that but was somewhat daunted at the thought that there were millions of financial transactions completed every day. He merely replied a little sarcastically that Fenton would have no problem in finalising his task if he could only intercept a sufficiently large transaction and subvert it to acquiring whatever equipment he required in order to protect the realm.

Fenton was similarly frustrated at the pace of movement on his security project. 'But I would need the money first in order to acquire the equipment. I've made a little progress but it's proving a slow bicycle race. Tiny clues, tiny advances, but, at least, the wheels are turning at last. The great art robbery has created an explosion of attention and no doubt warned any criminals about that we are after them. I'm hoping that it will lead them to a rash move that will reveal their presence at some time; but we need to get hold of the Softlyn equipment, anyway, just in case it might be turned against us.'

'We need a rash move, too. We know the culprits, but interrupting their operations is another matter. That equipment would come in useful for us if only we, that is you, could use it to gain access to their offices.'

'Yes. Ballantyne offers great prospects for the future. All we need to do is to acquire sole use of it,' Fenton replied in defence. 'If our ugly customers get hold of it, we'll be well and truly sunk.'

'You'll have to see the top man, if it's that crucial. Just make sure that Ballantyne is kept secure in the meantime.'

Fenton left the meeting feeling that his margin of safety was extremely thin. Pelham might still commission an entry of his own and remove the equipment, but Stapleton would still have the knowledge to rebuild and exploit it. Meanwhile, he was powerless to ensure the security of the equipment. The thought struck him that he should commission another entry by the Special Operations team in order to safeguard whatever equipment existed. He had done it once and he could do it again, but he thought it was too soon to broach the matter of purchasing Softlyn because he would need to make a persuasive case complete with figures and he had none yet.

The refectory area offered a welcome break as he sat with an afternoon tea in order to bury himself in his notes and to think of the next step. Somebody took a seat opposite him.

'Hello,' the woman said as he raised his eyes to focus on a very familiar face. 'I hadn't expected to see you here,' she continued.

Fenton overcame his astonishment to ask, 'Jessica! What on earth are you doing here?'

'I joined the Newcastle office about two years ago and I'm down here to update a computer program,' she told him, proudly displaying her identity card. 'My new skill. Before that, I worked as a hospital secretary and then enrolled in a class to become an expert in something. I'm the office expert in transmissions, now.'

'Congratulations! I'm still the same old donkey plodding along, but sometimes, I reach a solution that has defeated everybody else.'

'I've installed the update and now I'm waiting for the train. It's not booked until five thirty, so I'm just passing the time until then.'

'I assume you are living in your mother's house, now.'

'Yes. It's one of those solidly built *Homes for Heroes* erected after the First World War. My parents bought it in the fifties. It's too big for me, really, but it's where I grew up, so I ought to keep it, I suppose.'

'Happy?' he ventured.

'Oh, yes. Of course. Old memories, but all the residents have changed. And you?' she asked in her turn.

'Yes. Of course,' he replied with equal pretence. 'The house is a bit smaller but easier to care for. I even do a bit of gardening. Getting old, obviously,' he joked.

'Any girlfriends?'

'You should know that,' he said more in submission than defiance. 'You left and, now, nobody wants me,' he replied with his habitual dark humour and exaggerated modesty.

Jessica recognised a glimmer of the injustice she had done him, knowing that he had acted very decently towards her, but she disguised her remorse in a regretful smile of appreciation. She temporised for a moment by checking the timetable for the train, wondering how long it would take for her to reach the station and whether she could extend this unexpected meeting. No delays were reported but, with a sudden groan of feigned disappointment, she exclaimed, 'It's been cancelled! The next one is 8.30. That means after midnight arrival. I'll have to book a hotel and travel tomorrow.'

'There's a small hotel round the corner,' Fenton told her helpfully and, had he known, a little to her disappointment. But after a short hesitation, he added, 'Or, you could stay at my place if you like. Cuisine included.'

'Well! If it's no trouble,' she replied wondering whether he had divined her pretence. 'I'd like to see the new residence.'

The suburban train brought them to a modest area of neat bungalows that Jessica admired as they walked the short distance from the station. 'Looks a nice area,' she commented.

'Fortunately, the natives are friendly and most are retired. I quite like it here. Nobody interferes. In fact, I hardly ever see anybody about.'

He took out his key and ushered her in. 'It's a lot smaller than the old house. Two bedrooms and a spare room that I use as a study,' he told her as he showed her into the smaller bedroom where she left her luggage before joining him in the kitchen. He was anxiously examining the contents of the fridge. 'I should have bought something at the local shop,' he told her. 'I'm a bit short on rations, I'm afraid.'

'Let me have a look,' she insisted. 'There's enough for one meal. Stand aside and I'll be hostess instead of you,' she told him, happily seeking an opportunity to resume their old relationship.

'I can at least bring a bottle of wine to the celebration,' he responded.

From that slight setback and recovery, they managed a joyful conversation in which they updated themselves on their lost years. She told a few anecdotes and he filled in a little background of his recent exploits to which she, unwilling to demand more depth from his habitual generalities, listened attentively. Afterwards, they flicked through National Trust magazines after having selected some music, both thinking that life had not changed from the old days but that they had not been so bad after all. 'The embodiment of politeness,' she thought. 'If only he were not so private.'

Fenton lay in bed thinking how strange it was that, after years of silence, his long-term partner had become a colleague and, now, was in the adjoining room. He lay back idly thinking through a confusion of thoughts about his projects: whether he could assist Harold, what priority he should give to Ballantyne, when Jessica would have to leave and whether he should say goodbye at the local station as she left or accompany her to the main line station, and what else he would do to fill the days until the weekend.

He heard the bedroom door open cautiously and Jessica entering to take a few steps before slipping in beside him. 'I didn't unpack my pyjamas,' she explained, 'and it's a bit cold without them.'

'I'm glad you didn't ask for my spare ones,' he responded as he placed a warming arm around her, having quickly matched her in the state that nature had provided.

'I shan't have to leave until Sunday,' she told him later.

'Which one?' he responded.

Chapter 27

Marcus had viewed the television transmission with a little trepidation at how he could satisfy the inevitable pressure for a declaration of the gallery's involvement in the crime of the century. He was bound to come under scrutiny and to be criticised either for knowing nothing about what had now been revealed as a government initiative or for deliberately hiding the facts from the public. He called a board meeting for Tuesday but not before he had fielded several calls from the press for an announcement.

The board had all viewed the transmission and gathered at the appointed hour, each expressing their ignorance of and surprise at the revelations. Marcus announced that he had scheduled a press briefing for the following morning only to be pressured by the board about what warning he had received of the operation.

'Surely, you must have had some inkling of what had been planned.'

'What possible defence can we mount against what will be an unconstrained attack by the press.'

'We will be pilloried unmercifully by a pack of wolves.'

'They will be snapping at our heels and demanding resignations.'

Marcus quailed under the onslaught of his own team, in addition to fearing that the press would not have the slightest leniency. He wished he were somewhere else, but his notions of duty compelled him to stay bravely at his post and face the fire that was sure to be directed at him.

Laura announced that she had contacted her brother for comment and been informed that he had been notified of the test but had been bound by a non-disclosure agreement and had, in any case, been unaware of the turmoil that was raging about the matter far apart from his regular occupation.

Marcus felt a tiny gem of an argument he could adduce in the defence of himself and the gallery as a whole.

Next day, the press waited with expressions of delight at the slaughter they would be able to unleash. They had seldom had such a cause célèbre that was so suited for them to express their venom at a defenceless object of scorn and a pompous bureaucrat well known as an official of little achievement promoted to a sinecure for life. The knives were out and teeth were bared.

Members of the board entered the room stony faced and with no expectation of an easy passage. Marcus gave a few words of welcome to the press. 'May I welcome you once again to hear the latest report on the disappearance of the del Mano and,' he added with a faint smile, 'to the happy news of its recovery.' His remarks were received with total silence, which was reassuring but also disconcerting. They were gathering for the kill, he realised. 'You will all have learned from the television broadcast in which,' inclining a hand towards Spenser, 'our very knowledgeable art director participated, that the whole incident was one planned as a security test. You will also be aware that the test was not merely completely successful, but was an illustration of how a government agency can act with great capability in undertaking the task, and, therefore, a performance that brings a sense of comfort to us all.'

Spenser noted that he had been cited as a participant in the broadcast but sensed that that was merely yet another attempt to move the focus even for one brief moment from Marcus to himself.

Marcus continued with a short resume of the events so far

and the board's denial of any prior knowledge of the removal, only to be interrupted by cries of derision. 'Our readers will find that most improbable,' and 'The public will suspect a cover up,' and 'Poor management supervision.' Marcus blanched at the first salvoes but carried on as best he may.

'We had no prior warning. The whole incident was conducted without our knowledge or even awareness, we were not consulted and we were confident that our security system was functioning perfectly.'

'Not perfectly enough, though,' was the inevitable response.

'Aren't you aware that your systems proved inadequate for the protection you need?'

'Do you contend that management has been totally without fault?'

Marcus replied that management had undertaken a thorough review of security and they were in the process of protecting all displays with the most effective glazing and, in addition, had increased security patrols.

'Why did the main trustee not inform you of the government approach to him?'

'Did you not think of enquiring about it?'

Marcus was trying unsuccessfully to hide his increasing desperation at his predicament, but all members of the board had become increasingly annoyed at the unjustifiable accusations being levelled against his attempt at elucidation. Laura stood up, causing a momentary pause in the hostility. She introduced herself as the liaison officer between the board and the main trustee. 'May I ask you to consider the facts rather than to make unfounded accusations aimed at the chairman?' she said in a voice of authority that would brook no attempt at interruption. 'I undertook to inform my brother that our most treasured painting had been stolen. He expressed his concern, of course, but imparted no information about the theft. I have also told him of the painting's safe return. You may know that he lives in Italy and manages a large international engineering group rather than concern himself with the gallery. He delegates much of the work to his senior managers but is nonetheless a busy man. In his permanent absence and residence abroad he relies on the board to exercise control, but I have spoken to him several times in order to update him.

'I would remind you,' she continued in a voice of forbidding forcefulness, 'that we called in the Art Squad as soon as we were sure that the painting had been taken. The fact that they have not been able to identify the culprit tells you that even the keenest minds have been unable to detect the method of removal or who may have been responsible. I suggest that you now direct your questions to the government agency concerned – if you can identify them,' she taunted, resuming her seat amid the appreciative regard of her colleagues and a momentary abashed silence from the press.

'Can you tell us whether the painting was switched by gallery staff before the discovery of the exchange?' one of them had the temerity to ask.

Spenser had suffered more over the months than his colleagues and now stood up, attempting to conceal his rage at the question. 'That is a most insulting and provocative assumption,' he replied, bristling with a barely controlled indignation. 'I have held that painting in high regard ever since my first encounter with it many years ago. We have cared for it and guarded it for decades with the utmost devotion. You may be sure that the switch was not carried out by any of our staff and that they have been given no authorisation to do so, and I have certainly not done so,' he fumed. 'The removal was carried out by a government agency of which you must all now be well aware. Aspersions on any of our staff are beyond contempt. The del Mano is a great work of art, an Old Master, for which it is the duty of all of us to treat accordingly and not the sort of trashy article you can dash off in half an hour.'

Spenser resumed his seat as Marcus stood up, after having been granted a short interval of recovery in which he had regained a little of his old confidence. 'I think we have responded fully to your penetrating questions,' he said calmly. 'I shall be at your service at a later time if circumstances arise. In summary, I reiterate that security has been enhanced although the method of removal remains unknown to us. The painting has been returned undamaged and is again on display. Now, I wish you all good day. Thank you for attending what I hope has been a revealing meeting for you all.'

The press murmured among themselves as they left the building.

'Revealing! Nonsense.'

'Trashy articles! How dare he?'

'And we the guardians of the public.'

'It sounds like the end of the story unless we can identify the government agency.'

'Or fly to Italy and interview the main trustee.'

'Who is he, anyway?'

Marcus buttonholed both Laura and Spenser in order to thank them for rescuing him from a difficult position. 'I have had much experience with similar contentious meetings,' he assured them with a confidence that had been restored as quickly as the press had left. 'I could have held them off a while longer, but your assistance was most helpful; although I find it judicious to handle such impertinent questions more wisely, Spenser.'

Spenser felt his distaste for Marcus growing, but he managed a more politic, 'Thank you for that advice, Marcus. We can all benefit from better wisdom.'

Laura followed him to his office. 'You told those ignorant,

little people what we all wished to say, and we'll be forever supportive of you.'

Spenser gave her a trace of a smile at hearing kind words, kindly meant, but he wished he were at home again and holding Mariol, once more, in his arms; a saviour in his affliction. 'I'm getting very fatigued with the whole business, Laura. Thank goodness our holiday is not far off.'

Laura could see how distressed he had become at the worry he had experienced over the months and now at the unrestrained accusations of the press. She rang Frank and reported the proceedings to him and how heartbroken she thought Spenser to be. Frank was as receptive as ever and replied that he had a nagging conscience at having not informed them of all he knew. Even that gloss was being untruthful to his own sister, he thought. But he was about to marry Rosa and wished to dismiss the whole affair from his mind. It was he who was at fault but he had felt compelled to assess the effectiveness of Ballantyne before it could be used in anger against his own business. 'We can all meet at the wedding. Bring the children as well,' he ended on a lighter note.

Spenser had left for home soon after Laura had left his office. He knew he was a wreck, a shadow of his former self, but was glad that he had spoken up as he had. That afforded some consolation and he could not care whether they had been offended. He had been even more incensed than they and, in addition, had suffered several months of trauma whereas they had treated the calamity as an opportunity to taunt everybody with the licence of ink.

As he entered the house, Mariol rushed to him concerned that his early return indicated that he was unwell. She noted how drawn was his expression and suspected the worst. 'Spenser, you're very early. Is anything wrong?'

He hugged her, feeling safe once more with the only person

who understood him. 'We had a very difficult meeting with those newspaper people who posed nothing but insulting questions. Marcus was true to form as well, blaming me for everything. I'm finished with the gallery. Nobody cares about me,' he told her, feeling utterly dejected.

Mariol was horrified at his decision. The gallery was his life but she knew how deeply he had suffered. 'I care hugely about you, Spenser,' she told him in her most sympathetic tones and to his relief that he was home with her again. 'You have been under a lot of strain recently, but, together, we shall get through it all. Let's talk about it upstairs and you can regain a bit of your old confidence.'

Spenser was almost in tears of gratitude as he allowed himself to be helped upstairs and to relax in bed with his closest companion in the warmth of her embrace. She had known Spenser for fifteen years. Too short a time, but he had aged visibly over recent weeks and, now, she was alarmed. She wanted more than another fifteen years with him and held him as if he were a baby. He was a very sensitive being despite his sometimes forbidding outward demeanour to others, but she had never known him like this before, broken and downcast as if having suffered a serious illness. The prospect of losing him forever loomed in her mind. 'You're safe from all those Lilliputians, Spenser,' she told him softly. 'I'm here with you and we shall always be together.'

Spenser relaxed in the warmth and safety of her arms wondering how he could ever have managed without her. She was still with him when he awoke one hour later. He felt refreshed and so glad that he had met her. He remembered how they had sat at the café table and discovered each other's story, he the art director of an important provincial gallery and she professor of literature at the university. They had spent the remaining days of the holiday together touring and viewing the sights, a honeymoon before the feast. Shortly after the fearful day of parting had arrived, she had followed him home when the semester had ended and found an interest in teaching local students. They had both spent years alone having accepted what appeared to be their destiny, but a casual meeting in the crowd and a single conversation had ensured that they would never part.

Mariol had never before seen him so distressed and, fearing that he would be taken from her, shuddered at the contemplation of a future without him. Her childhood memories had flown so far away and she had neither lit a candle nor breathed the smell of incense throughout those many years. Now, in the depths of despair, she recollected those days of innocence from which, in adulthood, she had drifted away and, finally, against all expectations, had found a harbour of love and tranquillity in Spenser. She pleaded in her anguish, 'Dear God, keep him with me. Give us both more happy years.'

Hector had also welcomed a call from Bamber after the television transmission and made an appointment for the following day. They spent their first minutes reflecting upon the programme that had communicated just enough to satisfy the general public but, with the slightest amusement, they agreed that the investigators would, no doubt, express a sense of outrage at having been fooled by their own government.

Bamber confirmed that Maddox had given Pelham's contact number to Fenton, at which Hector responded, 'So, he was the main instrument in the negotiations. We shall have to ask him to placate the Art Squad, but it doesn't speak well of their capabilities; their outrage should be turned on themselves. I suppose they will claim that they flushed out the culprit even if Fenton were to give them the real story, but he will probably keep that a closely guarded secret.'

'You still have to give Grantley a decision whether to undertake sale of my business. I'd rather you acted for me, though, so that I can become independent and not be constantly in danger of being sold off without warning.'

'You won't have the capital for innovation in electronics. That's an industry that changes rapidly and leaves the old technology far behind,' Hector advised him. 'With adequate funds that we could negotiate, you could buy the group portion and, shortly after, sell Ballantyne to the government in order to redeem the loan.'

'Could you negotiate with the government, though?'

'I'll contact Fenton. He has already organised two successful field tests, which shows interest and indicates a good chance of reaching a deal.'

Jessica had told Fenton that the office would be asking embarrassing questions if she did not reappear on the Monday, since she had already reported completion of her task on schedule. She had left before midday and he had returned disconsolate and alone with the television programme to watch in the evening as his only entertainment. Jessica did not seem to harbour any thoughts of the sort of dreariness he supposed she must have felt before she had gone back to mother; but he had no hope of seeing her again – unless he could persuade her otherwise.

He was gratified at receiving a call from Hector on Tuesday afternoon with a request for him to come to his office to discuss the broadcast and the next steps, whatever they may be. That would be a diversion for him that he sensed may lead to progress in the Ballantyne project.

They both agreed that the programme had provided a convincing explanation for the mystery of the painting's removal, but also, that it would not satisfy the investigators, who would be far from convinced that it had all been a test of security. Their injured pride would more likely cause them to create the accusation that a gigantic publicity stunt had been staged in order to attract visitors to the gallery.

'That would certainly be an embarrassment for the board, but we can hardly intervene to explain that it was a test of vital national importance,' Hector contributed and Fenton concurred. He was not engaged in a business that could reveal its affairs to outsiders.

Hector relayed the news that Bamber had now realised how earnest Grantley was in selling Softlyn, but was anxious about it being absorbed into yet another group, possibly without him. That would also mean that any chance of Fenton acquiring Ballantyne would probably become very slim indeed. 'I have made a suggestion that he could buy the group holding with a loan that we could negotiate, but it would have to be one of very short duration. The possibility of him selling all rights in Ballantyne to an interested buyer in order to liquidate the loan could then become compelling. Obviously, he would prefer his creation not to fall into the wrong hands, but with a large loan hanging over him, he may be tempted to take any offer.'

'I see,' Fenton responded. 'But if I were to approach the Treasury, I'm quite sure that I would meet with a rebuttal. At first, anyway. I could argue that it was of vital importance to defence, but they are very skilled at declining to spend money on possibilities rather than certainties.'

'I shall have to tell Grantley whether we can act for him in the sale,' Hector told him. 'He has already had talks with one group that has expressed interest in the company. He tells me that he expects an offer by month end. Two weeks. You will have to act quickly if you don't want to lose out.'

Fenton left with a rough cost estimate from Hector and sought an interview with his superior, Burnley Hebton, in order to report that he had achieved a little progress in his pursuit of the international band that he was investigating. The response was approving, even if not overwhelmingly positive, but Fenton, remembering Hector's two-week deadline, felt under pressure. He suggested they call in Jessica Turner from the Newcastle office, who had knowledge in that sort of area and had recently acted successfully for them. Burnley considered for a moment whether she could undertake another assignment, but then agreed to ask Newcastle for a short secondment.

The Art Squad had also viewed the broadcast and were understandably shocked and annoyed at the disclosure of confidential information. Inspector Yardley had contacted Marcus next day in order to ascertain whether he had had prior notice of the news that a government agency had undertaken the switch, but he had responded that he was totally unaware of their involvement. Yardley was furious at the disclosure but also at his own inability to have found the perpetrator and that the squad was now confronted with a blank wall of secrecy from their own government.

He attempted to bite back his frustration that, despite all attempts to solve the case, they had come to no satisfactory conclusion before further investigation had been curtailed. Sergeant Forbes was also annoyed but sought to identify the real cause of their discontent as government perfidy. 'We haven't come to a solution because we were deliberately hindered at every turn by the net of secrecy thrown over the case by The Department.'

Yardley grasped the explanation with great eagerness. 'Of course! That's it. Defeated by our own authorities! They could have informed us of their involvement, but The Department is one that never reveals its motives.'

They had been infuriated at their own failure to identify

the culprit, but if others were to say incompetence, they could now take refuge in the thought that they had been enmeshed in the tangles of deception so beloved of the higher echelons of government.

Chapter 28

Fenton greeted Jessica at the station when she arrived on Saturday. 'What's it all about?' she asked. 'I hear it's very confidential; like everything else, I suppose.'

'So confidential that no details can be disclosed to anyone,' he responded.

'Not even to me? They said it was an enquiry into a secret weapon.'

'It is not so much a weapon, more a secret surveillance tool. You will be at the centre of the action, though, and we'll work closely together.'

'I thought you would have a hidden motive,' she smiled, knowingly. 'I'll have to reveal everything to you, I suppose.'

'We shall have to be totally open to each other.'

'I'm looking forward to my induction,' she concluded.

They spent the day in an update on the importance of Ballantyne to The Department's investigation of the suspicious currency transfers and the relevance of it to her current assignment with him.

'We need that device in order to gain sight of data currently inaccessible to us. We have field tested it successfully on two occasions and we want to acquire it before it slips totally out of our control. You may have heard the furore of the disappearing Old Master,' he continued. 'The main trustee of the gallery lives in Italy, a convenient distance from any disturbance that might have arisen, but I sought his permission for us to make a field test of security equipment at his gallery. He was very reluctant, at first, but I flew out to discuss the matter and to assure him that I was a genuine representative of The

Department. He quite understandably refused to participate until I informed him that it was Softlyn that had successfully tested the equipment on a local museum at the mention of which he told me that that company was part of a group he had only recently failed to acquire in a takeover offer. He seemed particularly interested in the company and agreed to a test of their equipment. I got the impression that he had some undisclosed motive but I thought it best not to enquire too deeply. We have our secrets and he has his.

'The trustee wanted to acquire Softlyn, presumably because he suspected the effectiveness of Ballantyne, and the group MD wants to sell the company because it does not fit in to the group's area of expertise. That could mean losing Ballantyne possibly to a party unfriendly to us or, at least, depriving us of its use; and we are desperate to use it in our struggle to find out more on the international currency launderers we are chasing.'

'So what do you want me to do?'

'If only we could get hold of the equipment and the instructions for use, we would be able to achieve a huge improvement in our effectiveness against the lawbreakers, but that will not be your job. That will be for you to write a very convincing report that will persuade top management of the necessity to purchase Ballantyne from Softlyn or even the company as a whole. Their manager is half persuaded to do a deal but the group management has only recently been appointed and is ignorant of the product. We want to keep it that way. The fewer people who know about it, the better.'

'So why don't you write the report yourself?'

'Because I'd rather have you down here and update me every day,' he smiled at her as she responded with a comprehending laugh. 'I'll give you a few ideas and we'll write the report together,' he continued more formally, 'but you can claim full authorship. You are probably aware that a report from an expert purposely brought in from outside will be more persuasive than anything written by the staff,' he ended with a reluctant note of sarcasm at the ignorance of managers sitting far above the fray.

'Yes,' Jessica agreed. 'Independent consultants are always respected more than the local man because they have been engaged at great expense for the purpose. Managers consequently focus on their report rather than the capabilities already at their disposal despite their having gained huge experience in the subject. But it's a good excuse to call on "the expert from the north" and my capabilities. It's about time that somebody recognised my importance.'

'I always have and I'll tell you more often, now.'

Grantley rang on Monday to inform Hector that he had been misled by Pelham because he had just received a letter declining to purchase Softlyn. He appeared at the Railton offices later that day in a very disgruntled mood. 'After all those assurances expressing interest in the company, they, suddenly, without further enquiry, dismiss the whole business,' he fumed.

'Did they give their reasons?' Hector asked in reply.

'No. They just say "on further consideration" without more elucidation. They travel all the way over here, express unqualified admiration and, now, withdraw without the least explanation.'

'It's either price or reconsideration of strategy,' Hector replied. 'What do you propose to do now?'

'Find some other purchaser and go through all those negotiations again, I suppose. I don't like the thought of giving up – Softlyn doesn't fit into our strategy. We are an engineering group, not electronics. Why on earth it was cultivated by Lowfield is beyond me.'

'Coral have probably come to the same conclusion. They are all engineering, too. Unfortunately, finding another purchaser might take a while.'

'With your contacts, I was hoping you would have a few suggestions.'

'There could be several possibilities. I'll make enquiries, but what are the chances of a management buyout?'

'I doubt whether Bamber has the capital for that, but we would lose nothing by enquiring.'

'Let me handle that,' Hector replied. 'Now that the business has almost attracted an offer, he may want complete independence in order to assure continuance of his position. Have you advised him of Pelham's response?'

'Yes. He was fairly non-committal, but I couldn't judge whether he was glad or not.'

After several more expressions of annoyance, Grantley left the matter in Hector's control and returned to his office.

Hector updated Bentley with the latest news but he remained free until the afternoon when, predictably and almost on cue, Bamber rang to invite himself for the following morning.

'I am not the least bit surprised at Pelham's letter,' he told the partners calmly when he arrived. 'I told you that we had each agreed not to proceed against the other, but Grantley is the sort of person who doesn't like to be thwarted. He will only find another company of interest and sell Softlyn to them.'

'You will have a certain amount of influence given your minority holding. That will give you the opportunity to join in the bargaining process, but Grantley will be decisive in the sale and you will, then, be obliged to submit to whatever deal he accepts. You mentioned the possibility of a management buyout, though. I could check whether Fenton could arrange a purchase of Ballantyne before you lose control to a new owner, or even whether he could acquire Softlyn as a whole.'

Bamber confessed that he had little choice now but to place all negotiations in Hector's care, who therefore contacted

Fenton with a request to meet at his office. He duly turned up with Jessica next day, whom he introduced as a key intelligence officer from The Department, thereby assuring Hector that Fenton was now keen to finalise an acquisition. He was pleased to note her several questions about the equipment and the range of valuations likely to be named. Bentley cautiously ventured the prospect, without expectation of success, of merely needing to ask The Department to raise the cash only for Fenton to confirm his presumption that they were very parsimonious.

Jessica asked about key personnel and their inventive skills. Fortunately, Hector had full details of Softlyn's business in his safe and offered to show them to her in the privacy of his office.

With the assurance that the papers would not be removed, they left her alone to begin a thorough review. Half an hour of an initial perusal was enough to inform her of the essential material, which she photographed in order to ensure that the contents were captured for later examination, and typed the remainder into her laptop. Fortunately, Fenton ensured that she was supplied with the means of survival and held court over the papers during a period of rest, but it was not until very late afternoon that she announced the conclusion of her task. She placed her laptop into her bag, closed the folder and surrendered it to Hector again.

He was sitting with Bentley and Fenton, who had been talking about Softlyn, but that subject had been exhaustively examined during the day, already. She joined their talk, which continued with renewed vigour at the prospect of a deal with The Department. 'I think I've read enough, Hector,' she said. 'I shall format the gist of it into a report but, first, it would be useful to speak to Bamber Stapleton about some aspects.' Hector immediately agreed to call him for discussions and they left soon afterwards.

'And what has the expert from the north achieved?' Fenton asked as soon as they were alone and out of earshot.

'Quite a lot, but it's only data, so far. I'll have to comb through it in order to prepare a first draft.'

'I shall ensure you get the thanks you deserve,' he replied, to which she thought that she was gaining a greater recognition than she had achieved in her previous years with him. She still thought that she had acted correctly in caring for her mother in her last years but perhaps she had been too cavalier in so easily dismissing him from her life. For all his apparent self-centred personality, she had now gained some insight into his daily concerns that he had been unable to share with her before.

'We can talk about the papers when we have spoken to Bamber,' was all she felt able to say at this time. She needed to adjust gradually into a resumption of their former existence, but it seemed that she was drifting steadily into the harbour on the incoming tide.

Bamber was encouraged to see that Hector had been able to achieve an early start to his disentanglement with Overdale. Jessica had been introduced by Fenton as a senior intelligence officer from The Department and she had shown her pass to prove it. She declared the willingness of The Department to acquire Ballantyne on condition that all papers, prototypes and finished products were surrendered to them following the purchase which she would recommend. She had been apprised of the two successes in as many attempts to defeat the existing security systems installed at each field test location, upon which Fenton made a mental note that they should ascertain the exact origin and description of the equipment that had yielded to Ballantyne's persuasion.

The participants discussed the value of the company and therefore the value of Bamber's interest. He expressed caution at any lack of generosity. He did not want a liability still to exist after Ballantyne had been sold, thereby leaving him with too great a burden with little left of his product range to bargain away. Having been informed of the values mentioned by Pelham, the partners suggested an initial bid at the mid-point knowing that some movement upwards would be required in order to close the deal.

Bamber drove Fenton and Jessica to the museum, where he introduced her to Maddox Byrne, who readily gave the manufacturer, model and serial number to her, noting that the security test was being taken seriously at higher levels and hoping that she may be able to suggest an upgrade. She reassured him that the museum would be most unlikely to suffer another incident. He had quite correctly contacted The Department for oversight of the test, and further use of Ballantyne would, in future, be very severely constrained. She reiterated the Department's thanks for contributing to their revue of security matters and they left together to return to the Railton offices. Byrne bade them goodbye with a more relaxed state of mind than for several months. He had little enthusiasm for the expense of upgrading the security system and was relieved that it need not be done, after all.

Their next stop would be the gallery after Fenton had first checked with the Art Squad to ascertain whether they had the data required. He was surprised to discover that that elementary information had not been collected. Inspector Yardley still felt uncomfortable at his failure to detect the culprit and now found himself embarrassed at this omission of data, but he recovered sufficiently by offering to conduct The Department's representative to the gallery, thereby hoping to reclaim a little credit from the management. Jessica accepted the opportunity to be introduced by Yardley who, being already known to the management, easily arranged an appointment for the following day.

As Jessica was meeting Yardley, Spenser had called Garrard into his office to 'talk about the future'. Garrard was concerned that the long silence about his retirement date was about to be broken, but bravely approached what was likely to be his doom. Spenser was feeling somewhat recovered from his depression, partly aided by the opportunity for him to impart good news at last. His role as the most knowledgeable director had led him unconsciously to assume a rather distant personality, but he had always maintained a polite respect and mostly good-natured conduct with all whom he met. He was now warming to the task of offering a further year to their most long-serving employee and felt a glow of benevolence warming his heart.

With an unaccustomed smile, he invited Garrard to be seated. 'I would firstly like to apologise for the delay in advising you of the retirement options available to you,' he said. 'The delay is inexcusable but I can only plead that I have been very concerned, probably more than most, at the disappearance of the del Mano, and ask for your forbearance,' he almost said 'forgiveness', 'at the lack of information'. He wondered whether to mention his distaste for the press interviews in which he had participated. They had also been a burden from which he was happy to escape.

Spenser felt that he had begun a little too unfeelingly in an inadequate choice of words, but he was less familiar with the diplomacy of staff relations than with his more flexible capability when speaking of art. 'You will know better than anybody,' he continued, 'that the gallery has embarked upon a programme of reframing that will take several more months to complete. Your retirement date is now approaching, which would entitle you to a final bonus and a regular pension payment, but you have been a key member of our staff for many years and, in order for you to consider all alternatives, I am pleased to offer you an extension of employment for another year with a postponement of the bonus should you wish to stay with us for a little longer.'

Garrard had been worried about his looming retirement scheduled for the month after next, and Spenser's first words did nothing to allay his fears at ending his association with the gallery and all the challenges that it posed. The last sentences offering him the alternative to retirement were, however, a huge relief.

'I have been a little troubled at the retirement that seemed to be approaching, Spenser,' he responded. 'I have loved this job ever since I started here forty years ago and gained the honour of working closely with so many great artists. I have also been much troubled by the del Mano disappearance. It has a special resonance with me and its theft was an enormous blow. But thank you for the offer of extended employment. I would much rather continue here and participate in the glazing project than to spend my days in idleness.'

'Excellent. I know that I shall be much relieved knowing that you are still part of the team,' he said only now realising that Garrard's possible absence had been the source of a deep-seated concern. His decision to continue at the gallery now provided a welcome alleviation to the worry that had afflicted him; it was not only Mariol who had been his saviour but also this quietly modest employee of many years who had contributed a degree of salvation. In a momentary lapse in his usually impassive demeanour, he assumed a more friendly countenance. 'Please accept my apologies for the rather formal presentation, Garrard. My normal day is filled with talking about art; I find staff matters a little more difficult, and,' he added scornfully, 'those press people have also been very painful to endure. I have been very disturbed by their insinuations of bad practice, but with an extension to your service you have now provided me with a great deal of badly needed comfort.'

Garrard had not been present at the press meetings but he also lived in Spenser's world of art and could imagine the distress that such confrontational irreverence could bring to a man steeped in its beauties. 'I watched the television programme,' he replied. 'I agree that your presentation reflected the depth of your knowledge, no doubt in great contrast to the pack of wolves who have confronted you. I wish I could have had your background but the workroom has been a very comforting existence and I'm glad to continue there, but even if I were to leave, I know that Hedrick would remain a huge asset.'

'Yes. Especially now that he is getting married,' Spenser reflected, greatly regretting that Mariol had dismissed that option as inappropriate to the modern woman.

Jessica met Yardley, both showing their passes to the other. Whilst driving her to the gallery, Yardley congratulated her that The Department had retained its reputation for secrecy in arranging the theft to which Jessica merely shrugged with the suitably non-informative reply, '"*There are more things in heaven and earth, Inspector, than are dreamed of in your philosophy*".' Yardley thought he should have known better than to have mentioned the matter. 'Typical of that lot,' he thought. 'They think they live in the clouds; far above the world and ever more mysterious to us mortals.'

Marcus welcomed them with fulsome greetings, which merely persuaded Jessica that he was simply a fund of words without purpose except to convey a semblance of competence and effectiveness. Upon ascertaining the reason for their visit, Marcus generously offered to conduct them to the security team, where they collected the relevant details but declined further entertainment other than a visit to the del Mano gallery. 'This is the painting about which we have experienced such commotion in recent months,' he informed them. 'An Old

Master four centuries old and the most valuable picture in our collection and now our most guarded. It would probably reach a figure of several millions at auction,' he boasted, 'but the envious collector must remain disappointed; the picture is not for sale. We exist for the benefit of the wider public and not for the individual,' he announced with a mixture of importance and sanctimonious self-righteousness.

Just as Jessica exchanged glances of repressed amusement with Yardley at Marcus's grandiloquence, Spenser appeared with Garrard to be greeted effusively by Marcus in his most impressive style. 'This is our art director, the fount of all knowledge about this and all other pictures in our possession. Any questions, any detail, he's your man. He is particularly knowledgeable on the *Girl* and gives daily lectures in a short season devoted to the painting as well as to the artist.'

Spenser noted once again how bombastic Marcus was. Yardley needed no introduction, but why he had reappeared or who the lady was remained undisclosed, neither had he, himself, been introduced by name. Yet another casual slight to a fellow director. 'I'm pleased to see you again, Inspector,' he said. 'I shall be leaving for Italy on holiday next week, but if you wish to know anything in the meantime, I am at your disposal.'

'I think we have all the information we require,' Jessica replied, authoritatively, in his stead. 'We shall return to base, now.'

Spenser watched them leave. 'I wonder who she is, Garrard.'

'Someone too important for us to know, and few people can be more mysterious than the *Girl*,' he replied, pleased to note that he had brought a brief smile to Spenser's face.

Spenser, with the benefit of Mariol's loving care, had almost recovered from his depression of the previous days but was, nonetheless, very greatly looking forward to his holiday. No clamouring pressmen, no business pressure and no Marcus; just an enjoyable time with a wonderful woman in a land full of art.

Garrard was also delighted at having just been offered a further year at the gallery. He walked on to the workroom in order to share his good news with Hedrick and received heartfelt congratulations from him very content that their working relationship would be extended. 'Spenser is nearly always expressionless and unbending,' he told Hedrick, 'but I discovered today that he is as human as the rest of us, and has probably suffered more than we had imagined.'

Hedrick had told him of his engagement upon returning from the Tilson family after the weekend, and was not only happy with his newly engaged status but also glad that Garrard had reason to rejoice in another year with a salary.

Marcus undertook a tour of the exhibits in order to ascertain that all was well and to bestow a few smiles of approval at the personnel whom he met before driving home to be greeted by his wife of several decades. Marcus informed her that he had attended yet more meetings with the Art Squad inspector but, this time, also with a high-ranking government intelligence officer. He confessed that Spenser was quite able to attend to their enquiries but he had felt it incumbent upon himself as senior manager to attend to security matters without burdening his staff. With her accustomed admiration, Mabel listened, quietly pleased to accept yet another confirmation of his stature and tenure of office.

Chapter 29

Hector rang Grantley to inform him that he had had conversations with Bamber that pointed to his preference to become independent of the group and that he had contracted with him as advisor in whatever negotiations would follow. 'Formally, this means that I can't also act for you, but as we have previously agreed that I should approach him for his point of view, I think we have all established at least a working relationship that should lead to a conclusion that would suit you both.'

Grantley agreed that the omens seemed good and that the task of selling off the company was near to finalisation. 'We have already had an indication from Pelham of the price he was prepared to pay. If you can match their top price, I think we can do a deal in very short order.'

Hector had expected that response but replied that Pelham had withdrawn and a buyer of a company in electronics would regard the company as fairly lacklustre and routine in products. 'I suspect that they would not offer that price simply for increasing their sales volume, Norbert. You would need to make a more attractive price for them of perhaps two-thirds that amount.'

Having only just heard that Hector was acting for Bamber, Grantley's reaction was predictable. 'Much as I would like to divest Softlyn, we are in no hurry to make a hasty deal, Hector. I could reduce the price by a small amount but I simply want to divest it and not give it away.'

'In that case, I'll try floating that level to likely candidates.'

Spenser and Mariol arrived at their apartment in Florence, which seemed to be rather noisier than they had remembered, but the sun was shining and they had left the gallery far away.

Spenser sank into a chair and smiled with relief. 'Here we are, at last,' he announced with a smile wider than Mariol had known for months.

'Time for a bit of relaxation, now,' she responded. She looked at him with a love deepened by the years and by her devotion made stronger by her fears. 'Yes. Here we are,' she thought. 'We've made it to another holiday and, let us hope, to salvation for both of us.' After her concern for Spenser's health, she thanked her God for his improvement and for the prospects of a further recovery in his well-being. She had felt the approach of an enormous sense of loss but he had rallied and was greatly looking forward to visiting the sights despite their being already so well known to them from former times. But she would ensure that he would not become overtired even if she had to be more severe and curtail a treasured visit.

They unpacked and considered what museums and art galleries to visit and those they could leave to a later time. That was a matter they had discussed already, but Mariol was only too eager to join Spenser in his reveries. The more they spoke, the more they enjoyed their company together, but anxious not to tempt him to be too energetic, she told him that they should not race from one to another. He agreed. 'You are quite right, my dear. I look forward to relaxation far away from all my daily toils and I shall surrender to your strict commands.' Mariol felt that they would emerge from all the troubles that he had endured and she had shared. Perhaps they *would* have another fifteen years.

Over the next few days, they visited several galleries, viewed the art and sculpture, and walked arm in arm through the streets and over the bridge. Passers-by nodded appreciatively as they passed, having seen an obviously loving couple of a more advanced age than those numerous young lovers who were more often the subject of their admiring, even envious, gaze.

The search for del Mano's studio was a doomed undertaking. There was no sign or clue or hope, it seemed, but they were satisfied with the strolls through the city that it demanded; and the frequent rests at café tables were opportunities to sit and view the architecture.

At one of the tables, Mariol chose a happy interval in which to feast her radiant smile on Spenser as she prepared to tell him of her decision. 'Do you remember our meeting in Amboise?' she asked. 'And how we sat at a table just like this one that changed our lives?'

'Of course. It was an unforgettable time spent with the loveliest woman whom I have ever known.'

'A rather uncertain woman who did not know her own mind. A foolish woman who could not decide upon the most important matter in her life,' she chided herself playfully.

'On the contrary. You were the most decisive woman whom I had ever met. An educated woman who could speak in depth on her subject. One who matched my ideals and one who chose to live with me in the best solution for both of us.'

'It was. But I have improved upon that. I have made a very important appointment for when we return,' she beamed.

'An appointment?' he replied, rather puzzled. 'What sort of appointment?'

'It's at a date two weeks after we return – at the registry office. We are going to get married.'

'Good heavens!' he exclaimed. 'You were adamant in not wanting to get married. Not for a modern woman, you said.'

'Well, now that I've had time to get to know you properly, I've changed my mind,' she replied with the broadest of smiles.

'My dear, we have been the most loving couple for fifteen years. We shall be married at last and, then, we shall be the most loving newlyweds whether in Florence or Skelton.'

'We shall be the happiest couple anywhere in the world,' she rejoiced wondering why she had been so severe on the previous occasion when he had broached the proposition. The holiday would also be the happiest she had ever spent.

Jessica drafted her report in which she described Softlyn as a company currently being divested by Overdale merely because the group had newly taken over Lowfield and was restructuring to the exclusion of electronics in which it had no expertise. The company had proved attractive to the Italian Coral Engineering group, which was moving into security and had already made an offer which was under consideration. Softlyn manufactured several advanced products but its main field of expertise was in security and entry products. The product of interest to The Department was Ballantyne, a security disabling product that would prove of great interest to overseas powers and would, in the wrong hands, prove disastrous to national interests. Its effectiveness had been tested very successfully on two occasions, the latest being a full test with a specialist entry team and without management knowledge. The consequent furore in the art world had been a matter of mystery given the total lack of evidence and had stubbornly proved resistant to the Art Squad's thorough investigation.

A foreign power could use the product to discover secret documents without leaving a trace of entry to sensitive sites. She quoted an estimated value slightly higher than the Pelham offer but cautiously expressed the opinion that a settlement at a slightly lower price could be obtained if an offer were to be made quickly.

Fenton read their joint document several times but decided to present it in hope that the suggested price would not prove too prohibitive. As the hour approached, Fenton stressed that the appointment be conducted in an atmosphere of restrained urgency that would convey the importance of gaining control of the product before it became marketed to another purchaser who may, like Coral, be based abroad and thereby prove to be beyond The Department's immediate observation.

They entered Hebton's office and Fenton introduced 'Jessica Turner, our expert from the north.' She immediately took command of the meeting with a determined presentation of the few options available. They needed access to closely secured documents in order to foil the activities of the money launderers but also to secure Ballantyne from being acquired by foreign governments eager to obtain secret defence information. The product had already been tested by Coral Ital, thereby confirming that it was known abroad and that there may be a suspicion of others wishing to gain possession. The device had met the totality of the tests to which it had been subjected and was available now but was likely to be disposed of by the new group management in their current restructuring as soon as funds were transferred from another bidder.

Fenton contributed that a reputable firm of consultants had been used in order to establish relations with the Softlyn management, but they had stressed the advisability of an early decision before the new group management discovered the potential of the device. They would then be sure to raise the price considerably, especially if approached by a foreign power.

Burnley listened almost in silence throughout the presentation, at the conclusion of which he took the report with a promise to read it and to forward it, if thought fit, to a higher level for consideration.

Upon their leaving the meeting, Fenton remarked to Jessica, 'That was a spirited presentation, but Burnley seemed to be less moved than I was.'

'Typical bureaucratic reaction. He doesn't seem very keen to make a case for expenditure.'

Burnley was not keen. The Department had many claims

on its resources and was bound to be scathing about potential rather than actual events, despite the successful field tests. He read it through and studied the schedules. At least Fenton had made some progress at last but he was only too conscious that the report mentioned a figure that he suspected would lead to immediate rejection. He would pass it to High Desk with a recommendation to purchase but without any hope of an early decision.

After a week in Florence, Spenser suggested a trip to Bologna in order to visit Pelham. 'Now that we are in reasonable driving distance, we may as well use this occasion to give him an up-to-date report on the disappearing del Mano,' he told Mariol. 'As well as simply to liaise with our main trustee.'

Mariol was a little deterred by the thought of finding one's own way driving across an unfamiliar country and suggested taking a less stressful train journey. Spenser remembered his promise to defer to her sensibilities and they agreed to check the possibilities at the station. That would be only a small change from their daily routine.

They boarded the train next day with a small overnight case and watched the countryside pass by. Bologna appeared within the hour and they emerged to another gem of a town. Spenser checked the address and they approached the taxi stand. Their first attempt was declined with bursts of polite refusal at the distance concerned but the next in line accepted and they continued their journey. The driver stopped for instruction from a local lady who, with a huge smile, pointed to the big house on the hill top. Numerous cars were parked along the road and several people were in the garden. 'Must be a celebration of some sort,' Spenser remarked, settled the fare and advanced to the house.

They were greeted by several guests who seemed to be

welcoming them but in a language which neither understood. 'Frank Pelham?' Spenser asked slightly bewildered by the press of people holding their glasses half full of wine. 'Si, Franco, Franco,' they corrected him, pointing them to the rear garden, where they encountered even more people. They were accosted by one of them, whom they understood from his rather stern expression must be a security man asking for their invitations. Spenser mimed in support of his English that they had no invitation and were about to be hustled away by him and another security man when they heard a woman calling to them. 'Spenser, Spenser, I hadn't expected to see you here.'

'Laura!' Spenser exclaimed. 'How fortunate we are to see you! We don't have an invitation and are about to be escorted away.' She signed to the security men that they were welcome guests and led them into the centre of the group, whilst explaining that she had come for the wedding.

'Wedding! We've just come to see Frank. We didn't know there was a wedding.'

But she had drawn them to the bride and groom and were introduced to the happy couple. 'Spenser Ferndale and his wife, Frank. Our art director.'

Frank turned his full smiles upon them. 'Welcome to the nuptial party, Spenser, I don't think we have ever met,' signalling the security man to put their case in the house. 'But it's a good thing you did not come earlier. This is Rosa, since this morning, my loving wife.' He said something to Rosa, who replied with an Italian that sounded welcoming.

'And this is my dear wife, Mariol,' Spenser told them, rather pleased to be using the much longed for word even if a little prematurely. She added her congratulations to the happy pair. 'We had not realised that there was a wedding in progress, Frank. We are on holiday in Florence but I thought we should visit our main trustee whilst we were not too far away.'

'He knows everything about art, Frank,' Laura added. 'Even appeared on television recently to talk about the del Mano disappearance.'

'I understand that it created enormous speculation,' Frank responded. 'Laura kept me in touch with developments but I was largely ignorant of the impact upon the media since I am hidden away in the wilds of Emilia-Romagna.'

'Our chairman had to bear the main assault from the scribblers but Laura put up a very daunting counter attack,' Spenser responded.

Laura complimented him in turn. 'And Spenser was also very dismissive in his remarks.'

'He was severely upset at the theft,' Mariol intervened. 'I thought he would never recover, but our little holiday has been his saviour,' she told them admiringly and with evident relief.

Rosa detected a slight accent in her speech and asked whether she was French, to which she, having had her nationality confirmed, was grateful to be able to regain her focus as bride rather than one who seemed in danger of becoming unjustly ignored. She explained that she would not like to miss this unexpected opportunity to practise the little French she had. Mariol responded by praising the pleasures and security of marriage. 'We've been together for fifteen years, the best fifteen years of our lives. Those times before I knew him were spent in idle pursuit of study and advancement, but I had no idea of what was in that other world that I had not explored. Now I think how foolish I had been. We could have had even more years if only we had met earlier.'

'I've known Franco for years already but he had a strong loyalty to his first love,' Rosa confided sadly. 'She died but it took over twenty years for him to reconcile himself to the fact that she would not return. But let's talk of happier times, the times before us, the times when we can create new memories.'

'Of course. We were drifting into the past but, now, we are in the future.'

Spenser and Mariol continued to praise the wonders of domesticity with their hosts before wandering off amid the numerous guests, but they were all speaking a language with which they were not familiar. On passing a couple attempting to converse with the natives, however, they heard the odd word of English intruding and, thinking that they might be the only ones with whom they could exchange a few remarks, ventured a rather hesitant, 'Hello, would you be English, by any chance?' The couple turned from the guests with whom they were exchanging conversation, thereby confirming the assumption.

The husband breathed a sigh of relief at their approach. 'Yes, we are. My wife is the one who can speak the language. But I have almost forgotten even my schoolboy French. I'm Bentley and this is Cordelia.'

'We are so glad to meet you,' Mariol informed them with some relief. 'We came to see Franco, but hadn't known that it was his wedding today. Fortunately, Spenser knows Laura, otherwise we were on the brink of being thrown out.'

'I used to live in that house over there and knew Franco well,' Cordelia told them. 'Getting married is a great conclusion to his regrets at the death of a girl he knew years ago.'

'Yes. We have just been given a little insight into that by the bride herself.'

'Rosa,' came Cordelia's reply. 'She's waited years for him. That's loyalty for you. But everything has turned out nicely in the end. They are just right for each other.'

'Just like us,' Bentley added. 'We met decades ago, lost each other, met again by chance and got married only one week ago, so we are having a late honeymoon.'

'You are not alone,' Mariol told them with a broad smile. 'I thought marriage was too old fashioned but I've grown up now and we are getting married in two weeks.'

Music sounded from speakers in the garden and several tunes played to the happy couple dancing on the patio to the applause of the guests. Laura took her teenage son onto the patio and joined the dance, Sylvano led her daughter onto the grass and several more couples joined the throng. Spenser had no experience of dancing, but Mariol saw the chance to hold him close as they swayed gently over the lawn, both almost in tears of pleasure thinking of the years to come.

Cordelia and Bentley manoeuvred close beside them. 'This is going to continue until after midnight,' they told them. 'Are you going to return to Florence, tonight? Or have you booked a hotel?' Bentley asked to an awakening of their slight concern.

'No. We had better find a hotel, but we shall have to get a taxi back to town, first.'

'Don't worry about that,' Cordelia intervened. 'Stay with us. We have a spare room.'

They were both full of thanks and kept close to them and Laura with her teenagers for the next hour talking about weddings, the past and the future. Laura expressed her regrets that Frank, in attempting to hold conversations with his numerous well-wishers, had been insufficiently available to them in order to speak about art and the gallery.

'Come round tomorrow afternoon, Spenser, at about two. After we've given them time to adjust,' Laura added with a smile.

Chapter 30

Cordelia and Bentley led the way to her house accompanied by Mariol and Spenser, each couple holding hands and reflecting on their perfect day, which was ending with a late evening walk into the future. Cordelia revelled in welcoming guests to her house, which she had expected to be her refuge but had become a holiday haven in her newfound matrimonial security. Mariol had made an announcement that she would never have imagined in the whole of her life hitherto. To be married! To join the world and its customs! To be the centre of everybody's congratulations! She had known happiness for fifteen years but the decades would now open to a lifetime of abundance.

After a day of celebration came an hour of conversation at Cordelia's house. 'I have lived in a cave of my own throughout my life,' Bentley told them. 'But I had never realised how cloistered I was until today when I found myself surrounded by everybody speaking a language that I could not understand. After years of negotiating complex deals, all conducted in a shoebox and not the open spaces, I can now emerge from the ignorance of my isolation and enjoy with you visions of light.'

Spenser responded with similar expressions. 'I have been steeped in art for several decades and have seldom known the importance of the wider world, but have focussed upon the brushwork and not the picture. A broader view stands open now that we are about to emulate the happy couple and be joined in wedlock.'

Mariol assured him with a loving smile that it was she who had spread the veil across his view. 'But the curtain has been raised to reveal a vista that we had not known before.'

Cordelia added her conversion to an existence more spacious

than the self-imposed limitations that had characterised her former days. 'This is the cottage that I intended for my retirement but I cast away my haunted past when I lifted my gaze to a future full of promise.'

Upon ascertaining that their hosts would return from honeymoon at the end of the following week, Spenser invited them to another wedding soon after that. 'But not yours. This time it will be ours. You will be very welcome if only to help with the applause.'

Cordelia expressed her newfound liking for weddings. Having only recently been married themselves, Franco having married that very day and, now, another wedding to be held within a few days would be a most delightful prospect.

They all woke late on the following day to the realisation that the sun was inviting them to an exploration of the village, thereby prompting a walk that proved a gentle appetiser. Spenser insisted on treating them all at the restaurant. 'This is a big adventure for us,' he explained. 'A delightful interval in our days visiting the sights.'

Bentley contributed the fact that he had found Bologna very appealing but that this was his first visit abroad. 'The south coast was as far as I cared to go. I seldom took a holiday, but with great good fortune, Cordelia and I met there again by chance after several decades.'

'He was very persuasive in encouraging me to stay,' Cordelia added. 'The past is always with us and tends to drag us back to the familiarity of the times we knew, but, happily, the future proved to be a stronger magnet and draws us ever onward.'

The clock ticked on with the quiet reminder that they should return to the big house. They reached it in good time for their informal invitation, which Spenser hoped Laura had confirmed with Frank. Whilst waiting for a few more minutes to tick by, they admired the view from a garden which seemed almost undisturbed by the previous day's celebration: the lake on one side, hills rolling into the far distance on the other.

Laura, having expected their approach, saw the group apparently standing appreciatively viewing the scene, the children were walking the footpath round the lake, and Rosa and Frank were in the garden trying to recollect to whom they had spoken the previous day.

'I hope they all had a good time, anyway,' Frank said.

'I certainly did,' Rosa responded. 'Fancy being married after all those years!'

'And we've had no regrets so far,' he replied with a smile.

'We know each other well enough by now, Franco,' Rosa reassured him. 'The future lies before us like the sea spreading to the horizon on a sunny day, and you may be sure that no stormy weather will disturb our lives.'

'And any waves will be merely ripples on the surface when viewed in the stillness of the night,' Frank responded in anticipation of the little disputes to which matrimony may be prone.

Laura stepped out to tell them that the visitors had arrived and then went back to conduct the arrivals round the house to the terrace. Their reception was one of smiles and congratulations, Rosa being particularly pleased at the sight of her supposed rival being no longer the threat to her long-held ambitions that had now been turned into triumphant achievement. But Cordelia had no thought of either victory or defeat. She had cleared her mind of all the nonsense that had blocked her tangled thoughts wound around the happiness that now shone its light upon her.

Frank greeted Spenser with a broad smile, informing him that, even as main trustee, he took little interest in the gallery.

His inclinations lay in the cut and thrust of business and not the static world of exhibitions, but a brief exchange with the art director would present an opportunity for a relaxing talk unrelated to his daily toil.

'You have a beautiful house, Frank, and a garden to match,' Spenser told him. 'Now I can understand why Laura is so often away from the gallery.'

Laura responded with the playful retort that she had to ensure that Frank was not concentrating too hard on business and neglecting his social responsibilities. 'The children like coming, too, and racing about the hills and the lake.'

'She's quite right, Spenser. Sometimes I can't leave work alone, but now that I am the epitome of the sermonising married man, I must be more aware of the world around me.'

'I look forward to emulating you, Frank. In just over a week, I shall join your ranks when Mariol and I cement our relationship of many years in a rather smaller celebration than yours. Perhaps I should also be aware of a world beyond the gallery.'

Mariol touched his hand. 'I shall ensure that you are not so focussed on the job that you become ill again,' she told him comfortingly. 'Not so much pressure from those media people and that posturing Marcus you so dislike,' she ended in a loving tribute that Frank could hardly overlook.

He conducted Spenser, Bentley and Laura into the house whilst Rosa revelled in her recognition in her first reception as chatelaine of the big house entertaining Mariol and Cordelia in the garden.

'Laura updates me from time to time and sends me the minutes of the board meetings,' Frank continued. 'But I leave management to the experts such as you and Marcus. I prefer to concentrate on today's creation rather than that of history.'

'I have the same regard for a well-produced work of art as you have for your engineering products, Frank. The value is to me totally unimportant; it is the devotion of the creator to his art that I admire. And of course, to its safety. Having survived for three or four hundred years, they demand our support for them to continue for several more centuries.'

'I hear from Laura that you were badly affected by the disappearance of our most valuable and oldest painting, for which I must apologise profusely. A representative of The Department, a man called Fenton, visited me last year with a rather astounding proposition, namely, to enter the premises and to spirit away *Girl with a Harp*. I dismissed the proposal with derision but he told me that an electronics company had successfully tested new equipment that would defeat all known security measures and had the intention of targeting the gallery regardless whether I consented or not. After his persistent pleas for permission, and verification of his position, I agreed to his request, but only on the understanding that the painting would not be damaged in any way and would be returned crated and unhandled within a few weeks.'

Spenser listened in horror that the main trustee could not have warned the gallery to increase security. A startled Laura wondered why he could not have released that information to her in her several calls to update him. Frank was seldom embarrassed but, this time, he had to admit that they both had good reason for their faith in his decision-making to be shaken. 'Actually, there is another reason in addition to security,' he admitted rather sheepishly in his defence. 'I like to keep in touch with new developments, and the particular electronics company that Fenton mentioned was one that I had been following for some years. I was aware that it may have an interest in targeting one or more of my companies and therefore, after a great amount of consideration, I agreed to the suggestion. At least, the attempt would be under government supervision rather than an uncontrolled attack by someone acting for a rival. I tried to forestall any action by launching a takeover of the group but, thanks be to you, Bentley, I lost out and my group would therefore have remained a possible victim to a hostile entity.'

'If I had known Cordelia to be your near neighbour, Frank, I would not have hesitated to propose a meeting with you. I know that my partner, Hector, met you when he was on holiday here, but he would have had no inclination to work on that project.'

Laura protested that not only the board but most of the staff had been traumatised by the theft. 'I wouldn't say that Marcus enjoyed his prominence in facing the media, far from it, but Spenser, in particular, was badly affected. Our most revered and valuable exhibit had disappeared without trace, and Spenser almost suffered a breakdown.'

Frank floundered in the realisation that his action had been unwise, even though it had led to an agreement with Bamber to obviate further attacks. He tried to defend himself by claiming that no theft had occurred because he had authorised the removal and specified strict safety precautions. Spenser's long suppressed resentment at those jibes from Marcus was now increased by a fury that finally drove him to an unaccustomed outburst.

'There was no guarantee that the painting would not be damaged in the attempt,' he fumed. 'You could have caused huge loss and not just in monetary terms. That is a great work of art that has been respected and safeguarded throughout the centuries and you colluded in the theft.' His anger increased as his habitual restraint was cast aside. 'Who cares whether your business could have been attacked? It could have been relaunched; but a great work of art is a work of genius that cannot be replaced,' he protested, becoming more vehement in his protest. 'Can we call upon the artist in his grave? Can we look upon a reproduction with the assurance that it has hung for centuries? Are Old Masters merely objects that can be treated with disdain? Can we lose the culture of the ages and retain only a history of human strife? Is art a mere indulgence or does it urge us to finer thoughts? Have you no care for the dedication of others to the public welfare?'

Upon approaching the house, again, the ladies heard a voice raised in protest. Mariol was horrified at hearing Spenser's uncontrolled voice raised in anger. She ran inside. 'Spenser, Spenser,' she pleaded as she rushed to gather him in her arms and holding him in what she feared might be the last occasion. She turned on the others. 'Stop tormenting him. He's all I have. He's very sensitive and still recovering. Spenser, it's all right, now. You're safe. I'm here. We'll go away. Go home. Go back to the gallery.' She had been concerned before but, now, she could only think that she was about to lose the most treasured relationship of her entire life.

She held him as he fought back the tears, knowing that he was in the safety of Mariol's protection. 'They don't care,' he told her. 'All they think about is money.'

Mariol held him closer, 'Yes, you're right. We'll go away now, and leave them to their gold.' Turning to Frank she shouted uncontrollably at him, 'Keep your stupid money, Spenser's worth more to me than all of you put together.'

Laura looked at them helplessly. She had never known Spenser so affected. She thought of the conversations she had had with him, of his depression at the disappearance, of the trials that the press had posed, and of his annoyance with Marcus. She joined Mariol in ushering him gently out to the garden where they guided him to a chair and Mariol sat with him in tears, fearing the worst and holding his hand, telling him repeatedly in complete disregard of the others that she loved him.

Rosa looked in astonishment at Franco, wondering what had induced this scene of love and despair. Franco looked back with the knowledge that he had, indeed, put not just wealth but also his own reputation before the art of which he was trustee. He had committed a selfish and thoughtless wrong that could hardly be righted. Laura looked at him with an unaccustomed accusation amid the consciousness of the harm that had been done.

Cordelia told Rosa to drive her with Spenser and Mariol to her cottage so that they could rest there until next day. Rosa was irked by Cordelia's resort to instruction in what was her own house now, but submitted to the request as the quickest way to clear the atmosphere of embarrassment. Frank helped Spenser into the car and said, 'I'm terribly sorry, Spenser. You are quite right. I should have known better.'

Spenser nodded a faint, tear-filled acknowledgement before being driven away. Mariol helped him into bed, where they lay together in the cure that Spenser had most appreciated on the occasion of his previous recovery. She held him gently and lovingly in her arms in an anguish of extreme distress at the thought of losing him forever and uttered another but more heartfelt prayer for his survival. He felt her presence and bathed again in her loving words that seemed to wash away the sense of betrayal by a trustee who had no thought for the art to which he, himself, had dedicated his life. But he was safe once more in the world he knew far away from those who did not care and close to the woman he loved.

They woke to an evening that offered peace and tranquillity. Their good intentions of the day had revealed the harsh reality beyond their sequestered existence, one of coping with the challenges of adversity rather than the cloistered calm to which he was accustomed. They had their preference, the others had theirs.

Laura was horrified at the sight she had witnessed and Frank was mortified that decisions made in the remoteness of the hills had led to this most unexpected repercussion upon a key member of the board. 'We would be nothing without him, Frank,' she told him with as much an admonishing tone as she was able. 'He knows everything about art and is vital to the existence of the gallery. He was so authoritative on the television programme not just in talking about the del Mano but also in defence of the gallery. I thought he lived for that alone, but I've now discovered what a loving couple they are. You saw how protective she was and how she has sustained him. We can't do without him, but we have all underestimated him. And that windbag, Marcus, is always mocking him, but Spenser is such a gentle man that he would never dream of protesting.'

'I have taken the gallery too much for granted, Laura,' Frank had sheepishly to admit. 'But I am beginning to wonder whether it would be more beneficial for me to concentrate on the business and hand full control over to you. I'm only main trustee because Granddad wanted it. I have been far too distant but, if I have learned only one thing from business, it is that close proximity has its advantages.'

'I'd welcome the chance to get more directly involved,' Laura replied in a calmer tone. 'But I would not want Marcus's constant sniping.'

'In that case, I'll invite him here to give me his own views. Let's see whether he can justify his existence.'

They were interrupted by Rosa's return. 'He seems to be recovering,' she announced. 'I don't think it was anything that Mariol can't handle. She said he needs a period of rest and calm and a return to routine. Cordelia and Bentley are there if anything serious happens but I think that unlikely. He's just very sensitive, that's all.'

Spenser and Mariol enjoyed a relaxing return journey to Florence next day and spent the rest of the holiday in a gentler frame of mind harmlessly viewing the sites once more; Spenser a little quieter, Mariol his loving chaperone.

They arrived back home happy to have returned to familiar places but saddened by having had that little altercation with Frank Pelham amid the rewards and stimulation of Florence. They had one day free before Spenser was expected back at the gallery, but they set out on a gentle walk through the nearby wood to the view beyond that they had always enjoyed. 'Do you prefer landscapes to portraits,' Mariol asked him as they gazed at the prospect before them. He replied that both had their merits and the one that whatever was his current view was always the equal of any portrait he had previously studied.

'I look at this view, for example, and believe it to be unequalled by any other, but then I turn to you and see the most wonderful portrait that excels all those that I have ever known.'

Mariol smiled with pleasure as they nestled happily together. 'I have booked a photographer for next week, Spenser. He will create portraits aplenty.'

Next day, Spenser returned to the familiarity of the gallery a little saddened to have left the joys of Florence behind but happy to renew his acquaintance with numerous reencounters of greatness and to retrieve the comfort of knowing that all was satisfactorily unchanged. He felt the security of his office wrap around him as he sat in his chair sinking back into familiarity. All was as it should be in what had been almost another home in the decades that had flown by so quickly, but he knew that his real home was the one where he was with Mariol and the one that would, within days, become an even more secure sanctuary when they were married.

His ruminations were interrupted as his door opened and Laura entered. 'Hello Spenser. We returned on Friday and took the weekend to recover from the celebrations,' she added, sneaking a moment of assessment to reassure herself that he looked no less lively than he had before the holiday. 'I hope you are feeling prepared for another period of strenuous activity after your big break,' she said with a broad smile, to which he assured her that he had never felt better in resuming the duties before him.

'I wanted to let you know about one of the items on the agenda at the meeting next Tuesday,' she continued. 'It must remain absolutely confidential until then. You are not affected but I wanted to dispel any apprehension you may have after your very productive comments at Frank's house last week. He has finally realised that he has too many projects to handle and thinks that delegation is not the only management tool he possesses.'

'I'm glad you didn't call the meeting for this Thursday. I'm getting married then, and I think I owe Mariol a whole day to celebrate.'

Laura took the opportunity to invite herself to the ceremony. 'You are a very private man, Spenser, almost of mystery,' she chided him gently. 'Evidently, not one who broadcasts his activities to everyone, I see, but, also, not one who cannot speak out when roused. Your little outburst has worked wonders with my workaholic brother, not only married at last but also looking in our direction. He invited Marcus to a strategy discussion last week.'

Spenser was intrigued but his curiosity was soon satisfied.

Chapter 31

Burnley Hebton had presented Jessica's report to High Up, who read it through with the sort of interest he reserved for routine until he noticed the reference to the Pelham theft. That was the gallery where a former acquaintance from his days in government administration was now chairman of the board. He remembered him as a man of integrity, even if one inclined to a soporific verbosity, who had been granted the sinecure of a quiet job in the art world more as a reward for long service rather than achievement. 'Old Marcus! That old duffer,' he thought. 'Fancy him being mixed up in the biggest art theft of the century.' But he knew instinctively that Marcus would have had nothing to do with the sort of technology that must have been used in the raid.

His curiosity prompted him to telephone his opposite number in Special Operations, Rick Merton, an ex-SAS man. After the exchange of codes necessary to prove the identities of the callers, he asked whether the SO people had had anything to do with the gallery theft, to which he was informed with the usual pride exercised by one who had conducted a successful raid that 'I authorised it at the request of one of your people. Fenton Barr, I think it was. Why do you ask?'

'I have a request from Fenton and an expert from our Newcastle office to acquire it in order to help track down international currency launderers.'

'I'm surprised that it has taken so long. It was a stunning piece of work by my squad. They had a month's training, photographed the one they wanted and framed a copy from the museum shop. The device was invented by some bright spark in electronics. Our man hid in a cupboard and swapped it at night before walking out next day through the shop. If it's on the market, I recommend you buy it before anybody else can get it. Otherwise, no security system will be beyond a breach.'

High Up called Burnley and, much to the latter's surprise, authorised the purchase. Burnley called finance, telling them to liaise with Fenton to establish a price. Fenton was more surprised than Burnley at the rapid decision and referred them to Railton and Barratt Consultants. Hector told them that the product was held by Softlyn and ventured a rather higher price than he thought practicable but, much to his well-disguised astonishment at their immediate acceptance, undertook to recommend the sale to Grantley.

He first ascertained that Bamber would be happy at the price but was a little disconcerted when the latter expressed uncertainty until Hector told him that the offer was at the top of anybody's assessment. A moment of reflection was sufficient for Bamber to realise the benefit of the offer. He had already decided not to deploy Ballantyne further, and, if it could be useful elsewhere, he may as well surrender the product to a responsible authority and continue to manage Softlyn. With his slice of the cake he would be able to pay off the mortgage and still draw a salary whilst pursuing his talents in a larger environment.

Grantley's first response was also that a higher price could be negotiated but Hector was adamant that it was at the top, even above, any figure that could be obtained elsewhere and clinched the deal by pointing out that it could be completed without delay rather than allowing the offer to lapse if a lengthy bargaining process were to discourage the bidder. Approval followed. Grantley's main consideration was to dispose of the company and, after a brief moment of reflection, thought that Hector had obtained an excellent price in addition.

Fenton told Jessica that she deserved a big reward, especially if she were prepared to stay longer at his house, 'Just in case your talents might be needed again,' he added.

'I shall be quite happy to deploy my talents as long as they may be required,' she responded with a knowing smile.

The great day dawned for Spenser and Mariol. 'Is this what they call a wedding breakfast?' he asked, to which Mariol replied, 'One no different from all the others, but the last before the start of a life to come.'

'At the stroke of the noonday clock, we shall be on the brink of matrimony. I've been waiting for fifteen years for that clock to strike but, now, my wait is over.'

'I was too dismissive of formalities, Spenser. We had a love that needed no greater force to bind us together, but I admit that I was foolish to think that we would not gain from the extra embrace of solemnity. A church service was barred by the differing conventions of birth, and a civil ceremony seemed to lack compulsion, but that has always been open to us and I have now accepted that vows are sacred wherever they may be sworn.'

The morning passed in ensuring that all was ready for a very small reception and in dressing appropriately for the ceremony. With their relief at the arrival of the catering team as the hour approached, they set off for the registry office in good time pleased to note that the guests were already assembled. Professor Tilson and Edith had brought Astra and she had brought Hedrick. Two of Mariol's A level students whom she had invited were there with their parents, too. Garrard had also been persuaded and told Spenser that he could not miss playing truant in this most worthwhile of causes. Laura and the conservator were there, and Cordelia and Bentley were in conversation with them all whilst the photographer quietly took any opportunity for a few surreptitious pictures. Spenser reported at the desk whilst Walter slyly asked Mariol whether she really wanted to take on Spenser permanently. She assured him with a huge smile and great conviction that nothing would change her resolution, now.

They took their places but the registrar quietly pointed out that no witnesses had taken their seats. Spenser realised that the necessity to nominate them had totally escaped his mind and, turning to the few guests for a solution, he quickly pressed an obliging Walter and a laughing Astra into those positions. Mariol's momentary concern was restored to equanimity and the preliminaries were read out. Her so long delayed embrace of formality now crowned her long acceptance of domesticity and conquered any lingering doubts of providence. She had known happiness for fifteen years but her devotion to her irreplaceable Spenser had now been blessed with the fullness of all that society could offer.

Certificates were signed and they were fulsomely congratulated. The bride and groom became immortalised as a product of the photographer's art and the whole group joined them in whatever combinations could be conjured by mankind. Finally, a very small convoy brought the party to the matrimonial home, where Walter proposed a toast and Spenser replied with heartfelt thanks to his new wife and her contribution to his, and their, happy day.

Garrard turned to the guests with an indication of wanting to add his congratulations to the happy couple. 'As the eldest member of this little group,' he started, 'I feel it my duty to add my good wishes to those that have already been expressed. But I also have to admit that I am the least qualified to do so since I have spent all my life as a single member of the community. Nevertheless, I can add my assurance to you both that, in your new estate, you have achieved an additional advance for which I have a considerable envy. The happiness of you as individuals is surely a large part of the joy that will contribute to your future lives, but it is rather the untold years of togetherness in a lifelong companionship to which you have now advanced that will be your greatest reward. You have reached that stage of completion in human life to which all must aspire, one where domestic bliss will pervade your lives and never diminish. A new life is before you in which you will walk on, forever united, through long years yet to come. The past is something to be valued and reflected upon with joy, but the future is a priceless jewel that will be worn with an affection hitherto unknown. Regrets and remorse are now abolished; love and happiness will now be your constant companions throughout this happy marriage.'

Both Spenser and Mariol smiled broadly at Garrard, confirmed that his words accorded with their thoughts. Spenser responded that he had finally met his match in erudition unaware that Garrard had, at last, been able to utter his long desired but repressed feelings to the world that he would have preferred to utter to Peri; but Astra and Hedrick thought that his words had been addressed to them and exchanged smiles of approval to Garrard and to each other.

The guests wandered about the house and garden where Walter reminisced about the television programme and wondered whether the gallery had seen increased visitor numbers. Edith congratulated Mariol and could not omit proudly mentioning the date for Astra and Hedrick's wedding, which was not far off now. Garrard told Walter that he had worked at the gallery for decades and that it was he who had encouraged Hedrick to join the workshop but he had also taken advantage of his own role as mentor to impart his encouragement to him in the matter of matrimony. 'Have no qualms at Astra having chosen an unexpected partner,' he said. 'Sometimes, one has to be carried on the tide rather than to fight against it, and I am sure that you will be well rewarded.'

His fulsome praise of Hedrick was also very welcome to Walter, who was persuaded that his future son-in-law was a craftsman with a secure future.

Hedrick responded that he had achieved an immediate acceptance and that he did not really need encouragement from Garrard, but admitted that he had been very helpful, nonetheless. Garrard smiled his quiet acknowledgement, not at all persuaded that his efforts had been to little avail.

Mariol beamed her delight at Astra's forthcoming nuptials. 'You are quite right to marry young,' she told her. 'I've waited far too long,' she confessed. 'I thought marriage too old fashioned but finally realised how self-centred I was. The result was that I've kept Spenser as my private joy throughout the years without enough consideration for his wishes.'

Hedrick looked at Astra, who smiled back at him, both thinking that they had heard a blessing of greater meaning than they could have imagined. He felt that he had already received great consideration in Astra having somehow even looked at him; she could have chosen anybody from what must have been several suitors. He felt more valued by her but Garrard had spoken to him with the wisdom of age and persuaded him to open his heart to her. *She* felt as if she were stepping onto an escalator that would carry her smoothly through the years. One that would ascend through any tribulations that they may experience after which she would look down at all the troubles vanquished.

Laura experienced another stab of pain as she looked back to her days of joy, the days when she had no thought of becoming a widow at that too early age. But she had her children to shield her from anguish and had resolved to usher them through life and into independence. She assured Mariol that Spenser would shine the brighter now that she had thrown wide the shutters upon the world. 'He will have no more regrets, or be too troubled by gallery politics. Just make sure you look after him. We can't do without a man of his ability.'

Modesty had been Spenser's constant companion throughout the years, but he found an extra delight in allowing Laura's comment to add to his contentment on that momentous day. He was almost bursting with the happiness of having gained a new status of equality with those who had also taken the vows of matrimony. 'I have total confidence in continuing to be cared for by my wife just as she has in the care that I shall continue to give her,' he said, and in a reference to the politics of the gallery, he continued with the foreknowledge of Laura's confidential update on developments, 'The gallery will receive new attention. In with the new, out with the old. And I do not refer to the art on display,' he said adding, to Walter's approval, 'That must be the main focus of our future endeavours.'

Bentley overheard the new policy, unable to betray a confidence in knowing that the gallery would be secure from another calamitous event. 'I feel quite sure that you will have attained a greater reputation as a safe haven for all your exhibits,' he declared with a persuasion that brought an even higher level of satisfaction to his listeners. Cordelia joined him in the promise that they would increase visitor numbers when they viewed the prize exhibit of *Girl with a Harp*.

Spenser took Astra aside for a moment to ask whether she and Hedrick may be thinking of moving away and thereby depriving the workroom of a valuable worker. She replied that they had no such plans but that she was in a quandary trying to work out her own future employment.

'With your background of studies you should be in a position to find something suitable. I wonder whether you have thought of lecturing on art. We have a studio that is almost unused and just begging for employment.'

Astra replied that she had insufficient training for that but she would consider the suggestion.

'A good route into it would be as a guide to visitor groups,' Spenser responded. 'I would like to offer tours of our displays, much of which has a very interesting background. The del Mano incident is sure to retain a little notoriety but other works are unjustly neglected by visitors. It would be quite a challenge to stimulate new interest in them but your knowledge could easily be enhanced in order to achieve it.'

Astra glimpsed a positive route into the sort of career she would like, and it would ensure that she and Hedrick could better afford to stay in the area. A glance at Hedrick and Garrard was enough to tell her that they would also approve of the move.

Some time later when the guests had departed with repeated wishes for their happiness, the newly marrieds took each other by the hand. 'We've done it, at last,' Spenser told Mariol who looked lovingly at him.

'My only regret is that we did not do it earlier,' she replied. They embraced and went back into the house.

Holidays were a long-lost memory when the board assembled for the monthly meeting the following week, at which Marcus welcomed their return to a new season of peace and tranquillity. He presented the accounts and noted that visitor numbers were increasing after the summer dip and that media comment was quiet after the months of unwanted publicity.

After the routine items had been despatched, the only significant item on the agenda was 'Announcements'. Marcus therefore continued, 'Now I turn to the major item on the agenda,' he told the meeting. 'I have a special announcement to make.' He paused for the members to sense the gravity of the matter. 'Two announcements, in fact,' he emphasised.

'In the week before last, I was honoured to be consulted by our main trustee about the future prospects for the gallery, how we had progressed with our glazing project and how we could increase our visitors beyond the high figures that we have achieved so far. Our trustee was concerned to improve upon the impact of our operations with a slightly more ambitious plan of publicity, attraction of younger visitors and public events. That was an excellent intention, I think you will agree, and accords with a plan that I had been contemplating for some time but had been held until the security matter had been resolved. We studied the very well-presented proposals that Frank Pelham had drafted to which I was in complete agreement.

'I felt, however,' he continued in a tone that conveyed the wisdom of great experience, 'that it would impose a considerable burden upon our resources and in order to allow it to be progressed with the greatest expedition, I suggested a reorganisation of responsibilities to those whose practical knowledge in such matters was best suited to the relevant task.' He paused to note the expectant silence that greeted his words. 'Since I have been chairman for over a decade now,' he continued, 'I have decided that this would be a good opportunity to hand over the responsibilities of that office to a younger and more practical head of development. Frank graciously accepted my suggestion with the consequence that I shall be leaving my role and observing developments with great interest from the border lines of retirement.'

Marcus sat back in his seat to await the expected expressions of regret, slightly disappointed at the calm reception of his news. 'That is most unexpected,' was the general tenor of the response.

'But you mentioned two announcements,' the conservator prompted.

'Indeed so,' Marcus responded eagerly and quickly resuming his habitual bombastic demeanour. 'I can now reveal the identity of my successor, but before I name the person who has been appointed to the high demands of that position, may I indicate my good intentions in offering any assistance that may be required in that exacting role. Frank mentioned to me, in confidence, that his pressure of work in managing his engineering group had distracted him from his oversight of the gallery with the consequence that he has decided to relinquish his position as main trustee. He will therefore appoint our very good colleague, Laura Denton, to that taxing position in his stead.'

The news was welcomed with a greater bustle of enthusiasm than that of Marcus's retreat from business, 'May I therefore request your indulgence,' he continued, 'for me to welcome our new main trustee and chairman to say a few words of thanks and to outline her plans for the future.'

A patter of applause from the three directors other than Marcus and Laura herself greeted her first words. 'I am most grateful to you, Marcus, for that splendid introduction but also for your service to the gallery over the decade.' Marcus nodded a condescending smile accompanied by a modest shrug. Turning towards the others, she continued, 'I look forward to working with you all in my new capacity as chairman. Apart from the departure of Marcus from the board, all other members will be retained with the same remit; but with Marcus's departure, I shall merge all my present duties including my former representative position into the role of chairman and conduct them as a single entity. That will reduce communication necessities as well as offering a reduction in expense.

'I would also like to congratulate you all on your stoical forbearance that has unfortunately been a consequence of the recent disappearance of the del Mano. I am happy to announce that the methodology of the theft and the identity of the operatives who carried it out are now well known to the government and all material connected therewith is in the safe custody of Special Operations. Further details will not be released but we may rest assured that, in the knowledge that we shall not suffer a repeat of that worrying event, the expense of renewing our existing security system need no longer be incurred.'

Murmurs of relief greeted the announcement and the meeting adjourned with polite farewells to Marcus. They wished him well in his retirement, to which he bravely replied that he could now concentrate upon his several ambitions of work in the community that he had long wished to develop. As Marcus took his farewell of Spenser, he told him, 'Don't forget that my expertise will always be available to you. Whenever you may need it,' he added generously.

Spenser replied that they envied him his period free of responsibility. 'You've exerted yourself too much, already, Marcus, and you deserve a break. Take a year or two to develop those new ambitions of yours, but be assured that we will contact you should the necessity arise.'

Marcus left the building no longer burdened by his heavy duties and with the conviction that his record would be hard to emulate. He arrived home to be greeted by Mabel, with a trace of anxiety in her face. 'How did it go, dear?' she asked, inevitably betraying a little of her concern.

'Splendidly,' he assured her with the authority of a man who had achieved an honourable retirement as an elder statesman whose advice would be eagerly sought. 'Laura gave a few words of thanks for my loyal service and even Spenser told me that he would consult me should they encounter any difficulties.'

'That's so nice, dear. Now you can focus on the autobiography you were planning.'

'Yes,' Marcus replied. 'I was thinking about that, but it is sure to demand a great deal of time to finalise,' he added with a practised smile. 'But I think I deserve a little relaxation before I commit myself fully.'

After Marcus had taken his final farewell, Laura smiled conspiratorially at Spenser, a man of great sensitivity but invaluable. Spenser returned her smile, acknowledging her understanding that he was free at last of ignorance, carping criticism, bombast and denigration. The stress he had endured over the years dissipated like mist penetrated by sunlight. He straightened up, a man of mature years but visibly younger, happily married with the best wife in the world. He drove home to be near her, but this time as she rushed to him, he lifted her up and swung her round. 'My dear,' he said. 'I am the happiest man alive.'

She knew he had confirmed that Marcus had gone. He had cast off his burdens and she felt all her worries blowing away with the winds of spring. Her faith was confirmed; she would light a candle and give thanks to God.

About the Author

David William Paley was born in Sandhurst and, until retirement, held several financial control positions in international companies. He lived in Germany for four years but now lives with his French wife in Buckinghamshire and speaks both French and German in addition to his native English.

His previous novels as William Paley are *The Magic Canopy, Oceans of Regret, Four Ways to Keep a Secret* and *Raking the Sands.* As David Paley he has published four Kindle books of poetry, including anthologies of French and German poems in '*101 French Poems*' and '*150 German Poems*' containing poems in their original texts followed by his translations into English. The second edition of his *Visions and Illusions* appears in both print and Kindle editions and contains ninety poems.

He has created a website, *www.poemswithoutfrontiers.com,* that displays several hundred English, French and German poems in their original texts with his translations from and into the other two languages.